KENNETH

As they picked their way, with the tide receding and progress less difficult, Kenneth brought up the other matter on his mind. "Yesterday, I spoke on the need for an alliance of all the Celtic peoples, to withstand the threat of the Angles and the Norsemen. Your father was doubtful, but Ewan was in favour. You went further. You said that there should be a *unity*, not just an alliance, unity to a great Celtic realm. That I also hold to. If it could be possible."

"Yes. Why not? This of four nations, all of the same blood and faith, makes for weakness. *One* would be strong, could regain our lost lands, Lothian, Cumbria and the rest."

"Four? I think of more than four. *All* the Celtic nations. Wales, Man, even Cornwall. I do not think that Ireland would ever join with the rest, too proud and great for that. But the Irish might enter into an alliance. They much suffer from the Norsemen also, in the north, in Ulster . . ."

Eithne stared at him, pausing. "Wales! Ireland! Cornwall! Oh, Kenneth – that is too much! Man perhaps, yes. But these others are too much to hope for, ancient, famous high kingdoms . . ."

"Yes, perhaps that is only a dream. But Alba, Dalriada, Strathclyde, Galloway and Man, that would be a possibil[ity] one realm! One mig[ht]

Kenneth

Nigel Tranter

CORONET BOOKS
Hodder and Stoughton

Copyright © 1990 by Nigel Tranter

The right of Nigel Tranter to be identified as the Author of
the Work has been asserted by him in accordance with the
Copyright, Designs and Patents Act 1988.

First published in Great Britain in 1990 by
Hodder and Stoughton
a division of Hodder Headline PLC
First published in paperback in 1992 by Hodder and Stoughton
A Coronet paperback
This Coronet paperback edition 1997

10 9 8 7 6 5 4

A CIP Catalogue record for this title
is available from the British Library

ISBN 0 340 56638 8

Printed and bound in Great Britain by
Clays Ltd, St Ives plc

Hodder and Stoughton
A division of Hodder Headline PLC
338 Euston Road
London NW1 3BH

Principal Characters in order of appearance

Kenneth mac Alpin: Prince of Galloway and son of Alpin
Alpin mac Eochaidh: King of Galloway
Eochaidh the Poisonous: King of the Scots of Dalriada
Angus mac Fergus: High King of all Alba
Donald mac Alpin: Brother of Kenneth
Athelstan: Son of King Athelwolf of the West Saxons
Conall Cruaid: A shipmaster
Diarmaid: Abbot of Iona
Princess Eithne: Daughter of Angus mac Fergus, High King
Ewan mac Angus: Brother of Eithne
Roderick the Second: King of Strathclyde
Howell: King of Man
Aed mac Boanta: Mormaor of Moray
Queen Cathira: Wife of Godfrey of Oriel
Godfrey mac Fergus: King of Oriel, in Ireland
Feradach: King of Donegal
Bethoc: Abbess of St Bees
Riagan mac Ewan: Lord of Ravenglass
Duncan: Lord of Arnside
Phadraig: Prior of Ballymeanach
Rotri ap Mervyn: Later King of Gwynedd, kinsman of
    Howell of Man
Feredith mac Bargoit: Mormaor of Mar, later High King
Brude mac Fochel: Mormaor of Moray, later High King
Thorgesr: Invading Norseman, calling himself King of Ulster
Maelsechlaind: High King of Ireland
Cerball: King of Ossory
Drostan: Mormaor of Angus, later High King
Gartnait: Mormaor of Mar
Nechtan mac Drostan: Mormaor of Angus

PART ONE

PART ONE

1

The young man fretted and frowned. This was neither time nor place to be troubling with cattle. The enemy were at their heels, this land of Lothian hostile, and the man Athelstan a shrewd fighter. They had foolishly given him time and opportunity to catch up with them – and they knew from their rearward scouts that he was doing so, hand over fist, with a large force of West Saxons and Northumbrian Angles. So they themselves should not be going down into these river-levels and flat ground, held up by this vast herd of cattle; they should be holding to the higher ground, mounting rather to this ridge to the south-west, a defensive position where they would have some advantage against attackers, leaving the wretched cattle meantime. But it had been thus all the way northwards from Northumbria, delay, delay, this greed for booty, ever adding to their plunder. Was this what they had come south for – spoil, gear, loot? He had complained, objected. But who was going to heed such as himself, young, unimportant, with three kings present, including the High King of Alba himself? He was a prince of sorts, certainly – but of only a minor sub-kingdom, Galloway, the Land of the Southern Gaels.

Kenneth mac Alpin gazed back whence they had come, down towards the wide valley of the Lothian Tyne. They had returned here from another Tyne, the Northumbrian one, that furthest south penetration of their cautionary thrust into the Anglian kingdom. It had been no major invasion, despite all the kings, for the Northumbrians had been getting aggressive of late, raiding deep into South Alba and Galloway, their pirate longships even assailing the coasts of Dalriada and the Southern Hebrides, taking advantage of the damnable Danish attacks now so frequent, seeking to fish in troubled waters. So they required a lesson. And had been given one, to be sure, the combined Albannach, Scots and Gallovidian army having trounced the Northumbrians no less than three times, as well as laying waste a wide swathe of their land, right down to Tyne. It was just unfortunate that it so happened that this Athelstan, son to King Athelwolf of the West Saxons, was himself raiding in Southern Northumbria at the same time, despite the fact that his mother was an Anglian princess. And little as he cared for the Northumbrian Angles, he hated the Celtic nations of Wales and Alba still more. So, a noted warrior and renowned campaigner, he not exactly came to the rescue of his would-be victims, but saw the opportunity to have a confrontation with the Gaels who happened to be available. He had been coming after them for nearly one hundred miles now – and because of these wretched cattle, over a thousand of the brutes, he was drawing close.

Kenneth had no wish to make himself unpopular with his elders and betters, these including his own father and grandfather. But nor did he wish to be trapped and defeated and probably slaughtered with them down there in this Vale of Peffer ahead, as they might well be. Admittedly, looking back, he could still see no sign of any following host – but from this viewpoint between the Tyne and Peffer valleys, no more than four miles distance was visible, because of the Biel woodlands. So Athelstan could be a mere five miles or so behind – and with their own rate of progress, with this cattle-herd to slow them, they were covering no more than three miles in the hour. The enemy's horsed host therefore could catch up with them in the next couple of hours. Presumably his seniors realised this; but they did not seem to be as concerned as they ought to be. He felt that he had to do something about it.

He rode forward to where, above the little lochan of Markle, the leadership group sat their fine mounts, approaching a heavily built man of middle years, square of feature.

"Father," he said, "is not this a folly? To be going down into this Vale of Peffer's levels, burdened by all these cattle-beasts, with the Saxons at our backs? We would be caught down there, on those flats, and surrounded, trapped. We should be on the higher ground yonder. This ridge. Where we would have the advantage. This Athelstan could come up

10

with us at any time."

"When we will deal with him," Alpin mac Eochaidh, King of Galloway, said. "Be not so fearful, son."

"What I fear is our own foolish carelessness," the younger man declared. "All, so far, has been over-easy for us, our people become too confident. This Saxon host presses hard. We are saddled with much booty and all these cattle, weakening us greatly . . ."

"Wheesht, boy – wheesht!" his father ordered. "Who think you to instruct? We have been at this game before you were born! Be not so free with your fools and follies!"

Kenneth bit his lip. "At least let me take my own troop along the high ground there. To protect our quarter. Then, if there is an attack in the vale, I could come down, make a diversion against the enemy flank or rear . . ."

"They are not even in sight, boy."

"We move slowly and they move fast. My scouts reported them last as nearing the Biel Water crossing. They could be halfway from there by now. We can see only so far, because of those woods. They could be on us in two hours. Less. If you will not change direction and make for the higher ground, let me do as I say."

Alpin shrugged. "It is not for me to say. Not with your grandsire here. And Angus mac Fergus commanding . . ."

They moved over to where three men rode at the very head of the long column, save for the forward scouts, with two others immediately behind bearing aloft colourful banners. Of the trio in front one was old, one middle-aged and one youngish, the last on a much poorer horse than the two fine animals alongside, and bearing himself much less assuredly. King Alpin reined close.

"Kenneth here is fearful," he announced. "And thinks that *we* ought to be also. He would have us hold to the higher ground. He fears that we could be trapped in this Vale of Peffer."

"Ha! A Daniel! A Daniel come to judge us – as Susannah would have it!" the elderly man commented quickly. "The good Susannah! Is that it, boy – is that it?"

Kenneth never knew just how to take this grandfather of his, one of the strangest characters ever thrown up by Gaeldom. Eochaidh the Poisonous, King of the Scots of

11

Dalriada. Now in his late sixties but wiry as he was lean, he was warrior, a devious plotter, one of the most cultured men in Christendom and with a waspish tongue – which was where his nickname of the Poisonous came from, his speech not any proclivity for poisoning.

His grandson drew a deep breath. "As to the lady Susannah I know not, sir. But – this of descending into yonder vale in our present state seems to me unwise, with the Saxon at our heels. We may have to do battle at any time. And that seems no place to do it."

"No? There speaks the voice of experience! *De omni re scibili et quibusdam aliis!* Out of the mouths of babes and sucklings! Hear you that, Angus, my friend?"

His middle-aged companion, a big man, handsome, iron-grey of hair and beard, unsmiling, inclined his head and said nothing. Angus mac Fergus, High King of All Alba, was, unlike the other, a man of few words.

King Eochaidh thrust his beaky head on its long stringy neck towards his grandson, distinctly vulturine, as they rode slowly onwards, at the pace of those cattle. "We learn – oh, we must learn. Old, witless as we may be. Instruct us, Kenneth mac Alpin – instruct us."

The young man looked at his father, and got no help there. "On the ridge here we would be better placed to withstand attack. Down there, with all these cattle, we could be trapped. Outnumbered, we could be surrounded in the levels. This Athelstan comes up fast. Our people are grown careless, laden with booty . . . "

"And on your ridge, boy, they would have more care? Could not be surrounded? The cattle better herded?"

"Leave the cattle, sir. Let *them* go down into the vale. If we withstand or defeat Athelstan, we can regain the cattle. If not, we lose the brutes anyway. We did not come to Bernicia and Northumbria to collect cows, surely!"

King Angus of Alba barked a brief laugh.

"Alpin, my son – how did you produce such a prodigy as this? *You* were never so brilliant, so notable a thinker! Nor, I swear, was that woman you were fool enough to marry! Shall we do as he says, Angus? Turn all around? Abandon the cattle? Climb yonder ridge and wait for the Saxon? Or continue with our unthinking foolishness, and pray for the good God's deliverance?"

None there considered that anything but a rhetorical question.

"God might indeed aid us. *Deo favente!* After all, He made this vale. He made it something of a swamp of waters, with burns running down off this high ridge beloved of the discerning Kenneth, to flood the plain of it and make the ground soft, too soft for horses to cross at any pace. He made this Peffer stream to wind through all the marshland of the vale, uncrossable – save for the one ford our guide here tells us of. At . . . where was it, fellow?"

The younger man sitting his horse behind, a local Lothian petty chieftain's son they had picked up at Dunbar, answered, looking nervous. "Prora, Highness. The ford of Prora. The only one in miles."

"Prora, then. God made the stream and the vale and the bog. And He made stupid dumb brutes of cattle that will bunch and wheel and run amok, given opportunity. And, if in their hundreds, they could block any ford, form a mindless barrier for some men to stand behind and for others to fail to win through, even Saxons! Shall we throw our poor selves upon the mercy of God – or heed Kenneth mac Alpin mac Eochaidh? *Dominus illuminatio mea!*"

Again Angus mac Fergus laughed as they rode on.

Alpin jerked his head for his son to leave them. "Back to your scouts, lad," he said.

But that young man, although now flushed of face and humiliated, was made of no wilting stuff, true descendant of the race of Fergus mac Erc who had come from Ireland to found Dalriada four hundred years before. Reining his horse round, he spoke, looking not at his sire or grandsire but at the High King of Alba.

"May I take my own troop of scouts along the high ground, Highness?" he asked. "From there we shall see further, better, watch the enemy's approach. Send you word."

"You are captain of scouts," Angus tossed back, with a shrug. Presumably that was permission.

Kenneth left them, to spur back. What a grandfather to be born with! Captain of scouts for the army he was. And although he had men far back, keeping an eye on the oncoming foe, and a few well forward, both down in that vale and up on the ridge, he still had some forty Galloway men of his own troop, riding with him in the main host. These he now reached, and calling to his younger brother, seventeen-year-old Donald, to bring them on, veered off, to head for the higher ground, south by west.

Up there, quickly the scene changed, for this broad spine of land separated the Tyne and Peffer valleys, and once on its crest the prospect opened out to far-flung vistas. Actually, the drop to the Tyne on this south side was steeper than to the Peffer, the greater river having carved for itself a narrow ravine-like course below the isolated, mighty summit of Traprain Law which rose like a stranded leviathan out of the lower Lothian coastal territory. When this came in view, Kenneth gazed at it, wondering. Its wide summit was deserted now, save for grazing sheep and circling hawks – but three centuries before it had been otherwise, the capital fortress of the Gododdin, the Southern Cruithne, another Celtic people whom the invading Romans had called the Votadini Picts. Their king, Loth, had given name to all this land of Lothian, he whose daughter, Thenew, had been the mother of the celebrated St Mungo, or Kentigern, friend of Columba. Six thousand people, it was said, had dwelt on the fortified top of that hill – and now not one. The Angles and the Lochlannaich, the Viking Danes, had seen to that, these savage incomers from across the Norse Sea, who still so menaced the entire Celtic polity.

But that young man had not come up here to mourn the vanquished and lost people of his own race, any more than to admire the view. Drawing rein beside an abandoned stone circle, some of its monoliths cast down or fallen over now, he turned in the saddle to stare eastwards. From here he could see much further back whence they had come, right to the coast at Tynemouth, and Dunbar beyond. But those wretched intervening woods at Biel still blanketed the plain between, so that it was impossible to see the Saxon host which his scouts reported to be thereabouts. At least they had not yet emerged from the tree-cover.

Leaving one man to keep watch here, Kenneth led his party westwards along that spine, at a trot, his mind still smouldering over his grandfather's scathing sarcasm. It had been unnecessary, uncalled-for, surely, and in front of the others. And he still believed that *he* was right, that the wiser course would have been to hold to this high ground and leave the cattle, despite all that of bogland and the ford. Yet he had to admire old Eochaidh, whilst almost hating him, for his learning, his abilities and what he had achieved, the most cultured monarch Dalriada had ever had. But that poisonous tongue . . . !

His resentment did not prevent him from making keen examination of the territory. For a mile or so the ridge ran fairly narrow and clearly defined, but thereafter it widened, with the higher part on the south side and the ground falling away somewhat on the north. This meant that Kenneth's party had to leave the ridge proper, in order to be able to keep the Peffer valley in view. Which in turn meant that they could no longer watch the Tyne valley, and this could be important. So he sent a couple of men to hold to the high ridge, to keep an eye on that side.

Riding thus they quickly drew ahead of the main army down in the vale. A sort of hanging valley was now opening before them, between the two branches of the ridge, with the slope down to the vale-floor, to the north, ever lessening. At another stone circle, Kenneth halted. He could see, well ahead of the cattle-herd and the vanguard of the army, the roadway through the vale suddenly making a right-angled bend to reach the Peffer itself, and to resume again on the other side. That must be this Prora ford. No point in them going further than this, then, meantime.

They dismounted, to watch the slow advance of their force, strung out for the best part of a mile behind the cattle. Anything less like an army being pursued by a seriously threatening host would be hard to imagine. Yet the leaders down there, experienced men all, knew the situation. Kenneth expressed his doubts and mystification to his brother Donald, but that cheerful youth seemed to have every faith in his elders and betters, and showed little concern.

They could see the cattle and drovers nearing the ford, when the scout Kenneth had left at the first stone circle came up at a fast canter, with news. The Saxon host was in sight, from there, and large, much larger than their own, in his judgment. And not only in sight and coming on quickly, but dividing into two – one section following the Scots-Albannach route up from Tyne towards Markle, heading for the Peffer, the other making straight on up the main Tyne valley, as though to pass below Traprain Law, but keeping to this side of the river.

These tidings set Kenneth urgently to think. Athelstan himself could not know the lie of this Lothian country, so he must also have local guides – and the Bernician Anglian chiefs who now lorded it over this former Celtic province would be apt to favour the Saxons, their own sort, rather than the retiring Gaels. So in making this division of his force, Athelstan must have been given information which could benefit him. Surely it must mean that there was a way by which the southern division, by thus heading up Tyne, could somewhere ahead cross over and get in front of the slow-moving Gaelic force, west of this Prora ford, and so trap them. Which would make nonsense of his grandsire's strategy.

Unfortunately, Kenneth himself had no local guide to instruct him – something he ought to have thought of. The one with the kings had said that Prora was the only ford for miles. But that could mean merely that there was none this side for a mile or two, and the same beyond. There *could* be another ford further on, at no great distance, for this outflanking division to reach, over the hill, to cross and come back behind his own people. That could result in disaster.

"Donald," he said to his brother, "ride you down to our father yonder, with all speed. Tell him of this – that they could be trapped by this enemy move, this division. That there must be another ford further down Peffer. And that Athelstan is in large enough force to risk splitting his host thus. Tell Father, not our grandsire."

The youngster nodded and rode off northwards downhill.

Kenneth was tempted to go himself across that hanging valley to the southern and higher ridge, in order to see the advance of this enemy detachment, to assess numbers and progress. But he had two men up there who were quite capable of doing that. What he could do, while they waited, was to go and enquire at some houses he could see in the hanging valley there, as to the lie of the land ahead. They had not come this way on their journey south to North-umbria but had followed the inland route through the Lammermuir Hills.

So, with only two companions, not to alarm the local folk, he rode the half-mile to the nearest cottage. He did not have to go quite so far, for before reaching it they came on a shepherd rounding up his flock with the aid of two barking dogs. They were eyed warily.

Waving reassuringly, Kenneth gave the man good-day and asked whether he was of Anglian blood? The shepherd promptly spat, which was sufficient answer. So then he briefly explained who he was and the situation of the two armies, with this diversionary force coming up the Tyne to the south. Was there any way such Saxon force could cross over the hilly ground ahead and then get across the Peffer further west?

The man nodded. That was simple, he said. Two miles further up the Tyne, before the village of Haydn's toun, they could turn off and climb the hill of Garmyltoun and so come down to the Peffer near the former chapel of St Pensandus at Druimm. There was a ford there, for pilgrims to the chapel.

So-o-o! Kenneth let out a long breath. It was possible, then – probable. How far? How many miles altogether?

The shepherd shrugged. Four or five to the ford. Not much more than one back to the Prora ford.

Thanking him, Kenneth reined round to head back to his party. The Saxon horsed force, even allowing for the climb over the hill, could be at this chapel-ford in an hour. Then back to Prora, on the far side of Peffer. There was no time to play with.

He was debating whether to hold to his first intention of waiting on this high ground until the battle started and then rushing down to stage a diversion at the Saxon rear, or else to hurry down now and inform the kings of the urgency of the situation, when one of his scouts from the southern ridge came to tell him that the enemy force was heading up the Tyne valley and past the base of Traprain Law. And even as this news was being imparted, shouts from the others drew attention to the appearance back eastwards of the first horsemen and banners of the enemy, coming over the

Markle shoulder. It was too late for any hurrying downhill now to be of any value.

Chewing his lip, an alternative tactic occurred to that young man. It would take an hour for the southern enemy to reach this chapel-ford – but *he* could reach there sooner, without that hill to cross. Could his little band achieve something there? Could forty men hold a ford? Not for long, against a large force, but perhaps for long enough to have some significant effect on the Saxon strategy? Much would depend on the width and length of the ford. But there was a possibility there, surely?

No sooner considered than acted upon. Slantwise, downhill north-westwards he led his troop fast over the braes and hummocks, as the land sank to the vale, their sturdy garrons sure-footed amongst the burnlets and scrub woodland, the gorse and dwarf hawthorns. They did not want to get too far down into the soft ground of the vale-floor, as yet, heavier going. Besides, they would be more likely to see this chapel better from higher ground.

In fact, they discerned it readily enough at least half a mile away, for buildings were few and far between in that undrained Vale of Peffer and the typical Columban stone and thatch little church, surrounded by its cashel of hutments and grass-grown earthen stockade, stood out clearly.

As they drew close they could see that the place was deserted, the thatch largely fallen in, the huts wrecked. No doubt the Angles or the Vikings were responsible for that, as for so much else, this Celtic Lothian a savaged land.

They wasted no time on the ruined fane on its slight rise of ground, fair enough Christians as they were, but headed down for the Peffer. To find the ford was easy, for there was a stone and log causeway leading to it through the soft terrain, no doubt laid down by devoted monkish labour. At the river itself, if Peffer could be called that, it was clear enough as to why there was no crossing for man or beast save at very occasional and special points. For this was no ordinary stream, more of a great drain winding through the levels, with little in the way of clearly defined banks, these mud-lined and reed-grown, sometimes expanding into what were ponds, almost lochans, and seldom less than one hundred yards across, on occasion three times that. A more effective barrier would have been hard to devise.

The ford itself proved to be at one of the narrower parts, naturally, but even so was some seventy yards across. It was not wholly a natural shallowing and firming of the stream-bed, for the monks had gone to the trouble of continuing their causeway under water, widening it somewhat. This bottoming had inevitably become overlaid with mud and silt as time passed, but it still made a fair crossing although not very wide. For Kenneth's purposes the narrowness was all to the good.

Splashing across, they dismounted, to prospect the pos-sibilities. The width, they reckoned, was no more than a score of feet – which meant that only three horsemen could seek to cross it riding abreast; similarly, of course, only three could line up abreast to defend it. Seventy yards from bank to bank meant that it was beyond the range of effective spear-throwing – that is, save by horsemen already part-way across. It would make a moderately good defensive position.

With no sign of the enemy, was there anything that they could do to improve it? Obstacles to add? Down on these soft levels there was little suitable material to use for obstruction, no large stones, no tree-trunks. And they had nothing to dig with but their swords. All they might do was to go back up to the chapel area, slightly higher set, where a number of these small, stunted hawthorns grew, and try to use these, either uproot them or hack down what they could with the swords.

That did not prove so easy, for although stunted, these little trees were ancient and firm-rooted, the wood very hard. Eventually they had to bring horses over again, and with tethering-ropes tied round the trees, used the animals' weight and strength to drag out a few. With others they merely chopped off prickly branches.

Hauling all this down, they sought to make an added barrier with it at their far side of the ford. This proved difficult also, for they had nothing very effective to anchor the hawthorns in place. The water was not deep here, no more than three feet, and the sluggish Peffer produced no strong current; nevertheless their desired barricade could drift away. They had to use the tethering-ropes again, these pegged down with wooden stakes on the bank, not very secure but the best that they could do. At least it kept the tangle of brushwood approximately in place.

All this took time, and before they were finished look-outs gave warning. The Saxons were coming into sight over the green ridges to the south, in what seemed large numbers. It would not be long now.

Hastening to drive in the last of their pegs and tethers, they waited. Suddenly their forty men seemed a very inadequate little band. Mounted they might look a shade more effective.

It was hard to judge numbers as they drew near. Kenneth suggested eight hundred, but others said more. Anyway, a daunting host for that band to challenge. They formed up, to line the bank of the ford.

The enemy came on fast, in a hurry to make their long circuit. They looked a tough, well-armed, well-horsed crew, fair-haired in general, with the typical Saxon down-turning moustaches, wearing padded ox-hide waistcoats as protective armour. None wore the multicoloured tartans of the Gaels.

When the leaders reached the far bank, they reined up, to stare across, assessingly. Then a horn was blown, and a man raised his voice, to shout.

What he said was incomprehensible to the Gaelic-speaking hearers, but there could be little doubt as to the meaning. Kenneth did not waste breath in reply, but raised a hand, palm outward to the foe, in clear denial of passage.

There was a pause as the Saxon leaders conferred. Men were sent up and down the bank to inspect and prospect the width of the ford and the possibilities beyond, some urging their horses some little way over the muddy margins and into the water – where they promptly were in trouble, sinking deep and extricating themselves only with difficulty. That lesson at least was quickly learned.

The defenders waited.

There was little delay about the next step. The leaders waved forward a foremost troop to venture the ford, swords drawn and short spears ready for throwing. It was those spears which worried Kenneth mac Alpin. He and his were similarly provided; but once they had thrown theirs, all forty, the enemy would still have twenty times as many. So theirs had to be harboured carefully. They hoped that the Saxons might be more prodigal, and provide some reinforcement. Kenneth said as much to his followers.

That first attempt must be made example of. The horsemen could come on only three abreast, however tight-packed behind. The tighter the better.

Kenneth let them come almost halfway across. Then, with only some forty yards separating them, he raised his spear.

"The horses!" he shouted, and threw.

It grieved him to aim at the dumb beasts, but this was war and lives, many men's lives, were at stake. The horses were not protected by padded cowhide or shields, and they made much larger targets. Half a dozen spears made short work of those first three animals. Neighing shrilly, in pain and fright, they went down in kicking, lashing turmoil, throwing their riders. And into the struggling confusion of flailing limbs and hooves came the next two trios, pressed on from behind. Three more spears launched brought down one of these, to add to the chaos.

A few spears came back to them from the rear ranks of the would-be forders, but in the rearing, sidling disarray of struggling horseflesh, these could not be aimed with any precision. None did any damage – and provided four replacements for the defenders.

The attackers retired in disorder, leaving the Gaels five spears down. The ford, already showing red, was a litter of injured horses and splashing riders.

Four spear-throwers on the north bank dismounted to collect the Saxon weapons.

There was some more horn-blowing and shouting from across the water, with fists shaken. More horsemen were dispatched up- and downstream, no doubt to look for alternative crossings further afield.

The Saxon leadership tried a new tactic. They knew the depth of the water in the middle now, and that men, dismounted, might wade it – and could cross eight or ten abreast, not three. And these close-knit ranks could use their shields to form an all but impenetrable moving barrier before them.

This proved to be an infinitely more effective manoeuvre. The first few spears cast by the defenders were fended off by the slow-wading shield-bearers, and although one stumbled and fell at the impact, his place was quickly filled from the rear. Some spears came back at them and one of the defenders' horses screamed in agony, with a gash along its croup.

Kenneth ordered a retiral far enough to get the horses out of range, then dismounted, to hurry forward again, leaving two men with the animals. He saw that now the Saxon horsemen were beginning to cross behind the screen of their dismounted men.

He cursed the fact that they had so few spears. Admittedly more were coming over at them, and one of his men yelled, with an arm wound. He halted his people some way back from the water's edge.

"Wait!" he panted. "Let them get to those hawthorns. Then . . . !"

Wading through water up to the men's middles was inevitably slow, and although this gave opportunity for the men behind the shield-bearers to throw their spears, these tended to fall short of the defenders' present stance, cast from a low position and from unsteady footing.

It was trying to wait there, watching the enemy get almost across. But in the circumstances advisable. And there were extra spears coming, the longer they waited.

When Kenneth saw the first of the waders reach the jagged hawthorn barrier, he burst into action, racing forward, spear poised. Down to within close range he ran, his men at his back, their own round targe-shields held before them on their left arms, and there hurled their weapons.

There was no missing now, and in the enemies' efforts to drag apart, surmount or force through the tied hawthorns, shields could not be maintained in position to form any solid cover. Entangled in the brushwood, those first ranks made an easy target. Great was the execution.

The trouble was, of course, those behind, especially the horsed men. Their spears came over with effect, at this shorter range, and some few of the defenders fell, Kenneth himself suffering a hit which, fortunately, thanks to his plaid wrapped across chest and one shoulder, was largely deflected so that he scarcely noticed the pain of it, only the impact. Had the Saxons been carrying more than one spear each, the story would have been different.

That barrier of wood and rope was now added to by injured and struggling men. There was no way that the horsemen could move, save backwards. This, inevitably, they began to do, rather than sitting as targets in mid-stream. Fortunately, most, in anger and frustration, flung their spears before reining round, none of which reached Kenneth's people.

The second attempt had failed.

Gathering up spears, the defenders found that they had now only seventeen. So far there had been no sword-work at all.

Such enemy wounded as were able staggered away back across the ford, some aiding their fellows, but leaving four or five motionless at the barrier.

So far so good. But Kenneth recognised that this could not go on for much longer. Once their stock of spears was used up, they would be overwhelmed. Swords, hand-to-hand fighting, would not stem the numbers against them.

Meantime the Saxons, so near, were clearly at a loss. Presumably they could see how short of spears their foes were, and would recognise that it was only a question of time. But meanwhile, further attacks were going to be equally costly for them, their only objective using up those spears – no pleasant prospect for men, however bold.

They tried dismounted men plunging into the water, with tether-ropes tied together linking them, up and down from the ford, hoping presumably to get a sufficiency across to distract and thin out the opposition. But these were quickly in difficulties, floundering, half-swimming, going under – this on account of the deep mud and slime which formed the floor of the stream where there was no causeway, not only giving no footing but sucking down any feet and legs which sank in. This attempt had to be abandoned also, although it was persisted in for some time.

Then there was a diversion. A single horseman came spurring, as fast as the terrain would allow, up the far side of the Peffer, from the west, obviously urgent. Kenneth's heart sank. Almost certainly that meant that somewhere along there one of the mounted detachments had found a way across the Peffer, another ford or at least a possible crossing.

In which case, it would not be long before they would have company this side, their defence outflanked.

Most evidently this was the message received by the Saxon leaders, for amidst much shouting, a further large company, fully two hundred men, was detached and sent off downstream at speed.

Kenneth had to think quickly. Was there any point in waiting longer here? Were they achieving anything? Presumably the main forces would be confronting each other, by now, at the Prora ford. Was his duty now not to hasten thither with all speed, to warn his seniors of the imminence of attack at their rear? Or should he wait a little longer, denying this ford to the enemy as long as possible? It could be that every minute might count back there. If only he knew what was happening eastwards . . .

He decided to wait, meantime, but to send one man off to Prora to inform the kings. It had taken some time for that lone Saxon rider to return, so that probably meant that any alternative crossing-place was a fair distance off. There might well be some delay. Much would depend on whether the finders of that crossing would wait there for reinforcements, or come on on their own. Kenneth tried to remember roughly how many had gone off to that side originally.

Clearly the enemy across the ford were now prepared to wait also. The defenders had time and opportunity to attend to their few wounds, none serious, one horse being the worst casualty. Kenneth's own shoulder was stiffening up, from the bruising. It was not this that preoccupied him, but the westwards situation. He kept gazing in that direction.

But one of his men saw them first, and pointed. There, half a mile away, horsemen had appeared on this north side, how many it was impossible to tell at that range over flat ground. But enough to change the entire position, undoubtedly. Kenneth bowed to the inevitable, and gave orders to mount and be off.

They were followed by shouts and jeers from across the Peffer.

According to that shepherd there was not much more than a mile between the Prora and chapel fords; but it seemed more as they rode eastwards. Their beasts could not go fast, because of the softness of the ground; and owing to the scrub and tall rushes and reeds, from these levels they had no distant views. In fact they heard battle ahead before they could see it, the shouting, screaming, lowing of cattle and clash of steel. Whatever the circumstances, the two armies had met.

When, at length, they got close enough to see what went on, Kenneth was little the wiser. Ahead all seemed to be unutterable confusion, a vast mass of milling men, horses and cattle, beneath which the Peffer itself was not to be seen – which must mean that the fighting was going on on both sides of the river, something certainly not intended by King Eochaidh at least. But battles are seldom carried out according to the strategists' plans. Where the Scottish-Albannach leadership group was based was impossible to tell. No banners now flew above the widespread pandemonium.

Kenneth glanced over his shoulder. As yet no sign of the pursuit. What was his best course? Just to plunge headlong into the mêlée might not be to any great advantage. If he could see the Gaelic leadership, he could seek to force a way through to it. But he could not. Would it be better just to wait this side of the battling thousands, form a thin line facing the other way, to confront their late enemy, the outflanking force, and at least lessen their impact on the main struggle? He and his would be overwhelmed and obliterated, of course, but it might aid the cause.

His dilemma was resolved by a wounded man, a Gallovidian but no hero, staggering to get as far away from the conflict as he could, clutching a blood-soaked sleeve. He, recognising Prince Kenneth, was able to point to where, showing only very slightly above the struggling mass, was a single hawthorn tree somewhat larger than most hereabouts. There, he said, the three kings had taken up their stance, God help them all!

Kenneth saw his course now more clearly. He would leave his followers in a tight bunch here, not to get involved in the general fighting meantime, but to await his orders – and to keep an eye westwards for their recent foemen. If he did not come back shortly, then to use their own judgment as to what was best. Drawing his sword, he spurred on alone, aiming in the direction of that tree.

It might seem an impossible project to attempt,

considering what lay between him and his objective. But, although young, Kenneth mac Alpin had considerable experience in warfare – few young men of Gaeldom, in those days, had not, especially those of rank. He knew that in any battle, men tended to be preoccupied with their immediate assailants – they had to be. A mass of fighting men and frightened animals might seem impenetrable, but in fact could usually be worked through by a determined rider on a horse held in close control, since few, if any, would be concerned with him unless he attacked them, being otherwise engaged.

So he rode into the strife on his chosen course, sword swinging. He made no attempt to smite, only to help cleave a way through, presenting the flat of the blade rather than the cutting-edges, pushing past and sometimes over friend and foe alike – it being not difficult to tell which was which, for the Gaels all wore the tartans, plaids, jerkins, kilts. Most men were fighting on foot, hand-to-hand, the preferred method in close combat. He was slowed down, of course, by the press, but himself suffered no direct assault, although glancing blows tended to strike his mount or his own legs, by chance. His principal concern was in keeping his horse in hand, if alarmed by the smell of blood, the noise, the fallen bodies it had to get over, as well as the actual battling. That, and holding to his due line, for in the thick of it all it was difficult to keep in view that not very high tree in all the twisting and turning involved.

The only contribution to the fight he made at this stage was when he saw one of the Albannach battlers, already engaged, being attacked from the rear by another Saxon. Kenneth used his sword then, and not the flat of it, to equalise that specific contest, before pressing on.

The fighting was thickest, fiercest, as he neared the hawthorn, where the enemy, in obviously greater numbers, sought to get at the Gaelic leaders, the three kings all but beleaguered by their tree within a tight circle of their guards.

That Kenneth was able to cut his way through to them was thanks to the enemy in the main having their backs to him in this struggle, while his own people, recognising his tartans, sought to give him passage. With difficulty he reached his objective, that group of still-mounted men.

None of them, not even his father, greeted his appearance with any noticeable joy or relief, all otherwise preoccupied. He saw young Donald there, so at least they would know of the outflanking force, no comfort as that would be. He reined up his foam-flecked beast beside King Alpin.

"You will have to break out," he panted. "Surrounded thus, you will go under. Another eight hundred come, this side of the river. Soon. Break out!"

"How can we break out, boy, held in tightly as we are? Too many against us, half our numbers still across that ford. We were caught getting the cattle marshalled . . . "

"Yes, yes. But, wait here and you will die. All of you. Cut your way through, to the north."

"How? We are too few to do that. We could never get through."

"*I* did!" When that was received only by a shake of the head, he went on. "I have my troop, back there. Waiting. Only forty – but enough to get you out. A wedge, a horsed wedge."

"Could you get them here?"

"I can – if I can get back to them!"

Angus mac Fergus, the High King, reined close. "If we could but get at Athelstan yonder . . . !" he jerked, pointing.

Some way across the heads of the fighting dismounted men, but this northern side of the ford, another group sat their horses, watching the struggle, undoubtedly the Saxon leaders, no more than eight score yards off but as out of reach as though a mile away.

"Kenneth here says that he could bring his troop of scouts to us. In a wedge. Forty of them," Alpin announced. "And get us out of this broil. Cut a way out, to the north . . . "

"Where you could direct the battle better," the younger man put in, anxious to spare his elders' feelings. "Order a withdrawal, to the higher ground there."

"Could you do it? Get them through this rabble?"

"I believe so."

"Well, then . . . "

Kenneth glanced over at his grandsire. But Eochaidh the Poisonous was determinedly looking elsewhere.

Wheeling his horse round, the younger man started back

whence he had come.

Riding down the battling members of the royal guard was not pleasant, but necessary – and probably his mount's hooves and weight did no very grievous damage. But once through that inner circle Kenneth could drive forward, sword flailing, with less compunction, amongst struggling fighters, since half at least were the enemy. He had not much time or opportunity for consecutive thought as he went, but an idea was taking shape in his mind.

Gradually the press thinned out and there was his scout company, still waiting, bunched, as ordered, however fretfully. He shouted and waved at them to form a wedge, a wedge. They stared and sidled, but little more. They were scouts, not really trained horse-fighters.

Angrily, Kenneth commanded and bullied and all but pushed them into approximately the formation he desired, the cavalry wedge, the spearhead device by which a horsed group, boldly led, could cleave its way through most other battling masses whether mounted or not. In that shape, solid, protecting each other's flanks, the inner men ready to replace casualties amongst the outer, a wedge of determined riders was almost impossible to stop. Kenneth had no time for perfecting his formation, but with his men roughly in position, placed himself at the apex of the triangle, and bringing his now bloody sword forward and down in a fiercely commanding gesture, spurred his long-suffering mount forward again for the fray, his group tight-packed behind.

In the event, it was extraordinarily easy to plough their way through, the weight and impetus of the forty sufficient to propel them almost without any sword-work, as they bore down upon the struggling fighters, the group's principal problem being to avoid jostling and collision with their own companions rather than opposition from the enemy; and, for that matter, from friends also, for of course they had to ride down the one as much as the other. A cavalry wedge could not be discriminating.

So, in almost less time than it takes to tell, they had burst through the battling throng and driven up to the kingly party at the tree. And there, if Kenneth had expected praise and acclaim, he was disappointed. For all there were otherwise concerned, staring, pointing upwards, not at the tree but skywards, despite all the savage conflict going on around them. Astonished, Kenneth too gazed up.

What he saw was sufficiently strange. There, against the deep blue of the otherwise cloudless afternoon sky, was a cloud-formation in the exact shape of a cross – but a saltire cross, like the letter X, white against azure.

King Alpin saw his son. "Look!" he cried. "St Andrew's cross! There, in the sky. Andrew – Peter's brother. His cross."

Kenneth knew the story, how the Apostle Andrew, seeking to convert the Gentiles to Christ's cause, was condemned to death himself by crucifixion, like his Master; and pleaded with the heathen to be executed, if so he must be, on a different sort of cross, that he might not seem to be trying to rival Christ's, the precious symbol of their faith. So they had made him a slantwise cross, the saltire or St Andrew's cross. And there, the likeness of it shone in the sunny sky above Lothian and the warring hosts.

Angus mac Fergus of Alba was shouting. "God has not forsaken us! See – He sends His servant Andrew to our aid. He will strengthen our arm, support us against these pagans. We may yet have the victory this day! If God gives us it, I swear that I will make Andrew the patron saint of my kingdoms. I swear it! Andrew – St Andrew!"

All around him, men took up the cry. "Andrew! Andrew!"

Kenneth was not unimpressed. But he had this notion in his head, now grown and developed into an urgent decision. The High King had said it earlier – if they could get at Athelstan himself . . . ! Perhaps his wedge could do that? It had got them thus far. Athelstan's group had their backs to the Peffer. If he could drive through the press that far, the Saxon himself would have to stand and fight, not merely direct the warfare.

He shouted to Angus. "Highness, I could drive at Athelstan. This wedge. Reach him, as you said. If Athelstan were to fall . . . !"

"You could, boy? You think it? Aye, then – do that. And God go with you – God and St Andrew! That cross will aid you . . . "

Without waiting further, Kenneth dragged his horse's head round, shouted to his troop to close up tightly, and yelling "St Andrew! St Andrew!" drove into the smiting, struggling mass again, due southwards for the Peffer bank, sword weaving a figure of eight pattern from side to side. His men, packed behind him, took up that cry – indeed all around them the saint's name was being shouted now, as the Christian Gaels took heart from the sign and sound of it, however dangerous it was for men battling for their lives to turn their eyes skywards even for a moment or two. Perhaps, of course, the enemy were also seeing that cross, as well as hearing the cries and sensing the renewed confidence of the opposition, and were thereby affected.

Whether or not that was so, the wedge cut its way forward with little more difficulty than heretofore, a hurtling mass of horseflesh and swordsmen smashing their bloody way through the all but stationary agglomeration of fighters, making directly for Athelstan's mounted group.

This last could not do other than wait for them, with the press in front and the Peffer behind – and these were no inexperienced nor timorous warriors. But they too were at a disadvantage, stationary or almost so, against driving force. Into them the wedge smashed in fullest charge – and the group disintegrated at the impact.

Kenneth's aim was to strike down Prince Athelstan with his own sword, if possible. But another Saxon horseman was in the way, and by the time that he had parried this man's spear-thrust and returned his counter-stroke, he was pushed past and on by the pressure behind.

The problem with any wedge was to turn it round without losing formation. This demanded space so that it could be contrived in a wide half-circuit. Where the pressure of fighting men made this impossible, there was nothing for it but to break up and turn individually and then seek to re-form, less than easy in close-packed battle. This Kenneth attempted now, but with only moderate success, his company quickly becoming dispersed in the general mêlée, in their efforts. With only half a dozen or so close to him, he sought to drive back to what remained of the Saxon leadership party. But now, of course, he lacked the valuable speed and impetus. He had to fight his way.

Despite being thus preoccupied, however, it did not take him long to perceive that Athelstan, with his distinctive helmet and magnificent white stallion, was no longer visible. Others of his group were identifiable, milling around now and not in any sort of unity. Then he saw the great white horse – and it was riderless.

Uncertain now as to priorities, he gazed around – and uncertainty is no recommended state on a battlefield. He was reminded of this in forcible fashion by being all but cut down by one of the Saxon mounted chieftains, and, raising his left shield-arm to ward off the blow, failed to so do adequately because the said arm had stiffened up after the almost forgotten stroke received at the chapel ford. It was a near thing, and only the prompt action of one of his own men saved him, as he reeled in his saddle.

A little unmanned by this, Kenneth was realising that he was not now providing the leadership required of him, when a slighter blow on his shoulder swung him round, to fend off another attack. But it was another of his own people, using his sword to draw his attention. And having gained it, the man gestured down, to the left. There, unmistakable, in a temporary gap amongst the combatants, was the body of Athelstan Athelwolfson, bloody and battered, obviously dead. Someone else had achieved what Kenneth had sought to do.

At least now Kenneth saw his duty clearly. The kings had to be informed, and quickly, for this news could change all. He turned to his half-dozen, leaving the rest dispersed, and signed to these to form themselves into another small wedge behind him, to drive their way back, through the battle, to that hawthorn tree.

He scarcely was aware of what he did now, so filled was his mind with the way matters had developed, that cross, and the change in spirit of the Gaelic host and the fall of Athelstan. Victory could now be theirs, if all this was properly exploited. What did not occur to Kenneth mac Alpin was that he was in fact, unsuitably, hastening to tell his elders and betters just how to achieve the exploiting.

So, all but automatically leading the way back through the press, he came to the three monarchs, where they sought to direct the fighting.

"Athelstan is down!" he shouted. "Dead! Athelstan fallen. We can win this day."

All eyed him, as the import of that sank in.

"He is dead. His chiefs scattered. If we drive forward now, all of us, we can push them into the Peffer. Leaderless . . . "

He pulled up beside his father, who leaned from the saddle to grip his son's shoulder, wordless.

"God, and St Andrew, be praised!" the High King Angus cried. "And you, boy – and you!"

"Aye – but strike now! Now! We can have them. As they learn that Athelstan is fallen . . . "

To state that the Gaelic host made a prompt change-over from the defensive to the offensive would be misleading, an exaggeration; but the situation did change, and noticeably. Everywhere the Gaels were enheartened and the foe the reverse. How quickly the news of their leader's death spread amongst the Saxons was impossible to know, but something, some sense of failure and defeat, did spread amongst them, and this in turn further encouraged the others. Battles are not usually won or lost at any specific moment or incident; but the trend can often be identified as starting at such. As now. The three kings left their tree and began to move Peffer-wards, not in any sudden charge, and still surrounded by their guards, but in a distinct and steady advance, to the continual shouting of St Andrew's name; and as surely the enemy were pressed back upon the river.

As the nearness of the Peffer at their backs was borne in on the struggling Saxons, more and more it obviously became their preoccupation. Some might try to swim it, but most clearly saw the ford, by which they had crossed here, as their only life-line. So there developed a recognisable drift backwards in that direction, and as the distance shortened, the drift gradually became a hastening, a rush, a rout. For it was only a narrow passage, and could take no large numbers at any one time. Safety across there became a personal priority.

In all this, Kenneth played his part, picking up some of his dispersed troop in the process. When he had gathered about fifteen of them, he recognised his opportunity. That ford. If he could cut that, then the day would be theirs, the enemy not only demoralised but divided into two. Fifteen men could make a wedge again, smaller but effective. Enough probably, in present circumstances. So it was disengage from hand-to-hand fighting, form up again into a spearhead, and then drive and burst their way through this rabble to the Prora ford, now some two hundred yards off.

It was really only bodies in the way now, little of active opposition. Headlong they ploughed onwards, inevitably slowing, by the very press of humanity, as they neared the water, their mounts rearing and lashing out in alarm. But they reached the ford and forced their way out on to it, driving men off right and left. In the middle, Kenneth raised his sword-arm, making a circular gesture, to swing his party now on either side of him facing back, a double line of horsemen, not a wedge any more, blocking the underwater causeway.

At first the fleeing Saxons came on, pushed by the pressure behind. Those still on horseback did best, some indeed managing to fight their way through. But by far the majority had chosen to do battle on foot, leaving their beasts on the south side, to make the opposed crossing, and few indeed of these were able to pass the horsed barrier. Trapped between the river and the advancing Gaels, everywhere men began to throw down their arms. The battle ceased to be that, even though isolated groups fought on doggedly.

The Saxons on the south side of Peffer saw that all was lost, and began to stream away eastwards as best they could.

The victors presently drew breath to survey the scene of carnage, count the cost – and assess the vast amount of booty, weapons, horses and prisoners they had acquired. Athelstan's body was found and dragged to the hawthorn tree. They would have prisoners pull down one of the nearby Prora cot-houses, for its stone, and build a cairn of this over the corpse – which, of course, was not entitled to Christian burial – and one day, Angus mac Fergus said, they would erect one of their carved Celtic crosses above it, not as any memorial, but as recognition, for all time to come, of St Andrew's intervention on their behalf.

Kenneth mac Alpin found himself the hero of the hour. He was even credited with the slaying of Athelstan, although denying it. He sought to discover who in fact had achieved what admittedly he would have wished to have done himself. He learned that there were three contenders for the honour amongst his own troop, claiming and counter-claiming, all apparently having assailed the prince more or less together. Undoubtedly they would squabble over it for the rest of their days.

King Eochaidh could not bring himself actually to praise his grandson – not to his face at least. But he did admit that his strategy had been somewhat invalidated by the existence of this unknown chapel ford downriver – for which he blamed their local guide who had not mentioned it, and who had conveniently disappeared once the fighting started. Kenneth's attempt to hold that ford, however unsuccessful, might perhaps have helped a little.

That was as far as the old poisonous one would go, as eventually the Gaelic host, having disarmed its Saxon prisoners, abandoned them and proceeded on its way down Peffer, to where that strange stream made its confluence with salt water at Aberlady Bay. They would camp there for the night, on firm ground near the village, and tend their wounded. The cattle would be rounded up and brought along.

For his part, Kenneth was uncaring as to praise or blame. What was exercising his mind now was this matter of St Andrew as patron saint. Of what? The High King had said, of his kingdoms. That included sundry parts and provinces of the mighty Alba. But it did not include Eochaidh's kingdom of the Scots of Dalriada. Nor, of course, their sub-kingdom of Galloway. Were *they* not able to claim St Andrew also? Why not? It had been as much their victory as Angus's. Could two nations, then, claim the same patron saint? Be united in this, at least? Might it not be a first step to a greater unity? A uniting of Alba and Dalriada – one kingdom? That now, would be something. He had thought of it, vaguely, often. One kingdom north of the Scotwater and the Clyde. One day, perhaps, even Strathclyde also. Was that a dream beyond all consideration . . . ?

Young men can dream dreams equally with old.

2

The joint Celtic armies continued their homeward march, in no haste now, with the wounded to consider and those cattle ever delaying, along the south shores of the Scotwater estuary, past the great lion-shaped hill and rock fortress of Dunedin and on up the narrowing firth, with the distant Highland hills ever beginning to beckon ahead. The first parting of the ways came at Ecclesbreac, at the marshes where the Carron River reached salt water and the main host began to swing northwards. Here the Galloway contingent, the smallest section, left to head southwards, at first to cross high, bare moorlands to the upper Clyde valley and so over the great watershed where Clyde, Tweed and Annan all rose, and then down Annandale and Nithsdale into their Solway country. Young Donald mac Alpin was given his first command here, there being little likelihood of trouble *en route* – for there was peace these days between the kingdom of Strathclyde and the Albannach and Scots. Alpin himself, and Kenneth, were to go on to Dalriada meantime, for a council meeting Eochaidh was calling. So Donald and his people, with their share of the captured cattle and booty, departed, and the march was resumed, for the Snawdun of Stirling and the vital crossing of Forth, at the very waist of the land.

The Scotwater estuary, for so long an impassable barrier except by ship, sixty miles from Dunbar at its mouth, suddenly narrows to the joint rivers of Forth and Teith, under the line of the Highland mountains. Here was the first crossing possible, a major ford, even a lengthy timber bridge. Over both towered the Snawdun, the mighty fortified rock, so like that of Dunedin, thirty-five miles back, both outposts of the Albannach kingdom. None might cross here save with the permission of the frowning fortress. And any crossing *had* to be here, for beyond Stirling westwards the plain of the Forth and Teith was a waterlogged waste, twenty-five miles long by five wide, bog, swamp and scrub-forest, haunt of wolf and boar, by man all but impassable.

Northwards now they headed for the narrowing of that other estuary, the Firth of Tay. Just short of it, where the River Earn came in to join it, was Forteviot, capital of the Albannach sub-kingdom of Fortrenn; and here the two hosts separated, not without a certain acrimony over the due division of those cattle, old enmities surfacing. In it all, Kenneth plucked up courage, perhaps unwisely, to put his question to Angus mac Fergus.

"Highness, this of St Andrew. You said that he was to be the patron of *your* kingdoms. Can he be of Dalriada also? Can two peoples have the same saint?"

"I do not know that. But Andrew shall certainly be Alba's."

"Better than that Bridget-woman you have had for long!" Eochaidh put in sarcastically. Alba's patron and intercessor was St Bridget, a Celtic semi-legendary abbess, her tradition mixed somewhat with a pagan sea-goddess – this less surprising than it might seem in a kingdom with a system of matrilinear succession. Dalriada's, of course, was St Columba himself.

The High King ignored that.

"The victory back at that Peffer was a joint one," Alpin put in, supportively.

"Aye – and I would judge that the Scots contributed more to it than did the Albannach," his father observed – even though he did not look at his grandson.

Kenneth had not intended to provoke an argument or any ill feeling. "Can we share a patron then, as well as a victory?"

"That I do not know." Angus shrugged. "I have not heard of such. You Scots will do as you like. But St Andrew is Alba's."

"And Dalriada's!" Eochaidh asserted. "As to more than one nation having the same patron, that is no matter. Have you not heard? Andrew is already the patron saint of Muscovy."

"Muscovy . . . ?"

"To be sure. I would have thought that a man of any

learning would have known that!"

"I have more to do with my time than read books and the like, Nephew!" That was coldly said. Eochaidh was not, of course, Angus's nephew, although his wife's uncle, but from the younger monarch to the elder, it was reproof.

Kenneth was more concerned that he had started this altercation. He sought to change the subject, at least somewhat. "The cross? What of the cross? We will use that? St Andrew's cross. White on blue."

"To be sure. We shall fly it as banner, my people's banner," the High King answered. "Not my own royal standard – that is the black boar on silver."

"And you are welcome!" Eochaidh snapped.

"If both nations had the same patron and used the same device as banner, it would make a sort of unity," Kenneth persisted, a determined young man. "We can unite to fight the enemy, as it is. We could be the more united . . . "

"We could also be finished as a people!" his grandsire said. "Do not be a fool, boy!"

"Let us be on our way," Alpin suggested pacifically. "The road is long . . . " The parting, then, was less than harmonious.

Eochaidh did not take long, on the way up Strathearn, to berate his grandson on his folly. "What makes you haver of unity?" he demanded. "Have you no sense, boy? Unity with Alba would be the unity of the mouse with the cat! Dalriada would be swallowed up, quite. Lost. They are ten to our one, and more. The land twenty times as great."

"We could be a deal stronger, united. Against the Norsemen and the Angles and Saxons who endanger us. We united for this punitive raid."

"We can act together, when necessary, short of uniting. Dalriada will remain Dalriada – mind it!"

There was no more to be said – not then.

The Scots had not so far to travel as had the Albannach, who must traverse all the mountain lands of Strathtay and Atholl, Badenoch and Strathdearn, to Inverness, Angus's largest community. But even so it would take them fully five days, at the pace of the cattle, westwards across the centre of the land, going up Strathearn, Glen Ogle, Glen Dochart, Strathfillan and over the watershed of Mamlorn to Loch

Awe-side and eventual salt water at Loch Etive, where they would enter Dalriada. Nothing was more apt to emphasise to all concerned the modest size of the Scots kingdom compared with mighty Alba.

Reaching the sea, or at least the Sound of Lorn at the fortress of Dunstaffnage, they turned south now, by the Oban and a succession of sea-lochs, with the mountains pressing close, until they came at last to something very different, a sudden widening to what amounted almost to a plain, rare indeed on that seaboard, the flood-plain of the River Add, a four-mile-wide spread of level land where the stream reached the sea, part waterlogged admittedly but with much tillable soil and good pasture for beasts, cattle-dotted. But it was not all level, this Moine Mhor, or Great Moor as it was called, for rising out of its centre was an extraordinarily abrupt conical hill, ringed at its rocky summit with three circles of earth and stone ramparts, but these containing no building – Dunadd, the Dalriadan capital hill.

The plain was ringed with settlements, hamlets, mills and farmeries on the firmer, slightly rising margins, especially to the north where there were a notable cluster of stone circles, standing-stones and burial-cairns, relics of the sun-worshipping druidical days. Hereabouts most of the armed force still remaining with their leaders left them, for their homes, again with some squabbling over cattle and booty. Only the highly placed lived at Dunadd itself, around the base of that hill.

Kenneth was glad to be back. Although he had lived for the last few years hundreds of miles southwards on the Solway shore of Galloway, since his father had been appointed king there, Dunadd was his home, where he had been reared. Prince of Galloway he might be, but this was where he belonged. He used to climb that hill every evening, summer and winter, before going to bed, saying up there such prayers of which he was capable and dreaming his dreams. Dunadd of the Scots. One day . . .

It was on the hilltop that Dalriadan council meetings were held traditionally, weather permitting. Perhaps there was good reason for this, no buildings there notwithstanding, for as well as enshrining so much of the nation's story, from its lofty pinnacle so much of the kingdom itself could be viewed, quite extraordinary – although Kenneth, for one, found the prospect distracting in the extreme for due attention to council debates. There were vistas to the east, of course, quite far-flung, but these were of hills and mountains and valleys. It was to north, south and west that the eye was held, by the limitless panorama of the West Highland seaboard, peninsulas, headlands, sea-lochs, islands to all infinity. The long isle of Jura, with its breast-like twin summits, blocked the prospect somewhat south-westwards, but all else was clear, right out to Colonsay and Oronsay, Coll and Tiree, with near at hand Scarba with its whirlpool of Corryvreckan, the inshore isles of Luing and Seil and Shuna, the Garvellachs and Columba's Hinba, mountainous Mull hiding Iona itself, hundreds of lesser isles and skerries, nameless, all adream on a sea of azure and amethyst, emerald and pearl, the pure white of the cockle-shell sand, which ringed them all, shining through to enhance the colours.

With that to survey, heeding any discussion was not easy.

Eochaidh was very much in charge, his poisonous tongue ensuring that comments, interjections and the like were kept to a minimum. His councils lost not a little through his chiefs' fears of being mocked, ridiculed.

Their principal preoccupation today was Norse raiding. This had been getting worse and worse for years. At first it had been pirates from the Orkney and Shetland isles, taken over by the Scandinavians. But now they were mainly from Norway itself, and Denmark. These had gained a foothold on the north-east coast of Ireland and from there were terrorising the West Highland seaboard, savage, bloodthirsty sea-rovers concerned only with loot, murder, rape. Defending all this island kingdom effectively against them was an almost impossible task. Pagans, they had a particular animus against Christian shrines and churches – and it seemed that there had been another raid on Iona while the Scots army was away in Northumbria. Iona was a favourite target for them, being the very birthplace of the Columban Church and all too readily accessible, small, with no large population to help to defend it.

Eochaidh was set on retaliation, of course, on major

punishment to discourage further attacks. The problem was how to get at the raiders. These were essentially seafarers, always in their longships, with little in the way of bases. Indeed most of them went back to Scandinavia after their summer-time hosting, as they called it, for them a pleasurable seasonal employment. So they were hard to find, could appear and disappear at any time, and had no villages or townships to wreak vengeance upon.

In the circumstances, few suggestions were forthcoming as to how to cope with this, other than sending a squadron of ships to parade round the Hebridean Sea, mainly as warning but also in the slender hope of chancing on some of the raiders. This had been attempted before, of course, but with scant success.

Eochaidh himself said that some such naval expedition had to be staged, however ineffective it proved, since not to do it would be as good as inviting further raids. And their people had to be given some encouragement. He would assemble a small fleet forthwith, and Alpin his son would hasten down to Galloway and raise more ships there. Then they would comb the isles. This latest raid on Iona must not go unchallenged.

It was this reiteration of the name of Iona which brought Kenneth's full attention back to the subject under discussion. Little Iona was his favourite isle, not only on account of its sacred links with Columba and the establishment of Christianity here, but as perhaps the most beautiful of all the islands, the very jewel of the Hebridean galaxy. That these savage pirates should be deliberately defiling this sanctuary was the ultimate outrage.

He spoke up. "Highness, let me go to Iona. Take a longship – two would be better. Enquire there. The raiders may have left some hint of where they came from, or where they were going, something to identify them. If we knew at least which crew of barbarians they were, we might be able to trace them. Some guidance in our search . . . "

"Why two longships for that, boy?" his grandsire barked.

"To give the folk there courage to speak up. A small show of strength. Earnest of our attention to avenge. And then to be seen to be going off after the raiders."

"And if they can give you no guidance?"

"I say that we must still show strength, resolve. Seen to be going in pursuit. Or else, I fear, the Iona folk will desert the island. It has suffered too much. Iona lost would be a sorry defeat for Dalriada."

There was a murmur of agreement from around.

Eochaidh shrugged. "Try it, if you will. I do not see it as like to be successful. More use would be your telling to the folk there of our new patron saint! Of all our people, they will be most thirled to Columba. But Columba has failed to save Iona thus far, tell them Andrew may do better!" And he looked round the councillors significantly.

The news of the substitution of St Andrew for St Columba had not been greeted with any marked enthusiasm by the elders amongst the chiefs, and those who had not been involved in the Northumbrian expedition.

"I will do that, yes."

"You will waste no time," the King went on, sourly, almost as though he regretted having seemed to have been over-accommodating. "I cannot spare two longships for long. We shall assemble a fleet here, and every vessel will count. Alpin, it will take you two days to sail down to Galloway, perhaps three. Four more to collect a squadron, three more to sail back. Ten days, then. Ten days from now we shall sail, in force. I want you back, Kenneth, by then, with your ships. No later. You understand?"

"Yes, Highness. Two ships, with full crews. For ten days."

They went on to discuss other matters.

Kenneth's mind was now occupied with this new venture and he was impatient to be organising it, but could not escape until the King closed the meeting. Then he was not long in getting to horse, to ride down the couple of miles across the Plain of Add, by a causeway through tilth and marshland, to Port an Deora, the haven for Dunadd at the head of Loch Crinan.

Here, a variety of craft were based, many fishing-boats drawn up on the strand, deeper-draught vessels moored at timber quays, a few longships, some cargo-carriers but no merchanting and trading craft – for Dalriada was not a trading nation, unlike Strathclyde to the south.

There were only half a dozen longships there, for Eochaidh did not keep any established fleet, gathering in the

41

galleys of his chiefs and lords when a fleet was necessary. Kenneth went out to examine these, from the jetty. Their masters and crews were not present, of course, only a couple of seamen as caretakers. They told him that most of the shipmasters lived up at Ballymeanach, the population centre for Dunadd, to the north; but that Conall, one of these, lodged with the fisherfolk in a cot-house here.

Kenneth, going to try to find this Conall, was saved the trouble when a middle-aged, gnarled man of square build and square features came stalking up, looking enquiring rather than welcoming. No doubt he had seen a richly dressed and well-mounted stranger examining the ships and sought the reason.

"You seek something here, master?" he demanded.

"I seek two shipmasters, friend. Are you one? Of long-ships?"

"I am. Conall. Of this vessel here. What want you with shipmasters?"

"I want fighters. Fighting ships and fighting men both. I am Kenneth mac Alpin, of Galloway. And I have a task for them."

The other gazed at him levelly, but said nothing.

"You man longships, friend Conall? To sail? To carry? Or to fight?"

"All three, at need. I get less of the last than I would wish. So you are the prince? Is it your Galloway men you wish to fight?"

"Not so. It is the Norsemen, the Scandinavian pirates."

"Ha! Those savages! Then I wish you well, Prince."

"I need more than well-wishing. I need two hard-fighting crews and masters. Can you find them for me?"

"I can. If need be."

"The need is there. It is will and spirit that is lacking."

"How do you fight these Norsemen, Prince? How to *find* them?"

"That we will have to learn. But it must be possible. Go to Iona first, where they have done so much of evil, of hurt. Learn what we can there."

"When would you sail?"

"So soon as may be. I am given only ten days. When King Eochaidh will require all ships to be assembled here for a great fleet. Yours amongst them, no doubt."

"Ten days . . . !"

"Will you do it? I cannot command you to do it."

"Aye, I will. I will need till the morn to collect the crews."

"Of fighters, see you."

"I sail with no others," Conall said briefly.

They left it at that.

So next morning early Kenneth was back at Port an Deora, to find two fully manned longships awaiting him, almost over-manned indeed, for as well as the thirty-two oarsmen each, for the sixteen long sweeps, the masters and helmsmen, there were about a score of others, as extra rowers and spare fighters, for each vessel. So he found himself with a force of over one hundred, as rough-looking a crew as it had been his lot to encounter, but certainly the sort who would not dodge a fight. They would require to be paid hereafter – but that was for the future.

Conall seemed almost impatient to be off. Apparently they had been waiting for almost a couple of hours. He introduced the other master as Murdoch, a younger man, lacking one eye.

The journey to Iona, although only some thirty-five sea miles, was no simple sail, despite being through some of the most spectacular waters known to man, and in fine weather a delight, at least to the eye. For the Sea of the Hebrides presents the sailor with challenges innumerable, reefs and skerries everywhere, in reality submerged mountain-tops, tide-races, overfalls, sudden shallows, downdraughts off the hills and the like – and this part of it, off Lorn, the most testing of all. The prevailing south-westerly winds are complicated by the mountainous islands and the narrow sounds or channels between, which act as air funnels, and gaps amongst the isles creating tidal surges, disconcerting for the unwary mariner. Actual sail-use has to be carefully controlled in all this, since wind direction can be erratic in the extreme, even in a breeze which elsewhere would normally be steady. So oar-work was important.

Out of Loch Crinan the longships turned northwards up the Sound of Jura, where they could hoist the single square sail to fair effect, tacking this way and that, the thirty-two oarsmen on each more or less resting. But less than three miles on they had to negotiate the Dorus Mor, the Great Gate, a quarter-mile passage between the tip of the long Craignish peninsula and the rocky islet of Garbh Reisa, and immediately it was hard oar-work, not only on account of the current of the inflowing tide in these narrows but because suddenly they had the wind full against them – this caused by the abrupt cliff-girt ending of Jura ahead and the narrow strait of Corryvreckan between it and towering Scarba funnelling the south-west airstream round to make it north-west. Shipmasters in these waters had to know their business.

In front now was the said Strait of Corryvreckan, the obvious access to the main western ocean. But not for prudent navigators. Therein lay the notorious whirlpool, grave of ships innumerable, a strange menacing feature caused presumably by a tide-surge round the conical peak of a submerged mountain-top creating a circular swirl of enormous strength with a down-sucking centre which even the largest craft could not counter. Of a winter's storm the roar of this could be heard even at Dunadd, an unchancy sound, although of a fine summer's day, as this, there was little noise. But that was no reassurance, for Corryvreckan could be as lethal in a calm as in a gale. Conall did not consider turning into the half-mile-wide strait, but continued on up what now became the Sound of Luing, much less inviting as this appeared on account of its positive rash of scattered islets, skerries and reefs, the great rocky cliffs and beetling crags of Scarba on their left. There was a safe passage through this welter of hazards to the open sea, demanding only careful navigation.

Lunga replacing Scarba on the left and Luing itself, six miles of it, on the right, they came out from the close waters at length, into the wide ocean, where oars could be dispensed with again, meantime, the south-west wind free to propel them, with tacking, for they were now sailing north-by-west. The prospect remained isle-dotted but differently, for these islands were more distant, the Hebrides proper, miles apart – Coll, Colonsay, Oronsay, Tiree and the rest, with further away still Muck, Eigg, Rhum and, just discernible, the jagged Cuillin Mountains of Skye.

But it was for none of these that they headed. Mull, next

to Skye the largest of all the Hebrides, lay due north, its great mountains blocking off all view in that direction. Mull's long, low south-western promontory, the Ross, lay like a great barrier before them, a dozen miles off – and round, just beyond the tip of that barrier, lay Iona.

Leaving the four Garvellachs on their left, one of which, little Hinba, had been St Columba's private retreat, they headed out over the sparkling waters, oars shipped and crews at ease, only the hazard of the Torran Rocks halfway to their destination to be avoided now.

Three hours after leaving Port an Deora, thanks to that helpful breeze, the two vessels rounded the tip of the Ross of Mull, and there before them, a couple of miles off, was their immediate goal. And even in all this galaxy of isles, this superabundance of beauty, it could be seen why this small entity had been given the name, unchallenged, of I, or Iona, *the* island. A jewel indeed, set within its ring of gleaming white cockleshell sand, aglow with colours, fertile with crops and flowers, dotted with cattle and sheep and whitewashed cot-houses, alive with birds, a picture of loveliness and peace.

And yet, although peace *belonged* to the place, as Columba had perceived and added to in his own notable fashion, these days it knew perhaps the least peace of all the Hebrides, the deliberate especial target for attack and sacrilege by the marauding Norsemen, who seemed to single it out for their grim attentions.

The longships drew into the haven and boatstrand of the bay on the east side of the island, a mere mile from the Mull shore. Even before landing, Kenneth could see something of the devastation, cottages roofless, their whitewash smoke-blackened, barns and sheds thrown down, boats on the strand smashed. At first glance the place might have been deserted, for no folk were to be seen. But smoke did rise above some of the undamaged cot-houses, so inhabitants there were still, but they were hiding, no doubt alarmed. Longships bearing down on Iona would be apt to have that effect.

Ordering the crews to remain aboard meantime, Kenneth went ashore with only Conall, deliberately both unarmed, to reassure, although the tartans of their garb ought to identify

45

them as friendly when this could be distinguished.

Kenneth had visited the island many times, of course, and knew his way about. The centre and heart of it was not far from this anchorage bay, on the east side, where Columba had established his monastery on the site of the ancient druidical college. Thither the pair made their way. Only one or two barking dogs acknowledged their arrival.

From a distance, the sacred precincts did not give much impression of damage, because here many of the buildings were of stone, not the whitewashed wattle and daub of normal construction. But on closer inspection it was to be seen that this was an illusion. The beehive cells, the tombs of the kings, the Reelig Oran and the tall stone crosses could not be cast down without almost as much labour as in the building of them, and this the Vikings had not troubled to do. But they could be wrecked and defaced internally, the tombs desecrated, monuments smashed, carvings battered, wall-paintings smeared with filth. The wattle and daub buildings, of which most of the monastery consisted – twisted sapling frames infilled with soil and stones and outwardly coated with clay, whitewashed to show the interlacing pattern of the saplings, beloved of the Celtic carvers and decorators – were comparatively easy to destroy, and these had all been demolished: the kitchens, the refectory, the dormitories and the rest, the loving labour of the ages done away with. What made men act so towards those who had done them no hurt? The Norsemen were pagan, yes, but so were many other races who did not act like this. Christianity represented no menace to them. They were not seeking to conquer a country. It was all blood-lust and a passion to destroy, it seemed.

Kenneth went first to examine the enclosure for the tombs of the kings, for here was where his ancestors were buried, the long line since Fergus mac Erc, four centuries of them. Some crosses were cast down, but otherwise no damage. No doubt the Vikings did not recognise the significance of it.

They made for the nearest surviving house where smoke arose from a cooking-fire, watched by an elderly man from the doorway.

"I am Kenneth mac Alpin of Galloway," he announced. "We are not long back from Northumbria, with King

46

Eochaidh. We heard that the Norsemen had been raiding again here. We came to discover what we can."

"King Eochaidh would be better guarding his own land than hosting to Northumbria," the old man declared bluntly. "Those devils of Danes crucify us here! They are fiends, brute-beasts! We can no longer live here, on Iona!"

"I am sorry. We seek to get at them. Teach them a lesson. But we must find them first."

"They slew my son. Raped my wife and daughter. Took my granddaughter and other young women away. Animals . . . !"

"*Where* do they take them?" Conall demanded. "Where?"

"Who knows? Think you that they tell us? Those that they do not slay!"

"We cannot punish them if we do not know where they are," Conall said.

"How many of them were there?" Kenneth asked.

"Two of their dragon-ships, this time. Five score men . . . "

"Two ships only? Then these must have been but part of a greater hosting."

"Enough! Enough to savage our island."

"Yes, friend. But if these were only part of a larger fleet, then the rest may not be far away. Two ships are unlikely to be hosting on their own."

The other shrugged. "Black Duncan thinks that they are based on Coll. He was away visiting his brother on Tiree. He says that he saw four dragon-ships anchored in Loch Eatharna, off Arinagour of Coll."

"Four! How long ago was that?"

"While they were raiding here. Four weeks past now."

"They may have gone now, then. But perhaps they are using Coll as a base for their devil's work. You have heard of no more raiding since then?"

"We have plenty to think on here without heeding for other folk's troubles!"

"No doubt. We can try Coll, at least." Kenneth changed the subject somewhat. "Tell me, friend, in all this destruction, what happened to the monks? Did they . . .? The precious books and writings? The sacred vessels of the church? The robes and vestments? Columba's own psalms?

47

All the precious things of Iona?"

"The priests and monks are dead. Every one slain. We buried them after – those of us who escaped. Much burying. Some of the writings and scrolls and relics were thrown about. We gathered them up. I have some here, in my house . . . "

"Good. Guard them well – for they mean much to our nation. So, the monks died. As others have done before them. I fear that we will have difficulty in persuading others to come here."

"They would be fools to come . . . "

They took their leave of this disillusioned ancient and headed back to the ships. There was nothing that they could usefully do on Iona meantime.

Clearly a careful reconnaissance of the Isle of Coll was indicated. Even if the Norsemen had gone, the islanders there might have gained some idea as to where they were gone or where they had come from. Coll lay some twenty miles north-west of Iona, only open sea between.

Kenneth debated with himself. If there were indeed four or six or more Viking ships there, then to arrive openly would be asking for trouble. So a descent by night would be advisable. It was now mid-afternoon and they could be there in two hours with this breeze – too soon. They might go to Tiree, the next island to Coll, and hide there until dark.

So they sailed west by north, in no hurry now, and keeping a sharp look-out for other craft. But apart from two or three fishing-boats, vessels were notable for their absence, no doubt the presence of Norsemen in the area accounting for that.

Tiree was a long flat island, the most level of all the Hebrides and the most fertile. Columba had used it as a granary, to supply food for his many monasteries and cashels. The two longships circled it warily, for Vikings could be active here also. But its very flatness helped to reassure – dragon-ships' masts would stand out conspicuously from any anchorages.

They drew in, eventually, to the most west-facing bay, furthest from Coll, there to wait, aware that their arrival would be creating dire alarm amongst the inhabitants. No enquirers came to seek their identity.

As the sun sank in splendour behind the Outer Isles, and the dusk took over the Hebridean Sea, they raised sail again, to head round the northern shores of Tiree's ten-mile length. This would help protect them from sight from Coll, the western tip of which lay only a mile or so to the north-east. By the time that they got that far, it was almost dark. Kenneth considered it safe to move in.

For two islands approximately the same size, and so close together, it was strange that these were so different in character. Coll was much less fertile, more hilly, although even so the hills were not high, with much more of rock and sand-dune, more typical of that seaboard altogether. The long north-west shore facing the ocean was devoid of sheltered bays and havens, all reefs and skerries; but there were three possible anchorages on the south shore: the main centre of the island, Arinagour, at the head of a fine sheltered sea-loch, Eatharna, this the furthest off; a narrow, shallow inlet at Breachacha halfway; and a wide open bay and boatstrand at the bottom end, where there was the little fishing community of Crossapol. Kenneth, who knew the isle of old, reckoned that the Norsemen, if there, would almost certainly be using Arinagour, where would be the best anchorage, houses, food and women. The Breachacha inlet was narrow and could be a trap. So he ordered Conall to put in at Crossapol Bay.

Just four of them put ashore in a small boat, to make quietly for the nearest fisherman's cot-house, all dark. Their knock at the door, at that hour, was bound to cause concern and fear, they realised.

It took some time to produce an answer. They heard whispering. Then a voice asked who called and why?

"Fear nothing, friend – it is Kenneth mac Alpin of Galloway. Come from Dunadd. We seek the Norsemen. Can you tell us of them?"

That produced more whispering. Then the door opened a crack and a man peered out at them.

"We heard that the pirates were at Coll. Or based here. Is that so, friend?"

Presumably reassured, perhaps in that there were only the four of them, the fisherman opened wider. "Yes, master, they are here – God pity us! The Danes."

"Where? How many?"

"Sometimes many, sometimes fewer. They anchor at Arinagour. Raid the isles from there. Demons, killers, destroyers!"

"Yet you survive, friend?"

"Only because we catch fish for them. Otherwise we would be dead. They come and use my wife whenever they wish."

"I am sorry. They are at Arinagour now?"

"Only two of their ships, at this present. Four sailed two days ago, northwards."

"Two! Then . . . " Kenneth looked at Conall.

"Aye." That man nodded. "Do they sleep on their ships of a night?" he asked.

"No, no. They will be in the houses, drinking and bedding the women."

"But they will leave guards on their ships?"

"That I know not, masters . . . "

Back they went to the longships, urgent now. There was little need to discuss plans – the thing was obvious. They raised sail and drew out of Crossapol Bay, north-eastwards. As they sailed, Kenneth told the rowers to tie cloths and sweat-rags round the oar-shafts, to prevent creaking and groaning noises.

It was some six miles up to Arinagour's loch, and well after midnight before they reached it. Here a rocky islet part-filled the half-mile-wide loch-mouth. They downed the sails and got out the oars, to probe up-loch carefully. Navigation in the darkness was chancy in such enclosed waters. They all but crept, watchers peering in the bows for rocks and skerries.

They had almost a mile to penetrate before, quite suddenly, they saw the outlines of two dragon-ships ahead of them, hitherto hidden against the loom of the land. No lights showed thereon – nor indeed from anywhere on the island.

Now all was tense on the two longships. Muffled as the oars were, they seemed to creak unconsciously against their rowlocks – although Kenneth assured himself that the splash-splash of the wavelets would cover that. He dared not risk bringing his own ships alongside the others, in case they bumped and roused any occupants. It was unlikely that guards aboard would deliberately stay awake of a night, in the circumstances; but they could not rely on that. Silence was essential.

Rather than launching coracles, small light boats which each longship carried, Kenneth asked for volunteers, swimmers, who would drop over the side, swim a few yards and then climb up on to the enemy vessels. He had no lack of response. He stripped off some of his own clothing in readiness.

With about a dozen others he slipped down into the dark, cold water, and swam the few strokes to the dragon-ships. Hoisting themselves up was the most difficult part of it, but the more agile, once up, assisted the others and all were quickly aboard the first vessel.

These Norse dragon-ships were approximately the same construction as their own longships, but somewhat larger, with more oars and a higher prow ending in the typical menacing dragon's head. The main portion of the vessel, long and narrow, was open, with the rowers' benches across, and a single central mast for the great square sail; but at bows and stern there was decked-in accommodation for shelter, sleep and storage, far from extensive. Kenneth led the way quietly, with some of his men, to the bows cabin, with the others going to the stern. Neither found any guard or watch-keeper.

A little surprised, Kenneth gathered his people to point at the second Norse craft.

They went through the same procedure as before. Aboard, they divided again. Once more Kenneth found no one in the bows cabin; but when their colleagues appeared from the stern one, they were grinning, and two were brandishing bloody dirks. Also they had increased their numbers by one, a youngish woman huddled only in a blanket, and fearful. Apparently there had been two Norse watch-keepers, and these had elected to spend the night in company, sharing this female captive, and all had fallen asleep. There were two less pirates now, at any rate.

Thus cheaply they had won two dragon-ships.

Kenneth debated with himself. They could sink these ships – or they could try to take them, as captures, in triumph. But their crews, on land? Depriving them of their ships was scarcely enough. They had come to teach these barbarians a lesson. The men first, then.

Back on their own ships, he spoke to the desperately frightened woman, seeking to soothe her by asking her where she was from. Whispering, trembling, she said that she was from Iona, her husband and child slain, brought here as a plaything for these Danes. With some other women. Assuring her that she would get home in due course, he asked whether she knew how the Norsemen were disposed, on Coll. They would not be far from their ships – they never were – but were they all together at Arinagour, or scattered? She said that some were in various houses of the township, but most were quartered in the church, which they had taken over and defiled, roosting there with captured women. By this hour, all would be asleep, most drunken.

Kenneth, considering, decided to divide up his five score men into five parties. Half he would take with him, for that church; and four parties of a dozen each would search the houses. A very few he would leave with the vessels. The woman, hatred of the invaders overcoming her fear, volunteered to come with them, as guide.

They moored the longships as close inshore as they might, and landed, Kenneth himself carrying the woman through the shallows. It was not far up from the boatstrand to the first of the houses, the church on somewhat higher ground, she said, behind a little inlet. Leaving the shipmaster Murdoch in charge of the four house-parties, with urgent instructions to avoid noise at all costs, he led his own party round the inlet and up to the church on the knoll.

It was no very large or elaborate building, merely an oblong of some seventy feet by twenty, stone-built, with a single door and small narrow windows, and a roof of reed-thatch. Close to it, they could hear the sound of snoring from within, the door left open.

Kenneth was not sacrilegiously inclined, and loth to damage sacred property. But this church was already defiled, and filled with sacrilegious and murderous pagans. It was due to be cleansed – and he could not be delicate about the doing of it. But, unfortunately, there were women in there also, Christian women, wronged women, a dire com-

cation. He consulted with Conall.

"We could burn them out – that thatch. But, the women . . . ?"

"They must take their chance."

"I cannot do that. They will have suffered enough, already."

"We have no choice, man, if we are to destroy these brute-beasts. We cannot do that, and spare the women."

"See you – the thatch will take some time to catch alight, to burn through. The smoke and noise will arouse them. There is only this one door, not wide. No more than two men can get through at once. And the windows are high and narrow. They will rush to get out. And we will slay them as they come. The women, I reckon, will be left behind. No?"

"That could be, yes. Let us be at it, then . . . "

Many of the Scots had flint and steel. Tinder was less easy, but it had been a reasonably good summer and there was dry marram-grass which caught fire readily. Also the thatch would itself be dry.

Bunches of burning grass were tossed up, all round, and quite quickly some lit the reed-thatching. In only a minute or two the roof was ablaze.

It took a surprising time for the situation to become apparent to those within – or at least so it seemed to the men clustered at the door waiting, swords and dirks in hand. A muffled shout or two reached them from the township houses, but in the church itself only snoring – which the crackle of the flames soon drowned.

It was, in fact, a woman's screaming which aroused the Norsemen to their danger. This was succeeded by shouts aplenty. Then the first of the would-be escapers appeared in the doorway – to be cut down by all who could get at him.

After that it was sheer savage slaughter, with the invaders denied all opportunity to strike back, their own crushing together at the narrow doorway itself hampering them from wielding weapons. Those in front were pushed on to their deaths by those behind. Quickly a twitching, thrashing heap of slain and wounded blocked the entrance. With the yells and shrieks from inside, the glare of the flames and the ever-increasing heat, it all made a fair representation of hell. What it would be like inside was beyond imagining.

Some of the Norsemen tried to get out through the meagre windows, but only the slimmest and most nimble could achieve this – and Scots with cold steel awaited those that did get through.

In the end it was some of the trapped men's despairing efforts to hack a way through the blazing thatch itself which precipitated a climax. For the hole made seemed to allow air to rush inside and greatly to encourage the flames. In moments the entire roof was aflame and falling in.

Appalled at the thought of the women within, Kenneth yelled to some of his men to come with him. None of the Vikings was now battling to get out of the doorway, which was all but blocked by the heap of the writhing slain. Over this horrible barrier he sought to clamber. The lurid, flame-lit, choking smoke restricted all view, the heat was breath-taking when he needed breath, the noise mind-reeling. It took him moments to perceive what was happening. Men were now seeking to climb out of the gaps in the fallen roof, fighting each other, clambering on top of bodies to do so, treading each other down, hair, beards alight, utter desperation taken over. He could distinguish no women.

He decided that there was nothing that he could do here. He turned and waved his men back, to lurch and struggle for the doorway again. And then, he perceived that one of the heaving bodies he was trampling over was that of a woman – or, at least, the head and long hair of a woman part-covered by fallen men and burning debris.

Urgently he stooped, to pull at and drag aside those male bodies to get at the woman, to heave her up with all his strength. Her arms freed, she flailed about, which did not help. But somehow he dragged her free and part-carried her to the doorway, to get her over the heap there, and out.

He turned back, waving to others to come, to do the same.

They got three more women out, thus, but one proved to be dead. By then Kenneth himself was all but suffocated, hair singed, with superficial burns, reeling and scarcely aware of what he did. Conall grabbed him and pulled him away by main force, to set him down on grass well back from that inferno of a devastated church. There he lay panting, only semi-aware of what went on.

When he had recovered sufficiently to rise and go forward again, it was all over, the building no more than a funeral pyre for the dead Norsemen and any women who had not got out. None of the enemy had escaped steel and fire. His men were cheering in triumph, most slightly burned but none incapacitated.

Kenneth found himself to be all but shattered by what they had done, but perforce had to swallow his misgivings. The detachments sent to comb the houses for raiders came back in twos and threes, wiping bloody weapons, satisfied with their part in the slaughter. Islanders huddled here and there, in bewilderment and terror. There were notably few men amongst them.

Distinctly dazed as he still was, Kenneth was sufficiently himself to recognise that they might still be endangered, despite this victory here. Those two dragon-ships were not likely to be the only ones in this part of the Hebrides. Others might well be near at hand. And the burning church could have served as a beacon. Tempting as it was for all to bed down here on the couches vacated by the Norsemen in the houses – with possible grateful female company – he insisted on a return to their longships meantime. They did not want to be caught the way *they* had caught the enemy. They would come ashore again in the morning.

There were grumbles but no actual refusals. And considerable booty in weapons, and liquor, gold armlets and clothing came with them.

They moved the four vessels seawards some little way, to hide them behind the shelter of the small islet near the loch-mouth, from which they could make escape, if necessary, either way. There, posting guards to keep watch, two on the islet itself, the others settled to sleep.

Their slumbers were undisturbed, save by the changing of the guards.

Sunrise saw the two longships emerging from Loch Eatharna into the open waters, to separate and sail north and south some distance, so that their crews might observe all the seas around in case other Viking craft should appear. But no shipping was to be seen on all the sparkling morning ocean – although, of course, vessels might be hidden behind islands. They returned to Arinagour.

Despite their drastic purging of Coll's invaders, the purgers did not find themselves to be greeted with much gratitude and acclaim by the islanders – the attitude being that once the newcomers had departed and other Norsemen returned, their vengeance would be the more dire. Kenneth recognised the force of this, but did not see what he could do, save to say that King Eochaidh would be bringing a large Scots fleet to scour the entire seaboard and seek to drive the Vikings away altogether.

He set his men to burying the enemy dead in pits dug in the sandy levels at the loch-head, a major task which they could scarcely leave to the women, children and aged men who had survived the pirates' savagery. If Kenneth was still somewhat shaken by the horror and scale of what they had done in the night, any feeling of guilt tended to be wiped out when they were taken to see something down at the boat-strand near the village. Here, where the fishermen dried their nets over wooden scaffolding, the Vikings had made use of the said scaffolding for another purpose. On it they had hung row upon row of heads, cut from the bodies of the men of Coll. These heads had obviously been washed, the hair and beards combed, with ghastly order and care, to festoon this vermin-board, a demonstration as extraordinary as it was grisly. Kenneth had heard of this horrible custom, but never before seen an example.

He was for taking the heads down and giving them decent burial, but the women and kinsfolk dissuaded him. The Danes had said that they were to remain there, as witness of their prowess; and if they were removed there would be reprisals, nothing more sure.

Kenneth decided that there was nothing more that he could do on this unhappy island, save seek to reassure in that King Eochaidh would endeavour further to avenge them and clear the seas of the hated raiders. Returning to their vessels, he divided his crews so as to man the two captive dragon-ships, and all four vessels put to sea. At least they would have something to show for their efforts when they returned to Dunadd.

Sailing due southwards now, the south-west wind not quite so helpful as when they had come, they had a score of miles to go to pass Iona, and the Ross of Mull, before, avoiding the menace of the Torran Rocks, they could turn eastwards to head for the Sound of Luing and the sheltered inshore waters thereafter. Their ships were undermanned now, also, but speed was not vital.

That is, until in the early afternoon, just past Iona, they spied sails to the west, no fewer than seven, in close formation, square sails. These need not be Norsemen, admittedly; they could be longships from the outer Isles coming to Eochaidh's muster. But seven together was more than was to be expected from that quarter. Kenneth became uneasy. Even if they were Vikings, of course, they might not be interested in his ships, or perhaps even spot them against the background of Mull and the inshore isles to the east. But . . .

It was not long, however, before the Scots came to the conclusion that the other flotilla had as sharp eyes as their own and *were* interested in them sufficiently to be changing course towards them. They were probably five or six miles away but definitely drawing closer.

Kenneth consulted with Conall. Manning four ships with the numbers for two, they must inevitably be at a disadvantage as to speed, save in a directly following wind. And if these were Norsemen, and attacked, they could hardly hope to prevail against seven of them. What to do, then? Should they abandon the two captured vessels, retrieve their crews and so make better time – after the delay that must involve? Or should they disperse, all four craft fleeing separately and so seek to break up the pursuit? That would almost certainly ensure some loss, even though some might escape. Or just carry on hopefully, in an attempt to reach the inshore islands of the mainland and try to lose the enemy amongst them? Uncertain, they decided to follow the last course, meantime.

It was not long before they discovered that this would by no means serve. They were being overtaken; clearly these were swift and powerful dragon-ships, intent now on catching up with them. Kenneth, judging distance, came to the conclusion that there was no hope of reaching even the Garvellach Isles, much less the Sound of Luing, before being brought to bay. He doubted also whether he could risk slowing up to transfer the crews from the captured craft. Their situation looked grim.

He turned to Conall. "Corryvreckan?" he jerked.

The other stared at him.

"It could be our only chance, if these aim to attack. They are clearly Norsemen. They will overtake us well before we can make any landfall. But the Gulf of Corryvreckan. Think you they will know of that? Have heard of it? They might not follow us into that."

The shipmaster, tough and bold as he was, looked appalled. "Not that! Not Corryvreckan!" he got out.

"It would give us a chance, at least. Columba did it – took his ship through it. Not the whirlpool itself, but the strait. *We* could do the same. I reckon that we could make the mouth of it before these catch up with us. If they know of it – and probably they will, for it is the best-known hazard in all this Western Sea – they may well not dare to enter it . . . "

"Nor should we, I say!"

"Would you rather stand and fight? Four half-manned ships against seven fully manned? And the fiercest sea-fighters in the world?"

Conall was silent.

His doubts were not misplaced. The half-mile-wide Strait of Corryvreckan lay between the long island of Jura and the precipitous Scarba, now some eight miles to their south-east. At its centre was the extraordinary phenomenon of the mighty whirlpool. If the Norsemen had done much hosting in the Hebrides, then they would almost certainly have heard of Corryvreckan, and might well shun it.

"We can hug the Jura shore," Kenneth went on. "If it comes to the worst, we might have to abandon the ships, land . . . "

"Or drown!"

"Better than have our heads hung on a Viking tally-board!"

Kenneth's mind was made up. He gave the order for the steersmen, however reluctant, to change course the necessary points southwards, even though this must lose them some little benefit of the wind. The oarsmen must pull the harder.

It was a race now, indeed, with those miles to cover to the strait-mouth and the dragon-ships overhauling them ever more rapidly, their extra oar-power telling in these conditions. What the Norsemen thought of it all was not to be known, two longships and two of their own dragon-ships heading deliberately for that yawning gulf.

Kenneth's preoccupation was now divided. Could they reach the strait-mouth before they were intercepted? And what would he do once they were therein? Major questions, both.

In the event, they made it with only minutes to spare, for the Norsemen were no more than four hundred yards behind the Scots ships as they entered the dread gap between the craggy tip of Jura and the awesome, cave-gaping precipices of Scarba, near enough to see the fierce dragon-prows, the painted black ravens on the square sails and the gleam of sunlight on steel, even the winged helmets of the Viking leaders standing in the bows.

Now Kenneth could, and must, concentrate on this dire gamble to which he had committed them, the peaceful afternoon placidity of it all having to be sternly discounted. The strait was some two miles long but only a fourth of that across, looking even less on account of the towering land-masses on either side. The whirlpool was reputed to be towards this west end and worst at the north or Scarba side; but since itself was some four hundred yards across, with its pull apt to extend further still, that would affect more than half of the strait's width – and at different states of the tide said to reach even to the Jura shore.

He headed Conall's ship slantwise across the opening, at not too steep an angle, for he was anxious not to have the pursuit think that there might be a safe passage close to the Jura shore. This oblique course not only had Conall exclaiming, but let the Norse ships draw even closer. But Kenneth was too engrossed in his own calculations to heed. He was eying the sea surface ahead intently. Columba, he had been told, threw rowers' sweat-rags into the water to gauge the pull of the maelstrom by the speed at which these were carried away. He had a heap of rags ready. The first two cast in bobbed about innocently enough.

He glanced back. His three following ships were keeping very close, almost dangerously so, apprehension evident on all forward-peering faces. The Norsemen were now a bare three hundred yards behind. But even as he looked there was a change in their tight formation. This was caused by the leading ship pulling round, actually in the strait-mouth, to all but broadside-on, the others edging in to cluster about it. Clearly a conference was taking place. Kenneth hoped and prayed that caution would prevail – although caution was not a normal Norse reaction.

His next rag thrown went dancing away from the side in an easterly direction. So the pull was beginning. The rowers were not complaining yet – but they would when the current really began to grip their oars. He maintained course.

The Norse ships remained more or less stationary. It must be quite a hard decision for their leaders to make. But meantime the Scots were able to draw ahead again.

Then Kenneth perceived that caution was not going to prevail behind. The Viking ships came on.

His silent cursing was interrupted by shouts from his oarsmen. They were feeling a distinct tug now. Conall took matters into his own hands – after all, it was his ship – and ordered a sharper course for the Jura shore. Kenneth reckoned that they had now a lead of some six hundred yards or more.

They were not far from the Jura shore when there was a development. They could hear shouting from the enemy. Evidently they too were now feeling the pull of the whirl-pool. And this produced an unexpected reaction. Four of the dragon-ships of the pursuit came on after the Scots but three did not exactly turn back but swung away, to begin to beat up and down, clearly to wait beyond the drag of the current.

Kenneth urgently debated with himself. If he and his people sought to land on Jura, the Norsemen would follow and they would be outnumbered two to one – more, if the other ships then came to join in. So that was to be rejected. What, then? How he wished that they were not saddled with these two captured vessels. He threw another rag, but here it floated off not so fast as the last one.

He turned to Conall. "See you – we must do something. These two captured ships. They much hamper us. If we head in closer to the shore, then abandon them? Get our crews back. That should give us increased oar-power. Perhaps hold up the enemy a little, as they regain them . . . "

Conall was glad to agree to any improvement. He bellowed instructions to the crews of the two dragon-ships.

Within four score yards of the shore, just west of the most prominent jut of Jura's northernmost tip, their captured craft were brought alongside the other two and a hasty transfer of crews achieved. Then off again, extra men now on each of the oars.

Having to round the thrusting point of Carraig Mor meant heading the ships north-by-east for a little way, that is towards the whirlpool, and quickly they felt the drag of it. Although this alarmed the crewmen, it gave Kenneth an idea. If they could in fact take such a course hereafter, to the limit of safety, they might decoy the Norsemen into doing likewise and even, as it were, risk cutting a corner to head them off and gain on them. Then they might get caught in the tidal pull and fail to get out? Or at least get sufficient fright to make them draw off, give up the chase? A slender hope – but the situation was becoming desperate.

He said as much to Conall, who was the reverse of enthusiastic.

Listening was the helmsman at the steering-oar. He spoke up. "Ferchar Odhar, here, on the second oar, is a Juraman, lord. He spoke to me back there, as we took the others aboard. His father, a fisherman, used to sink lobster-pots round on the other side of this Carraig Mor headland. There is an inshore reef there, enclosing shallow water. Where he used to put his lobster-pots."

"What use is that to us, man?"

"Anchor there our two ships, on a rope. Ferchar says that his father used to do that, when the current was strong . . ."

"A long rope! Praise be – that could be it!" Conall exclaimed.

"Have we rope long enough?" Kenneth demanded.

"Plenty of rope always aboard both craft."

"Can we do this? Have we time?"

"Once round the headland, lord, we will be out of sight of the Danes for a while. If we hasten . . ."

"Good! Then we try that. This rope . . ."

Kenneth and Conall shouted instructions to the other vessel. All their rope required. The two craft to be tied together. The ropes knotted to form one very long anchor-cable. Anchor dropped behind this reef of Ferchar's. Then head out towards the whirlpool, as far as the rope allowed. The rope would hold them, God willing. Without the rope, the Norsemen, if they followed, would be at the mercy of the current. Then win back thereafter, men pulling on the rope to aid the rowers. It should serve . . .

Doubts were expressed, but it was a possibility and no better suggestions were forthcoming. Round Carraig Mor was not exactly a bay but a re-entrant angle where they would be hidden from the pursuit for a brief time. There, hastening shorewards again, Ferchar Odhar pointed out the position of the underwater reef, not far along. Making for this with all speed, Conall chose a secure anchor-hold behind it while others tied the two longships close together. Then they lowered the anchor on its now very lengthy cable, and without delay turned to row out northwards again.

Just in time, for the first Norse ship was now rounding the headland not much more than three hundred yards away. Straight out for the Scarba shore the Scots rowed. Soon the oarsmen shouted that they had almost no need to row, so strong was the pull becoming.

The second shipmaster was at the stern of his vessel watching the rope. At this stage it was, of course, under water, and so would not be seen by the Norsemen. If it began to rise into visibility, he was to shout warning.

Kenneth saw, as he had hoped, that the Vikings were indeed seeking to head them off and make time by cutting across. They would believe, presumably, that if it was safe for the Scots it was safe for them.

Despite himself Kenneth could not help gazing down at the surface-water around and ahead of them, so deceptively smooth and harmless-seeming. Without that rope . . .

The Norsemen were drawing ever closer, their two leading ships now near enough to see the bearded faces of the leaders under their winged helmets. Soon they would be within range of throwing-spears. Kenneth reckoned that the vortex of the whirlpool could not be more than three hundred yards ahead.

Then came the warning shout from the rear. The anchor-rope was beginning to rise to the surface.

This was the moment of truth. Would the anchor and rope

hold them? The rowers were ordered to dig in their oars and back-water with all their strength. They hardly needed to be so exhorted.

The rope came up, and held. With a jerk, they were stationary.

But the Norsemen were not. They came on, still rowing hard.

The moment when the true situation dawned on the enemy was entirely evident to the Scots. Men were poised for spear-throwing on the first dragon-ship, so close were they, when shouting arose, not in threatening challenge but in alarm. Probably the rope had been seen now, also the back-water pulling of the Scots. Most certainly their oarsmen would recognise that they were no longer in control of their vessels. Dig in as they would they could by no means halt the onward surge. Fast, faster than their most speedy progress hitherto, they lurched onwards, to the north by a little west.

Despite their own danger and fears that their anchor might not hold, Kenneth and his people watched. Swiftly the first and second dragon-ships were carried past them, next to panic now evident aboard. The other two vessels were some way behind and could be seen to be seeking desperately to pull round westwards, the menace perceived.

All on the Scots craft had stares riveted on the two foremost ships as they plunged on, tending to swing broadsides-on now, no stopping them. The yells had died away as men faced their fate. These were pagans, and perhaps they accepted that their Thor and Odin would be waiting to accept them into Valhalla of the heroes, with its five hundred and forty doors. Some oarsmen continued to row furiously, but most abandoned their long sweeps and stood up. All faced the front.

Kenneth chewed his lip, a prey to a variety of emotions.

They saw the first ship turn right round as it swung away east-about, at great speed now. Then it was swirling north and then west in a fairly tight circle, the second vessel beginning to go through the same circular motion. It was when the two were momentarily almost in line of vision that Kenneth perceived a significant fact. The first was now noticeably lower in the water than the second. Even as he gazed, it sank further. It was being sucked down as it neared the vortex.

It seemed almost beyond belief for the Scots to wait there and watch this happening. No words were being spoken now, breaths almost being held.

The second dragon-ship was now becoming low in the water. Yet, from this distance, there appeared to be no reason for it, no turbulence, no obvious swirl on the surface. Only those rotating ships with the steadily lessening free-boards.

Then a sort of groan went up from the Scots as suddenly there was no freeboard visible on the first ship, only its dragon-prow, stern-platform, sail and mast. And swiftly these were gone also.

They saw some men diving overboard from the second vessel, but these heads disappeared almost immediately. Then their ship went under exactly as had the other. The innocent-looking surface of Corryvreckan gleamed in the late afternoon sunshine, as before.

The watchers turned to eye each other, for the most part speechless.

It was only then that Kenneth bethought himself to look for the other two dragon-ships, to find that they were further away than when he had last seen them. Stern-on now, their oarsmen pulling their hardest, they were managing to make some headway back whence they had come. Evidently they had not waited to watch their colleagues' end. For the moment, at least, these were no further menace.

The Scots' thankfulness for that was muted by preoccupation now with their own situation. Their rope had saved them from the whirlpool, but could it get them back? These two escaping craft had been considerably further to the rear, where the drag was less strong. If not . . . ?

It was decided that all should transfer to the second long-ship. There, four men to each oar, everyone else, save the steersman, to pull on the rope.

This all took some time to organise, and meanwhile the two Norse craft were making ever better progress away. And it *was* away, for they were clearly heading seawards now, back towards their waiting compatriots at the strait-mouth, not lingering near the Jura shore. Presumably they had had sufficient of Corryvreckan.

When all were in position, Kenneth and Conall gave the order to pull in as much of the rope as they could. This proved ominously difficult, for the cable was now stretched taut, and no amount of hauling seemed to have any effect. It was only when the rowers were commanded to pull that any least impression was made – and even then the rope was almost jerked back out of the pullers' grip.

Urgently men sought to get sufficient rope inboard for some thirty to grasp, while the oarsmen dug deep, groaning with the effort.

For what seemed a long time no success was evident. Then Kenneth perceived that more men were in fact on the rope, so it must be coming in, however slowly – which must mean that they were moving the ships. He shouted encouragement to pull and row harder, harder. Foot by foot more dripping cordage came in.

The strain on the sweating, gasping men was enormous. But with their lives depending on it, men can excel themselves, although those drowned Norsemen had not been able to save themselves. The Scots ships moved southwards, even though the movement was imperceptible to those on board, only the increase in the amount of rope drawn in indicating slight progress. There were setbacks when muscles flagged and dearly won rope was lost again. If the anchor, caught in behind that reef, lost its grip? But it had held thus far, and during the major strain, when they were closer to the whirl-pool. And to be sure each yard they made eased their task just a little, the further they got from the vortex. Presently all could feel it, hard work still but the rope coming in faster.

The fleeing Vikings had now almost joined up with the three ships waiting at the strait-mouth. Somehow, Kenneth did not think that they would venture back.

At last the Scots' ordeal was over. The oars were now taking them to the Jura shore and the rope coming in almost without effort. God was to be thanked. When Kenneth looked westwards, it was to see the five Norse ships heading off for the open sea.

Anchor retrieved, and the two longships separated, keeping close to the shore now they headed back westwards beyond Carraig Mor, to collect the abandoned dragon-ship prizes. These they found aground but apparently undamaged. Then, all four manned again, it was eastwards once more, all but hugging the shore, sufficient risks taken for one day.

Relief was profound as it was general when they left the Strait of Corryvreckan and could turn southwards down the Sound of Jura, with a mere dozen miles or so of sheltered waters between them and Dunadd.

It was dusk before they reached Port an Deora, and to a more rousing welcome than they might have expected, for quite a fleet was assembled there now – and never before, it was safe to say, had two Norse dragon-ships been brought into Dunadd's harbour. Astonishment, question and acclaim were the order of the night.

It is to be feared that the heroes were just too weary to appreciate it all.

A few days later King Eochaidh led an impressive Scots fleet to sea, to sail up and down the Hebridean Sea – and did not catch a single glimpse of a Viking ship. They did put heart into some proportion of the inhabitants of the islanded seaboard, however; and wherever they went the exploits of Kenneth Norse-Slayer were recited and amplified, in the cause of morale, to that young man's embarrassment. If his grandsire approved, he did not say so, but ascribed any successes to the influence of their new patron saint Andrew. Kenneth, for his part, felt that it was more to the credit of St Columba.

3

As it fell out, this loyalty towards Columba on Kenneth's part became further demonstrated very shortly thereafter; for only a few days after the return of the fleet to Dunadd, they had a distinguished and unexpected visitor from Ireland. This was none other than Diarmaid, Abbot of Iona, who it appeared had been summoned some time earlier by the High King, Angus of Alba, to bring back the relics of St Columba from Kells in Ireland. These had been sent there, for safety from the raiding Norsemen, some thirty years before by Constantine, Angus's elder brother, when he was King of Dalriada. To regularise this transfer, the Abbot of Kells – which had been Columba's own monastery before he came to Dalriada and Iona – was made also Abbot of Iona. And now he came returning the precious symbols of the Columban Church to where they belonged – or, not quite, for they were, it seemed, not to go back to Iona, as still endangered, but on to Scone, in the central Fortrenn province of Alba, where Constantine had established an alternative religious centre for the Church, and now Angus was enhancing it. The relics brought were very varied, from Columba's portable stone altar-cum-font, on which kings had been seated on their enthronement, to the famous little Brecbennoch reliquary which had been used to contain the anointing oil, manuscripts, copies of the Psalms in the saint's own handwriting, other documents and illustrated gospels, carvings, crosses and vestments. All these were brought ashore from the Irish ship – and Kenneth was not the only one alarmed at the risks taken in bringing them, the consequences had this vessel been intercepted by the Norsemen.

Their safe arrival was a cause for great rejoicing on the Scots' part. But there was another side to it, for the relics appeared to be due to be taken on by the Abbot Diarmaid to Fortrenn, forthwith, to the Albannach High King; and however much co-operation there might be, these days, between the two kingdoms, the Scots looked on Columba as their own. Admittedly he had converted the larger nation of the Albannach also, but here in Dalriada had been his base, Iona, from which all his endeavours sprang. There was a general feeling that the relics ought to remain here, even though Iona itself was no place to deposit them meantime. After all, Constantine had sent them away when he was still King of Dalriada; the fact that he had become High King of Alba thereafter should not affect the issue. And now his brother, Angus mac Fergus, was calling them back to Alba . . .

Abbot Diarmaid was sympathetic, but declared that this was not a matter for his decision. He had been summoned, with the relics, by the successor of the monarch who had sent them to Ireland, and he was in duty bound to deliver them to King Angus. Any discussion or negotiation thereafter should be between the monarchs themselves.

Eochaidh was displeased.

Kenneth, who on this occasion agreed with his grand-father, recognised the abbot's predicament. He suggested to his father that they could at least try to change the High King's mind in this matter and get him to agree to the retention of the relics here. Once they were in Fortrenn, at this Scone, it would be more difficult to get them back, that was certain. If they sent a messenger with their request, and meantime entertained this abbot here, it might serve. It would entail a delay of only six or seven days. As an after-thought he added that perhaps now, after the adoption of St Andrew as patron, King Angus might be less concerned over the Columban relics; and that, to excuse the delay, he himself might go back to Iona meanwhile and collect such further items as remained there, which the cottagers he had spoken to had hidden away.

Alpin said that he would put all this to Eochaidh.

That difficult man for once concurred. He would send a letter to Angus, and meantime seek to detain Abbot Diarmaid.

So it was back to Iona, using Conall's longship again – and this time avoiding the Strait of Corryvreckan. On the island they discovered that not only their previous elderly informant had secreted sundry sacred articles but others had done likewise. Some were distinctly loth to give them up, but using the King's command Kenneth was able to gather in quite a collection of precious items – writings, a saint's bell, illuminated tracts, two crucifixes in green Iona marble, a communion chalice and even a bishop's crozier pulled out of a cot-house's thatching. Well satisfied, he returned to Dunadd after three days.

In the interim Eochaidh's attitude had hardened. No matter what Angus decided, in response to his letter, he was not going to allow Columba's altar, in especial, to leave Dalriada. On it all the kings of their line had been enthroned, since the saint had set Aidan mac Gabhran upon it, almost three centuries ago, himself included. It had nothing to do with Alba.

When the courier returned from Fortrenn, his message was, as feared; King Angus required the return of the relics, all of them. As heir to his brother Constantine, their disposal was at his decision.

Eochaidh sent for Kenneth.

"See you," he said. "You are the great one for putting all to rights – or so they say! Here is a task for you. Contrive to have that stone altar lifted from the church here, where it lies with all the other relics. Only the altar. Get some ruffianly crew to do it – and pay them to keep quiet. Some of your shipmen friends, belike. Have them take it to some secure hold. Far hence. I do not want to know where, not meantime. Nor you, either. So that we can tell Angus and this abbot that we do not know where it has been taken. You understand? Get it away this night – for the Irishman goes on in two days. We will say that scoundrelly men have done it, that there is much feeling here, in the matter. That we will seek for it, but . . . "

"But, Highness – this is beyond all! A shameful deceit. Over so sacred a treasure. And none will believe it . . . "

"I care not for that. It will be gone, and none to know where. Save your man. He will tell us, at some future date. That stone must not leave Dalriada."

"King Angus will be wrath."

"It may be so. But he can do nothing about it. Besides, you will take him these other items which you found on Iona

69

in the altar's stead. Say that we give him these, in token of our regret . . . "

"*Me*, Highness?"

"Yes, you, boy. You will go with this Abbot Diarmaid to Fortrenn, as my envoy. Tell my regrets about the altar. He thinks well of you, for some reason! After that battle in Lothian. You will serve best. So – see you to it . . . "

Distinctly doubtful, Kenneth went thereafter once again to Port an Deora.

Whatever his doubts about the entire proceeding, he found none, nor any reluctance, on the shipmaster's part. Conall expressed himself as entirely ready to co-operate, and even began to suggest hiding-places for the altar when Kenneth hastily stopped him. He must not know where it was to go, at this stage – so long as he was assured that it was safe. That was essential, of course. Let Conall, and two or three others of his men, be at the Dunadd church, the one near the palace, that night late, say around midnight, with a stout garron to carry the thing and some harness to tie it. He would meet them there.

It was not really dark when Kenneth left his quarters to make his way to the church; but nobody seemed to be about the township at that hour, he was thankful to note. He found Conall and four of his crew lurking behind the church, with a sturdy, shaggy garron and a roll of strong fish-netting, which ought to serve for carrying their burden.

The church door was not locked. But it was dark inside, with the windows small. Kenneth had brought a candle, with flint and steel, and hoped that, thus lit, they would not attract attention from outside.

It was eerie in there, by that small flickering illumination. The relics were all stacked to one side save for their objective itself, which was, suitably, placed up beside the permanent altar, just in front.

Candle raised, they examined the shrine. None, of course, had seen it before. It was smaller than Kenneth had anticipated – although if he had considered he would have realised that it could not be very large, since it not only had to be portable but also to be of seat-height, if kings could be enthroned thereon. It proved to be a solid oblong block of dark stone, almost black, and of a somewhat glazed texture, decorated overall, save for its top, with intricate carving, typical Celtic interlacing and herring-bone margins, with elaborate spirals culminating in raised bosses. It was about twenty inches high, the same in breadth and perhaps two feet in length, with spiral carved volutes projecting at each end to facilitate carriage. The top was plain, save in the centre a distinct shallow hollow, for holy water when used in baptism. Kenneth had heard that it was, in fact, carved out of a meteor, exceedingly hard and shiny stone, significant as having come down from heaven. They gazed at it there, the Scots' most prized and famous stone, typifying their nation's destiny, around which all sorts of tales and legends had already accumulated, wondering.

But this was no occasion for wondering, however moved they might be by what they saw – although they did indeed wonder, when it came to moving it, that Columba had chosen quite such a weighty object to take around, for it required all of them to carry it, straining. The story was that the saint had had an old white horse for this duty, with presumably some sort of strong pannier to strap it to, and ample manpower normally to hoist it up – the same old horse that wept tears the day Columba died. They hoped that their own transport arrangements would be adequate.

In fact, Conall's net was an excellent idea – possibly the saint had used some similar device. Wrapped round the altar, and with a couple of spars brought to thrust through the netting, it was not too difficult to raise on to the horse's broad back – even though the animal protested somewhat. Tying it in place there was a problem, but seamen were good with rope and knots and they got it reasonably secure. Clearly Columba must have had some kind of cradle or framework for it.

The seamen would take their precious cargo down to Port an Deora, necessarily slowly and with care, and load it aboard their longship. Thereafter, where it went was to be Conall's secret. Since he came from the area where Loch Etive opened on to the Firth of Lorn, some forty miles to the north, it might well be somewhere in that vicinity, which he would know well. So be it.

Two days later, when the Abbot Diarmaid prepared to resume his journey, there was a great to-do when the altar was discovered to be amissing. None seemed more concerned than King Eochaidh, although Kenneth was less assertive in his distress. The abbot, after his initial upset, was very stiff-faced about it, and may well have suspected official connivance without saying so. He acknowledged the additional relics, provided as compensation, with raised eyebrows – and at least Kenneth could expand somewhat on how he had come by these.

They left on their eastwards journey in a somewhat strained and silent atmosphere, a company of about forty, with as many led-horses as ridden ones.

That journey, of about one hundred and thirty miles, was necessarily a very roundabout one, with mountain ranges and long lochs to be circumnavigated, although, as an eagle might have flown, it was only about half that. They had to set off northwards for some ten miles until they could swing off eastwards for the foot of Loch Awe, a twenty-five-mile-long freshwater loch, up which they must travel in a north-easterly direction to reach, near its forked foot, Dalmally, where opened the start to the great pass of Drumalban, which would admit them to central Alba and Fortrenn. This Dalmally was about forty-five miles from Dunadd, and since a pack-horse train cannot travel fast, it took them two days, halting overnight at Ardchonnel, where was a remote Dalriadic stronghold on an islet, the only one they would see on their journey. At Dalmally the second night, under the mighty peak of Beinn Cruachan, the abbot looked distinctly askance at what obviously lay ahead, eastwards, a mass of great mountains rearing heads into cloud and seeming so close-ranked as to deny all passage save perhaps to deer and eagles. Clearly Ireland had not prepared him for the like. That was Alba, Kenneth informed.

However, in the morning, when they entered the mouth of Glen Orchy and started to climb, Diarmaid gradually began to accept that there was a way through this frightening lofty wilderness of barren rock and heather, of frowning, shouldering cliffs and screes. He admitted the greater admiration for his fellow-countryman, Columba, who had conquered all this, and its inhabitants, for Christ, those centuries ago. Soon they left Glen Orchy for a lesser but higher valley, Glen Lochy Kenneth named it, a dreary, rising corridor through the mountains. Up and up they rode all that day, Kenneth pressing them on, for although it was only some fourteen miles to their next halting-place, it was hard-going all the way, rising to a great height, and with no sort of shelter or resting-place until they were through the pass itself.

At length, at the summit, between the yawning jaws of the final defile, in the purple shadow here despite the brilliant sunset behind them, they reined up to gaze eastwards to a fairer scene. Widening valleys, open straths and spreading forests seemed to stretch to infinity, mountain-girt still but lesser heights these, more rounded, kinder – Braid Alban of Fortrenn. They were halfway to their destination.

They began to ride downhill, thankfully, to pass the night at Tigh-an-Druim, the House of the Druim-Alban pass, a hospice run by monks.

After that their travelling developed an easier and less urgent character, down fair Strathfillan, with its open pine forests, to Glen Dochart and its loch, under shapely mountains, and up to a lesser pass at the head of Glen Ogle, with all wide and splendid Strathearn ahead, the mountains diminishing to mere hills, the land growing ever more populous and fertile.

Three days of this and they came, down Earn, to that river's confluence with great Tay, where the latter was beginning to open out to its wide estuary and the ultimate Norse Sea. Here, at Forteviot, was what had been the capital of Fortrenn, one of the sub-kingdoms of Alba; but now it had gained in status, with the High Kings more and more using it, recognising its centrality as against far-away Inverness, its convenience, also its proximity to the Fife sub-kingdom which was so vulnerable to Norse and Anglian invasion and terror. Constantine had much favoured it, and now his brother still more so.

On arrival at this Forteviot, on rising ground above the Earn, a strong site where the river made a major bend, enhanced by artificial ditching and marshland as moat, they found King Angus to be absent. He had gone, apparently, to a place many miles to the north, where the Tay emerged from the mountains, and where the two saints, Columba and Mungo, on their one joint expedition as elderly men, had set

73

up a church, monastery and religious centre. There, in recent times, King Constantine had brought the teaching fraternity from Iona when that ravaged isle became untenable for them, to establish a religious college for the Columban Church – hence the name of it, Dun Keledei, the Fortress of the Friends of God. Angus mac Fergus, it seemed, took a great interest in this centre, as he did at Scone, which he was making the dynastic focus-point. For an embattled monarch under constant threat of attack by Norsemen and Angles both, he appeared to be much preoccupied with religious and ceremonial affairs.

The travellers were kindly received by Queen Finchem, a plain-faced but strong-minded and dignified woman, daughter of a former sub-king of this Fortrenn. Alba was divided into seven sub-kingdoms, from Ross in the far north to Fife in the south, with Moray, much the largest, its former seat of the high kings at Inverness, Buchan, Mar, Angus and Fortrenn in between. These lesser kings were called the *ri*, and they appointed the High King, or *Ard Righ*, usually of the Moray line but not necessarily so, the most able in statecraft and war being the standard of choice, not primogeniture, with matrilinear succession still important.

Angus and Finchem had four sons, Ewan, Nechtan, Finguine and Bran, with one daughter, Eithne, the first-born and about Kenneth's own age. The Princes Ewan and Nechtan were away with their father, and the other two were but boys in their early teens.

Abbot Diarmaid was made much of, and little said, at this stage, anent the missing altar. But Kenneth was quite warmly welcomed also, his part in the Lothian battle much talked of, and exaggerated; moreover, he was of course in cousinship here, for his late grandmother, Ergusia, had been Angus's elder sister.

There was some discussion about further procedure. It was not known just when King Angus would return, although it was not expected that he would be long delayed. But he was also to visit Scone, it seemed, no doubt on the way back, and this might take him another day or two. Abbot Diarmaid was an elderly man, and had had enough of travelling; but Kenneth was otherwise minded – and he rather hoped that he might see King Angus first, before the abbot related his version of the disappearing altar. So when the lively young woman, Eithne, suggested that they might ride on to Scone, hoping to meet her father there, he agreed. Queen Finchem raised no objection, saying that the good abbot should remain with her at Forteviot and the young people could go to Scone, some dozen miles to the north. Not to go further, however, for the High King could return by more than one route to Scone and they might miss him.

So next morning the four of them set out – for young Finguine and Bran were not going to be left out – with a small escort. Kenneth found that he got on very well with Eithne, a fine-featured, dark-eyed girl, who was attractive without being actually beautiful, full of spirit and laughter. He had no sisters of his own, only the two brothers, Donald and young Gregor, and decided that he would have liked one such as this – although he was sufficiently masculine to acknowledge that he would probably enjoy this one's company the better for her *not* being his sister. In otherwise clean-cut and regular facial lines, she had a slightly uptilted tip to her nose, which somewhat intrigued him.

They had to cross Earn by the Forteviot ford and there-after climb the escarpment on to Dupplin Muir before turning eastwards for Tay. As they went, Kenneth asked about this Scone and why it had become important. He could understand about Dun Keledei, with the saints' connection. But Scone . . . ?

"Scone was important long before Dun Keledei became so," Eithne explained. "It was an old pagan sanctuary, set there of a purpose. For this was where good overcame evil, the kindly land overcame the unkind sea, fertility triumphed over barrenness. You see, it is at Scone that the salt water coming up from the firth is turned back by the fresh water coming down Tay. It gets no further than Scone. So there is the triumph of what makes for good, man's survival and advantage. Therefore our pagan fathers chose it as sacred, set up their circle of stones there in praise of the kindly sun, guardian of the waters, and made it the place where the kings of Fortrenn should be enthroned."

"A pagan place . . . !"

"Yes. But my uncle, and now my father, seek to make it Christian. Columba did that, did he not? Used the pagan places of idolatry for the true worship of Christ-God. That is why my father wants these relics of the saint at Scone."

"Your father is a man of much feeling, I think."

"Oh, yes. But, perhaps too much, Mother thinks. For what we need at this pass are great warriors, she says, not men of feeling! I do not know . . . "

He did not answer that.

"My father much venerates St Columba, too. That is why he called me, his only daughter, after Columba's mother."

"Ah, yes. I, too, venerate Columba . . . "

They rode in silence for a while.

They reached the Tay well before Scone, opposite Moncrieffe Island, where it was already river rather than estuary, but too broad and deep for any ford. Apparently Scone was on the far side, so they had to go another three miles upstream before they could cross, at Derder's ford, and then turn downstream again a mile to reach their destination.

This proved to be no very dramatic-seeming entity, despite its story, merely higher wooded ground beside a sort of peninsula in the river, with a small church, a priest's house, some cottages and the stone circle. And it was obvious, by the lack of activity visible, that King Angus had not yet arrived.

They called on the priest who, on account of the importance of the place, was entitled an abbot, although there was no abbey or monastery as yet. He knew nothing of any visit by the High King; but was suitably welcoming towards the little royal party.

Since they must wait, Eithne offered to show Kenneth round the features of the place – which the boys obviously considered would be a bore, and preferred to go looking for pearls, for which this part of Tay was famous, their sister warning them not to get drowned. So she and Kenneth were left alone – which suited the young man very well.

She took him first to look at the stone circle, on a mound clear of trees where the sun could reach it from whatever quarter it shone. Kenneth had seen many such, but this one was notable, its thirteen monoliths exceptionally tall, and with a central massive altar-table for sacrificial victims. They eyed it a little askance, even though their ancestors had worshipped here, realising something of the horrors witnessed by that bloodstained table.

"Why the killing?" Eithne asked. "Why the human sacrifice? The sun that they worshipped is kindly, not cruel, a blessing to men, not a savage tyrant to be placated."

"I do not know. But – was it in fact the sun that they worshipped? Some say that our forebears saw the sun only as representing the unknown god. The kindlier face of the god. With storms, thunder and lightning and darkness the harsh and savage face. So the sun had to be besought to intercede for men. The sacrifices may have been for the other side of the god, to help the sun's pleas for them."

"It seems so wrong, now."

"Now, yes. But in those days they were ignorant of Christ and the loving God. Until Columba came to teach them. He taught them that their unknown god was in fact no devil, no killer, but kind, loving, the friend of man. He used their stone circles as sites for his churches. But not here, it seems. He never came to Scone?"

"I think not." She looked at him curiously. "You speak strangely, Kenneth, for a fighting man, a warrior, a – a slayer of men. My father has told us of your doings at the great battle in Lothian, how you largely saved the day, caused the deaths of many Angles and Saxons. I did not think that, that I would greatly like you! Nor hear you to talk of loving mankind, kindness and the like!"

He shook his head. "It is strange perhaps, yes. I am a fighter, it seems. It comes naturally to me. The fight, the struggle. These I relish. But not the killing. I do not enjoy that. It can sicken me. But . . . there must be fighters. Or the evil will prevail, will it not? Someone must stand up for the right. If a man is assured what the right may be."

"That is the rub of it. For those you fight may also think that they have the rights of it, no?"

"That could be. Then, I do not know. A man has to use his judgment. He may be wrong. But not always, surely. There are times when the right and the wrong are clear, most evident. These Norsemen, now. I have been fighting against *them*, since Lothian. In the isles. Their cause cannot be right, I swear. Not that they have any cause, I think. Only blood-lust and savagery. Attacking defenceless folk, slaying men, women and children for pleasure. Burning, raping, tormenting. They are evil. If you could have seen what they do . . . "

"They are terrible, yes – a dire scourge. But – are all you fight like that? This, in Lothian. These Saxons and Angles? Were these not pursuing *you*, after your raiding in their Northumbria? Who was doing the burning and slaying then, Kenneth mac Alpin?"

He frowned. "We went there to teach them a lesson. After all their raids and cruelties here. Or in Fife. *You* know that. They must threaten even you, here in Fortrenn."

"Oh, yes. We have to be ever on our guard against them. That is why my uncle Constantine, and my father, came here from Inverness. But it is this of right and wrong that I wonder over. How is one to judge it? As a reason, or excuse, for war, fighting, killing? My father and my mother much speak of this. I think that she is more of a warrior than he is!"

"Even Columba fought in war. In Ireland. The great battle at Cooldrevny. Against paganism. And these Norsemen are pagans."

"It is said that he repented of it, all his days. And that he said, later, that pagans are only as yet unconverted Christians!"

Kenneth turned away. It was hard to have Columba, whom he all but worshipped, held up against him.

Impulsively she laid a hand on his arm. "Forgive me! I should not belabour you so. Who am I to be judging right and wrong! And to you, our guest. Come – I will show you the Mote Hill. And, I promise, no more judgments!"

They moved over some way further northwards, beyond the church, to where amongst trees was another mound. A very different one this, not very high, rising in regular shape out of level ground, clearly artificial but grass-grown.

"Here is the Mote Hill," Eithne said. "Where the oaths of allegiance were given and taken to the kings of Fortrenn. It is said that all this mound of earth was thrown up, over the years, by the chiefs and landholders when they came to give their oaths. You will know how it is required that they give it standing on their own ground. Possibly it is the same in Dalriada? So, to save the kings journeying to all their lands, they brought each a sack of his soil with him, here, to empty and place a foot upon as they took the oath. And all this earth, left here, has grown into this mound. I cannot really believe that, but such is the tale of it."

"It seems over-much, yes, for that. We do have the same custom at Dunadd, but we do not preserve the soil. And there is *less* of it, for only enough of it is brought by each chieftain and lord to fill the imprint of a foot, carved on a stone. They put the earth in that, then place their foot on it, and so take the oath standing on their own soil likewise. On the top of Dunadd Hill. We still do it. I think that the stone footprint was there before the Scots ever came from Ireland – an Albannach custom, like this here, which we adopted."

"You are all half-Albannach now anyway, are you not?"

"I suppose that you could say so. Through intermarriage, over three hundred years. My own grandmother, your aunt . . . !"

"Yes. And my uncle, Constantine, King of Dalriada before becoming High King of Alba. Think you that there *should* be two kingdoms, Kenneth? Should they not unite in one?"

"Often I have thought so, yes. We share so much, as well as the land. And face the same dangers. We would be stronger, united. But . . . there is the danger, for Dalriada, that it would be swallowed up in Alba. Lost, in the greater realm. There are ten Albannach for every Scot. It would be difficult for us to keep our identity. And it is worth keeping. The Scots."

"I see that. But it should be possible to do so?"

"We have an alliance meantime, at least."

The climbed to the top of the Mote Hill, and the girl told him that this was where her father planned to place St Columba's famous altar one day, since it was the enthroning place for kings.

Kenneth cleared his throat. "I do not know that it is the most suitable place."

"Why not? For the enthroning stone. And this is a holy place – the *Caisg Creideamh*, to give it its other name."

"Ha – that!" This young woman had a genius for rubbing Kenneth mac Alpin the wrong way, attractive as he found her. "I would not call *that* a holy name! Easter Belief! I would call it rather *Caisg Mearachd*, Easter Error!"

She eyed him. "You hold to the old way, then?"

"To be sure. That surrender of Nechtan mac Derile was sheerest weakness. And wrong. Done to appease St Boniface and the other Romish priests, who had hold over him. A . . . a treachery!"

"Surely not. How could it be wrong? All Christendom holds Easter thus . . . "

"Not all. The Irish Church and our Columban Church do not. Nechtan had no right to change the date . . . "

A century before, Nechtan mac Derile, High King of Alba, had changed the date for the celebration of Easter, from the Celtic to the Romish usage, by royal decree – this on the urging of Boniface and other Anglian missionaries from Lindisfarne, a strange decision considering that he had not long before decisively defeated the Angles in a great battle in Angus. But he was a strange man. The argument depended on the period of Lent which preceded the feast of Easter. This represented the forty days and nights of Christ's fasting in the wilderness. The Celtic Church, therefore, calculated Easter as forty days after the beginning of Lent. But the Church of Rome held otherwise. The popes decided that since the forty days must have included six Sundays, and Sundays could not be fast-days, therefore the Lenten overall period must be forty-six days; so Easter Sunday must be held a week later than the Celtic celebration. The Irish Church, always independent of Rome, declared this to be a nonsense. Did Christ, in the wilderness, halt his fasting every week, to return for the day to his friends and their tables? Nothing more improbable. So they would not change. Nor would the Columban Church – not in Dalriada, that is; but in Alba, Nechtan's decree held, despite the protests of the clergy. And here, on this mound, apparently, Nechtan had announced his decision.

Kenneth pointed out something of all this, perhaps over-vehemently, to some head-shaking on Eithne's part. They descended the mound and returned to the abbot's house not exactly in silence but a deal less talkative than heretofore.

Kenneth shared a room that night with the two boys, the elder of whom had found two small pearls, to his great glee and the sulks of his brother, while Eithne was found a couch with the cleric's daughter. At least Nechtan had not decreed that the Columban clergy should be celibate, like the Romish ones.

In the morning, Eithne was all smiles again and carefully eschewed controversial topics for the time being, Kenneth glad to do the same. She proposed a short expedition, while they awaited her father, to the former Roman camp, a couple of miles to the north. This time, the boys came too.

Disharmony having to be avoided, by mutual consent, produced its own faint air of constraint, but that was no great price to pay. And they found the Roman camp full of interest, although it was eight centuries since it had been built and soon thereafter abandoned. There was still much to be seen: massive gateways, with grooves in the stone pavements made by chariot wheels, inclined roadways up, for the said chariots, stables for the cavalry horses, fragments of mosaic pavement, a stone water-tank, still holding water, even a vaulted strong-room. This was really only a marching-camp, Eithne explained, set there to protect the Derder's ford – the same by which they themselves had crossed Tay the day before. There was another and larger fort on the other side of the river, where Almond joined Tay. Clearly the Romans had considered this crossing very important, in their Agricola's brief invasion of what they called Caledonia back in that same century of Christ's life. They had not got much further north than this.

That ford, the only one for many miles, had its importance for them this day also, for, looking down on it from the high ground of the camp, they saw across the river a long file of horsemen approaching from the north-west, a large banner carried at its head. This was almost certainly King Angus, so the four of them remounted and hurried down to the ford to meet him.

In very much a family reunion, Kenneth hung back. He knew Ewan, a nineteen-year-old, who had been on the Northumbrian expedition, but this other son, Nechtan, was new to him, a handsome youth. Angus greeted Kenneth amiably, but reserved his attentions for his daughter, of whom he was clearly very fond.

Kenneth wanted to speak with the High King alone, if possible, but he found no opportunity until they were back at Scone, when he managed to approach him with the others being shown Finguine's pearls and where they had been dredged up.

"Highness," he said, "I have to tell you that Abbot Diarmaid and myself have brought you the Columba relics from Ireland. But one is amissing, the altar. It was taken out of the church at Dunadd by some interlopers, the night before we left for Fortrenn. Where it is now no one knows – save those who took it. I am sorry . . . "

Angus looked at him narrow-eyed. "So! The altar! The most important of all. Gone! You expect me to believe this, young man? The altar which Eochaidh wanted to retain at Dunadd. Suddenly and conveniently lost! Do you take me for a fool?"

"No, Highness, no. But I can only tell you what happened. I saw the altar, in the church with the other items, the day before. We were deciding how many horses would be needed to carry it all. And next morning the altar was gone, but the rest still there. My grandsire sends his deep regrets. He will be making search for it, you may be sure . . . "

"But not over-closely, I think! He knows where it is, I swear."

"No, Highness – he does not. That *I* can swear! He knows not – none of us knows where it has been taken. Some desperate men. There is much feeling in Dalriada about this stone, you understand. That it should remain there, if not at Iona at least somewhere safe in Dalriada. Why, King Eochaidh asked that it should remain. Now, some determined men must have taken it into their own hands."

"Ordered to do it by whom?"

"Who knows? But none need have ordered it. With the feeling running high amongst all the folk it could be taken and hidden anywhere, and by anyone."

"I am displeased, nevertheless. As Eochaidh the Poisonous shall learn! This stinks in the nostrils, young man!"

"I am sorry, Highness, that you feel so. But – King Eochaidh, in token of his regrets, has sent you many other relics, apart from those from Ireland. These I myself uncovered on Iona recently, where they had been hidden by islanders, to save them from the Norsemen. Chalices, crosses, a crozier, vestments and the like. He hopes that you will accept these."

Angus looked a little less stern, and nodded.

Taking that as encouragement, Kenneth went on to say what he had really come to say, however doubtful as to its reception. "Highness, all this of St Columba and his relics. They are of great import, yes. But more to Dalriada than to Alba, I think? Since there was his base, his centre. And he was himself of the line of mac Erc. And now, you have adopted the Apostle Andrew as patron saint, superseding Columba."

"So . . . ?"

"Would it not, therefore, seem more suitable to make a St Andrew's shrine? After that Lothian victory. A centre where *he* should be venerated. In gratitude and reverence."

"That may be so. But – what have we, save that cross in the sky? We cannot make a shrine or sanctuary out of a cloud! And that took place in Lothian, not in Alba."

"No, Highness. But there is, I think, a possible answer to this. In Galloway, where my father is king, there is a story, a tradition, which I have heard more than once. As you will know, St Ninian brought Christianity there, from Rome, some five hundred years ago. To Candida Casa, at Whithorn. Two centuries before Columba. But his mission failed, in the end, and the pagans triumphed – although not before one of his saints, Patrick, escaped to bring the faith to Ireland . . . "

"I know all this, young man – knew it before you were born."

"I crave your patience, Highness. Hear me. Others of Ninian's mission had travelled afar. One in especial had been to the Holy Land and to Greece, even to Constantinople. Andrew had died at Patras in Greece and was buried there. But Constantine the Great, the Emperor, took the bones from there to Constantinople. And there this Galloway missionary, called Riaguil, commonly Rule, was privileged to be given a finger-bone of the apostle. He brought this back to Galloway, his most prized possession . . . "

"A bone! A bone of Andrew? God save us – this I had never heard. Part of the apostle? In Galloway?"

"Not in Galloway now, no. Nearer to here than that, Highness! The tradition is that this St Riaguil, Rule or Regulus, a play on words, was sent from Whithorn northwards to convert *your* people, the Albannach. He got so far as Fife, at its eastern tip, and there, in a storm, he was shipwrecked. All aboard but himself were drowned, the tale goes. In gratitude for his deliverance, he built a church there, enshrining the bone of St Andrew. And there, in due course, he died, ministering to the Fife folk. They called this church Kilrymond, the cell on the mount of Riaguil."

"Lord – never have I heard of this! Of the saint or of the place. Is this true, think you?"

"That I cannot swear to, Highness. But it is the tradition in Galloway. Riaguil would probably be a Galloway man. Why should a story like that, naming a place in Fife, be invented? It could be mistaken in details, but surely the names mean something? Is there a place called Kilrymond in Fife?"

"I know not. But will find out. This is of great moment, man – a wonder! Why have I not heard of it? A piece of Andrew himself! In Alba. It could be that this is why the saint intervened for us, in Lothian. When would this be, this visit of Riaguil?"

"I am not certain as to that. Possibly about the same time that Patrick, who was a Strathclyde man, went to Ireland. That was at the start of the fifth century after Christ. It could have been earlier . . . "

"You must find out for me, Kenneth mac Alpin. Find out all that you can. I want to know it all . . . "

At this stage the young people came back, full of chatter about pearls and how they grew and why Tay should be the only river to have them. The subject of St Andrew was not pursued meantime – but Kenneth was well content.

That evening Eithne had the abbatial quarters to herself, for the High King and his escort travelled in some style, with fine pavilions of painted sail-cloth for shelter, so that Kenneth and the young princes passed the night in fair comfort if not privacy. Before retiring, the girl told him that her father seemed to be pleased with him – which was encouraging.

In the morning, Angus's business with the abbot completed, they left for Forteviot, Kenneth riding beside the monarch, and the subject of St Andrew predominant. Angus mac Fergus was clearly much concerned and set on making the apostle's name and fame mean much in Alba. Kenneth could tell him no more than he had already done; but apparently that had been enough at least to put the subject of the missing altar into abeyance meantime.

Back at Forteviot, Queen Finchem surprised her husband by knowing of Kilrymond in Fife – not its story but its location. She said it was not so very far from the mouth of the Tay estuary, a few miles only to the south, where the Muckross peninsula jutted into the Norse Sea. So, yes, the place existed, although what there was of it she did not know.

Abbot Diarmaid's mission, in the event, therefore developed on a somewhat lower key than probably he anticipated.

Kenneth's task over, he was for off. King Eochaidh would be anxious to hear the result of this encounter; moreover he had no wish to find himself saddled with the duty of escorting Abbot Diarmaid back to Dunadd – he found that cleric's company less than enlivening, and his pace slow. And, as it happened, he was more or less hastened on his way by King Angus, who urged him to find his way down to Galloway just as soon as possible, there to discover all that he could about this St Riaguil or Rule and the St Andrew story, and, of his goodness, report back here to Forteviot. He could scarcely make a royal command of this, for Kenneth was not a subject of his, but he was very urgent about it. Kenneth promised co-operation.

He was not surprised when Ewan mac Angus announced that he would ride with their departing visitor, to see him on his way as far up Earn as Inchaffray, a friendly gesture – but was surprised when Eithne declared that she would come also. He was a little wary.

He had no reason to be. They were not far on their way when she put it to him that in fact Alba had more claim to Columba than had Dalriada. He had come from Ireland to convert the pagan Albannach, had he not? Not to the Dalriadans, who were already Christians. It was only when he discovered that the Dalriadans' faith had sadly waned that he put off time to revive belief there, before turning to his main concern, Alba.

That put Kenneth on his mettle, of course. "Alba may have *needed* him more – but it was to Dalriada, to his own people, the Scots, that he came, to set up his first and main monastery, at Iona. Not in Alba. He only made visits to the Albannach, always came back to Iona."

"But his principal work was with Alba, surely? What he came for, from Ireland."

"That does not make him any the less a Scot. Of the line of the mac Ercs. *Our* saint!"

She was not convinced. "Surely where a man does his greatest work is where he should be most honoured? Christ Himself, after all, although born in little Bethlehem, is renowned rather as of Jerusalem."

They were still debating the point, to Ewan's amusement, when they came to the ford through the marshes of mid-Strathearn at Inchaffray, where was the parting of the ways. There, saying their farewells, Kenneth was surprised to receive a smacking kiss from the argumentative princess, and an urging to come back to Fortrenn soon.

He proceeded on his way north-westwards, bemused.

4

There was no problem, at least, about a return to Galloway. King Eochaidh, after receiving Kenneth's report without any appearance of gratitude, seemed glad enough to see the back of him. It transpired anyway that King Alpin and Donald had left Dunadd for home two days previously, with the Galloway ships; so his own departure was anticipated.

The problem was travel. To reach Galloway by land would entail a ride of some five hundred difficult and circuitous miles, also crossing the entire kingdom of Strathclyde. That would take almost two weeks, and was hardly to be contemplated. Whereas going by sea, the distance was less than half that, and infinitely more convenient. Thoughtlessly, his father had left no vessel for him; but Kenneth reckoned that he deserved some recompense for his mission to Fortrenn and the saving of his grandfather's face, and made no bones about requesting a sea-going ship to take him home, preferably Conall Cruaid's. And since Kenneth, and Conall also, was in a position to reveal what Eochaidh would prefer kept secret, this was acceded, if with ill grace – the King, however, declaring that the vessel must be returned without delay.

So they left Port an Deora two days later, to head down the long Sound of Jura and proceed on down the still longer coastline of the peninsula of Kintyre, the longest in four kingdoms. Going south, thus, the prevailing winds were unfavourable, so that progress was fairly slow, with much tacking and oar-work. That first evening they got only so far as the sheltered bay of Machrihanish, still some dozen miles from the Mull of Kintyre, Conall preferring to negotiate the treacherous waters off that mighty headland in daylight. Here they were only a bare score of miles off the Antrim coast of Ireland, plainly to be seen.

Next day, although the wind had risen considerably, they

made a fair crossing of that great area of waters where the forces of the Atlantic Ocean, the Hebridean and Irish Seas and the Firth of Clyde met in heaving turbulence. This was nothing like the Gulf of Corryvreckan, no whirlpools and overfalls and downdraughts, for the sea was deep here; but the clash of tides and currents and mighty surges resulted in enormous waves, broken water, and spoutings under a mist of spray.

Across this, in Strathclyde waters now, they were none so far from the North Galloway coast, but still with many miles to go, for Galloway was a large sub-kingdom with a lengthy coastline, and Alpin's capital was situated round on the great Solway estuary, on the eastern shore of the central of its three great peninsulas.

When, after passing the soaring Craig of Ailsa, they rounded the ultimate tip of the Rhinns of Galloway, with the island kingdom of Man now on the horizon ahead, Kenneth assured Conall that they had not far to go now, round the next large headland, that of Whithorn itself, then up only seven or eight miles to Garlies.

Conall had never been so far south as this. He had tried to inform, on their way, where he had hidden that altar; but still Kenneth did not want to know. It could be sheerest hypocrisy, but since he assuredly would be seeing King Angus again, he had to be able to deny any knowledge of the stone's whereabouts. He could not explain this to the ship-master without implicating King Eochaidh.

Once round the Burrow Head, the tip of the central peninsula of Galloway called the Machars, they were facing into the huge estuary of the Solway, forty miles across which lay Cumbria. They turned due north now, and in only a mile or two came to the Isle of Whithorn, where St Ninian had established his first Christian cell. They passed this now, the wind at last in their favour, and about another six miles up a rock-bound coast with low green hills behind, came to a wide, shallow double bay enclosed between modest headlands two miles apart. At the head of this was a sizeable township, and on the higher ground behind it, fortress walling and ramparts, enclosing a large hallhouse.

"Garlies," Kenneth pointed. "My father's house.".

Six longships were tied up at the township's harbour. They

moored alongside these.

Kenneth's father and brothers could not give him much, or any further, information as to his quest anent St Riaguil, however interested they were in his story and project. He would have to go down to Whithorn, where the monks would know, if anyone did, either at the priory or at the isle itself.

Next morning, then, he rode down alone through the grassy, cattle-dotted slopes of the Machars, southwards. It was good country, splendid pasture, with fertile stretches for crops, not much woodland and therefore, with the sea all around, windy. Populous too, and providing substantial manpower for its lords. But somehow Kenneth had never felt the affection for it that he did for the Hebridean sea-board of Dalriada and its isles. That was home to him, even though he was Prince of Galloway.

In four miles or so he came to Whithorn itself, not the isle thereof which they had seen from the ship. This was the town some way inland from where Ninian had established his abbey and seminary of Candida Casa and where the saint was buried. Kenneth made for his monastery, a place now of strangely uncertain status, thanks to its peculiar and un-settled history. Ninian, of course, had been of the Romish persuasion, consecrated a bishop by the Pope. So the estab-lishment he set up was of that Church. That was in AD 397. But after he died in 432 and his mission was overwhelmed by resurgent paganism, with St Patrick taking Christianity to Ireland, the flame of faith remained alight only in that land; and when in turn it was brought back to Galloway, it was by missionaries of the Celtic Irish Church, the same which produced Columba. And this differed from the Romish Church in many ways, not only in the date of Easter and celibacy for its priesthood. So Candida Casa at Whithorn was renewed as a *Celtic* Church monastery. However, Galloway, the Land of the Southern Gael, detached as it was from both Alba and Dalriada, was an obvious target for the invading pagan Angles, and again Candida Casa went down. But, in the late seventh and early eighth centuries, parts of Anglia were converted, and from Rome, including Deira or York, and this became their religious centre. In 727 the new Archbishop of York founded a bishopric of Galloway, largely for political reasons, Romish again, and centred it at Whithorn. There were five bishops of Galloway until, in 796, joint Albannach and Dalriadan intervention regained Galloway for the Gaels, and drove out the Anglian bishops. Thereafter Galloway was elevated to the status of sub-kingdom of Dalriada, and Alpin mac Eochaidh was sent down to rule it. Nothing very positive had been done about Candida Casa and Whithorn, save to install Columban Church monks there, under a prior. So now the former Ninianic seminary, former Romish abbey, former Anglian cathedral, was a mere Columban priory of a few monks and lay brothers.

Kenneth, aware of all this, went to call on Prior Duncan.

That amiable old cleric would have liked to be helpful but could not tell him much – not about St Riaguil, that is. About Ninian he was knowledgeable, and proud to be, as it were, that great man's successor – he called him St Ringan, the local name. He enthused over Ninian's royal parentage – which Kenneth doubted, since there had not been a kingdom of Galloway, to his knowledge, until his own father had been sent here to make it such – his pilgrimage to Rome, his friendship with St Martin of Tours, to whom he dedicated his monastery. As to Riaguil, all he could say was that he must have gone north to Alba in the early 400s, when Ninian's mission was at its most vigorous, and never came back. He did advise Kenneth to go down to the isle, however, where the old monk Ronan kept the chapel; he was a local man and often spoke of Riaguil – with how much accuracy who could tell?

So it was on another four miles through the green hillocks to Isle of Whithorn. This was not really an island, not quite, but a very narrow-necked little promontory jutting into an enclosing bay and making a sheltered fishing-haven. On the rocky summit of this half-isle, what they would call an ornsary in the Hebrides, Ninian had allegedly built his very first chapel, presumably before he made his pilgrimage to Rome, to be superseded by the larger establishment inland when he came back a bishop. A rude and simple thatch-roofed rectangle of whitewashed stone, it was now in the care of the old monk Ronan.

This custodian, a wizened, cheerful little weasel of a man, was entirely ready to talk about Riaguil, for whom he seemed to feel some sort of affinity. Not that he could tell a great deal more than Kenneth had already heard. He said that Riaguil – he called him Rule – actually came across from Ireland to Ninian's seminary. When he was trained and ordained priest, he went back there, with St Patrick, and established his own monastery on the River Shannon, far to the west. But for some reason he came back to Ninian at Whithorn. He then went on pilgrimage to the Holy Land and Constantinople, and in due course returned with the finger-bone of St Andrew. Later he was sent north on his mission to Alba. He was a great traveller, was Rule.

Kenneth explained his especial interest in St Andrew. How much fact did Ronan think there might be in the legend of the bone?

The little man was almost indignant that there could be any least doubts about it. Rule would not lie about anything so sacred.

"No – but he might have been misled, deceived. One man's bone, after all, would be very like another's! Or the relic might have been invented, over the centuries. Not by Riaguil but by the storytellers."

"No, no," Ronan declared. "No invention, Prince. Och, I can show you the proof of it."

"Proof . . . ?"

"Aye, proof. Did you ride here from Whithorn? Aye, then you passed it."

Mystified, the younger man shook his head.

"There is a standing-stone near the roadside, not far from the town. Did you not see it? I call it St Rule's Stone. On it is carved an inscription in Latin. Do you have the Latin, Prince? It is much worn now, rubbed away. But clear to be seen still is the Latin for . . . *brother of Peter the Apostle.* Andrew was the brother of Peter."

"This is extraordinary! But – why? Why there? On a stone."

"Who knows? Perhaps that was where St Rule had his cell. And carved it himself before he went to Alba. What else could it be? There is no place dedicated to St Peter in Galloway. Nor indeed to St Andrew. Whithorn itself was dedicated to St Martin of Tours. So this, to the brother of Peter, speaks of Andrew's bone, held by Rule. Can you explain it otherwise, Prince?"

Kenneth admitted that he could not. He said that he would examine this stone on his way back.

Ronan wanted to take him to see the *diseart* of St Ninian, a retreat such as all the Celtic and British saints seemed to require, in a cave at Physgill, above the shore three miles to the west. But Kenneth had been shown this as a boy; and it was not so much Ninian he was interested in at present but Riaguil and Andrew.

On his return ride he paused to examine the stone, clearly visible at the approaches to the town of Whithorn, a simple monolith of grey stone now much weather-worn and mutilated, possibly having been damaged by the pagan Angles. Kenneth's Latin was only indifferent and the lettering was defaced. But, below an encircled cross, rudely carved, were letters. Blurred, was what seemed to be FRATER LOCI STI PETRI APVSTOLI. Certainly that would mean brother of Peter the Apostle. But, of course, the word brother could refer to a later monk or priest who was a devotee of St Peter. But admittedly it *could* mean Andrew, Peter's true brother.

Was this sufficient to take back to King Angus?

Whether it was, or not, it was all that he was able to gather. Nobody at the hallhouse-palace could suggest any other source of information which might add to his scanty gleanings.

Kenneth decided to take the High King at his word and return to Fortrenn at once, rather than wait on in the hope of something turning up. Besides, it was a very long journey, and Conall's ship would be returning to Dunadd in a day or so and could drop him off in the Clyde estuary, at Dunbarton, the Strathclyde capital, which would vastly shorten the distance. King Alpin approved this proposal, for he had a suggestion to put before Roderick, son of Eugein, King of Strathclyde, and Kenneth could act the envoy.

Thus expeditiously the return to Fortrenn was commenced, a deal more speedily than Kenneth had envisaged. Back round the Galloway peninsulas and into the Irish Sea they sailed, and once therein the wind was behind them and they made good time. They reached the mouth of the Firth of Clyde, in sight of the Craig of Ailsa, that evening, and put into a bay at the mouth of the Girvan Water, still in

Galloway, for the night. All next day they sailed up the long firth, and by evening reached Dunbarton, near its head.

The Strathclyde capital, in the light of the sinking sun, was a sight to set fire to the imagination, an abrupt conical hill seeming to rise directly out of the water, where the firth began to narrow to a river, up the steep sides of which walls and ramparts and gateways clung, seemingly in defiance of gravity, these enclosing tall buildings, palaces, halls, chapels, all clustered almost one upon another, aglow in the golden light. Behind this hill, which at closer approach proved to have twin peaks, stretched a large town, almost a city, with its waterside lined with quays and jetties, these thronged with shipping, a great port. It all made Galloway's Garlies and Whithorn seem very modest if not dull. Even Dalriada and Alba could not rival Dunbarton, the Fortress of the Britons, in its wealth and appearance, trade the secret of its power rather than armed strength.

King Roderick the Second received Kenneth without enthusiasm. After all, not a few of his predecessors had died at the hands of both the Dalriadans and the Albannach – even though the last great battle, seventy years before, at Mugdock, not very far from here to the east, had been won by the men of Strathclyde, when the then High King Talorcan, a predecessor of Constantine and Angus, had fallen. And now the Gallovidians were wanting help.

Kenneth sought to bring history to his aid, older history than these comparatively recent troubles. "Your forebear and namesake, Highness, Roderick Hen, son of Tothail, entered into just such an alliance as we propose, and against the same foe, the Angles of Northumbria," he declared. "On the advice and behest of none other than St Columba himself. It was for Strathclyde's benefit then, as well as that of Dalriada and Alba. As it would be now. The Angles and the Saxons do not change. They have already cut off Galloway from our fellow Celts and Britons, and yours, in Wales. Think you that they will be content with that? They invade the east of Alba, Fife and Angus, continually. They occupy Lothian. We beat them in battle there, yes – but that will not halt them. For they are many, many. Strathclyde will not escape their attentions. But, united, we can hold them."

Roderick, a still-faced, stolid, youngish man, did not seem impressed. "*You* may be threatened by the Angles," he said. "We see more danger from the Norsemen, the Danish pirates. They constantly attack our ships, slay the crews and steal the cargoes. They are the greater menace."

"Not to your *realm*, Highness, surely? To your prosperity and trade, yes – but not to your kingdom. For they seek only booty, spoil, bloodshed, not to take over lands. As do the Angles."

"Trade is the life of Strathclyde. These accursed Danes and Vikings could ruin my people."

"Then an alliance against the Danes as well as the Angles, Highness? For they endanger Dalriada also, raiding our shores and islands. Only weeks past I was battling with them. And taught some, at least, a lesson."

"*You* did, Prince Kenneth?"

"I, and my two longships' crews. We burned two of *their* crews, on Coll, and captured their dragon-ships. Then sank two more in Corryvreckan."

"Corryvreckan? The whirlpool? I have heard of that. Sank, you say? How that?"

Kenneth explained briefly. Clearly he had King Roderick's interest now. He thought to make the most of it in his father's cause. He went on to tell of the Dalriadan fleet's subsequent sweep of the Hebridean Sea.

"These Danes base themselves on the Irish coast, as well as on the Orkney and Zetland Isles," Roderick said. "An attack on them there, by our combined fleets, would effect more than any sweeping of the seas, or even your own small assaults – admirable as they may be."

"I agree, Highness. The Irish themselves would thank us, and join us, I think."

"And Man? If Man would join in . . . " It was evident that Roderick was concerned only with the Norse threat, not the Anglian, prepared perhaps to deploy sea-power rather than land-armies. But that could be used.

"So, Highness – an alliance against the Danes *and* the Angles. That would serve all well – Strathclyde, Galloway, Dalriada and possibly Alba also. I go now to Fortrenn, to see the High King. I might persuade him. As to Man, I know not. The kings there are of Welsh blood, are they not?"

"Yes. Howell, son of Rotri, is King of Man. They came from Wales. They also suffer much from the Scandinavians, so near to Ireland. Howell has many ships. If he could join in such an alliance . . . "

Rashly, Kenneth said that he might consider going to Man, after he had seen King Angus, as this idea of a grand alliance built up in his mind. If all the Celtic-British realms would unite to act together . . .

He did not get an actual commitment from Roderick to join such an alliance, but had to be content with an undertaking that the King would seriously consider the matter. At least that cautious man presented Kenneth with a fine horse for his onward journey.

All the way north-eastwards, by the upper Clyde, the Kilpatrick Hills – called after St Patrick who had been born here – and the Fintry Hills beyond, Kenneth turned over and over in his mind this growing conception of a major alliance of the Celtic peoples. His father had sent him to Roderick only to seek a compact with Strathclyde. Its former province of Cumbria, at the other side of Galloway, was now invaded and taken over by the Northumbrian Angles. The Britons of Strathclyde were Celts, Cymric Celts as distinct from Gaelic ones, as were the Welsh. But with Roderick's preoccupation with the Norsemen, which also applied to Dalriada and Alba, and now it seemed with Man also, even perhaps Wales itself, a much wider possibility presented itself. These six realms, if they could be united instead of hostile to each other, or at least in a military alliance, could alter the entire situation, not only get rid of the Scandinavians and contain the aggressive Angles and Saxons, but form a great Celtic nation, powerful enough to rank amongst the foremost principalities of Christendom, to cherish and further the influence of the Columban Church and advance the culture and artistry of the Celts as against the barbarous loutishness of the Scandinavian and Germanic invaders, to the benefit of all.

Was all this folly, a dream that had come to him almost unawares, impossible of achievement? Most would undoubtedly say so. But had not others done the like? Alexander the Great. Charlemagne, his grandsire's friend, had welded an empire out of warring states. Could a Celtic

Charlemagne or Alexander arise . . . ? A High King of Alba might do it, the largest and most powerful of the six realms. Not Angus mac Fergus – he was not of the character to achieve such leadership; it would require a warrior, but a thinking, far-seeing, talented warrior. Some successor perhaps. The Irish? Could they be brought in? They had a High King also . . .

Such thoughts occupied Kenneth's mind all the way to the wide and flooded strath of the upper Forth, boundary between Strathclyde and Alba. Here the Great Moss was like an enormous moat, twenty-five miles long by five across, and acted as barrier between the two, undrained bog and swamp and scrub forest, dotted with lochs, ponds and myres, pathless save to the deer, the wolves and the boar. Eying it, Kenneth likened it to his Celtic unity conception. It looked impassable, but was not – for it could be got round although not crossed. He would remember that.

King Roderick had told him how to get round the Great Moss of Forth, west-about over the higher ground of Gartfarron, Gartmore and Aberfoyle, under the shadow of mighty Beinn Lomond where the Forth was born, then eastwards into Menteith, the mouth of the River Teith, which flowed parallel with Forth to the north, at a loftier level. This was no way to try to take an army, but practical for a determined horseman. Being that, and no idler, Kenneth managed to get as far as Aberfoyle that first night, a distance of some thirty difficult miles, he reckoned. There was a small monkish hospice here, within a former great stone circle.

The following day's journey was longer as to distance but less roundabout and taxing, through the hills of Menteith, the skirts of the highland mountains now, to follow that river down past the Dun of Teith to where the Allan Water came in from the north, at Dunblane; up this to the watershed between it and Earn, and so eastwards now to Forteviot, some forty miles.

Kenneth was surprised by the warmth of his reception by the High King and his family. He recognised that Angus was eager for any information he could bring as to saints Riaguil and Andrew, and pleasantly surprised at the speed with which it was brought. But that need not have produced the

96

kindliness and friendship shown to him by all, even the formidable Queen Finchem and her opinionated daughter. He wondered what he had done to arouse this reaction.

It was autumn now, and after the evening meal it was pleasant to sit round the fire in the great hall, sipping honey-wine made apparently by Eithne. Angus was very much a family man, and allowed his young people to express their opinions – so the discussion was lively.

It centred round the authenticity or otherwise of Andrew's finger-bone, of course its present whereabouts and St Riaguil's mission. The inscribed stone at Whithorn, needless to say, aroused great interest, and all seemed to take it as applying to Andrew and therefore to his relic. Save for the Queen, who held that brother of the Apostle Peter could apply to almost any missionary-saint who had made the pilgrimage to St Peter's shrine at Rome. This was contested by all the others, who asked why Riaguil would put up a stone to any wandering missionary. Finchem replied that the stone might well apply to Riaguil himself, his own monument, since presumably he had gone to Rome on his way to the Holy Land and Constantinople. *He* could be the serving brother of the apostle, and no reference to any bone.

Kenneth thought that he saw where Eithne had inherited her fondness for debate.

On this occasion, however, the girl was on the positive side. "Nobody would invent the story of Riaguil and the finger-bone," she asserted. "Why should they? The bone might not be really Andrew's, I suppose, only thought to be. But, equally, no one can prove that it is *not*, can they?" This to the acclaim of her brothers.

Her mother smiled. "That argument could apply to almost any heresy!"

Her husband spoke up. "I have been making enquiries here, amongst the clergy. There is record of an Abbot Tuathalan of Kilrymond, in Fife, who died about seventy-five years ago. So if there was an abbot, there must have been an abbey or monastery. Whether it is still there, none here know. It is at Muckross, the remotest corner of Fife."

"Then we must go and see," his daughter declared.

None contested that.

"Do you know when this Riaguil came to Alba?" the

97

Queen wondered. "Are there no records of that?"

"It must have been early in the fifth century, the Prior of Whithorn said," Kenneth told her. "St Ninian died in 432, and he sent Riaguil while he was still actively seeking to convert the Albannach, not when he was old and failing."

"Four hundred years is a long time later to be seeking a finger-bone!"

"And eight hundred years still longer after St Andrew's death, for his cross to appear to save us in Lothian," the High King said.

"When shall we go?" Eithne demanded. Evidently she intended not to be left out of any exploring party.

Her father was not discouraging. "Tomorrow, no. I have a council with the mormaors of Angus and Fife, at Scone. But the day following, perhaps. It will take us some time to ride to Muckross. It will be twenty-five miles at least – a day's journey . . . "

"The morn's morn, then . . . "

5

It was a lively party which set out for the eastern extremity of Fife, the High King scarcely as animated as his offspring but eager enough to make progress with his great project of linking Alba indissolubly with the Apostle Andrew, which he saw now as a God-given task, elevating the status of his realm. The young people perhaps did not see it quite so loftily, but more as a challenge and adventure. Kenneth perceived it as part of his personal commitment to saving Columba for Dalriada and Galloway. Queen Finchem elected to stay at home.

They rode eastwards down Earn, to cross the mouth of Glen Farg and so to Abernethy, the old ecclesiastical centre of Fortrenn, now being superseded by Scone and Dunkeld. On by the south shore of the widening estuary of Tay they went, on a golden October forenoon, by Lindores, Flisk and Balmerinoch to Wormit, an area much devastated by Norse raiding. There, on high ground, they could at last see the open sea ahead, with comparatively flat and level land between, the coastal plain of Fife Ness, instead of the green hills which had flanked them hitherto. Southwards, down into the plain, they turned.

Angus explained that this area ahead was known as Muckross, or Mhuic Rhos, the promontory of the boar, long a famous hunting-ground of the kings of Fortrenn. He was not himself much of a hunting man and had never followed the chase here, but had heard much of it, the best country for wild boar south of the Highland Line – and, of course, the high kings of Alba's symbol was the wild boar. An Moine Mhor, the bogland of the upper Forth, might be better, but it was practically impossible to hunt there. Kilrymond would be somewhere on the coast hereabouts. Since Riaguil's ship had been wrecked there, it presumably would be at a rocky or reef-bound part of the shoreline – and most of this seaboard ahead seemed to be low and sandy.

As they rode through the dune-country, moorland of heather and whins and scrub oak and birch, Kenneth sought tentatively to interest King Angus in his concept of a great Celtic alliance, not stressing outright union at this stage. The other sounded only moderately interested, not committing himself to anything, not even to co-operating with Galloway and Strathclyde against the Norsemen, indicating that he had enough trouble to deal with the pirates on these eastern Tay and Forth shores without getting involved in the Western Sea. Ewan however took up the notion enthusiastically, and when Eithne heard the discussion, and joined in as of right, she too was for united action. Oddly enough, it was the girl who announced presently that if she had her way Alba would take the lead in forming a unity of the Celtic nations, not just an alliance. That was the only way to maintain and advance their Gaelic heritage, she declared, in the face of these invading hordes. Her father shook his head indulgently, and even Ewan looked doubtful, but Kenneth said a word or two in support and promised himself some discussion with her hereafter. That could do no harm, since undoubtedly this one had some influence on her brothers, if not her sire.

However, after fording the River Eden, they began to see the coastline rising ahead to small cliffs, as well as thrusting out seawards to a long headland, no doubt Fife Ness itself, so converse came back to the matter on hand. This looked more like where ships might be wrecked in bad weather.

Near this modest Eden estuary they found a fishing-haven, which seemed to have escaped the Norsemen's attentions. Here they made enquiries, and learned that Kilrymond was about three miles ahead. They could see its clifftop, indeed. Yes, there was a little religious community there, a monastery with a few monks. The fishermen paid these a tithe of their catch. It served as a hospice for travellers – although there were not many travellers these days, because of the devilish Danes.

They found the monastery without difficulty, somewhat decayed and perched in a distinctly exposed position on a windy summit above the breaking waves. The cliffs here were not high, compared with some Kenneth knew, but it

100

was hardly a typical spot on which to site a religious community. That would be Riaguil's doing.

These were Columban monks, and there was great excitement when they discovered that they were to entertain the High King, protestations as to the poorness of their provision, the inadequacy of their quarters, and so on. Nevertheless, they produced a very substantial meal, simple, quite varied, of both fish and beef, curds, honey and oat-cakes. When asked how they could do this at short notice, they were shown the underground earth-house where ice, stored from winter, was kept in stone-lined deep and dark premises, this keeping provisions fresh. And the monks had their own farmery.

It was not long, of course, before the questioning started. What was known here about the bone of St Andrew? Did they especially reverence that apostle here? What of Riaguil?

Prior Malcolm – he did not call himself abbot – did his best for them. None knew where the famous bone was, no. But that it existed, he thought that there could be no doubt. This St Rule's cell of Kilrymond existed only because of it.

To save time, Kenneth told the prior what he had been able to discover at Whithorn. Did he know any more than that?

This Malcolm did know a little more, particularly about the early story of the bone. It appeared that when the Emperor Constantine the Great was about to invade Patras in Greece, allegedly to avenge the martyrdom there of Andrew, Christ's first disciple, three hundred years before, but really for military and political reasons, an angel had appeared in a dream to Regulus, Bishop of Senlis in far-away France, ordering him to go to Patras and remove the relics of the apostle, which the Emperor was asserting he was going to bring back to his capital of Byzantium, which he was renaming Constantinople in his own honour. Regulus hastened to Greece, to arrive before Constantine, and managed to collect certain items, the bones of three fingers of the right hand, part of an arm-bone, a knee cap and one tooth. Other remains eventually the Emperor laid hands on, and took to Constantinople . . .

"Regulus?" Kenneth interrupted. "Regulus, Bishop of

Senlis, you say? I heard that Regulus and Rule were the same – a play on words, regulus meaning rule in the Latin, and Rule being how Riaguil was pronounced."

"No, no, Prince – that is idle chatter, men confused. But Rule and Regulus have their link, yes. For on his visit to the Holy Land, the Irish Rule, a devotee of St Andrew, heard of this Bishop Regulus and the relics, and believing that their names having the same meaning indicated some divine purpose, went to Senlis on his way home to Whithorn, and from Regulus obtained this finger-bone of the apostle, in gift. That is how he came to have it."

There were exclamations all round, at this, a much more circumstantial and believable story than that this unknown monk from Galloway could have been presented with the relic by the proud and warlike Emperor. Undoubtedly it made the entire proposition seem the more authentic. But there was no hiding the royal visitors' disappointment that the vouched-for bone's whereabouts was unknown. The best that the Prior Malcolm could do for them was to inform that it might be in a cave somewhere along this coast. It seemed that, when paganism regained its ascendancy in the early fifth century, and Ninian's Christian mission went down, the druids, the pagan priests, inherited the bone, considering it a notable and very potent charm which they could use for their own devil-worship. The last such recorded to operate hereabouts had lived in some cave nearby, presumably with the bone. He had put a curse on anyone violating the cave, with the direst penalties. The local folk still superstitiously dreaded this and would not enter any of these caves. Which it was – for there were many along this coast – none knew, so all were shunned.

There was the inevitable reaction from the young people. The caves must be searched. They were not concerned over druids' curses. The bone must be found. That should not be so very difficult, after all. Such a small thing as a finger-bone would almost certainly be kept in some sort of container, a casket perhaps, a box or at least a bag.

Prior Malcolm said that he and his monks had had a look, now and again, but without success. Kenneth for one got the impression that these also had not been wholly unmindful of that curse.

Tomorrow, they would search *properly*, it was asserted. The six of them, in pairs – none expected the High King of Alba to join in anything so elementary; but any of their escort who cared might help.

In the morning, however, Angus declared that he was going to visit a place about six miles further along the coast eastwards, near the mouth of the Cameron Water, where reputedly the largest boar in all Alba had been slain. This animal, which had terrorised the district for long, had eventually been disposed of by the concerted efforts of the entire population, and when killed was found to have tusks no less than sixteen inches long by four inches in thickness, an unheard-of size. Since the boar was the symbol of the high kings, it was felt that this king of boars' head should be in the possession of the Albannach monarch; and Angus would go to collect it from the local chieftains while his children searched for the other more sacred relic. Where the King went, his escort went also.

So the young people set out on their own. Searching caves in cliffs was not the sort of activity girls would be much good at, Eithne's brothers decided; and the older couple were not going to be hampered by youngsters either. They paired off therefore, Ewan with Nechtan, Finguine with Bran, which left Eithne with Kenneth. She announced that she would have selected him anyway, since the task had to be done thoroughly, and her brothers were always too impatient.

The youngsters, of course, started on the first cave they came to along the shoreline, not very large and easily accessible by clambering over the rocks, in great excitement. Their elder brothers chose another nearby, larger. A third was quite close at hand, halfway up a cliff. Eithne and Kenneth passed on. The reddish sandstone of this seaboard seemed to provide caves readily.

Nevertheless, after that they seemed to run out of such, and after half a mile or so, the pair had to leave the shore, which became too steep and narrow, with the tide coming in close, to climb on to the higher ground. Yet Prior Malcolm had said that there were caves right along, and some particularly fine ones where the Kinkell braes came down to the cliffs. They could see the headland of Kinkell Ness ahead, so the caves must be hereabouts somewhere.

The trouble was, of course, that from the clifftops it was difficult if not impossible to see the openings of caverns below. When the tide was fully out it might be possible to get along the shore itself. But meantime . . .

Then Kenneth noticed gulls, or rather the stiff-winged fulmars, flying in directly to an area below them and not always flying out again. This must imply some sort of cavity, surely. If only they had thought to bring a rope, he could have let himself down. But they had not visualised *descending*.

Eithne was not to be put off by gravity. "See," she said, "this cliff is not so very steep. We could get down here, I think. There are ledges on it. If we were to work our way down and along . . . ?"

"Not very easy, I fear . . . "

"It is not ease we seek, is it, Prince Kenneth?"

"No. But . . . " He frowned. His masculine pride resented being made to look feeble by any woman. He went to the edge, to peer down.

It was just possible, a steep grassy slope first then the naked rock, but ribbed, striated, forming horizontal shelves and ledges, with a fair amount of turf and greenery between. And fairly obviously there *was* a hollow of some sort, probably a cave, beneath.

"This may be folly," he declared.

"Let me go, then."

That, of course, was enough to set the man on the downward track. Turning his back to the sea, he commenced the descent, face to the cliff.

It was not difficult at first. Once past the grass slope, he found the rock firm and with suitable hand-holds, the ledges wide enough to base the feet, or at least the toes. It was a matter of feeling his way, left or right as much as down. The slant was much less than perpendicular.

That is, until presently he came to a stretch which was, and this coinciding with a sheer rock-face for a dozen feet or so below. He was held, for his shelf petered out. Nothing for it but to go back some way and try another route.

His glance turning upward and to the left, he was vouch-safed the vision of a considerable expanse of female lower limbs. Eithne, her not-over-long skirt now kilted high and tucked in, was following him down. Swallowing, he permitted himself only a moment or two of this delectation before he called out that he was held, that they would have to go back, find another way. He began to add that she ought not to have followed him, then recognised that this was no occasion to start one of their arguments, and held his tongue.

She had her say, nevertheless. "Eyes downward, I think, Prince!" she called. "Where safe, that is."

His response was indeterminate.

In the event, there was little further call for embarrassment. Not that that young woman had seemed or sounded embarrassed. For when he got to the next downward possibility, he found Eithne had discerned it first and was now below, in the lead. She seemed to be entirely competent at this activity; indeed, she began to direct him as to how to proceed.

In it all he had almost forgotten what they were looking for, until the young woman called and pointed. Over to the left yawned a large cave-mouth, in and out of which the birds were gliding.

The base of that cliff eased off to grass again before reaching the rocky shore, and they were able presently to edge along this directly to the cave's entrance, the girl now modestly lowering her skirts. This cavern opened quite some distance above the tideline, indicating presumably a different sea-level at one time, higher than the others they had seen.

"This could be a hopeful one," she said. "Up here, the winter seas and spray would not enter. A better refuge."

Inside, although the high roof quite quickly slanted down to some seven or eight feet, the cave was long and dry, but at first sight featureless. The sandstone did produce one or two little shelves and crevices, but none appeared to contain anything more interesting than bird-droppings and the dried seaweed from nests. Of course, the further in they went the darker it became. However, all the party had brought flint, steel, tinder and candles. Lighting two of these, they probed further.

It was the flickering flame's highlighting of the uneven texture of the stone walling which revealed to Kenneth the significant detail, a little cross within a circle, roughly inscribed on the sandstone above one of the ledges, at about face-height, modest but vital testimony. Here had been a Christian retreat, a *diseart* of some Columban missionary, possibly St Riaguil himself, who had carved this token of his faith. Without the candle's sidelong illumination it would not have been visible.

Eithne was much encouraged. If this was a Christian sanctuary, then it might well have been the druid's also. So the bone might well be here.

But search as they would they found nothing else, deep as they crept to where the cave became no more than a fissure in the cliff. One or two hollows and niches they came across, but nothing within any. Disappointed, they extinguished their candles and moved outside.

"Where can it be?" the young woman demanded. "If *you* were a druid, old and dying, where would you hide a precious charm, Kenneth?"

"I do not know that I would hide it at all. Rather pass it on to someone else. Give it to another druid. Or, if he was the last of them all hereabouts, someone who accepted his beliefs."

"In that case, it is gone. Gone for ever. No – *I* would have hidden it. So that it was near me when I died."

He shrugged. "Who knows? But this may not have been *his* cave. See – there is another, yonder. Smaller, but still a cave, I think."

Further eastwards still some hundreds of yards was a lesser opening, somewhat lower down the cliff. To this they worked their way. They explored it, but profitlessly.

The beach seemed to be improving again, widening a little ahead, so they decided to stay low and scramble over the difficult stretch immediately ahead, if they could, to this better shore where they would be able to see any further caves more readily.

The traverse of those tumbled boulders and seaweed-hung rocks, all clefts and gaps, entailed much jumping, balancing, hand-holding and general clutching, about which neither made complaint. Indeed when they reached fairly level rock and sand, Kenneth for one was almost disappointed.

However, ease of passage and simplified viewing did not

make for more success in their quest, for they saw no more caves. Soon, in fact, the cliffs began to level off and they recognised that probably there was no point in going further.

"The others may have done better," Eithne said, almost as though she hoped not.

They turned back.

As they picked their way, with the tide receding and progress less difficult, Kenneth brought up the other matter on his mind. "Yesterday, I spoke on the need for an alliance of all the Celtic peoples, to withstand the threat of the Angles and the Norsemen. Your father was doubtful, but Ewan was in favour. You went further. You said that there should be a *unity*, not just an alliance, unity to a great Celtic realm. That I also hold to. If it could be possible."

"Yes. Why not? This of four nations, all of the same blood and faith, makes for weakness. *One* would be strong, could regain our lost lands, Lothian, Cumbria and the rest."

"Four? I think of more than four. *All* the Celtic nations. Wales, Man, even Cornwall. I do not think that Ireland would ever join with the rest, too proud and great for that. But the Irish might enter into an alliance. They much suffer from the Norsemen also, in the north, in Ulster . . . "

Eithne stared at him, pausing. "Wales! Ireland! Cornwall! Oh, Kenneth – that is too much! Man perhaps, yes. But these others are too much to hope for, ancient, famous high kingdoms . . . "

"Yes, perhaps that is only a dream. But Alba, Dalriada, Strathclyde, Galloway and Man – that would be a possibility. Think what it could mean – one realm! One mighty realm."

"Yes. Greater Alba!"

It was his turn to pause and look at her assessingly. "Hardly that!"

"No? What, then?"

"As to name, I know not. But it could scarcely be Alba."

"Why not? Alba is much the largest. Ten times as many folk as Dalriada. Four times as large as Strathclyde. Galloway is only a sub-kingdom. Man even smaller. What else could it be named but Alba Mor, Greater Alba?"

He shook his head. "The others would not have it, Eithne. As though they were to be swallowed up by Alba. Can you see Strathclyde agreeing to that? Or Dalriada? No. The name will fall to be decided later – if ever it comes to pass. But not Greater Alba, I think."

"Then you may find the Albannach hard to persuade, Kenneth."

"We must persuade first and think of names later. It is the unity that is important."

"That is true, yes. It will not be easy, I fear."

"You said yourself, that time – is it ease that we seek?"

They left it at that.

Discovering another small cave, which they had not seen from above, westwards of the one with the cross, they gained nothing there either. They decided that they could probably remain at shore-level now, with the tide ebbing. This entailed more gallant male assistance to a female, however agile and competent she appeared. He was becoming quite knowledgeable as to his grips and holds.

They met the two younger brothers skimming flat stones into the wavelets, sure sign that they were bored with searching and had found nothing. These said that Ewan and Nechtan were still at it, but with nothing to show for their efforts. They did not believe that there was a bone, at all. It was all just a story.

Their sister was quite sharp with them.

Nevertheless, when they made contact with the other two again, it was a somewhat subdued party which returned to the monastery that evening.

But King Angus, when he got back, was otherwise. Apart from the highly impressive trophy of the wild boar's head, which he showed off with pride, hideous thing as it was, he had gleaned some information which might be of value in their search. The chieftain at Pitmilly, from whom he had received the boar's head, had told him that there was a tradition in his family that there had been a Columban saint called Ethernan, who had been a missionary hereabouts two centuries before. He was an Irish monk brought over by Columba, with another, St Monan, to assist the ageing St Kenneth, Columba's friend, at Kilrymond. Ethernan had eventually succeeded Kenneth as abbot, and had for some reason taken a great interest in Inchmay, an island in the mouth of the Firth of Forth estuary, not far away, which he used as a *diseart* or retreat. The tradition was that he had taken there some very precious relic, and dying on the island, the relic had never come back. What it was no one knew now for sure; but the general opinion was that it would be the famous finger-bone of St Andrew.

This new clue in their quest much enheartened the unsuccessful searchers. It was agreed without debate that a visit to this Inchmay was called for. Prior Malcolm was ordered to arrange a fishing-boat of some fair size to be ready to take them out to the island next morning, weather permitting.

October is often one of the finest months of the year in that country, calm, golden, with hazy sun, the seas quiet. So they were fortunate in their little voyage, for conditions could be very much otherwise in the Norse Sea off Fife Ness. They set out from the Kilrymond haven in a fair calm, in an eight-oared, high-prowed and broad-beamed fishing-coble, sufficiently roomy for them all, given these conditions, with about a dozen sea-miles to go.

Such breeze as there was, being easterly, did not help on their outward journey, so that it was all oar-work. The young princes offered to take a turn, but the fishermen would have none of that, scarcely hiding their doubts as to the abilities of royal rowers. They went skirting the coast the cave-seekers had explored, rounding the headlands of Kinkell, Buddo, Hartle and Cambo, to the savage, thrusting point of Fife Ness itself, to the reefs and skerries of which their oarsmen gave a wide berth.

Round that point Inchmay was pointed out, three or four miles ahead. Kenneth for one was surprised. He had looked for some small islet or stack of rock, to form a saint's refuge for meditation and spiritual renewal; but this was a major island, with tall cliffs, low hills and a serrated coastline, possibly two miles long. All the passengers eyed it a little doubtfully. A place of this size was not going to be as readily searched as they had anticipated.

Only one of the fishermen had ever actually landed on the May, as they called it, and that many years before. He remembered that the landing-place, on a notably uninviting coast, was at the southern end of the island, where there was a sheltered inlet. He also remembered that there had been an old hermit living there. Whether he was still alive nobody knew. Nor why he should have been there in the first place.

Was he a holy man? Kenneth asked – but none could tell him.

They rowed down the eastern side, gazing at its cliffs and crags, all whitened by the droppings of seafowl. They saw no caves here. At the south end the land dropped considerably in level, to a horseshoe-shaped cove, too small to be called a bay, within rocky arms, where there was the landing-place.

Disembarking, there was only one way to go, northwards. Seen thus, the island, although long, was very narrow, only perhaps a quarter-mile wide, so that from a quite well-defined central track the cliff edges were very apparent on each side. It was not going to be too difficult to search, after all. Everywhere around seabirds were circling, screaming.

They had not gone far up the track when they saw ahead of them, cupped in a grassy hollow, a stone beehive-shaped cell with vaulted roof, typical of those built by the ancient Celtic missionaries. Next to it was a broken-down timber shed. And tethered nearby on long ropes were two goats. It looked as though Inchmay was still inhabited.

They moved up to the low arched doorway of the cell. King Angus stooped to peer inside. A strong smell of unwashed humanity emanated. It was totally dark within, once the light from the narrow doorway was blocked off.

"Is there anyone there?" the High King called.

There was no answer.

They were for moving on when Eithne, keen of hearing, spoke. "I heard something. In there. Movement. A stirring."

Kenneth was bending, to creep in, when a head and shoulders emerged from the low doorway.

They were presented with an extraordinary sight. The head seemed hardly human, only the eyes peering out of a tangled mat, the grey hair of the head and beard and brows all grown together into an unlovely ravel so that not even lips were visible. As more emerged, of much the same colour and texture, but now seen to be filthy, stained and ragged clothing, part undoubtedly goatskin, it was hard to tell where this ended and humanity began again. The visitors stared.

"Who are you?" Angus demanded.

There was no answer.

"Are you the hermit?" Kenneth asked.

Still no reply.

Eithne tried. "We have come from Kilrymond. Seeking St Ethernan's shrine. Is this it?"

The apparition looked from one to the other, but found no words. He remained on all fours.

At a loss they eyed each other. Then Kenneth knelt, to pat the ancient's shoulder, or where the shoulder should have been. "We are friends," he said. "We wish you well. Friends, you understand. Come to your island, in peace. Fear nothing. You understand what I am saying?"

After a moment or two the shaggy head nodded.

Encouraged, Kenneth went on. "St Ethernan came here, long ago. We seek traces of him. You will know of St Ethernan?"

Another belated nod.

Was the man dumb, he wondered? "Was this his cell? Where he had his *diseart*?"

A nod.

"Can you tell us anything of him?"

A tongue came out of the bush of hair, possibly to lick hidden lips.

"Eth . . . er . . . nan," came forth thickly.

So at least he could speak. "Can you tell us anything of the saint? On this isle."

That seemed to be too much. Silence resumed.

Eithne tried once more, kneeling down also since that seemed to help. "We come seeking a relic. A precious relic of St Ethernan. He is said to have brought it here. Do you know of this?"

Those surprisingly keen if watery blue eyes gazed at her. Then suddenly, still on hands and knees, the man turned and crawled back into his hut like some scuttling animal into a den. Afraid that she had gravely upset the creature, the young woman was exclaiming, when back he appeared, looking almost eager now. In a dirty, clawlike hand he was clutching something, which he held out to the girl.

It was a cross, a crucifix contrived in wood, not very expertly, the arms not exactly in line, an attempt at simple interlacing carved on the shaft, all quite small. They looked

111

at this rather humble offering questioningly.

"*You* made this?" Eithne wondered.

The other shook his head vigorously, and produced an uncertain sound of two syllables. None there quite caught it.

Kenneth spoke. "You did not make this? Did Ethernan?"

Again the decided shake of the head. "Mun . . . go!" That at least was clear.

"Mungo! You mean . . . *Saint* Mungo? The great Kentigern? *He* made this?"

The nodding was now equally positive.

"But . . . but this is not, not very well fashioned. Not perfect. Would he, would Mungo . . . ?"

"Mungo," the other got out. "Young." And beamed on all.

They eyed each other, Eithne still holding the crucifix. They had got two words out of the hermit now. Possibly he could speak well enough, but having lived alone on this isle had not done so for long. How to encourage him to better efforts?

"I am Angus mac Fergus, the High King of Alba," the monarch said. "We are looking for the finger-bone of St Andrew. Ethernan may have brought it here. Do you know of that?"

The hermit did not seem impressed, but he nodded.

"Is it here? The bone?"

A shake of the head.

Kenneth, who was less interested in Andrew's bone than were the others, being a Columba man, concentrated on the crucifix. "This of Mungo," he said. "How do you know that it was his? Can you tell us?"

"Mungo!" Clearly that name had a releasing effect on the anchorite's little-used tongue. He did more lip-moistening. "He made. When young."

"Ha! That would make sense, yes. How do you know this, friend?"

Slowly, as the result of much patience, questioning and encouragement, the story came out, the hermit's eloquence increasing as they went on and the use of words came back to him. Ethernan, it seemed, had missionarised all the northern shore of Forth, with his colleague Monan, working from Kilrymond, and had even built a secondary monastery on another isle, far to the west, which he called after his master, Columba – Inchcolm. Further west still, in Fife, were the remains of an earlier Christian establishment, of St Ninian's period, at Culross, fallen on evil days. Two aged monks were all that remained there. Ethernan wanted to revive this, but he had too much on his hands already, and died before he could achieve it. However, he did acquire this crucifix relic there, of which he was very proud.

They waited with various degrees of patience for the point of all this.

Mungo was actually born at Culross Abbey, it seemed. His pregnant mother, the Princess Thenew of Lothian, was cast adrift in a coracle without paddles by her pagan father, King Loth – from whom Lothian took its name – for the sea to take her, just because she *was* pregnant, but not to the princeling her father had chosen for her but to a Lammermuir shepherd, it was said. She had drifted down Forth as far as this Inchmay, where the coracle grounded. She had remained on the island for a while, but lack of food forced her to enter the coracle again, on an incoming tide, and in it she drifted, up-firth now, until at length the boat grounded at Culross. There she was taken care of by St Serf, the abbot, and when her child was born, Serf christened him Mungo. Mother and son remained at the abbey, where the lad was reared in the faith, until he was old enough to himself become a missionary and he went to convert the Britons of Strathclyde and to found Glasgow, near Dunbarton. As a youth he had carved this crucifix. St Serf kept it and treasured it, as did Ethernan two centuries later.

"But this is a wonder!" Kenneth declared, perceiving much use for this relic. "Mungo's own work. Mungo, who is patron saint of Strathclyde and whom the Welsh venerate as St Kentigern, their Lord of the Hounds of God. This could mean much."

"But it is not Andrew's finger-bone," Angus pointed out.

"It could mean more, Highness."

"I think not." The monarch turned back to the hermit. "You have no word of the bone, man?"

Back to a shake of the head.

"This, then, is the relic we heard that Ethernan brought to Inchmay?" Eithne said. "Not a bone, a cross."

"So we have wasted our time." That was Ewan.

It was Kenneth's turn to say, "I think not."

The hermit, perhaps concerned over lack of appreciation of his treasure, or even at disagreement amongst his visitors, waved an almost apologetic hand and turned to crawl back into his cell. They thought that they had probably seen the last of him, but in a moment or two he reappeared, bearing a wooden bowl filled with milk, presumably goat's. This he presented to Eithne.

She hesitated, then took it and sipped, smiling. She handed it over to Kenneth. He gulped a mouthful and found it sourish and strong. He looked at King Angus, who shook his head. None of his sons looked eager, either. So he gave the bowl back to its owner, the courtesies exchanged.

"You have been here long?" he asked. "Alone. A . . . a man of God?"

"Long." The other looked vague. "Long. I came long ago."

"Why to this isle? Alone."

"I sinned." That was humble. "A woman. Sent here, as punishment. To tend the beacon."

"Beacon . . . ?"

"Beacon." The man pointed to the nearest hilltop. "Warning fire. For ships." He sighed gustily. "Now no more."

"You mean that you kept a fire burning here? To warn shipping, to avoid wreck on this island? That is why you are here?"

"Ethernan made the beacon. Long ago. Many ships struck here. Fire warned them." Another sigh. "Now not."

"Why? You have stopped it? The beacon."

"No wood."

"Ah." They had seen no trees on this island. "Where did the wood come from before?"

The hermit gestured northwards. "Crail. Hospice of Kilrymond. Cut wood. Brought it in boats." He pointed to the broken-down shed. "Kept it there. Now no more."

"A pity. So – you could now return to the mainland? No longer remain here alone."

The other both hung his head and shook it. He would stay here, obviously.

Angus had had enough of this, and began to move back towards their boat. But his young people, having come all this way, wanted to explore the island, and he gave in to them. Kenneth took the crucifix, to hand it back to the hermit.

"This cross of St Mungo," he said. "It is precious. You have kept it safe. But – what is to become of it? When you . . . move on, friend?"

The man shook his head uncertainly.

"Many, in high places, would wish to have custody of this, who venerate St Mungo. It could achieve much, I believe."

The hermit took it, and held it to his shaggy person. "It will be here," he said simply. "When I am gone."

"Yes." Kenneth nodded. "I understand. I will remember that. Guard it well. We thank you . . . "

They went the length of the island, climbing the little hills, examining the great stone fireplace on one of them, for the beacon, skirting the dizzy cliffs, the High King impatient to be gone. Kenneth took the opportunity to speak his mind while the others were stalking seals.

"Highness, this of St Mungo's crucifix. I see it as important. *You* would prize St Andrew's bone as of great value to you and your realm, now that he is your patron saint. Something to hold and cherish, for your people to venerate. But Mungo is patron of Strathclyde, and of great importance to the Welsh. So far as I know, there are few, if any, relics of Mungo in existence today. So you have here, in your Fife province, something of great worth to these other Celtic kingdoms."

"So?"

"This could notably strengthen your hand in any negotiations. For an alliance or a unity. Strathclyde in especial, I believe, would concede much to have that crucifix. Man also, possibly, for King Howell of Man is Welsh. And Mungo, or Kentigern as they called him, went to Man. So here is a key to open important doors."

"Important to you, perhaps, young man. Less so, for me."

"You may well have reason to be glad of allies, Highness. If the Norsemen strike at the *east* coast of Alba as they are doing on the west, and the Hebrides. And in Ireland."

"It may be so. We shall see."

"The word of this crucifix could greatly aid any envoy to the other kings."

"Yourself, you mean?"

Kenneth shrugged.

"You are not my envoy, yet, Kenneth mac Alpin. You may be Galloway's or Dalriada's. But not Alba's. Remember it!"

"I would not so presume, Highness."

"No? That is well." Angus relented a little. "You did well for me in Galloway, at Whithorn. This of St Riaguil and the bone. You have my thanks for that. And you will have still further thanks if you can uncover anything more as to this bone, for I am determined to have it if I can."

"I do not know what else I may do in the matter. But what I can, I will." He looked at the older man questioningly. "May I ask, Highness, why has this bone, and St Andrew, become of quite so much consequence to you? But a year ago, few ever spoke of Andrew. The Lothian victory was important, yes. That cloud a notable sign. Now, of a sudden, it is all of the greatest moment, for you, it seems."

"I have my reasons." The High King stared out over the sparkling waters of the firth southwards, to where the Craig of Bass, North Berwick Law and Traprain Law reared on the Lothian shore, between the last two heights of which the battle with Athelstan had taken place, as though he sought for something there. Perhaps he found enough to encourage confidences, for he appeared to decide that it might be worth telling Kenneth. "I had been looking for some such cause ever since I became High King," he went on slowly. "Alba is a difficult realm to govern. Almost too large. One reason why I do not seek to make it larger, by this of union with others. I am High King, yes – *Ard Righ*. But there are seven *ri*, lesser kings, each all but independent. Wide-scattered. To hold all together is not easy. My *ri* nominate the *Ard Righ*. Some act as though they had *made* me, and could unmake! Some as good as rebel. So I seek for something to hold all together, and some sign that I am more than just the man they nominated. That I am their sovereign lord. This of Andrew and the cloud was such a sign, God-given. That cross in the sky, given for me! A new patron saint for Alba, to unite the nation. The first-called apostle. God's symbol

116

and blessing. You understand? You will be King of Galloway one day, Kenneth. Probably King of Dalriada also. Kingship demands much of a man. More than just wielding a sharp sword!"

"I understand, yes. I see it. Why Andrew is so important. And his bone . . . "

"Yes. The patron saint must have a shrine, a national shrine. And an *empty* shrine does not carry the same weight. I want something to put into St Andrew's shrine. Part of his person, the bone, would serve best. I will set up a shrine at Kilrymond, a place for pilgrimage, for all Alba. I require a relic. I have heard of no other than this bone. At your Whithorn, there was no word of anything else which St Riaguil brought back?"

"No. But I will go and ask again . . . "

The young people came back, full of seal-talk, and a move was made for the boat. Kenneth was thoughtful.

With the breeze behind them now, the fishermen were able to put up a square sail, and the coble made much better time back to Kilrymond.

They would leave for Forteviot in the morning.

That evening, Eithne suggested a walk northwards, round the sandy point known as Out Head and the bay beyond, where the rocks and cliffs gave way to sand-dunes and the beach was open for miles, towards the mouth of Tay. None of her brothers was so inclined, and her father was closeted with Prior Malcolm. But Kenneth did not have to make any great sacrifice to offer his company, nor did he suffer rejection.

It was already dusk and in the shadowy dunes it was quietly secluded, private-seeming. They did not talk much. At least, it seemed no occasion for argument.

"I like the gloaming," the girl declared presently. "There is peace about it."

"Yet I think that you are not the most peaceable of women."

"You think that?" She eyed him. "I am sorry that you should, Kenneth. Am I shrewish, a vixen?"

"No, no, nothing of that. But you are a woman knowing her own mind. And speaking it. Nothing wrong in that."

"But difficult? Awkward to deal with?"

"Not that, either. But strong."

"And men do not like strong women?"

"As to that, I know not. For myself, I do not find it so."

"You are being kind then."

"I do not find that difficult. Towards you."

They walked in silence for a while. When, after helping her across an incoming burnlet through the sands, her arm somehow remained within his, he certainly did not break free.

And yet, and yet . . . ? Perhaps he ought to be breaking free, in more ways than this one? Not allow himself to become too interested in this young woman. The only daughter of the High King of Alba, she was not for him. There were many men more important and suitable who might aspire to wed the Princess Eithne nic Angus, especially as the high kingship, by matrilinear custom, could descend through the female line. All those *ri*, for instance, the seven lesser kings or mormaors of Alba, themselves or their sons, could seek her hand. Loftier folk still – the high kings of other Celtic realms. Kenneth mac Alpin, of the sub-kingdom of Galloway, must look elsewhere.

At the next opportunity, he detached his arm. She did not seem to notice.

They talked, and they did not talk – and Kenneth's distancing process gained little momentum.

He even got a farewell kiss from Eithne when he took his leave in the morning. There was no point in going back with the others to Forteviot when he could save a day and a half's riding by proceeding directly up Forth, for the Great Moss and Strathclyde, where, at Dunbarton, he could find a ship to take him to Galloway, and return his horse to King Roderick. He would tell that monarch of the St Mungo crucifix, planting the first seed.

King Angus announced, before they parted, that he was going to give one-tenth of his royal revenues from the Fife province for the establishment and maintenance of a splendid shrine to St Andrew here at Kilrymond, and hoped and prayed that it would not be long before he had something to enshrine in it. And he was relying on Kenneth mac Alpin.

6

The winter conditions were not to be recommended for even Kenneth's sea-going, and he remained in Galloway over the following months. He was not inactive, however, with no lack of local tasks to occupy him in his father's realm, as well as his own favoured sports of stalking roe-deer with bow and arrow, hawking for wildfowl on the Solway marshes and spearing flat-fish and even salmon in the shallow sandy estuary bays.

But he was not forgetful of his longer-term interests, and did much thinking. He was no dreamer but he could and did visualise the steps which might be taken towards the eventual fulfilment of his conception of a united Celtic nation, or at least a federation, which could withstand the Teutonic and Scandinavian hordes which were invading and devastating all northern Christendom. It was perhaps quite unrealistic, hopeless of attainment, but the vision was there and he felt that he had to work towards it if he could.

Towards that distant end he could at least attempt some small steps here in Galloway. He went more than once to Whithorn, to probe for any further links with St Andrew, for King Angus. And there he heard from an old monk something which set him off on a new line of investigation.

This ancient, now with a wandering mind for daily matters, and therefore seldom much heeded by his younger colleagues, was crystal-clear as to long-ago recollections. He told Kenneth that, sixty years before, as a young man, he had been sent to Hexham Priory by the then abbot here, with a copy of St Ninian's psalms, much prized, for the Prior of Hexham. This priory, of the Anglian, Romish Church, was situated in Northumbria, near its Cumbrian border. And there he had seen relics of Andrew the Apostle. Indeed, the priory was dedicated to St Andrew. These had been brought there, he thought, about a century before that, by St Wilfred, the bishop. He did not know just what these comprised, but thought that there were quite a number of them.

This, needless to say, intrigued Kenneth. He was soon contemplating a visit to Hexham Priory.

There were, of course, problems about this. Cumbria was, in theory, part of the kingdom of Strathclyde, which extended almost as far south as the Welsh border. But it had long been occupied by the Angles of neighbouring Northumbria – one of the reasons why Kenneth hoped that King Roderick of Strathclyde would join an alliance, to help win his territories back. But, although thus invaded and dominated by the Northumbrians, the native Cumbrians were of Celtic stock and so not unfriendly towards fellow-Celts from north and south, however differently their new overlords might feel. It would not do for a prince of Galloway to visit there, but as an ordinary traveller he would probably go unmolested. Admittedly Hexham was over the border into Northumbria proper, but not far, he understood. It ought to be possible.

King Alpin, a quiet and rather gentle man, thought that his eldest and enterprising son was headstrong to the point of folly, but, seeking to dissuade, did not forbid. So, in early March, with the worst of the winter over, it was hoped, Kenneth set out alone – although his brother Donald volunteered to come with him. Or not quite alone at this stage, for the first part of his journey was to be by sea, saving days of riding. So a scow-like, flat-bottomed boat had to be used, suitable for the shallows of the vast Solway estuary and capable of carrying Kenneth's horse. Donald at least would accompany him as far as the Cumbrian shore.

It was a sail of some forty uncomfortable miles across the bays of Wigtown and Kirkcudbright and the suddenly narrowing firth, with the seas whipped up by a fitful but gusty breeze. Fortunately, heading due east, the prevailing wind was behind them so that the boatmen were able to put up a sail and largely dispense with the oars, much speeding their progress. The horse most evidently did not enjoy the voyage.

They landed at Moricambe Bay, on the North Cumbrian shore, just as daylight faded, deliberately choosing a lonely area of unpopulated marshland and sands where their arrival would probably remain unnoticed. Carlisle, the Cumbrian capital, was only a dozen miles away, the seat of Anglian power here, and therefore to be avoided; but this area to north and west of it, because of the far-receding tides and windswept sand-dunes, was practically empty. The boat had to remain in the bay overnight anyway, since the ebbing tide left it high and dry, so its occupants bedded down for the night as best they could amongst the dunes, the horse tethered. Just before dawn the depth of water permitted a departure, and Kenneth said goodbye to his brother, and was left alone, to breakfast on cold meat and oatcakes. At first light he mounted, to pick his way eastwards, through the level lands bordering the Solway.

He kept carefully to the marshy area behind the dunes where he was unlikely to meet anyone at this hour. There were a few cattle here, knee-deep in the reeds, but he saw no one until he came, after a few miles, to the hamlet of Whitrigg, where he exchanged cheerful good mornings with one or two, all he saw. He was dressed nondescriptly and had chosen a very ordinary horse, so that he could be looked upon as an ordinary young Cumbrian farmer. By another hamlet, Glasson, he came to the Rockcliffe marshes, where the River Lyne joined the greater River Esk in a vast area of undrained flooded land. The former river was Cumbrian, but the latter was in Galloway – for the strange situation was that here he was within a mile or two of his own eastern border – although it would have taken him over one hundred miles of difficult riding to reach this point by land. Of more significance was that he was now too near to Carlisle for his liking, only five or six miles – indeed he could just see the walls of the great fort. So he clung to the banks of the Lyne, northwards, until he thought it safe to strike off eastwards to Scaleby, and thereafter reached the notable Roman Wall at Walton, now seven centuries old but still impressive, a strange relic of another age. He was in more populous country now, but being ten miles from Carlisle felt reasonably safe.

He was now heading up the River Irthing for the Gilsland Gap through the hills which formed the border between Cumbria and Northumbria. The Wall and its Roman road followed the river, which came down through this pass. He had now come some thirty miles in his roundabout journey, and his mount, not of the first quality, was growing weary. He had passed the monastery of Lanercost, where there would be a hospice for travellers; but he felt that such might be best avoided, the sort of place where he might find Angles. So leaving the road, river and Wall some miles short of the gap, amongst the hills, he made for an isolated farmery in a dead-end valley, to seek shelter. A thin cold rain was falling, and a night out of doors again was not to be recommended.

He was received with distinct suspicion by the farmer and his sons, of Wardoughan, but this disappeared when he made it clear that he was no Angle, and spoke to the men in their own tongue and similar accent. Indeed, from their attitude towards the occupying Northumbrians, Kenneth was encouraged to reveal that he was in fact a Gallovidian, with no more love of the Angles than had they. Thereafter he received warm if simple hospitality, as well as good advice as to his journey the following day.

It seemed that, once through the Gilsland Gap and the hills immediately beyond, he would be into the great South Tyne valley, with Hexham only some twenty miles ahead. So he could reach there by the following evening without difficulty. Only, he would be advised to avoid Gilsland itself, where there was a major Anglian garrison, apt to be a menace to all and to terrorise the neighbourhood – the source of his hosts' hatred of the invaders. Also the Haltwhistle vicinity beyond, where there was another fort. The farmer would direct him, by a route through the hills, clear of both these.

As to Hexham itself his informants thought that there should be little risk of trouble. It was very much a churchmen's town, with no fort or garrison, the folk native Northumbrians. Indeed, the clerics would be apt to be hostile to the Anglian King Alfrith, for he had only recently, at the request of the Archbishop of York, reduced Hexham from a bishopric to a mere priory, and there was much resentment. The new prior was said to be unpopular and uncomfortable, with the deposed bishop still living locally, and supported by monks and townsfolk both.

So next morning Kenneth was escorted up on to the lofty moorlands of Blenkinsopp Common and told to ride southwards, never leaving the high, empty ground, to Featherstone Common, thereafter to turn east to the lower ground, to cross the infant South Tyne at Featherstone ford itself, and climb again to the still higher Plenmeller Common. This would take him well south of both Gilsland and Haltwhistle, and far beyond. After that, avoiding the important ford at Haydon, he should make for the secondary valley of the Dipton Burn, which would bring him down to the Tyne in the Hexham vicinity.

Much beholden to these helpful hosts, he set off southwards.

All that day, in mixed sunshine and showers, Kenneth rode the high moorlands of Cumbria, the common grazings of farmers, cottars and villagers. Thus early in the year there were not many cattle out from their winter quarters, and he saw few cowherds and shepherds. Only the descent to the Tyne ford at Featherstone presented possible danger, but he had the crossing to himself and was quickly up again into the anonymity of the vast Plenmeller Common, lofty indeed, with even some low cloud chilling him with its damp smirr. His one difficulty was in eventually locating the minor valley of the Dipton Burn, amongst so many another, but in time he found it, and when he did it led him down to Tyne again and he was within a mile or two of Hexham.

The little town on a whaleback mound of the wide vale was compact, and clustered round a fair-sized church and group of monastic buildings, these very different from the Columban establishments, with tall stone towers and walls, guarded gateways and barred windows, an almost castellated air about them. Kenneth went straight thither, guessing that there would be the usual travellers' hospice – a feature which provided much of the regular income of such places, and a major convenience. He was received without question. After refreshment, and remembering what they had told him at Wardoughan about the unpopular new prior, he asked for the sub-prior first, which seemed the wise move.

A middle-aged, stooping and short-sighted cleric was brought to him, neither amiable nor hostile-seeming.

Kenneth had thought carefully about his approach, and had come to the conclusion that no young Cumbrian farmer role would be likely to serve his purpose. So he said frankly that he had come specially to Hexham from Galloway, on a mission of piety towards St Andrew. Whether this impressed the sub-prior was not apparent, but it did elicit the information that the other's own mother had come from the other side of Esk, Kirkandrews, in Galloway – which was partly why he had come to be a novice at St Andrew's monastery of Hexham.

Kenneth had, in fact, forgotten the existence of Kirkandrews, a small village and church at the extreme eastern end of Galloway, and to the significance of its name. He was, of course, not a native of Galloway but of Dalriada, and had never actually visited the Esk valley, so far from the palace-fort at Garlieston. Now, he was alerted, and took note to enquire further. It gave him, too, some slight link with the sub-prior.

He still did not admit that he was the Prince of Galloway, but said that he had come from Whithorn, which, as the other would know, had a strong connection with Andrew through St Rule. He implied, without actually saying so, that he had been sent by the Priory of Whithorn on this errand, and this seemed to be accepted at first.

Kenneth now chose his words very carefully. "Whithorn has no single relic of St Andrew, save for a stone inscribed with words about the brother of the Apostle Peter," he said. "We are eager to obtain some such token, to present to the High King of Alba, who has adopted St Andrew as the patron saint of his great realm. So I journey here." That was his first cautious step.

The sub-prior, whose name, it seemed, was Maldred, did not comment on the relic issue, but appeared to be interested in the statement about Alba. "Why has the High King made Andrew patron?" he asked.

"Have you not heard?" Kenneth took a chance. "Some time ago, there was a great battle in Lothian. Against the Angles and Saxons. The High King, with the kings of Dalriada and Galloway, were endangered in this. Then there appeared in the sky a strange cloud, shaped exactly like a saltire, the cross of St Andrew, white against the blue.

124

This enheartened the three kings, giving them the belief that the apostle was interceding for them with the Almighty. The High King vowed that if they were preserved and given the victory, he would make Andrew the patron of Alba, in place of St Columba. And so it was."

"Ha! I had heard of that battle in Lothian, yes. And the defeat of the Saxons and death of their leaders. But not this of a cross. We were not told of that."

"No. The Angles and Saxons would not boast of that, I think!"

"They would not – a plague on them!"

Those four words were what Kenneth required, to go further. Sub-Prior Maldred was anti-Angle, like the Cumbrians. So there might be opportunity.

"This of St Andrew is important, therefore," he went on. "For it could act as a uniting bond between Alba, Dalriada, Galloway and Strathclyde, against the invading Angles and Saxons. Aye, and the Norsemen too. And Cumbria is part of Strathclyde."

"So-o-o! This is not just the piety of the Priory of Whithorn, I think! There is more to it than that, young man?"

Kenneth wondered whether he had gone too far and too fast. "A gift from Whithorn to the High King of Alba would help the King of Galloway also," he said.

"It is King Alpin of Galloway that you represent then, I judge, not Whithorn's prior? *He* would have sent a monk, no?"

The man was shrewd, however short-sighted. "Both would wish for this," Kenneth ventured. And rather hurriedly explained. "King Angus of Alba has founded a shrine to St Andrew, at Kilrymond in Fife. Where Andrew's finger-bone was brought by St Rule, long ago. But the bone is lost. Some relic is required to put in the shrine, to make it venerated. And you have relics of St Andrew here, it is understood."

"They are our most prized possessions. Think you that we would part with any of them? For any king. Have you lost your wits, young man?"

"I . . . we . . . had hoped that some small item might be spared. In so good a cause. We would pay well for it. St

Wilfred brought back a number of relics to Hexham, did he not?"

"A number, yes – but not all of St Andrew. No – it is not to be thought of, my friend. They are a sacred trust. They remain at Hexham. I fear that you have wasted your time, journeying here!"

Kenneth tried another throw. "The prior? He might be prepared to think differently."

"Not so." That was cold. "He would not dare! Besides, Prior Thomas is not here at this present. He is gone to see his friend the Archbishop of York."

So that was it, mission failed. One final attempt. "Your former bishop? He might be able to . . . advise me."

"You know of that, the bishop?" The other was surprised. "How could good Bishop Oswald do, or say, aught to help you?"

"Give me guidance where else I might seek. He was custodian of these relics until recently, was he not?"

"I think that you would waste still more of your time, young man. And his."

"Perhaps. But he does dwell nearby still, does he not?"

"Yes." Maldred relented a little. "You are very determined. Bishop Oswald lives in a house in the Netherport Vennel. The former Almoner's House. But what will visiting him serve you? He is no longer in charge here, to our sorrow. Not that he would have parted with any relics."

Kenneth could be sufficiently stubborn. "He could give me guidance. As to any other source."

The other shrugged. "That I doubt. But – go if you will . . . "

Kenneth himself wondered why he was doing this. But the evening was still young, and he had nothing else to do here. He left the monastic buildings for the town.

He had no difficulty in finding the bishop's house, where he lodged with the widow of the former almoner. He proved to be a rubicund, elderly man, cheerful, and apparently not at all depressed by his deposition. Getting past the widow-woman was Kenneth's only difficulty.

He had no great hopes of this interview. He briefly explained his quest, stressing the worthiness of the cause and the usefulness of St Andrew in uniting the anti-Anglian forces, Bishop Oswald beaming and nodding the while. But when it came to gaining relics from Hexham, the old man's goodwill profited nothing. In no way could he recommend any such transfer, gift or sale. It would be a betrayal of their trust.

In vain Kenneth pleaded the wider good, the increased veneration of St Andrew's name and fame this could achieve in the Celtic lands. The bishop did not contest that – but not at Hexham's expense.

His visitor was on the point of departure when the other came up with that same name which the sub-prior had mentioned. What about Kirkandrews? he suggested.

Kenneth admitted that he had never visited the place, knew little of it, save that it was a small and unimportant village in lower Eskdale.

"It is not called Kirkandrews for nothing," Bishop Oswald said. "There is an antimension there of the saint. I have seen it myself."

"Anti . . . ?"

"Antimension. Do you not know of such, my young friend? You, coming from Whithorn Priory? An antimension is a cloth, usually silken, a napkin of sorts, in which is sewn fragments of the relics of saints, martyrs. You will be aware, no doubt, that something of the power of the Holy Spirit within a martyred saint remains in the bones – which are therefore greatly more to be prized than other relics not of the body. Even the smallest bone, or portion thereof, retains this holy power. So, for those not fortunate enough to possess a full bone, a fragment might be broken off. Such fragment, sewn into an altar-cloth, makes a much sought-after treasure. There is an altar-cloth at Kirkandrews, with a fragment of the bone of St Andrew sewn into the hem at either end. Perhaps it was brought from Hexham. Or from Whithorn, in Ninian's time, by your St Rule. Who knows?"

Kenneth drew a deep breath. "These are true fragments? No mere pretended pieces of bone? Sufficient to serve an unimportant little church, to impress the ignorant?"

"My son, that is not to be thought of. None would so risk their eternal souls. For to so falsify the name of a martyred saint would be to incur damnation. You should be aware of that."

"You think then, Bishop, that I might have some success at this Kirkandrews?"

"I do not say so. But, it is a very poor and lowly church. And there are two fragments in its antimension. One could be as effective as two. If sufficient inducement was offered . . . "

"Yes, I see. That is well thought of. Bishop, I thank you. I shall call at Kirkandrews . . . "

Better a fragment than nothing.

Next morning therefore, Kenneth commenced his return journey, following exactly the route by which he had come, by the high commons, avoiding populous places and roads, however delaying such progress. He was back at Wardoughan by dusk, and well received.

He wanted more advice – how to get to Eskdale, in the Kirkandrews vicinity, without running into problems with the occupying Angles. And once again he was not disappointed. This would in fact be easier than the eastern journey, the farmer told him. He should cross the Irthing, the Roman road and the Wall at the nearest point below this Wardoughan and climb into the northern uplands beyond at once, on to Midgeholme Moss and on westwards by Burtholme Common. Thereafter he would have to ford the King Water, but that was shallow everywhere and should not trouble him. Then over Walton and Broomhill Mosses, avoiding Hethersgill village, to the Lyne. Three miles on there was a ford at Clinty. Once across that, it was but four empty miles to the Esk and the Galloway border. To cross Esk he would have to use the Netherby ford. Then Kirkandrews was but a mile or two off.

This proved to be an accurate assessment, next day, the fords the only points which required care, where he was apt to meet other travellers. But except at Clinty, where two herdsmen were droving cattle across, he was not near enough to exchange greetings with a soul all day.

At Netherby, the last of Cumbria, he discovered a Roman fort guarding the ford of Esk; but fortunately the Angles had not thought this worth continuing, no danger-point, and it remained deserted. He crossed the wide river into Galloway, his mount belly-deep, with major relief.

There was no problem in finding Kirkandrews, for it lay

almost immediately opposite the Netherby fort, the only group of buildings in sight. And a less than inviting welcome to Galloway it made, although the surroundings were pleasing enough, a mere scatter of miserable, low-browed cothouses and tumbledown sheds and barns. At first the church amongst these was not evident, so like the other hovels was it, the thatched roof grass-grown, the narrow windows unglazed, the air of neglect all too apparent. But at least the door was open, indeed looked as though it was never shut.

Dismounting, and watched curiously from sundry doorways, Kenneth hitched his horse to a rail and went inside. It was fairly dark within, with some of last autumn's leaves still on the stone-flagged floor. The interior was as plain as without, a wooden cross on the stone altar the place's one decoration. There was no altar-cloth beneath it.

Disappointed indeed, Kenneth looked around him. Seldom had he seen a less inspiring place of worship. He perceived an aumbry, a mere small hole in the stone walling to the right of the altar, but in it was only a plain pewter chalice and platter, for the celebration of the eucharist. Nothing more.

Going out, he proceeded to the nearest cottage, where an old woman and two children watched. Giving her good-day, he asked where he would find the priest of this sorry little church.

She eyed him almost pityingly. "The priest? He lives at his bigger kirk. The Kirk o' Liddel," she said.

"Liddel? Another church? Where is this Liddel? I have heard of the Liddel Water and Liddesdale. Where?"

The woman pointed northwards, vaguely. "Yonder."

He saw a man watching from another doorway and moved over to him. "I am told that the priest lives at Liddel Kirk. Do you know where that is? How far?"

"It is where Liddel joins Esk, master," the man told him. "St Martin's Kirk of Liddel. Three miles, no more."

"And the priest of Kirkandrews lives there?"

"Aye. He has the two kirks, and Liddel the greater."

"Three miles northwards?"

"Up Esk, yes. Then ford it, above the joining."

"Then this Liddel is in Cumbria?"

"No, master, in Galloway. The Liddel Water is the

border, after Esk."

"I thank you . . . "

Having come thus far, and it still only mid-afternoon, Kenneth decided that he might as well go the three more miles, unhopeful as his quest now seemed. He rode on up Esk-side. At least he was learning something about his own principality of Galloway. The woman had said St Martin's Kirk of Liddel. St Martin of Tours had been Ninian's hero and guide, after whom he had named his Candida Casa at Whithorn. So there could be some link.

Half an hour later he had no difficulty in finding the place, for it stood plainly on the grassy peninsula where the two rivers met, a much larger church in a burial-ground, with a better house and farmery nearby. Even across the river he could see two men up on the church roof, presumably repairing the thatch.

There was a good ford over Esk just above. Nearing the church, Kenneth saw that one of the men up there on the roof was wearing monkish garb, kilted up. At least this kirk was not being wholly neglected.

He hailed the pair. "Are you the priest here? And at Kirkandrews?"

One waved, and came down his ladder. He was a youngish man, red-headed, boyish of looks. Down, he rearranged his brown robe.

"Greetings in God's good name," he said. "Can I aid you, sir?"

"It is my hope that you can, friend. I am Kenneth mac Alpin, and have come far in my quest."

"I also am Kenneth, sir – Kenneth mac Colman. God's unworthy servant here."

"As to that, we shall see. I have come here from Kirkandrews. And before that, from Hexham."

"Hexham? In Northumbria? You are . . . ?"

"Not Northumbrian, no. I am Kenneth of Galloway. Seeking relics of St Andrew."

"Kenneth of Galloway?" The other stared. "You are not . . . *that* Kenneth? The prince?"

"I told you – Kenneth mac Alpin. I travel thus, not to be known by enemies. In Angle-held Cumbria and Northumbria."

The other Kenneth was at a loss for words.

"You are said to have, at Kirkandrews, certain relics of the apostle. I called there, but saw only an empty, neglected little church. Was I informed wrongly at Hexham?"

"No. No, Prince. We have at Kirkandrews a precious antimension of the apostle."

"I did not see it."

"It is kept in a kist, hidden behind the altar. Being so precious and the church so near to the border. The Angles . . . "

"I thought that perhaps you had brought it here. For safety. That church being in such state."

"No. St Andrew's relics must remain at Kirkandrews. It grieves me sorely that the church is so. But what can I do? Two churches to maintain, and few people. None to help me. No moneys . . . "

"You are repairing this one, I see."

"I have to do it myself. With this one helper today. God's Church is poor in things of this world, Prince Kenneth."

"No doubt. But that might be altered, in some measure."

The priest looked questioningly.

Kenneth decided on the direct approach. He told of the Lothian battle, of King Angus and Kilrymond shrine, of the need for some relic to put in it, so important to the High King. Well before he was finished, his hearer was shaking his head unhappily.

"I could not give you the antimension, Prince. It is not mine to give. It belongs to Kirkandrews. From of old. It is not possible."

"There are two fragments of bone in your altar-cloth, the bishop at Hexham said. Two. And he told me that one was just as effective as two. If I could have one . . . "

"Do not tempt me!" the other cried. "I dare not give away even one."

"I do not ask you to *give*. I will pay for it!" Kenneth took off his calf-skin jerkin and rolled up the sleeve of his shirt beneath. Round his upper left arm was a golden torque, in the shape of a coiled serpent. He drew this down and held it out. "That would sell for much. Enough, I think, to repair both your churches. That, for one of your fragments of bone. It is gold."

131

The priest nibbled his lip in indecision and distress.

"It is not only the money, friend, you should consider," Kenneth went on urgently. "It is what this can mean. In God's cause. In Alba. St Andrew's name enhanced in a great new shrine, to his honour. Whithorn Priory would have given it, if they had had the like. Little Kirkandrews could be famous, for supplying Alba with its need. And it still retain its own piece of bone."

"You mean, cut the antimension in two?"

"That, or take one fragment out and give it to me. And this gold is yours."

The other gulped. "Could it be God's will . . . ?"

"That I know not. But it *could* be, yes, since it will further God's cause in Alba. And beyond, it may be."

The priest swallowed. "It is not the gold," he said. "But . . . "

That one last word was sufficient for Kenneth mac Alpin. "Shall we go back to Kirkandrews?" he suggested, touching the other's arm.

The cleric appeared to have no horse, so, mounting, Kenneth took him up pillion behind him, and set off across the ford and down Esk. They made a silent journey of it.

In the church at Kirkandrews, bowing before that plain little altar, the other took Kenneth to peer behind it in the semi-darkness. From there he dragged out a small wooden chest, obviously ancient, and opening this drew out a silken cloth, yellow, creased and fissured with age. This he reverently unwrapped and spread it over the altar. It was fully six feet long, and at each end hemmed over by a few inches. Kenneth reached out to touch one of the hems. He could feel the hard small portion of bone within.

Despite all that had gone before, he was strangely moved. He was here touching part of Christ's first-called apostle, an awesome thought. And proposing to *buy* it! Was that utter sacrilege? Would he be punished for this? Yet the cause was good. And this little church would receive a new accession of life – and still retain its other relic. He was not going to resile now, at any rate!

"Do we cut this in two? Or take out the bone?" he asked thickly.

The other could not speak, from emotion and uncertainty.

The more decisive Kenneth decided for him. He drew the dirk from his side. "Cut here, near this end, will leave you a sufficiency for your altar-cloth still," he declared. "You agree?"

The priest moistened his lips.

Before the man could decide on an objection, Kenneth applied the dagger to the silk, about six inches from the end. It cut easily enough, the knife sharp.

In moments it was done, the hemmed-in fragment of St Andrew in his hand. He sheathed his dirk, slipped off his jerkin, pulled down the golden torque from his arm and handed it to the still-doubtful cleric. "Yours," he said.

The other, in accepting it, still clung to the rest of the antimension as though it too was endangered. Kenneth helped him spread it again over the altar, smoothing it, to prove that it looked well enough. Then, bowing to the said altar and cross, he moved outside, stuffing silk and bone into the pocket of his jerkin.

They rode back to Liddel Kirk no more talkative than when they came.

Kenneth had thought to seek shelter for the night at the priest's house; but now he knew an almost childish urge to get away from the man, with his prize, before he might change his mind and demand the bone back. So, depositing the other Kenneth at his church door, he said that as it was barely dusk, he should ride on for another hour or so, for it was a long road back, by land, to Garlieston.

One gesture he did make, before departing – why, he might have been hard-put to it to explain. He asked the priest's blessing. Strangely, this seemed to give some comfort to the other, who, holding up his hand, bestowed it almost gladly, fervently. So they parted friends of a sort, if companions in doubt.

Thereafter, it was just a matter of one hundred miles of riding, riding, by Gretna, where he passed the night, by Annan and Dumfries, by Dalbeattie and Kirkcudbright, by the Fleet and the Cree, by Minnigaff and Wigtown, to his father's house at Garlieston, protected by his trophy? Or otherwise?

7

Back at Garlies, Kenneth's return and announcement were
distinctly prejudiced by other news – not that Alpin and his
family were so interested and concerned over the St Andrew
saga and its possibilities as was he, anyway. There had been
major Norse raiding on the Rhinns of Galloway coast while
he was away, with heavy local casualties and much damage
done, the nearest yet that the Scandinavians had come to
Garlies. Fishermen said that they were still in the general
area, last seen heading eastwards. They might well be back,
attacking elsewhere on the lengthy Galloway coastline.
Something had to be done about it, and quickly.

Clearly all at Garlies were waiting for him, Kenneth, to do
that something.

King Alpin had at least summoned all available Galloway
longships to muster in Garlies Bay.

So it was an immediate call-to-arms, all concerns otherwise in abeyance meantime. Eleven longships had already
assembled, and two or three more were expected from
further away. But every one would be required, for this was
no minor raiding but a full-scale Norse hosting by a fleet of
dragon-ships. How many was variously assessed, enough, at
any rate, to devastate much of the Rhinns of Galloway east
coast, the populous side of that long peninsula. Where they
were based, and where they might strike next, was anybody's guess.

Alpin, never an ardent warrior, and less so now as he grew
older, was well content to leave the leadership to his eldest
son, with Donald aiding. Kenneth summoned all the longships' masters up to the palace-fort for a council of war.
Because of the parts he had played in the Lothian battle, the
Corryvreckan incident and the capture of those Norse ships,
no doubt all exaggerated in the telling, he was listened to
respectfully by chiefs and shipmen, despite his comparative

youth.

First of all, he wanted to know, had any of them any recent and fairly reliable information as to where the Scandinavians were now, where they had gone after leaving the Rhinns coast? One skipper, from Balmae on Kirkcudbright Bay, said that his local fishermen had seen a large fleet, and it could only be the Norsemen, heading due eastwards for the Cumbrian coast. No one else could give any guidance, although some were prepared to take this as good news – until Kenneth pointed out that since these Vikings came from the west, either from Ulster or the Hebrides, they would probably come back this way from Cumbria, and might well inflict further damage.

The next point was, how many of them had ever actually fought against the Norseman, at sea? Only three had, although others had fought Anglian ships. He therefore warned the skippers that these were not just bloodthirsty pirates but the most effective and dangerous sea-fighters in all the world, to be challenged only with caution. By that he did not mean with reluctance or hesitation, but with real respect for a cunning and potent enemy. So the Galloway ships would act in closest contact and under his direct orders. Remember always that the dragon-ships were both larger and faster, with more oarsmen, than their own vessels.

He told all the skippers to acquire nets from the local fishermen – King Alpin would pay for them. These were for close-range fighting, if it came to that, with a supply of stones, a tactic he had thought out after the Corryvreckan incident. Extra oarsmen to be included on every craft, and ample throwing-spears and shields.

Now, had any of them points to make, questions to ask?

There was no real discussion. Some of the lords and chiefs had their say, indicating readiness to tackle the Danish devils, but few of the shipmen gave tongue.

It was decided to wait only one more day for late arrivals. Since they would be heading eastwards presumably, anyway, they might meet any reinforcements from that far part of the kingdom – although they might be just as likely to meet returning Norsemen.

That evening, two more vessels arrived, one from the Nith

estuary, the furthest east of any yet, and this crew reported the smoke of many fires along the opposite Cumbrian coast of Solway. It looked as though that must be their destination meantime.

Next morning, fifteen longships sailed out of Garlies Bay, in close formation, to the distinctly anxious farewells of the population, Kenneth wishing that he had the man Conall from Port an Deora to master his own vessel. With a westerly wind they made quite good time, despite poor visibility, and at midday, off Balcary Point, met two more Galloway ships coming from Annan. So now they made a sizeable fleet. Reports as to the numbers of the Norse squadron varied, but it was probably about a dozen vessels. Kenneth by no means permitted himself any over-confidence. The newcomers declared that the fires had now died down over in Cumbria, so it looked as though the raiders had moved on.

By nightfall they were off that coast. It was strange for Kenneth to be back here again so soon after his very different visit of only the week before. They put in and anchored for the night in the shelter of Moricambe Bay, and sent men ashore to see if they could discover the latest news of the enemy. But these returned to say that the only houses they could find in this unpopulous area were burned, and their people's bodies either hanging from trees or lying unburied, some beheaded.

Some two score miles southwards, next day, off St Bees Head, they saw two fishing-boats, and although these tried to escape, they bore down on them easily enough, and vastly relieved their crews by merely asking if they had news of the Danes. They were told that the evil ones had been seen the day before, heading due westwards, out to sea. That presumably meant either Ireland or the Isle of Man – although once in the middle of the Irish Sea the raiders might turn northwards for the Hebrides.

Kenneth had to make his decision. Man was only thirty miles away, Ulster more than twice that. He was a day behind the enemy. If it was Ireland, there was little that he could do, for the Norsemen had more or less taken over the entire Ulster coast, even set up a sub-kingdom there, and to try to assail them would be to court disaster. So, if the killers

136

had had enough of hosting for the moment and were heading for home, there was nothing useful to be done. But if they were going to raid Man, on the way, then . . .

He ordered a change of course, due west – which meant oar-work.

Actually they came in sight of Man, or at least of Snaefell, its highest mountain, quite soon, despite poor visibility. The island kingdom was over thirty miles long by a dozen wide, and approaching it thus they would come to its northern end. Kenneth had never been to Man, but some of his people had, and they told him that this was the least populous end, with Rushen, where King Howell had his capital, near the southern tip.

They were still about ten miles off when they recognised that some of the haze ahead was not just part of the day's mistiness but smoke blowing towards them from Man, and sufficient smoke to represent many fires. It looked as though they would not have to seek much further for the enemy.

Kenneth calculated. The raiders were, in fact, at their most vulnerable, if that word could apply, when they were at their raiding, dispersed, their ships stationary and only part-manned. His night-time attack, on Coll, was not likely to be repeatable; but it might be possible to take some advantage of a raiding situation. With all that smoke and haze their approach would probably not have been observed from the island. If they could remain out of sight until dusk . . .

Orders were signalled to the fleet to go no nearer Man meantime, to beat up and down until further instructions.

Two or three alternative possibilities of action preoccupied Kenneth mac Alpin. Which, if any, he might pursue would depend on what conditions they found prevailing on shore. And he could only discover that by being there. So he just had to wait.

With the shades of evening, the glow of fires irradiated the smoky gloom somewhat – but not enough to endanger them, he assessed, to show them up. And that illumination at least revealed where the burnings were taking place, and there were many of these, some strung together, some isolated – which seemed to indicate dispersal of the Norsemen. There were dark stretches also, which might offer them an unobserved landfall.

Moving a fleet inshore in the semi-darkness required very considerable caution, irrespective of enemy watchfulness, for the Manx coastline was in the main rockbound and precipitous – and the bays and coves were where the dragonships would have to be. However, in thirty miles of seaboard, surely there would be some possible anchorages for them, where no fires showed. So it was a matter of moving in as close as they dared, and then, from this north end, near the Point of Ayre, creeping slowly southwards until they might find an unoccupied inlet. This entailed, of course, not only most careful navigation and searching scrutiny for reefs and skerries, but the sending in of scouting ships to explore each bay and creek for possible shelter for so large a number of craft and to ensure that such was not already being used by the enemy. This was a slow process, but time at least they had.

The first two dark gaps in that cliff wall they tried proved too narrow and shallow for their requirements but, after another mile or two, where fires seemed close, they did find a bay large enough to take them all, close-packed, and empty, surrounded, it seemed, by broken cliffs. Admittedly this could become a trap and they must be out of it by daylight, but meantime it might serve.

Now for some action. Ordering most of the crews ashore, Kenneth sent parties climbing up, to turn left and right, inland. They were to find out, as quickly and silently as possible, the situation as to the raiders, where their ships were, whether these were dispersed, and the like. The remainder, the oarsmen in especial, could have an hour or so of rest.

They did not have to wait long for the first report. Less than a mile to the north, in a fairly wide bay which they had passed earlier and avoided because of the red glow at its head, five dragon-ships were anchored off a boatstrand. There seemed to be a fishing-haven there, and sounds of mixed revelry and screaming came therefrom, some of the houses alight. There was no means of knowing whether the moored ships were guarded.

Kenneth was digesting this, and wondering whether he could possibly get away with the same tactics as he had used at Coll, when another scouting party returned, from the south, to announce that, a little further off in that direction there was a basin-like inlet with a very narrow mouth. In its pool there were three more dragon-ships. There appeared to be no village or any houses there, but some way inland were burning homesteads.

Kenneth made up his mind, once more. The larger task, to the north, could wait meantime. If there was still revelry going on, it would be better later anyway, after midnight, when sleep took over. But this other southern prospect sounded hopeful. That narrow mouth to the pool . . .

There was no point in taking all his ships for this attempt. If they could not do it with six vessels they could not do it with sixteen. So he selected half a dozen skippers and crews and had them re-embark, to follow his own craft closely, oar-shafts bound with cloth to prevent creaking, leaving Donald in charge of the rest.

It proved to be quite difficult, for it was now completely dark, save for the fire-glow, to find that entrance – for the scouts had only seen it from landward. Indeed they went past it, and only when it became evident, from the fading red sky inland, that they had overshot their mark, did they turn back and discover a dog's-leg re-entrant, steep rock at one side and grass-grown knoll on the other, no more than forty paces apart. It made quite a bottle-neck to the pool beyond, this perhaps four hundred yards across.

Even in the gloom the three dragon-ships stood out, moored close together. No lights showed thereon, nor any-where immediately ahead.

Kenneth issued his orders. Two longships were to move up slowly, as quietly as possible, on either side of each enemy vessel. All six must endeavour to do this at the same time, so that no warning might be given to sleeping crews, if any. Then, at his signal, a wheepling curlew's call, board the dragon-ships simultaneously. It should not prove too diffi-cult.

It did not, even though the approach of the six vessels was less silent than Kenneth had enjoined. But the timing was good. He was afraid of bumping ship against ship, and whistled his signal just as soon as he gauged the last longship in position. There was a concerted rush, dirks and swords drawn, on to the three larger vessels.

All their care and precision was unnecessary. No single guard was found on any of the other vessels, anti-climax itself.

Whatever the chagrin of his crews, Kenneth himself was well enough pleased, his first objective gained. He had learned his lesson at Coll as to the dangers of burdening himself with captive craft which required manning. But these three ships could serve his purposes. He ordered his skippers to take two of them in tow and pull them out to that constricted entrance, and there to sink them across the narrow channel, so that they completely blocked it. The third ship he left where it was, undamaged, so that the Norsemen, when they returned, would try to get it out but would be unable to do so. Others might come to help. Who knew what opportunities that might possibly lead to?

The passage closed behind them, meantime it was back to their waiting crews in the bay.

Although this had taken less time than had been anticipated, it was now after midnight and time to be on to the next endeavour. Kenneth's thoughts on this one had not gone much further than his Coll experience, although he well recognised that he was unlikely to find conditions duplicated. On the other hand these Norsemen, in their arrogance, did appear to assume that they had nothing to fear from their victims, and could leave their vessels practically unguarded. Presumably the thought of a punitive force behind scarcely occurred to them, their experience being otherwise.

When they reached that larger bay to the north, it was evident that conditions here were somewhat different, and difficult. The fires ashore, although dying down now, were clearly near to the water's edge at the head of the bay, with a fishing-village near the shore, and five dragon-ships moored close in. So any attack on the ships would quickly become apparent from the shore, unless all there were deep in drunken sleep; and a counter-attack could be mounted with minimum delay. So this looked less hopeful. These dragon-ships could carry as many as one hundred men on each, as against their own fifty. So they would be dealing here with a sizeable host. And there were probably other groups of the raiders not so far away, as fires indicated. This might not even be the main body of the enemy.

At least, it seemed probable that they could put some of the enemy craft out of action. Kenneth marshalled his fleet into as tight a formation as oar-space would allow, not unlike a cavalry arrowhead, and led the advance into the bay.

It was not a deep inlet, and they had only a few hundred yards to go, Kenneth on edge for signs of alarm. None developed before they reached the first of the dragon-ships. Two of their own vessels moved in close to deal with this.

It was the second ship which started the trouble. Shouts and yells arose when it was boarded, and although these were fairly quickly choked off, the damage was done, for shouts now resounded from other ships, and soon this was re-echoed from the shore.

Kenneth had to react swiftly. Controlling a fleet in narrow waters and darkness is no simple task, and he had never had any experience of it previously. His first concern was not to lose any of his ships, either by capture or by running aground. Secondly, his aim was to destroy enemy craft, if possible. No large-scale battle here, afloat or on land, was advisable, with other Norsemen and their ships almost certainly not far away. He shouted to his men on the two enemy vessels to try to sink them, and speedily. All these large sea-going craft had hatches in their bottoms which could be opened so that they could be beached and dried out for scaling and repairs. When found, and opened, afloat, the ships would fill and sink. His men had to be given time for that.

Ordering the rest of his ships was less simple, amidst all the competing outcry. What he wanted was to form a line, of about half of his remaining craft, between the other three dragon-ships and the beach, a barrier to prevent the Norsemen ashore from reaching their vessels, this while the rest of his crews attempted to take the said three ships.

It did not quite work out like that, unfortunately, for manoeuvring many long-oared craft in shallow water and confined space is a recipe for chaos. That is what developed. Quickly Kenneth recognised that this way lay disaster, and that they must extricate themselves from the situation somehow. With many of the Vikings ashore now wading out from

141

the beach, he blew his bull's horn in a series of short blasts, the signal for immediate retiral.

Immediate was a less than exact description of what followed, however prompt the various skippers were to seek to disengage. To Kenneth at least it seemed a considerable time before he could count all his ships clear of the noisy confusion, and heading for the mouth of the bay, leaving continuing chaos behind.

What had been gained by this attempt? Kenneth sought an assessment, by hailing the other ships as they reached open water. Two dragon-ships sunk, probably a third – at least, it had been sinking, and although its crew might be able to close its hatch and stop this, it would have to be beached and drained out before it would be seaworthy again. Damage had been done on the two remaining vessels, and a number of Norsemen slain. At what cost? A few of his men wounded or injured, and half a dozen oars snapped, seemed to be the worst of it.

So now what? Six dragon-ships altogether were out of action for the present, but very few of the Norsemen disposed of. Unfortunately they did not know how many vessels the enemy had hereabouts altogether. The raiders stranded on land would almost certainly be able to communicate with others unaffected, so there undoubtedly would be counter-measures – for these Scandinavians were not the sort to accept reverses meekly. Moreover, there would probably be some attempt to free the ship cooped up in the pool to the south – that had been part of Kenneth's idea in blocking that channel.

Out of this debate with himself, he came to the conclusion that his strategy now should be to try to use this situation further to advantage. To slip out to sea and hide beyond the horizon at daylight would be advisable; but that would leave him unaware of the Norsemen's movements. Some sort of watch was required; but any of his own longships would stand out obviously, and probably would be hunted down. A fishing-boat would be best, lying well out between his fleet and the Manx coast. How to obtain a fishing-boat? There would be other fishing-havens down this coast not so far away, almost certainly. They still had four hours or so of darkness before dawn. They would head southwards looking for such a place, try to obtain a boat, and then head for the open sea.

No more fires showed as they progressed southwards. There were no large bays for some distance, however. The first two small ones they came to, with a single ship sent in to examine, revealed no communities. But the third did produce a little group of cot-houses at its head, slightly larger, where the cliff-girt seaboard sank somewhat, three fishing-cobles drawn up on the sandy boatstrand. No signs of life showed at the houses – probably their occupants had fled inland – and the cobles' oars had been hidden, also the nets. But the longships always carried spare oars, even though these would be somewhat long for such craft. One of the cobles was taken, with a volunteer crew of six to man it, and towed off to the north-east.

About four miles out, they dropped the coble. There, in daylight, its crew ought to be able to see any movement of Norse ships off the Manx coast. The Galloway fleet would proceed another five or six miles further eastwards, to wait, with one longship, under Donald, left in between to act as link. This, it was hoped, would provide Kenneth with the information he required. As the first faint paling of the sky ahead heralded the dawn, the fleet downed sails and shipped oars, to lie up, in the middle of the Irish Sea. Men could sleep, however comfortless were their couches. Kenneth himself did not allow his eyes to close.

It was some considerable time after sunrise before Donald's ship came hastening eastwards. The fishing-boat had reported five dragon-ships sailed south to the mouth of the narrow inlet blocked by the sunken vessels, and remaining there when last viewed.

Kenneth calculated. It looked as though his bait of the trapped ship in the pool behind was proving effective, five dragon-ships remaining. That would add up to an original fleet of nine or ten, depending on how many had got out of the northern bay. He thought it unlikely that they would be able to extricate the trapped vessel past those sunken hulks. But they could rescue the stranded crews. In fact, although the Viking fleet might be now reduced to five, their man-power would presumably remain almost unaltered, possibly not far short of one thousand men. His own fleet would outnumber the enemy three to one, but themselves be outnumbered in men, and outclassed as to speed and manoeuvrability. He must seek to act accordingly.

He ordered all speed westwards, unfortunately the wind, now in their faces, delaying them.

However, when they drew near enough to the Manx shoreline to see details, it was to perceive that the Norse ships were still clustered close to the cliffs, no doubt at that blocked entrance, although that was not evident at this range. Unfortunately, if they could see the enemy, the enemy would be able to see them, and a surprise attack impossible. Still, some of the Norsemen might well be either ashore or seeking to free the other vessel.

Urgently the Galloway crews rowed shorewards, Kenneth all but counting every stroke. It was in vain, of course. While they were still more than a mile from land, they saw the Norse ships hoisting sail and standing out towards them.

No trained sea-captain, Kenneth's strategy had to be based on the methods he would have used in land warfare, adjusted by common sense and instinct. The enemy, obviously intent on challenge, despite their reverses hitherto, were coming on in fairly open formation. Divide them, then. Two wedges. That should be possible. Then all turn to assist the leadership. Elementary field tactics, but with general application.

He shouted commands to his leading shipmasters to form arrowheads, eight and seven, hoping that what they were doing would not become too apparent to the Norsemen in time for them to close up tightly. He ordered his second wedge under Donald to fall in behind his own group meantime, so that their formation would not be apparent from any distance.

Those Scandinavians certainly did not lack boldness, continuing to advance head-on in determined style, their banks of oars throwing up a mist of spray. They had the wind behind them, of course. Whether their present formation was deliberate or not, they did not seem to change it. As they neared, on the breeze Kenneth could hear the rhythmic, gasping chant of the enemy rowers and their colleagues, a frighteningly confident sound.

When no more than a quarter-mile apart, Kenneth gave

his signals. The rear group of seven pulled out to the right, separating from his own eight, which drove straight on, oarsmen straining.

It was those oars, of course, which complicated Kenneth's problems. Projecting on either side of each vessel for a dozen feet, they kept the ships much further apart than he would have wished, so that the wedges were scarcely tight-packed. He had devised a plan to try to counter this, and had shouted it out to the nearest skippers, to relay to the others. His own vessel, in the lead, heading the wedge, would draw in all oars just before impact with the enemy, and the two next craft, one on either side, would close in, shipping their near-side oars, with all power on the outer ones, their prows to come halfway along the leader's flanks. Thus the first three craft would seem to form almost a single entity, propelled by only one-third of the oar-power. Admittedly this would reduce the force of their drive, but this might not be too serious when effected only at the last moment, as it were. The rest of their wedge would fill in behind, rather further apart, and help to propel the leaders onward. That was the project. Whether it would work and have the desired effect, remained to be seen.

It seemed that the Norsemen had never experienced any such assault; at least they made no obvious moves to contain it, no change in their advance. The two squadrons raced towards each other to dramatic effect.

Holding himself in, Kenneth waited until the leading ships were only some hundred yards apart before giving the next signal. Up and then inboard came all his own ship's oars. In close surged their two flanking craft, near-side oars shipped. In only a matter of moments their timbers were grinding against his own vessel amidships, left and right, their outer side oars furiously active. As one craft they drove in on the enemy formation, their supporters astern, deliberately to swing in against the leading Norsemen. Right down the side of this dragon-ship Kenneth's sharp prow sheared, snapping off the enemy oars like twigs, spearing, knocking aside and overturning the rowers in splintering, screaming ruin. A few throwing-spears came at them, some finding marks. Then they were past, leaving the temporarily disabled vessel to the attentions of their followers.

There was another enemy ship directly ahead now. This was not so easy a target. Its crew could see what had happened to their leader; moreover the three Galloway ships' speed had inevitably dropped considerably, for of course the leftmost rowers had had to raise oars high as they sheared down the foe's side. So this assault had to be very different.

These Norsemen, presumably expecting a similar attack, reacted to resist it, swinging broadside-on. Too late to alter direction, Kenneth's trio could do no other than crash bows-on into the dragon-ship's side amidships, with an impact which toppled all the crews in heaps. But it also had the effect of bringing the two flanking craft up level with Kenneth's, their bows also ramming the enemy.

For quite a minute there was utter confusion on all vessels, as men picked themselves up, disengaged from oars and reached for weapons. The Norsemen were no laggards, and their kind always aggressively minded; but although they could have sought to board the Galloway ships first, by the very nature of the attack, defence was instinctive. It was Kenneth's crews who led the way over the side, swords and dirks in hand, short spears stabbing, yelling their challenge.

It could be no disciplined assault, with difficult approaches over the three bows, awkward footwork thereafter on the rowing-benches, across enemy oars askew, and against the Norse resistance. It would have been worse had the foemen been ready and marshalled to repel. But most of them had been rowing, weapons not in hand, and they too were hampered by the benches and the fact that their attackers were coming in on three points. Also, on this occasion, they were outnumbered.

Kenneth restrained himself, recognising that his duty was to direct, not to lead with the sword. He hung back, at the prow of his own ship, pointing, gesticulating, yelling commands. And every now and again he glanced briefly around him, for he had a whole fleet to think of, not just these vessels here.

It was hard to estimate just how the fight was going, both near at hand and further distant, at this stage. Chaos seemed to prevail everywhere, men and ships milling and circling. At least they had the advantage in numbers of vessels; and probably in men also, now, for the chances were that, interrupted at their efforts to rescue that trapped ship in the pool, considerable numbers of the Norsemen would still be ashore.

Two of their own wedge of eight were now dealing with the leading enemy vessel which had suffered partial disablement. Of the remaining three, two had swung off to go to the aid of the other wedge; but the third was bearing down on the far side of this dragon-ship – as though Kenneth's three were incapable of handling it themselves. He dismissed momentary irritation; at least it ought to help bring this encounter to a speedier conclusion.

Even so it was hardly speedy. Those Norsemen fought like lions, grievously outnumbered as they proved to be. None seemed to consider yielding. Kenneth, more or less trapped here, and concerned for the rest of his fleet, was becoming agitated in his role of overall commander, so much less satisfying than personal battling, when a thought occurred to him. Those hatches, in the bottoms of the dragon-ships. In those which they had already sunk, they had all been placed near the stern. If they could reach this one, and open it . . .

"Come!" he shouted, to panting men nearby not actually for the moment locked in combat, slapping shoulders and pointing, and led the way sternwards. Three followed him, stepping over fallen bodies.

They found the hatch without difficulty, under sail-cloth and cordage; but raising it was less easy. Eventually the four of them, with their sword-blades, and no Norsemen free to interfere, got it up – and the water surged in. They dragged the heavy wooden lid over to the side and threw it into the sea.

Back at the fighting, it was surprising how long it took for the fact that the ship was filling with water to register with the combatants, all of whom were of course preoccupied with other matters. Even when it was slopping about almost at knee-level, only a few seemed to get the message, on both sides. But gradually it dawned, and then an extraordinary change came over all. Men broke off battling, more or less by mutual consent, to stare down and then rather wildly around them, the water now half-filling the vessel.

If fighting may come almost naturally to many men, to leave a sinking ship comes more so. Suddenly all still on their feet found it necessary to be elsewhere. Not only the Galloway men but not a few of the surviving Vikings scrambled over into the now four longships, where quickly they were overpowered and yielded, others actually jumping overboard, a strange reaction. That particular encounter ended forthwith.

Kenneth partially reversed the situation by ordering men back from his own craft to drag out the bodies of their fallen comrades, wounded or dead, or indeed drowned, while still the dragon-ship sank deeper. They left the Norse fallen where they were.

When approximate order was restored in the Galloway ships, Kenneth's ship led a move over to the second wedge's battle, taking place about a quarter-mile off. Although the slightly smaller group, they had found themselves having to deal with three dragon-ships, not two. They had of course been reinforced by two of the first wedge, but even so there was a less uneven struggle, and from a distance Kenneth could not be sure how the advantage went, in the huddle of ships. Even when close, it was not clear who might be gaining the upper hand, if any. Most of the fighting seemed to be going on on the dragon-ships, but that did not necessarily imply any ascendancy.

However, one of the Norse leaders, a realist evidently, must have reached his own conclusion in the matter, for before Kenneth's four could come up, one dragon-ship abruptly drew out from the cluster, as it were shaking off the opposition, and headed off westwards, oars lashing the water.

Although that did not end the battle, it did mark the beginning of the end. Now, with thirteen longships against the two, there could be no hope of a Norse victory, or even of an escape, for having seen how that one vessel had got away, the Galloway ships encircled the two closely, giving them no opportunity to break free. The Norse crews fought on, selling their lives dearly, but there was no question as to the result.

Kenneth thought to speed this up and thereby reduce casualties amongst his men. He called for those fishing-nets and stones they had taken on at Garlies, and loading the nets with the stones, had men throw them out over the struggling

148

fighters, friend and foe, in the dragon-ships.

That was the last straw. Although it affected all beneath the netting, hampering men in the use of swords, dirks, even fists, it trammelled and upset the enemy most, outnumbered and dispirited as they were already. Helplessly individuals began to throw down arms, such as were not already entangled in the net. That was it.

There remained only the first vessel tackled and badly mauled. Kenneth's two support-ships seemed to have that one well in hand. The waterlogged craft had now sunk.

Victory his, Kenneth surveyed the scene, and the cost. They had three dragon-ships as captured trophies, if they wanted them. They had not a few prisoners, mainly wounded, which they by no means wanted. And they themselves had sustained considerable casualties, few dead but many wounded, some seriously.

While his crews were congratulating themselves, boasting and tending the injured, Kenneth had other things to think about. What now? There would still be Norsemen back on land. Should he try to do something about these, or be content with what had been achieved? That ship which had escaped: it might well come back, after dark, to try to rescue the stranded men. Let it, then. Was not his first duty now to his own wounded? Get them adequate attention, if possible, and quickly. That would have to be somewhere on Man itself. So, forget the stranded Norsemen meantime; he could let King Howell of Man deal with them.

What to do with these prisoners, a nuisance and a danger? Most of his people were for slaughtering them out of hand, throwing them overboard – as undoubtedly the Norsemen would have done to them. But that was more than Kenneth could swallow. He decided to get rid of them, yes – but not that way. Put them aboard one of their own dragon-ships, disarmed and with only a few oars, no sail, and no food, and let them save themselves as best they could. There were some demurs at this, but Kenneth insisted. Before they herded them aboard, however, they stripped them of all ornaments, brooches and necklets, of which these pirates seemed inordinately fond, Kenneth himself doing rather well, for he removed a gold torque from one of the leaders' upper arms, not unlike his own which he had given to the priest at Kirkandrews, but twisted in decoration. Grimly he told himself that it would pay for Alba's bone-fragment.

Actually, he did not let its late owner go with the other captives, retaining him and another proudly defiant individual, obviously both leaders, as hostages. It occurred to him that they might just be useful.

So, pushing off their surprised captives in one of their own craft, and putting skeleton crews on the other two, the fleet formed up and set off southwards. At the south end of Man was Rushen, King Howell's seat and capital.

Well recognising the alarm which the sight of a large company of ships bearing down on the bay near Rushen, past Langness Point, would arouse in the Manx folk, especially with two dragon-ships amongst them, but concerned for his wounded, Kenneth had all his casualties transferred to two vessels, and leaving the others lying well out to the north-east, sailed these two round between that southernmost headland and the offshore Calf of Man, and into the great sheltered anchorage, in mid-afternoon. Even so, half a dozen Manx ships, longships and trading craft, hastily put out to investigate and intercept, and escort them in, suspicious in spite of the Galloway banners.

Kenneth's request to be taken to see King Howell, and his call for aid for men wounded by Norsemen gained them more friendly attention; and his mention thereafter that he was Kenneth mac Alpin, Prince of Galloway, was actually greeted with respect. It seemed that word of his Corryvreckan exploit had reached even Man, in some form, and he was accepted as something of a hero.

It was not difficult thereafter to arrange for the wounded to be brought ashore, and tended by a colony of nuns established here – the bay was called St Mary's in honour of their patroness – and for one of his ships to go back to inform the rest of the fleet that they could come on in without creating any upset. Then Kenneth, with Donald and some of his people, found an escort to take them to the King's palace-fortress at Rushen, on the high ground some two miles inland.

They were met halfway by a troop of armed horsemen hastening down to the township and haven – this because, from up at the palace vantage-point, they had seen the Galloway fleet standing off and were preparing for trouble. Much relief was expressed, and all turned back.

King Howell proved to be an elderly man, frail-seeming but nowise lacking in spirit. Having been prepared to resist Norse invasion, he was the more welcoming towards Kenneth and his brother – especially when the former presented him with the two Viking prisoners to use as hostages, and told him that he could have the two dragon-ships also, when they came in. Howell could send his forces north forthwith, to the area which the Norsemen had devastated and where the single ship was trapped – which he named the Clay Head and Laxey Bay neighbourhood – hoping to catch them there. Man had been greatly troubled of late by the Scandinavians.

That was the opening which Kenneth sought. Over a hastily produced banquet he expounded his cherished project of a great Celtic alliance, leading possibly and eventually to a united Celtic kingdom, of which Man could be part, emphasising the strength of such a realm and how it could clip the wings of the Anglo-Saxon invaders, as well as the Norsemen.

Howell listened with interest, and more than that, with an expressed measure of support. Having been reared in Wales, he was very much aware of the Anglian and Saxon threats, as well as the Scandinavian. Also his was a tiny kingdom and required all the allies it could muster. He was concerned over the matter of sovereignty, however. Speaking for Man, he was sure that the Manx would be reluctant indeed to give up their status as an independent kingdom. If a military alliance was not enough, then some sort of federation of the Celtic states might be forged, keeping their individual thrones and identities.

"An empire?" Kenneth wondered, rather doubtfully. "Sub-kingdoms within an empire?"

"Not sub-kingdoms, no. Would the High Kings of Alba and Ireland ever agree to be reduced to sub-kings? No, full sovereignty would have to remain."

"Then there would be no ruling voice, no decision. Many equal kings would but seldom agree."

"If they appointed a commander of armies. Not a king but

a general. That would be necessary in an alliance, also. Such as the mighty Arthur, the Briton."

"That might serve. Such might become a Charlemagne. So a ruling monarch would be best, one great realm."

They left it at that, Howell sympathetic but not convinced. He would, however, join meantime in any alliance against the invaders of the Celtic lands; and also urge his Welsh cousins to do the same. His son Rotri was much in Wales – he was there at this present – and he would have him act as ambassador and persuader.

With that Kenneth had to be content.

Next day, after a simple burial service for the fallen, leaving one ship to keep in touch with the wounded at the nunnery, to bring them back to Galloway when sufficiently recovered, the fleet, minus the two dragon-ships, set sail north-eastwards for home. Kenneth would have liked to go on to Wales, while he was so near, a mere sixty miles or so to Caernarfon Bay; but his father would probably take exception to that. Also, he recognised that his duty was to get his crews back to their anxious families as soon as possible. Being commander of a host had more sorts of responsibilities than one.

8

Kenneth's and Donald's return to Garlies partook of something in the nature of a triumph, despite the casualties sustained and the consequent sorrow of many households. The brothers and their crews were made much of, and their sea-battle hailed as the first major victory over the dreaded Norsemen. Galloway, it was hoped, might now be spared further raidings. Kenneth was not so sure of that, but did not say so.

However, his preoccupation was now with affairs elsewhere, considerably further north. He had business to do in Alba.

So soon as he decently could, therefore, he sought leave of absence from his father, and a ship to transport him, and set sail for Dunbarton in Strathclyde.

King Roderick was not a forthcoming sort of man, but he received Kenneth well enough. He was glad to hear of the Scandinavian defeat but did not enthuse about King Howell's agreement to a Celtic military alliance, indicating that he gauged the Manx contribution would be so modest as to be of little consequence. Alba was the vital factor. Until Alba's adherence was assured, the project was no more than a daydream. However, he did not resile from his own less-than-eager agreement to participate if others would.

Kenneth, allowing his ship to return to Garlies, borrowed a horse again and set out on the long road to Fortrenn, with quite a measure of anticipation.

That anticipation, in one respect at least, suffered a distinct setback at his very arrival at Forteviot; for although the first of the royal family he saw, in the garden of the palace, was the Princess Eithne herself, she was not alone, but had a young man with her – and he had his arm around her shoulders in an entirely familiar fashion.

She stared up at sight of Kenneth, and came running –

which was satisfactory enough. But the man came too, more slowly, and looking frowningly at the girl's impulsive greeting and smacking kiss. He was a good-looking character, tall and well-built, but with a fleering eye and an authoritative manner.

"Who have we here?" he demanded. Admittedly Kenneth, who seldom adopted elaborate clothing, especially when he was riding the land alone, was looking less than impressive after his long journey.

"This is Kenneth. Our friend. Kenneth mac Alpin, Prince of Galloway," she announced. And, in turn, "Here is my cousin Aed. Aed mac Boanta, Mormaor of Moray. Come . . . visiting."

The two men eyed each other, in more or less instant dislike. Neither required further introduction. Although they had never met, Kenneth knew a sufficiency about the other. He was, in fact, his own kin also, Aed's mother being his own grandmother's sister, both sisters of King Angus and the late Constantine. Aed had been appointed Mormaor of Moray, one of the *ri*, or sub-kings of Alba, by his uncle; and had the unusual distinction of using his royal mother's name, Boanta, after his own, his father unfortunately having been a nobody. What Aed knew about Kenneth was evidently not such as to greatly commend him.

Eithne looked from one to the other. "You also are kin," she said. "We all descend from King Fergus." She sounded almost a little anxious, for that young woman.

Kenneth nodded. "I am glad to meet a cousin," he lied.

"The hero of the whirlpool!" the other commented. "We do not all have the like to fight the Danes for us!"

"You have trouble with them in Moray also?"

"Sufficient." That was curt.

"It is good to see you, Kenneth," Eithne declared. "We have looked for you, for long."

"Have you?" He was surprised. "I have been much . . . occupied."

"We . . . my father, hoped that you would be back, ere this. With some word as to St Andrew. You said that you would seek for something."

"I did. But then I had to take up the sword. More Norsemen. And then on to Man. I have come as quickly as I could,

Eithne."

"Norsemen again? I . . . I am sorry. But glad that you are come. I have much to tell you . . . "

"Indeed you have!" That was the mormaor.

"Yes. Shall we go to see my father . . . ?"

Kenneth was aware of some tension as they went into the palace, on the girl's part, not Aed's. She took the new-comer's arm and gripped it tightly.

They found King Angus alone, actually drawing an elaborate design for a stone St Andrew's cross he was going to have carved for Kilrymond, a most ambitious conception, all interlacing and strange beasts and birds within the arms of the saltire, surrounded by a wreath of flowers. He looked up, irritated at being interrupted, until he recognised Kenneth.

"Ha – Kenneth mac Alpin – come at last!" he greeted. "With good tidings, since you have taken so long, I hope? Success, man – success?"

"A measure of success, yes, Highness."

"What mean you? A measure . . . ? Yea, or nay?"

"It is yea, I judge." He delved into a pocket of his jerkin and drew out the piece of silk, yellowed and ancient, and held it out.

"What is this? Cloth?"

"Feel inside, Highness."

"What . . . ?"

"A piece of bone. A bone of St Andrew. From Kirkandrews, on the Galloway Esk."

The High King stared.

"Kenneth, is it truly that? Truly Andrew's?" Eithne asked.

"I am so assured. Brought to Kirkandrews from Hexham Priory, in Cumbria, which is dedicated to St Andrew. St Wilfred brought relics there, from Rome and Byzantium. Two fragments, vouched for by the bishop, brought to Kirkandrews – why it is so called – in an antimension."

"A what?" Angus demanded, fingering the fragment.

Kenneth explained what an antimension was and how the priest there would nowise allow both fragments to leave, but had been so reluctantly persuaded to part with this piece – at a price.

Aed mac Boanta scoffed. "A likely story! To cozen the simple. It could be anything. A piece of cow's bone. Or sheep's. Anything."

"It has been in that silken altar-cloth for centuries, revered by Christians as clever as are you, Cousin Aed! Any bone could be make-believe, yes. Even the lost finger-bone at Kilrymond. But when a church and township have been so named because of it, from of old; and it was brought by a bishop from near where Andrew died – then who am I, or you, to say that it is untrue?"

"It is a mere chip. So tiny a piece. What is that worth? What use?"

"The size of it is of no importance," Angus asserted. "So long as it is part of the blessed Andrew. Assured of that, I am satisfied. Tell me of this St Wilfred, Kenneth. I have heard of him but know little. An Angle, by the name?"

"He was indeed an Angle, Highness. And no friend of our Celtic nations, although he was trained a priest at Columba's abbey of Lindisfarne, two centuries ago. But he was a strong man and a great missionary. He converted many Angles, indeed the King of Northumbria, Oswin. And founded this Hexham Abbey. He took the Romish side, against the Columban Church, at that conference at Whitby. Oswin's son, King Alfrith, appointed him Bishop of York, but he refused to be consecrated bishop by a Columban Church bishop. And so he went to Rome on pilgrimage, and was consecrated there. When he came back, he brought St Andrew's relics with him, to Hexham, which was raised to a bishopric, since another had been appointed to York. He dedicated it to St Andrew. Wilfred died there. That is all I know, told to me by the last bishop. I went to Hexham."

"You did? In Cumbria?"

"Yes. But I could win nothing of the apostle there. That bishop sent me to Kirkandrews, in my own Galloway, telling me of this antimension. It was my only hope . . . "

"I think that you did wonders!" Eithne exclaimed. "To risk going into Cumbria, where the Angles rule. That was brave, noble! On our behalf, Father. Was it not?"

"Yes, yes. We are beholden." Angus was turning the bone-fragment this way and that. "Here is a wonder, yes! Part of Christ's first-called apostle. Who saved us from the

156

Angles and Saxons in Lothian. This came to us, now, *from* the Angles. A wonder!" He was evidently accepting the fragment as genuine, rejecting Aed's doubts. "Now I have a relic to put in my shrine at Kilrymond. I shall build a great church there, in honour of our patron saint. And name it St Andrews. A place of pilgrimage for all the Albannach, for all time."

"And all of Kenneth's doing," his daughter reminded him.

"This part of it, yes. We are grateful to Kenneth mac Alpin, to be sure. He will not go unrewarded, never fear."

"A man of parts!" Aed observed. "Finding use for whirl-pools and bits of bone! I wonder what next?"

Kenneth thought to comment on that, then decided to hold his peace.

"My sister's son will learn," the High King mentioned, shrugging. "No doubt Eithne will teach him much. They are to be wed."

Kenneth drew a quick breath, and turned to stare at the girl.

She spread her hands, silently but eloquently.

Aed was less wordless. "Do you not congratulate me?" he demanded.

The best Kenneth could do was to bow stiffly.

"Aed is unlikely ever to be High King. But at least he can wed the High King's daughter," Angus said.

Kenneth recovered his voice. "If that is Your Highness's will," he got out. And then, "Have I your permission to retire? I have travelled far and fast."

"To be sure, my friend. Eithne will find a servant to show you to your chamber."

He bowed, and followed the young woman out.

For moments neither uttered. Then both spoke at once, and stopped again. Kenneth was feeling the reverse of loquacious, anyhow.

"This – this – is not my doing. My wish," Eithne got out at length, in a rush. "I do not want to marry him. But my father says that I must. Aed is the most difficult of the mormaors. Wed to me, he may be the less difficult to handle, my father thinks. For Alba's good. And of aid to Ewan when he becomes High King. My father is not a well man. He worries about such matters. Why he is so concerned over this of St

Andrew. He thinks not to live so very long. So plans thus. I am sorry, Kenneth – sorry!"

"It is no concern of mine," Kenneth told her, almost roughly, stalking on. He was, in fact, all but shattered by this development. He had never really admitted to himself how much this young woman had come to mean to him, never thought it all through. But now he knew that she was important to him – and it was too late.

She took his arm. "Kenneth, hear me. I tried to dissuade him. My father. Told him that it was *you* that I wanted. That I loved you. But he would not have it. I . . . "

"You said that!" He had stopped now, to turn and gaze at her in that painted corridor of the palace-fort. "You said, you said . . . that you *loved* me!"

"Yes. For that is the truth. Should I not have said that? Even though true. Was it wrong? Unwomanly?"

"My dear, my dear!" He reached out, to grip her, and immediately she was in his arms. They kissed, urgently, unreservedly, clinging to each other.

Then Kenneth at least recovered something of his senses. They could be observed, servants see them, tell Angus. This was folly. He thrust her from him.

"This will serve nothing, lass," he declared. "Only trouble. Your father – he would be wrathful. Punish you. We cannot vanquish your father. He is the High King. If he will not heed you, he is not like to heed me."

"No. Not now that he has announced it to others. I . . . " She paused, drawing further back, as a servitor appeared along that corridor. "Come – I will find a room for you."

On an upper floor of the great hallhouse, Eithne showed him to an empty bedchamber. The door closed on them, she came to him again.

"Oh, Kenneth – if only we had known before! *I* knew that I wanted you. But not that, that you could feel the same. You do, my dear? You do?"

"Can you doubt it, lass? I have been a fool not to declare it, not to seek your hand, ask your father. Not that he would have heeded me, perhaps. Prince of only a sub-kingdom like Galloway. One day I may be King of Dalriada. But . . . "

"Yet he owes you much over this of St Andrew. But – no! We would both be fools to think that he would change his mind now, go back on his announcement. As to Aed, all know of it, the other *ri*. Aed would be wrath indeed. He is proud and powerful, Moray the greatest of all the mormaordoms. There would be dire trouble in Alba. It is too late to do anything now."

"I know it, I know it. Eithne, my dear – forgive me that I did not speak sooner. Did not think of this. The blame is all mine."

"Hush! No talk of blame. How could you know? But at least we know *now*. That we love each other."

"But too late!"

"Is it ever too late, Kenneth, my heart, to love? Even though I am wed to another – whom I do not love? I am still, in my heart, yours, love *you*. And you me. Is that not so? Is it wrong? To be a man's wife and love another? It must have happened many times. I do not care if it *is* wrong. I will not, cannot, stop loving you just because my father says that I must wed Aed mac Boanta. And you? You will go on loving me, Kenneth?"

He groaned. "How can I help myself? Yet – my love in another man's arms, in his house, in his bed! To live with that! God help me, or I shall run crazy-mad!"

They clung to each other the more tightly.

Then it was Eithne's turn to push him away. "I must go," she all but sobbed. "If it was learned that I was here, in this room, alone with you. If it got to Aed's ears, or my father's . . . "

"Yes." He went to open the door carefully, and peer out. "No one here. Off with you, then. My dearest, if we do not see each other alone again, hold on to this. I shall always love Eithne nic Angus, whatever happens. And rejoice that she loves me. Strange rejoicing, but true, true . . . "

In the open doorway they kissed for the last time, before she all but ran from him. He stared at the closed door behind her, thereafter, for long, unseeing.

At the repast in the great hall that evening, he was seated between Queen Finchem and Ewan, whilst Eithne was on the other side of her father, at the dais-table, next to Aed. It is to be feared that he made a silent meal of it and far from good company for those beside him. He returned to his chamber thereafter as soon as he decently could.

It was long before he slept, however, thinking, thinking. He accepted that it was of no use to try to change the High King's mind now. To run off with Eithne was a temptation. She might well agree to this. But it would be to make her a hunted fugitive, disgraced, a shunned woman. That would serve nothing. He had to face facts, however unpleasant.

His impulse now was to get away from Forteviot just as quickly as was possible. The thought of being in the company of Aed mac Boanta, in especial Aed with Eithne, was more than he could stomach. So he must get away. But first he had other business with Angus mac Fergus – this of the alliance. The High King was in his debt, over the St Andrew relic. He must seek to use that to advance his international project, if not his personal desires.

Unfortunately, in the morning, he could not contrive a private meeting with the monarch, who was arranging a hunt on Dupplin Muir for his Moray guests. Kenneth had no wish to become involved in this, eager only to be away. The best that he could do was to waylay Angus in the stableyard, awaiting the horses being saddled, explain that he had to be gone, and more or less abruptly raise the issue of Celtic military co-operation.

The High King seemed disappointed that Kenneth was going thus soon, having hoped that he might accompany him on another visit to Kilrymond to instal the relic in its temporary shrine. However, grateful as he had to be over the said piece of bone, he could not just dismiss the alliance project out of hand, less than eager as he sounded about it.

Oddly, Kenneth found support coming from an unexpected quarter. The Mormaor Aed was standing there, with Angus's four sons, and, unasked, joined in the discussion, declaring that a united front against the Norsemen was indeed required, and overdue. There had been an increase in Norse raiding in Moray as elsewhere of late, from Orkney and Zetland, and something more than mere defensive tactics had to be done about it. He had approached the Mormaors of Ross, Mar and Angus on the matter, and they all agreed that some major expedition north to Orkney and Zetland was required, to strike at the Viking bases. If this could be done in conjunction with the forces of the other Celtic nations, so much the better – even though they might not be able to rely on Kenneth mac Alpin's whirlpools in this instance! Although he understood that there were such things in those northern seas also – roosts he had heard them called.

Kenneth let this pleasantry pass, telling himself that he had to be glad of support, even from this quarter. It did give him opportunity, however, to mention his battle against the Norse dragon-ships off Man so recently, and how he had used this to gain King Howell's adherence to the alliance plan. Also he told them that King Roderick of Strathclyde was prepared to join in – he did not emphasise his luke-warmth.

Ewan mac Angus's enthusiastic acclaim for the idea clinched the matter. His father, probably aware of the implied reproach in Aed's account of his contact with the other mormaors, that he, the High King, had done nothing about it, agreed now to one joint venture at least, as worth trying. Alba would contribute. What of Dalriada? Was Eochaidh the Poisonous prepared to co-operate?

Kenneth said to leave his grandsire to him. He did not add that, in the matter of the *Lia Faill*, St Columba's altar, he had a hold over that awkward individual.

It was left, therefore, that Kenneth should co-ordinate arrangements for a major joint venture that summer – although Aed asserted that *he* would do the organising for eastern Alba at least. Thereafter leaves were taken and the hunters set off, Kenneth to prepare for his own departure.

Eithne, it seemed, was keeping to her own room this morning, pleading female sickness. Kenneth considered calling upon her, but decided that this would only add to their mutual distress and heartbreak. So he went in search of Queen Finchem, to say his goodbye and to ask her to convey his farewells and admiration to her daughter for him. The older woman, eying him searchingly but not questioning him, promised to do this, with a sort of pitying expression. Possibly she knew something of Eithne's feelings in the matter. Nothing was said of the forthcoming marriage.

Kenneth mac Alpin took his leave, a man torn.

PART TWO

9

The great bay of Loch Crinan was a sight to behold. Safe to say that never before had the like been seen, there or elsewhere, such a host of warships, nearly two hundred vessels at anchor, the naval strength of five nations, or at least the major part of it, assembled in the mellow August sunlight – for it had taken that time for Kenneth mac Alpin to get thus far in his so ambitious project, so much convincing to be done, so many hurdles to overcome, so much personal travelling and advocacy involved. But now, at last, he could gaze out over it all from the conical hill of Dunadd, surveying, counting, assessing – and having to remind himself that this was not achievement but only the means to achievement, a beginning, that is all. Nevertheless, he could not but know a certain pride. What he saw before him was, after all, of his own doing, and only his.

The assembly-place of Dunadd had been chosen advisedly. It was important that the existence of this great gathering of ships and men should not be known to the Norsemen before it was impossible to hide it any longer. This was the hosting season for the enemy and their ships would be apt to be raiding anywhere in the Hebridean and Irish Seas, so warning could be given to the areas of the Northern Irish coasts where the Scandinavian bases were situated, the targets for this expedition. So a hidden rallying-point was necessary, and this sheltered area behind the long island of Jura was ideal, close to the Dalriadan capital where Norsemen were unlikely to venture unless in major strength, and with some twenty-five miles of enclosed waters to assemble in, and facilities for feeding crews and entertaining leaders readily available.

So here had come the war-vessels from Man and Galloway, Strathclyde and Western Alba, even three from Ceredigion in mid-Wales – not that the Welsh were yet a party to this alliance, but King Howell had persuaded kinsmen of his to come as a gesture of support and goodwill. All kinds of craft were there, mainly longships of various designs and sizes, merchanters converted for the occasion, even the four dragon-ships from Man and their own Port an Deora, which Kenneth had captured. Estimates of numbers of men involved varied between ten and twelve thousand, a mighty host – a deal too many for King Eochaidh, who found himself having to feed and supply them all meantime, and seek to protect the womenfolk of Port an Deora, Dunadd itself and Ballymeanach from their attentions – or at least to make some gesture of doing so.

The ultimate responsibility for all this preyed not a little on Kenneth's mind, for although there were princes, chieftains and lords amany in all that array, none so far sought to take over command of the whole from himself, the initiator of it all, however senior they might be; and there were no kings actually going to sail with them. In his early twenties, to be commander of such a fleet and host was a sobering thought. If anything went wrong, as it so easily could . . .

He was standing now near the summit of Dunadd Hill, with his grandsire and father, surveying the scene, fretting somewhat, his glance apt to turn northwards, up the Sound of Jura, whence he assumed that Ewan would come. Ewan mac Angus had been put in charge of the Western Isles fleet of the Albannach by his father, his first command; and although most of it was already at anchor down there in the bay, the young prince himself was not yet with it. He was coming north-about in a ship of his own, the long way round from Inverness. He was to journey so far with the East Alba fleet, on its way to Orkney and Zetland at the same time as this larger expedition, designed to split the Norse strength and defences, that venture under Aed mac Boanta. Ewan would leave Aed's fleet off Caithness and strike through the Pentland Firth, between Orkney and the Alban mainland, and then turn down southwards through the Hebrides, to make for this rendezvous. He should have been here before this, for they were due to sail that evening. Kenneth hoped that he had not fallen in with Norsemen *en route*.

That was not what concerned King Eochaidh. "When you have finished with your Irish adventures, young man, I do not want you bringing all this multitude back here, I'd remind you. They have cost me sufficiently dear already. Almost worse than the Danes!"

"A small price to pay," his grandson declared. "Iona would tell you that."

There had been still another dire raid on Iona, two months previously, in which St Blathmac, an Irish prince turned missionary, had been martyred whilst seeking to revive Columba's abbey and mission – folly according to some, including Eochaidh, but not in Kenneth's judgment.

Alpin's concern was otherwise. "How are you going to control all these ships and host, my son?" he demanded, not for the first time. "It is too much for any one man. They will go their own ways, all different nations, and little heed you. This has never been done before, never attempted."

"Perhaps not. I must take that risk. But they all know that we face a dangerous and cunning foe, and that the more united we are, acting together, the safer all will be . . . "

He paused as they saw two more longships heading up the Sound of Jura from the south. They were speculating on their identity when Kenneth perceived the royal boar emblem of Alba on the sails. Only a member of the ruling house, or a special envoy, would be apt to display that sign. Could this be Ewan? Coming from the wrong direction . . . ?

"Perhaps he did not know of the narrow Sound of Luing, and passed it? And avoided Corryvreckan," Donald mac Alpin suggested. "And so sailed the way round Jura, by Islay."

"It could be . . . "

The two brothers went hastening downhill to ascertain. Ewan mac Angus would probably be the next High King of Alba, his presence here of major importance. Moreover, Kenneth got on well with that impetuous young man.

It proved to be as Donald had surmised. They were Ewan's ships and, not knowing this complicated seaboard very well, had missed the narrows of the Sound of Luing and the Dorus Mor, and so had had to circumnavigate the twenty-five-mile-long Jura. Ewan however was in excellent spirits, and much impressed by the huge assemblage of shipping he found awaiting him. Also full of the fine fleet of

167

forty ships which Aed mac Boanta was taking to teach Orkney and Zetland a lesson.

It took some time before Kenneth was able to ask, as casually as he could sound, how Eithne fared? He was told that the marriage had been in June, and she was now living at Inverness, where Aed had taken over the former royal palace. When asked if she was happy, her brother shrugged.

They sailed eventually at sundown, to turn down the sound where Ewan had just come up, strange timing and proceeding for a vast fleet, but Kenneth's decision. It gave them the half-light of the gloaming to get down past Jura, so that it would be as dark as it ever was of a summer night in those parts when they reached the open sea. The Irish coast would then be only some thirty miles to the south, and they could be off it by sunrise, thereby achieving complete surprise, it was hoped. Meantime, leading the way in his friend Conall's longship, Kenneth used his Dalriadan vessels to act like sheepdogs herding a flock, keeping all to the safer channels of those dangerous waters. He wanted no mishaps at this early stage.

In that comparatively narrow sound, the fleet stretched for miles behind, making Kenneth all too well aware of how out of touch he was, inevitably, with much of his force. In the open sea it would be different.

By the time that they reached the wide mouth of the sound it lacked only an hour to midnight – yet, their eyes accustomed now to the dusk, it seemed less dark than Kenneth had anticipated, even though details at any distance were vague. He reckoned that they had six hours till sunrise – but they were heading south-by-west, which meant directly into the wind, so that it would be a night of rowing, and at the speed of the slowest. So, Rathlin Island in five hours, the Irish coast at the Giants' Causeway an hour later, the mouth of Lough Foyle still another hour – that is, an hour after sunrise. If only it had been, as so seldom, a northerly wind.

In open water, the great concourse of ships formed up gradually into five squadrons, inevitably by nation, Kenneth still keeping a few vessels to act as links and whippers-in. The sea was reasonably calm, the wind light. Rowers were to be changed every hour, and most of the rest could sleep.

Kenneth himself remained awake throughout, as did his shipmaster Conall. They discussed strategy and some of the problems which must inevitably arise in seeking to control, use and provision so large a force, particularly policy and methods of dividing it up for individual attacks and sweeps, where conditions called for small-scale operations. In fact, Kenneth would infinitely have preferred to be leading an expedition one-tenth or less the size of this fleet, from a tactical point of view; but he did not fail to remind himself, and Conall also, that this was not just a necessary counter-attack on the Norsemen but a gesture and manifestation of Celtic unity, the first such indeed since the time of the semi-legendary Arthur of three centuries before, a major demonstration rather than merely a military campaign. It was important, of course, that it should be successful and produce results for all to see; but its main objective was just to be taking place, proving the ability for five nations to act together against a common enemy. This aspect of it all had to be kept foremost in Kenneth's mind, the wider impact rather than mere tactical victories and minor successes.

As well as all this, in those hours of rowing over the nightbound sea, Kenneth thought to ask Conall as to the whereabouts of that precious altar of St Columba's – since he now reckoned that it would be safe enough for him to have this information, King Angus in his preoccupation with St Andrew not having so much as mentioned the matter for long, and so unlikely to question him. He learned that in fact the famous relic had been taken to the semi-ruinous fort of Dunstaffnage, on its promontory in mid-Lorn, north of the Oban, a former royal stronghold of North Dalriada, now more or less abandoned, which protected the mouth of the important Loch Etive, famed in tradition and legend. Conall, who belonged to those parts, believed that it would be quite safe, hidden there, for the place was locally considered to be accursed and not to be visited, because here, it was said, the betrayal of Deirdre and the sons of Uisneach had taken place. And since Deirdre was of the same Irish line as eventually produced Columba, it seemed a suitable resting-place. So there the *Lia Faill*, the Stone of Destiny, lay hidden until such time as Kenneth mac Alpin should decide on its restoration to the sight of men.

Pondering as to when that might be, the conditions which could permit it, and the influence the mystic stone might possibly have on his own life and destiny, Kenneth approached the Irish coast.

In the grey dawn they passed the tall cliffs of Rathlin Island, about six miles off the said coast, keeping well to the west of it so as to make their landfall at the Giants' Causeway, that spectacular feature of the North Irish seaboard, alleged to have been the commencement of a mighty roadway constructed by giants of old to link the Celtic lands of Ireland and Alba. There the great rock masses would establish their exact position, necessary for Kenneth at least, on an unknown coast, and arrival before sun-up. Portrush was said to be about seven miles to the west, and the entrance to Lough Foyle, roughly the same distance beyond, their immediate destination.

Kenneth had chosen this location for the first of their attempts more or less at random, or at least out of his own preoccupation with Columba. For he had no precise information as to Norse bases in Ulster, save that they were dotted along the northern coast. Lough Foyle was by far the largest inlet of that seaboard, some fifteen miles long it was said, and giving access to some of the most fertile and populous areas of the country. It would almost certainly be used by the Scandinavians; indeed some of the expedition's shipmen had heard that it was from there that many of the raiders came. Moreover Derry, near the head of the lough, was where Columba had established his first monastery and from where he eventually set sail for Dalriada and Alba. So this seemed as apt a location as any at which to start.

Even in the poor light there was no mistaking the Giants' Causeway when they neared the mainland shore, towering columns of basalt reaching as high as four hundred feet in places. The fleet turned westwards about a mile offshore. So far they had not seen any other shipping.

By an hour later, however, off a fair-sized coastal township which must be Portrush, they did see fishing-boats putting out for the day's work. At sight of the fleet these promptly turned and headed back to land, no doubt in dire alarm. What they would make of this vast concourse of ships was anybody's guess, but representing trouble almost certainly. That did not concern Kenneth. What did was the possibility of Norse ships being in Portrush haven. He sent two vessels speeding landwards to ascertain. These came back quite quickly, to report no dragon-ships, or other than trading-craft and fishing-cobles there.

So it was on to the mouth of Lough Foyle. Still without any appearance of enemy vessels, they discovered an unlooked-for-feature – which no doubt some of the Strathclyde shipmen, who would probably have traded here, could have informed Kenneth about – the fact that the lough, which seawards looked like a very large and deep bay, was not just what it seemed. For what appeared to be the closed head of this, some five miles up, proved to be otherwise, actually only an abrupt closing-in to a narrow channel leading to the inner lough. This strait or kyle was created by a long promontory of sandy dune-country projecting from the east side, and higher land on the other. For how far this persisted could not be discerned from the approach; but what was clear was that the fleet, if it was to enter and proceed, must do so in elongated file.

Kenneth was sending back signals to that effect when the situation was suddenly further changed. Into sight from that narrow opening appeared two vessels, one behind the other – and none there had to be informed that they were dragon-ships.

Kenneth once again had to make up his mind in moments. The pair were less than half a mile away – whether there were more behind, he could not tell. The host of ships at his stern were in process of marshalling into a miles-long column. His prime duty was to order and control his force, not to dash off on adventures of his own. But these Norsemen, on sight of the great fleet, were almost bound to turn tail and hasten back whence they had come. And that would be to warn whatever lay beyond, in the inner lough, assuming that there were more Scandinavians there, their own surprise lost. They must be intercepted, if at all possible.

In urgent decision he shouted to the two longships closest to his own to follow him with all speed, and to his oarsmen to row their hardest, to make an attempt to attack the enemy. The rest of the fleet must do as they thought best at this juncture.

Those Norsemen were, in fact, slow in turning about. They would be astonished, of course, at the sight. They would not know who or what this great assembly of ships represented, sailing out of the early morning sea. For a brief minute or two they continued on course. Possibly that was only to get well clear of the mouth of the channel in order to give them space to turn in a wide half-circle, for the sandy point on the east might well extend quite far as shallows. At any rate, although turn they did thereafter, the delay allowed Kenneth's three leading vessels to shorten the gap very considerably, so that they were only hundreds of yards behind as they entered the narrows.

The dragon-ships, with the greater oar-power, would probably be able to draw ahead, but at least it would mean that the enemy would not have much opportunity to go warning others about the oncoming fleet. Glancing back at the said fleet, Kenneth likened it to an oncoming stampede of cattle jostling to enter a defile. This was scarcely how he had envisaged his descent on Norse bases.

The narrows proved to be quite brief, with the lough quickly broadening out thereafter to its former width, level and seemingly marshy country on the east, woodlands backed by low hills on the west. There were obviously many more miles of the lough. The quite large town of Derry was said to be near its head, grown up round Columba's abbey. There was, he thought, another renowned and still older abbey on the west, where Columba had trained, at Moville, as well as sundry other villages and havens on that side. Also a smaller town, Limavady, on the flat eastern shore where a river entered the lough. That was as much as he had learned about this Foyle area. So there was a sufficiency of places where the Norsemen might base themselves in populous and sheltered locations.

It all was making an almost crazy situation, two dragon-ships leading, by only hundreds of yards, an endless file of miscellaneous craft out from the narrows and down the centre of the lough. The Norsemen had the edge as to speed, but only by a little. From the land it would look as though they were in fact leading a procession. Where these two might have come from they could not know; but obviously, if they were to swing off, to left or right, to their own haven,

172

to join others or to give warning, then they must lose way and the pursuit would gain.

On up-lough, then, the strange, long array of ships drove, in a spray and splatter, oarsmen rowing flat out, a ridiculous development. How would it end? Eventually they must come to the head of Foyle, presumably at this Derry, when there could be battle; but before that they would have passed havens and loughside communities which Norse ships were using as bases, probably – indeed it was unlikely, for their raiding purposes, that they would base themselves right up at the head, so far from the sea. And large towns were seldom their objectives, being more trouble than they were worth, for casual raiding.

Kenneth kept gazing to either side, looking for such locations. The lough had widened again to fully four miles across, so that in the centre they were too far from land to distinguish details easily, or to see individual ships moored or at anchor. All he could do was to order detachments of his fleet to peel off and go to inspect each community they passed – and he certainly did not require all this host of ships following him, anyway. He shouted back commands to that effect, to be relayed from vessel to vessel, and hoped that it would be understood and acted upon. This fleet-control was indeed a headache.

So far no other Norse craft, or any other indeed, had made an appearance, the sight of this host being sufficiently daunting no doubt. Kenneth had seldom felt less decisive and confident as to his course.

Then he saw what appeared to be a fair-sized township on the left, eastwards, where a river seemed to come in. That probably would be Limavady. If so, it might well be worth a visit, not too far from the sea and not sufficiently large to be a problem for the raiders. Anyway, he had to disentangle himself, as leader, from this profitless and undignified chase, somehow. So he shouted for his two flanking craft, both Galloway longships, to continue on after the dragon-ships, with part of the fleet, whilst he swung off eastwards with about a dozen others, to make for that river-mouth.

It was extraordinary how suddenly thereafter Kenneth mac Alpin felt himself to be a different man, himself again, not burdened by that unmanageable host of vessels, leading now only a small group towards a limited objective. He was, he decided, not made of the stuff of great commanders.

Not that he let such recognition preoccupy his mind to the detriment of present action, scanning all the prospect ahead with keen eyes. The river-mouth, despite its low-lying banks, became clearer all the time, with houses on the south side, not so many houses as he would have expected as a town, with what looked like marshy meadowland to the north. There was a recognisable church, and beyond it, rigs of cultivation stretching southwards and eastwards.

But it was not all this that held Kenneth's attention: it was the cluster of shipping in the river-mouth, at a distance difficult to identify as to types but many with quite tall masts. There might well be Norse craft amongst them, but if so none seemed to be pulling out to confront them.

Nearing the basin of the river, certain facts became evident. Although there were quite a number of vessels there, most could be seen to be not afloat but lying derelict-seeming, beached or abandoned, heeled over, a sorry sight. But there were half a dozen craft upright and moored together, with a few fishing-boats on a boatstrand nearby. Almost certainly the larger vessels were dragon-ships.

Shouting and pointing, Kenneth ordered his group to close up as they headed for that anchorage.

Soon they could distinguish the dragon-prows of the ships, fierce carved and painted creatures of differing design but all savage, menacing, some with lifelike human figures held in their jaws. There must be a great trade for wood-carvers in the Scandinavian lands of a winter.

There were signs of activity on the moored ships and ashore as they advanced, but no actual casting off or putting out of oars. No large numbers of men either, aboard or evident amongst the houses. It looked as though the crews were elsewhere.

As the Celtic ships came up, they could see men leaving the moored craft and jumping into the shallows to wade ashore. Ordering some of his crews to board the enemy vessels, Kenneth led the rest inshore, to land, himself sword in hand now.

It was strange how peaceful all seemed here, despite their warlike approach. Indeed this might have been a town of the

174

dead for all the activity which greeted them. The Norsemen who had left the ships had disappeared amongst the houses; and the population, if any survived, were keeping under cover. Some dogs barked, that was all.

Looking back, Kenneth got waves from the dragon-ships indicating that all were deserted. He glanced from the shut doors of the cot-houses down to the boatstrand area on the right, where nets hung on poles to dry. The Norsemen almost always spared some fishermen, to provide them with food; and those beached cobles looked in good enough order. He moved over towards the line of hovels and smoke-sheds there. Doors were shut here also, but almost certainly there would be folk within.

He rapped on the first door he came to, but there was no response. He had two of his men put their shoulders to it, to smash it open. Inside, cowered two men, a woman and a clutch of children.

Announcing that they were friends, not to fear, Celts from across the sea come to slay Norsemen, Kenneth sought enlightenment as to conditions here. At first the fishermen were too terrified to answer; but at length he got the older man to speak, to babble. It was some time before he could make out the sense of it, for though the actual words were approximately the same as his own, the accent was very different, remarkable considering that these folk were only a day's sail from his own land. Eventually he gathered that the Norsemen, having wreaked their savagery on all this lough-side area and port, had started to range further inland, and were now devastating Limavady itself. It was only thus that Kenneth learned that this township was not Limavady, which larger place was some six miles inland, but only the harbour therefor, named Portincaple, the haven of the chapel.

This information called for further decision. They were here to destroy the Scandinavians, and Kenneth's inclination was to go after them and seek to surprise them at this ravaging of the Limavady town, and there teach them their lesson. But that would take some considerable time, with the place seemingly miles away. And he had a scattered fleet out there, perhaps not awaiting but certainly requiring his leadership and direction.

They had these dragon-ships at least. And without them the Norsemen's fangs were to some extent drawn. So, dispose of them, a hasty search of the houses of the township for hiding fugitives, then back into the lough to resume command of his host. The Limavady raiders could possibly be considered later.

He ordered some of his shipmasters to take the six dragon-ships in tow, go out with them to open water and sink them. Others of his men to look for Norse crewmen in the houses, but to be quick about it – probably all had fled inland by now, anyway.

Presently, then, Kenneth was out in mid-lough again. Now there was no problem as to what to do with vast numbers of ships tailing after him like a flock of sheep, for the fleet was wide-scattered. Where they all were there was no knowing – various counts by Conall and himself reached between seventy and eighty craft, in groups and even pairs, dotted all over the scene, near and far, prying into bays and creeks of the lough. Most had probably gone on after the two fleeing dragon-ships, and might not stop until they reached Derry.

Watching the last of the captured vessels sink, Kenneth decided that his best course was to proceed up-lough also. All would presumably end up at the lough-head eventually, and he could reassemble his command. If any were getting into difficulties with Norsemen, the best that he could do was to leave most of his present group hereabouts, where they could be seen, to act as rallying-point and reinforcement if necessary, himself and the others to go on southwards. This was all rather like learning the shepherd's trade.

He saw, at a distance, sundry others of his vessels on his way up-lough, but it was difficult to discern, at a range of miles, just what went on. At least none gave the impression of being in trouble; but whether they were finding Norsemen he could not tell.

Kenneth did not in fact have to go right to the head of Lough Foyle to find the major concentration of his ships; for about four miles up there was no missing them, clustered over on the right or west side, where the lough was starting to narrow. He headed over to investigate.

Beyond the press of vessels, most of which appeared to be

more or less inactive at the moment, it was possible to perceive quite a port, in a bay backed by low wooded hills.

The first vessel they came to, a Strathclyde converted merchanter, its skipper shouting that there had been a great battle but that it was all over now, the Norsemen all satisfactorily dead. Kenneth could scarcely credit this of any great battle, there having been no time for such; but any struggle in which large numbers of ships took part could seem to be a major conflict to a merchant shipman. He urged his longship on through the press.

Eventually he recognised his brother Donald's vessel, by its large Galloway banner, and approaching, discovered a sort of conference going on aboard. Leaping from one ship to another, he was excitedly greeted, relieved also it transpired, for evidently nobody there knew quite what was to be done next. It seemed that there had indeed been a battle of sorts, if hardly a great one. The two dragon-ships which they had been chasing had turned in here, to this haven, called Carrowkeel apparently, where there had been three other Norse craft anchored. The enemy had by then been about half a mile ahead of the pursuit, and so had had time to give some warning. Also the crews of the three other ships must have been near at hand if not aboard, for by the time that their own first vessels arrived, the Norse were in some state to resist attack. It had been a hasty and confused affray, with no opportunity for manoeuvre or strategy on either side, just attempts at boarding, spear-throwing, hand-to-hand fighting and swordplay, with more and more of the Celtic ships coming up to join in. The Vikings had fought hard, but sheer numbers had overcome them and victory was won. Their own people had suffered a number of casualties, some of the enemy had escaped ashore, but all the rest were dead, for they had taken no prisoners. All five dragon-ships were captured, yonder. Now they were pondering on the next move.

As ever, the decision had to be Kenneth's.

Information required, he made his way ashore, where many of his crews had already landed. Carrowkeel was in an uproar of course, as the people, such as had survived the Norsemen's attentions, were less than reassured by this new invasion, by fellow-Celts as they were, it being too soon for them to look on the newcomers as liberators, and the fear of further Norse retribution thereafter inevitable. Folk were however already dismantling the usual hoarding which displayed the washed and hair-combed heads of local men, hung there as trophies and warning, weeping women and wide-eyed children removing the grisly relics to be reunited with their torsos in Christian burial. As a nice compensatory touch, some of Kenneth's crewmen were dragging the bodies of slain Vikings, to lay them out in rows beside the said hoarding – that is, after detaching all brooches, armlets and barbaric jewellery beloved of the Scandinavians.

Kenneth sought amongst the distracted folk for someone of knowledge and responsibility to question, but of course such men had been the first to be killed off. Eventually he found a crippled ancient, barely able to walk, who had escaped the invaders' hate as not worth the slaughtering, but who proved to be intelligent enough, if as critical almost of his own people as of the enemy. Out of much general and scornful accusation, Kenneth extracted some of the information he required. This Carrowkeel, it seemed, was the main and furthest-up base of these devilish Danes on Lough Foyle. They might raid some way beyond, but did not go as far up as Derry, for that fortified town would require siegery and large assault, in which these fiends were not interested. Yet the Derry inhabitants, spared the savagery, had no thought and care for those less fortunate, prepared to sit behind their walls and do nothing, so long as the invaders did not assail *them*, in what amounted almost to a shameful truce. Churchmen ruled there, of course – and the ancient all but spat – and these limited their intervention to prayers. King Cathal of Donegal was useless, safe in his Innishowen retreats; and old Conchobar the High King, was worse, a toothless fumbler – this from one also toothless but by the sound of him no fumbler.

Kenneth told him what they had done, and about the shipless Norsemen now raiding Limavady, and asked if he knew what other Norse bases there were on Lough Foyle; but the other knew little as to that and seemed to care less. All he could assert was that this Carrowkeel had been the Danes' main centre, God curse them. And they would be back, nothing surer, when the coast was clear again, and the more vengeful.

Kenneth could say little that reassured as to that, but did declare that he would go on to Derry meantime and seek to persuade the authorities there to adopt a more aggressive stance, helpful towards their neighbours – this received with scepticism.

Leaving Donald in charge at Carrowkeel, with instructions to try to contact all their other vessels left behind elsewhere in Foyle, and to see if any needed help, Kenneth took two longships as well as his own and set off up-lough.

According to the ancient it was about ten miles more to Derry, five of them in the narrowing lough, the rest up the River Foyle at its head. There were still a couple of hours to sundown, so they ought to reach there before dark.

Kenneth, to be sure, had long been eager to see Derry, from which his hero Columba had set sail for Dalriada almost three centuries before. Then it had been only his first monastery, amongst his beloved oak-woods – the name was merely a corruption of *darroch*, oak-tree. Now it was said to have grown into a sizeable walled city, but centred still on the abbey which gave it birth. Columba had founded other abbeys, notably Kells, the largest, near the High King's seat of Tara, but Derry was his first and favourite, from which he had exiled himself to go and bring the Albannach to Christ.

Seen from the river, the town was not on any very strong site, rising ground admittedly, with its oak-woods now largely cut down. Walls and ramparts had been erected, but it was still no fortress. The great church, built in honour of Columba, stood out prominently.

The arrival of the three longships may have occasioned some alarm in the town, but if so it was not obvious, with no precautionary closing of the gates behind the riverside quays. The old man had said that Derry was ruled by churchmen, so Kenneth, landing with Conall and only a few of his men, decided to head straight for the abbey and large church – which certainly was not difficult to find.

Clad as they were for war, they did attract attention, to be sure, in the early evening streets, but no interception or other attentions than those of barking dogs. They clearly were not Norsemen, and were probably taken for visiting fellow-Irishmen. At the abbey gatehouse, Kenneth announced himself as the Prince of Galloway, and asked to be taken to the abbot. A young monk was detailed to take them onward.

It was with mutual surprise, at the abbatial quarters, that they recognised each other, for the cleric was none other than Abbot Diarmaid of Kells, he who had brought the Columban relics back to Dalriada, and whom Kenneth had escorted to Fortrenn. Considerable explanations had to follow.

After accounting for his own presence in Derry, Kenneth, who had never much liked the other, learned that Diarmaid was only temporarily here, from his own Kells. The previous Abbot of Derry had died, and until a suitable replacement was found, Diarmaid had come up to take charge – for he was, in theory, Abbot of Iona, Columba's successor, and Derry also was to some extent his responsibility.

There was no really hearty welcome for the visitors, and news of their impact on the Norsemen hereabouts was received with muted enthusiasm. Kenneth's subsequent urgings that Derry's people should take a more active part in seeking to keep Lough Foyle free of the invaders produced still less reaction – possibly the abbot saw this as all liable to upset the live-and-let-live understanding they had with the Scandinavians. At any rate, no commitment was forthcoming to do anything specific. Kenneth could not help thinking how different would have been that earlier Abbot of Derry's attitude, Colum mac Felim O'Conall O'Neill.

However, Diarmaid was of some use to them, for his excuses, if that is the word, for King Cathal of Donegal and the High King Conchobar having done little or nothing to protect or aid the area produced the information that the Norse raiding was far worse elsewhere and on a much greater scale, demanding all the available resources of the various Irish monarchs. The worst hit areas were further south, down the east coast, where there were richer pickings and from whence they could raid the Isle of Man, Cumbria and Wales more readily, the kingdoms of Ulaid, Oriel and Dalriata, down to Meath. That was where the Norse had established themselves in force, on a much more permanent basis than hereabouts, especially in the Strangford and

Carlingford Loughs. Before strangers criticised those in positions of responsibility, they should ascertain the true and overall conditions.

Only moderately chastened, Kenneth took note.

He was, at least, offered accommodation for the night in the abbey guesthouse, although Conall and the others went back to their ships. He found an elderly monk to show him all the items of interest connected with St Columba, before retiring.

In the morning, when taking his leave of Abbot Diarmaid, he again urged him to try to persuade the men of Derry to sally out and assail the Norsemen who were attacking Limavady, and who must be finding themselves considerably disadvantaged lacking their ships. Whether anything would come of this he was unsure.

It was back, thereafter, to Donald at Carrowkeel.

There he found most of his great fleet reassembled and at anchor off the haven, only a few vessels missing apparently, off on their own ventures presumably. Donald had heard of only one of their ships actually lost, but two more captured dragon-ships, brought in proudly, made up for that. Casualties amongst the men were not negligible, but might have been much worse considering all the conditions, especially the comparative inexperience of so many of the crews in this sort of campaigning, and against notoriously dangerous foes.

Kenneth ordered all to prepare to sail. They would pick up the missing craft on their way down-lough. They had made a start, at least, even though, considering the size of their force, the results so far had been modest. Now they might find a greater challenge.

10

It was four whole days later before the looked-for challenge developed, for they had had to come some one hundred and fifty sea-miles, in formation and therefore at the speed of the slowest; and large numbers of men require a lot of provisioning, so that constant calls at harbours and villages had to be made, to forage for food and drink – and since this was very much a gesture towards Celtic unity, no offence towards the local population was permissible, and all meats, fish and victuals obtained were to be paid for, all a process which took time. After leaving Lough Foyle, they had turned eastwards again and sailed along the northern Irish coast, past the Giants' Causeway and Rathlin, calling in at Ballycastle, before rounding Fair Head and heading southwards down the Irish Sea. At Larne, hiding behind its Island Magee, they heard of Norse raiders who had in fact been using the narrow Lough of Larne as a base but blessedly had now left, it was thought to join their fellow-pirates in force at Strangford Lough, some forty or fifty miles further south, this being the principal Norse centre on all this coast. So the fleet had crossed the wide mouth of Belfast Lough, which it seemed the Vikings tended normally to leave alone, presumably because of its large population and defences, and on down the Donaghadee peninsula shoreline, anchoring for the night at Ballyhalbert. And now, towards midday, they were nearing the mouth of Strangford Lough itself, and going warily. So far they had seen no Norse vessels, only fishing-boats, all the way.

Kenneth had been fortunate enough to pick up, at Ballyhalbert, as guide, a young man, son of the local chief, who had seen his brother decapitated by the invaders and his mother and sisters raped, and was burning for vengeance. He knew the Strangford Lough area well and had assured them that they needed a guide, for it was a difficult, lengthy and islanded place where the unwary might well come to grief. Another point which their informant, called Tadg O'Rourke, made, was that this long Donaghadee coastline, more than twenty-five miles of it, was in fact only a very narrow and flat peninsula, in most places a mere three miles across, enclosing the twenty-mile-long Strangford Lough behind. A danger here was that the sight of this huge fleet sailing down inevitably would attract much attention on shore – it had done so at Ballyhalbert – and almost certainly reports of it would be carried across the short distance to the loughside villages where the Norsemen were based, warning them. So surprise could be discounted, if attack here was considered.

Kenneth, indeed considering attack, took heed. He asked what young O'Rourke would advise. To wait in the open sea for the Norse to come out to fight? If they so chose. Or to enter the lough and seek them there?

The other was obviously impressed by the large numbers of the Celtic fleet; but also was all too well aware of the fighting skill, naval ability and sheer aggressiveness of the Norsemen in their ships. Eager for action against them as he was, he was doubtful as to the best strategy. He explained that although the lough was over twenty miles long, six of these miles comprised a narrow entrance channel, less than a mile wide. And once beyond this, the main lough was complicated by innumerable islets, drumlins, and also pladdies, that is submerged reefs, so that although the average width of it was about four miles, the navigable channel was often less than half that. The Vikings would know it all well, needless to say, and could use its intricacies against any attacker who was less knowledgeable.

Kenneth, weighing up all this, recognised that it would be wise to wait outside, where he could bring his large numbers to bear in the open sea – if the enemy ventured out. But if they did not, and remained safely inside? He could scarcely just sail on, leaving them unassailed, he who had brought all this host to teach the Scandinavians their lesson. He would have to venture into the lough somehow. Or would he be better advised to land some proportion of his men, on this peninsula or on the mainland opposite, and seek to attack the Norsemen's bases ashore? Or both?

Neither O'Rourke nor Conall, Donald, nor any of his leaders, could give him the counsel he needed, any suggestions proffered tending to be vague and contradictory. He again knew the aloneness in responsibility of the commander.

He came to his own conclusion. They would wait outside meantime – but not all of them, all the time. With a few supporting craft, he would himself probe in through the narrows of the lough-mouth, to prospect the situation and the passageway, ready to turn back at speed should the enemy appear in force. Then, if there was no Norse emergence, they might seek to creep slowly into the lough by night, to get past the dangerous narrows in darkness and so, it was to be hoped, put themselves in a fair position for a sweep up-lough in daylight. This decision was received only doubtfully, but nothing better put forward.

The fleet, then, waited off Ballyquintin Point, the extreme southernmost tip of the peninsula, for most of the day, an uncomfortable proceeding in a northerly swell. No Norse ships appeared out of the lough-mouth.

In late afternoon Kenneth chose half a dozen longships to accompany his own, and leaving Donald in charge of the rest, rowed round the headland and into the lough's entrance.

The narrowness of it all was immediately apparent, and daunting in that it seemed to get even narrower ahead, with bends in it. The shores were rock-ribbed and steep. It was, in fact, a water-filled pass, and obviously could be a death-trap. A very few ships could hold it against a large fleet, like a single swordsman in a doorway.

However, so far as Kenneth could see, there was no ship seeking to do that, no haven or place to hide a vessel, at least as far as the first bend. Cautiously he led his group on.

Two small headlands opposite each other over a mile up narrowed the strait still further, and they went very heedfully past these in case there were ships hiding behind. The same at the first major bend, another mile – nothing round either.

All the way, Conall and the other skippers were testing depths and watching for reefs and underwater hazards; but there appeared to be little to concern them at this stage, deep water more or less right to the sides. So a night-time passage would not face that danger.

It transpired that, all the way up, that narrow strait was clear of lurking craft. Near the northern outlet there proved to be a small community on the west shore, with some fishing-cobles drawn up, that was all. From here they could see the lough widening very considerably ahead.

Leaving his other vessels in the last little bay before that outlet, Kenneth had Conall steer his craft as close to the western shore as he dared, to edge slowly forward, not to be noticed, if possible, by a waiting and watching enemy in front. He was thankful that he had taken this precaution when presently he gained a view of the widening waters. Three dragon-ships lay off out there, idling, about half a mile away.

Hoping that they had not been spotted, in the lee of the land and in the lengthening shadows of the sinking sun, they lingered for a few minutes. When it was clear that the Norse vessels were not moving closer, obviously placed there to guard against any invasion of the lough, Kenneth ordered a quiet retiral. The enemy evidently knew of the fleet's presence and threat. There was to be no surprise here.

Returning to the others of his group, he told two of the skippers to remain with their vessels where they were, ready to make a swift dash back to the fleet in the open sea should any of the Norsemen attempt to make a sally out through the narrows. With the rest, he rowed back down the strait.

It was almost dusk before they rejoined the waiting fleet. There he learned that, about an hour before, four dragon-ships had come into view from the south. They had been hugging the coast and so had not come into sight until they rounded a major headland, which O'Rourke named Killard Point – but when they did, had fairly promptly turned tail and hastened whence they had come. They might well have been making for this Strangford Lough. So now Norse forces further south would probably receive warning of a large and almost certainly hostile presence in the area.

Digesting this, Kenneth perceived that it could add to his problems; but also that it might mean that the Norsemen in this lough were not at their fullest strength, and therefore might be the more readily overcome.

At any rate, he decided to go ahead with the plan which had been forming in his mind – that is, if no Norse sally emerged from the narrows meantime. Well after dark the great fleet would row, slowly and carefully, up the six-mile strait and into the main lough, so that when dawn broke they would be in a position to sweep up-lough in full strength, and force the enemy to battle.

So it was more waiting, in that swell. No warning of trouble came from the ships left in the narrows. Kenneth used the time to send the most careful instructions round to all skippers.

By midnight it was as dark as it would ever be, and he gave orders to move.

It was to be doubted whether so great an array of ships had ever before, in these seas, moved in darkness through so narrow a miles-long strait. Only oared vessels, carefully steered and controlled, could have done it, although the oars themselves were something of a handicap because of their length, which demanded considerable space on either side of each ship. So they could not marshal themselves quite as closely abreast as Kenneth might have liked, however tight formation they could keep astern.

The earlier prospecting now paid off, and Kenneth led the way with fair confidence, O'Rourke reminding him of the positions of headlands and narrowings. He reckoned that nowhere was the navigable channel less than half a mile wide, which meant that even with the oars problem they could risk going ten abreast, and still be able to negotiate those bends without too much difficulty. So the slow-moving column was not so long as it might have been, a score of files of ten. There would be stragglers, of course, but probably no real difficulties.

In fact they achieved that passage in two hours or so, an hour less than Kenneth had allowed. At the little bay on the west where he had left their scouts, they picked up these two longships. All they had to report was that the three Norse vessels on the watch had sailed off northwards with the darkening, evidently anticipating no action by night; and no ships had approached these straits thereafter.

So now they had some hours to fill in till daylight. O'Rourke said that there was no haven on either side before

Killyleagh on the west, some three miles up. Whether the three Norse craft would have put in there they could not tell; but it seemed likely, if they were going to resume their vigil at the narrows at dawn.

Kenneth decided that they should move up almost as far as that, at least, in the darkness, and there form a cordon, and wait.

O'Rourke kept warning about those drumlins and pladdies.

It was difficult to know when they had gone far enough, for no landmarks stood out in the gloom and no lights gleamed ashore. But at length their guide declared that he thought they were in about the right place, and a halt was called.

Now the task was to reassemble the fleet in a very different formation, a belt or barrier right across the lough. Because of the reefs and islets which it seemed were confined to the sides and shallows, not the centre, the width to be barred off was considerably lessened. Even so it took all their vessels to form any effective cordon across two miles of water, especially as Kenneth reckoned that they would be more effective two deep than one, should a breakthrough be attempted. Other ships could always move in to any threatened section, of course. So much would depend on the Norsemen's numbers as well as their reactions.

Thereafter it was waiting once more.

Dawn seemed a long time in coming, but when it did it was to prove that O'Rourke had not been far out in his calculation, for he was able to point to Killyleagh township on a little bay just ahead.

From this position it was not possible to see directly into the bay and haven on account of two of these islets or drumlins intervening. Not wishing to disarrange his carefully marshalled barrier at this stage, Kenneth took half a dozen ships with him and sailed on.

Sure enough, three dragon-ships were hove-to in that bay. But they must have had sharp-eyed watchmen, for well before Kenneth's craft could move in on them, the crews had their oars out and were heading out northwards at speed.

It might just have been possible to cut them off before

187

they got out of the bay, but Kenneth did not so attempt. A different strategy was called for here. Let them go. Those ships would not get out of Strangford Lough without cutting through his cordon. He turned back thereto.

Now the movement and manoeuvre was very different from their night-time advance, to move the fleet thus formed up in line abreast, up-lough. It would not be possible in any exact fashion, of course – but so long as the barrier looked fairly solid from a distance, that should serve.

It was a slow progress inevitably, but the three Norsemen were well ahead now anyway, going fast. Where was the next haven? Kenneth asked O'Rourke.

There was Killinchy on the west and Kircubbin on the east, almost opposite each other; but he had never heard of the invaders using the latter. The western havens and bays were much the more favoured, with better anchorages, larger villages, more women and a mainland background to raid rather than just a narrow peninsula.

It was not long before they saw, far ahead now, one of the enemy ships turning in on the left, the west. That would be to warn Killinchy. And before their slow-moving formation got near, another two dragon-ships had joined the trio. That was well enough. They would have to turn and fight eventually.

In fact, by the time that the Celtic fleet had got two-thirds of the way up Strangford Lough, midday, they had eleven Norse ships rowing ahead. And quite suddenly the situation changed, in more ways than one. Islands loomed ahead, not just off the shores but in mid-lough, larger than any they had seen hitherto; and the enemy vessels, from rowing in scattered flight, turned round and formed themselves into a close group, to come back in obviously purposeful style.

There was to be battle at last. O'Rourke declared that he should have guessed it. Beyond that clutter of islands, the upper lough shallowed and became more reef-bound than ever, no place for fighting ships.

Kenneth, who had been heading for this encounter all along, was as prepared for it as he could be. Obviously the Norsemen were going to adopt the tactics he would himself have used, that is, not attempting individual breakings-through the cordon of ships but making a tight-grouped fist-like drive to smash their way past in one section. Let them attempt that, then.

When they were only some hundreds of yards apart, Kenneth gave his signal. The centre of his barrier slowed, but the two ends of it did not, but pulled the faster, each end to swing forward and in, like two horns. At the same time, other vessels closed in on the centre, in front of the advancing Norsemen, to thicken the barrier. The two horns met behind, and the enemy was encircled. The circle began to tighten.

Although the Norse ships were outnumbered almost twenty to one, they were larger, faster vessels, with bigger crews of more experienced fighting men. So the clash was a little less uneven than it might have seemed. The surrounded dragon-ships drove on, since they could do no other now, and Kenneth, seeking to judge timing and distance aright, went to meet them, shouting warning as to oar-drill – for that was vital now.

As the ships met, all but head-on, oars and oarsmen could have been sheared off and down like cut corn. So, at the last moments to avoid losing impact, the rowers on all craft raised their long sweeps high, upright, not all with entire success for the oars were heavy. Through this forest of upraised shafts, grappling-hooks were thrown, attached to ropes, spears were hurled, and men, swords and dirks in hand, sought to come to grips and blows. All around, the Celtic vessels pushed in.

However carefully visualised and prepared, Kenneth's planning thereafter went by the board. There was absolutely no way whereby he could exert control of the fighting in any degree, even on ships nearest his own. Men went fighting-mad on both sides, leaping over on to the others' ships, yelling, thrusting, slashing, stumbling and falling, some overboard. Those oars were a menace to all, tripping and impeding men, getting smashed and piercing flesh, on every ship. Chaos, savage and bloody, reigned.

For himself, Kenneth, recognising that his commanding role was in abeyance meantime, thought to attempt his secondary duty, to seek out the enemy commanders. Who, if any, might be in overall command of the Norsemen he could not be sure. But he had headed his own vessel at the leading dragon-ship. And at least the leaders on each craft were evident by the great winged helmets they so proudly wore, the bigger the wings the more important the individual. There were two so crowned in the front ship, and one, blond-bearded and huge, proved his leadership by leaping, straight after the impact, on to Kenneth's vessel, battle-axe weaving, shield high.

Kenneth, making swift judgment, guessed that this was not the senior chieftain, for another, older, with greying shaggy hair, wearing a longer-winged helmet, was standing still on the stern-platform of his own ship, sword in hand. Possibly they were father and son. This should be his target, possibly commander of all. The younger was engaging three of Conall's crew with scornful, shouting laughter, and Kenneth was for a moment undecided, when he saw Conall himself slip round behind the blond giant there, careful, deliberately to plunge a spear into the armhole of the other's protective padded-leather jerkin. The battle-axe dropped amongst the tangle of bodies and oars. That was scarcely noble fighting – but then Conall was a realist and no noble.

That decided Kenneth. He ran forward to the bows of his own craft, which were nearest to the stern of the other, pushing through the struggling press. The Viking chief saw him coming. So did some others, who moved to intercept. But the older man presumably recognised a foeman worthy of his steel, no doubt by clothing and bearing, and waved them aside, to stand waiting.

Kenneth had a throwing-spear, but, facing that warrior, was not going to use it. Half-turning, in what was really a gesture, he hurled it at the nearest of these other Norsemen and, pointing his sword directly at their leader, leapt from his own craft on to the other.

There was no preliminary skirmishing, no manoeuvring for position. This had to be done as to a formula, no advantages sought, the price and privilege of leadership.

They were none so ill-matched, for although Kenneth was much the younger, the other was taller, with a longer reach, and by no means aged. His sword undoubtedly was longer also, a great brand, and doubtless he would be the more experienced.

The Viking waited for Kenneth to lunge first, and then

parried the stroke away almost casually. His return thrust was equally formal and parried easily. But after that, as by mutual consent, the niceties observed, all abruptly changed. The swords began to flicker and flash and dart almost like snakes' tongues, the men's arms twisting, swinging, jerking, their bodies bending, arching, swaying, even though their actual stances remained remarkably steady, as convention required, with no dancing around.

No detailed exposition of such a duel could be possible. Training, keenness of eye, instinct, determination and agility all contributed, and in all these it seemed the pair were fairly equally endowed. But in the end it was probably years which proved the deciding factor. Kenneth was possibly twenty years the younger, and as the pace began to tell, his more youthful muscles and stamina told. Every now and again the Viking missed a stroke, over-reacted, or had to step back. A long red gash appeared on his forearm, his sword-arm.

Only too well aware that time was not now on his side, the older man fought the more urgently – and the less accurately. One of his mighty strokes, although warded off just in time by Kenneth's round targe or shield, did all but overbalance him by its force. But the said force was not without its effect on the wielder also, with the sword heavy. Round the Norseman swung, staggering a little, arms high to balance himself. On his left arm was his own shield, and this upraised momentarily left his lower half unprotected. Recovering himself first, Kenneth saw, and lunged – and no leather jerkin was proof against such a thrust. The older man's mouth opened, in a sort of shock of surprise, wide, soundless, and knees buckling under him, sank to the wooden decking, to pitch forward motionless.

Panting, Kenneth stared down at him. But not for long. There was a battle to think of, if not to control.

Gazing round, it was difficult to discern, in the mêlée, how the general struggle went; but definitely he could now see very few of the winged helmets, which might be significant. And, looking more carefully, he came to the conclusion that most of the fighting was going on aboard the Norse vessels, not his own.

What could he usefully do? On an impulse, he stooped to

remove the winged helmet from the fallen chieftain; and putting this on his sword-tip, over the blood, raised it aloft. With this trophy held high, he leapt back on to the prow-platform of his own ship, where fighting seemed to be all but over, and shouted to Conall to try to force their craft on through the crush of jostling vessels, all crew to cheer and cheer, while he held up his symbol of victory.

This procedure was not easy, the press of ships preventing rowing, oars having to be used only for pushing and propelling against the sides of other craft. But some progress was achieved – and the cheering at least was vehement, heartening.

Whether this had any real effect on the outcome was impossible to say; but the tempo of the struggle was most certainly slackening and there could be no questioning who was gaining the upper hand. Numbers had to tell, once they could be brought to bear, and that was now happening. The Norsemen fought courageously and effectively, none actually yielding, although some plunged overboard, to drown rather than be hacked to pieces.

So there was no concession of victory; and just when the fighting could be said to be over was uncertain, amongst so many ships. But presently that seemed to be the position. The Celtic fleet had won its first real naval triumph.

With much horn-blowing and shouting, Kenneth took charge again. All craft to put in to the nearest land – which actually was a large island, well over a mile long, which O'Rourke called Isle Magee – where they could assess the situation, tend the wounded, count casualties and bury the dead.

Fortunately the isle, the largest of these drumlins, was sandy and grass-grown, and even had a few fishermen's hovels – which implied fresh water. It provided a satisfactory resting-place meantime.

Casualties were in fact fairly high, inevitable with the way those Norsemen had fought, with hundreds of wounded to be given what attention was available. There were only a few of the enemy amongst these. Much burying followed, with the sandy soil easing the labour of it.

Kenneth held a council of leaders and skippers. What to do now? With all those casualties and the wounded to think of, most felt that they had done enough, and should now head for home. To some extent Kenneth accepted that. They had achieved quite a lot, and the Norsemen based on Northern Ireland must be having a deal to think about. Those dragon-ships which had turned tail at the mouth of the Strangford Lough and returned southwards would almost certainly have warned their fellows down the coast of the presence of this huge fleet; so there might be few opportunities for further assault anyway. But just to head for home now was to leave their task uncompleted. This entire expedition was to be a demonstration of Celtic unity. This Ireland was a Celtic land. They must use what they had done to further the cause. He looked at O'Rourke. Which kingdom was this? Who ruled it? And from where?

Their guide said that this was all part of Oriel. King Godfrey mac Fergus. And his capital was at Newry, upriver from the head of Carlingford Lough, some fifty miles further south.

They must go to Newry, then, and see King Godfrey. Present him with a couple of their captured dragon-ships and the wounded Norsemen, and demonstrate the value of Celtic co-operation. Such attentions had won over King Howell of Man. Let them try it here.

They saw no more Norsemen on their way south across the wide Dundrum Bay and on under the frown of the Mountains of Mourne, which here came down to the sea in cliffs. At Carlingford Lough itself, turning in, Kenneth called at the village at the mouth, and learned that the Scandinavians – God slay them! – had indeed been here, but two days before had suddenly packed up and sailed away. So far as was known there were no more of them up-lough.

This lough was very much smaller than either Strangford or Foyle. According to O'Rourke, it was about ten miles to the head, and thereafter a river, in a narrow gorge-like valley, led another six miles or so up to Newry. Whether King Godfrey would be there, of course, he could not tell, for Oriel was a large kingdom comprising Armagh, Monaghan, this Louth, and part of Fermanagh. The monarch could be anywhere – but of recent years he had spent most of his time at Newry, to discourage the Norse from raiding deeper into his territories. Kenneth reckoned this to be a distinctly negative policy, but refrained from saying so. Learning that it was possible to sail a ship right up the narrow river at the lough-head to Newry itself, he decided to do that, with one other longship, leaving the rest of the fleet here in sheltered waters at the mouth, but suggesting that some of the vessels should make a brief sweep southwards along the coasts of Dundalk and Drogheda to the Boyne, as it were to show the flag and possibly drive off any remaining Norsemen in this general area. Donald agreed to take charge of this. The remainder of the crews could rest and recuperate.

Next morning, then, Kenneth's two ships left the rest and proceeded up-lough. This averaged about three miles in width and gave a very different impression from those others they had seen, being much more like one of his own West Highland sea-lochs, this because of the quite high hills flanking it on either side. O'Rourke, whom he took with him, named these mountains, but the Scots and Albannach would scarcely have so called them; but they were major hills nevertheless, especially the Mourne ones on the east, the first such they had seen in Ireland.

Two hours' rowing brought them to the head of the lough and the quite dramatic river-mouth, issuing from a long and straight defile. This seemed to be deep enough to be fairly readily navigable.

It was, however, not quite so accessible as it looked. The ramparts of two forts guarded the entrance on either side, and when Kenneth's longship approached close there was seen to be a massive iron chain across the mouth, barring all progress. Halted, they gazed up at the forts, and signalled.

Even though their approach must have been observed from the forts, there was no hurry as to reaction. There was nothing for it but to wait. This presumably was King Godfrey's way of discouraging the Norsemen.

Eventually a few men came down the hill from one of the forts, to a shelf above the water where there was a winch-like contrivance for raising and lowering the chain. Demands were shouted at the newcomers as to who they were and what they wanted.

Kenneth's reply that he was the Prince of Galloway come

to visit the King of Oriel did not seem greatly to impress. So he added, taking a chance, that they were kin, in cousinship.

This, stretched sufficiently far, had some truth in it. Fergus was a family name in the mac Erc line, the rulers of ancient Dalriata, from which Fergus mac Erc and his brothers Lorn and Angus had come, four centuries before, to found Dalriada in Alba. Kenneth was a direct descendant of those mac Ercs, and so was this Godfrey mac Fergus of Oriel, himself sprung of the Dalriata royal house, Oriel now including Dalriata.

However far-fetched, this did appear to influence the guards, for they turned to their winch and, three men to each of its handles, began laboriously to turn them. Creaking and clanking, the heavy chain rose, hanging with seaweed. Kenneth had expected it to sink, rather, well below the surface, to allow the vessels to pass over; but instead it was raised, to stretch across about a dozen feet above the water. The point of this immediately became apparent. Ships with masts still could not pass, without unstepping the said masts; and a Norse dragon-ship would take some time to do this, rigged as it was. Unseating and lowering their own masts was a nuisance, but there was no getting past otherwise. It certainly was a device to delay intruders. They left the masts down meantime, in case there were further such barriers.

Once past the entrance, however, they encountered no more hazards as they rowed up that strange river; which in fact was more like a man-made canal. It would be a dangerous avenue of invasion, for there were no prospects on either side because of the hillsides, no effective landing-places, and innumerable points where defenders could bar passage to ships, which would anyway have to be moving in single file. This Newry, then, would be fairly safe from attack from the sea.

There was a strong current in the river, entailing hard rowing. It took them over an hour to reach their destination, a fair-sized town behind ramparts of earth, stone and timber stockades, set where the hills drew back and the valley widened. There was no great fortress on a rock here, but an abbey and large hallhouse appeared to share higher ground overlooking all, the latter undoubtedly the palace.

They were not challenged at the riverside berthing-place, scarcely quays, although watched with interest by numbers of folk. Presumably anyone who got past the entrance-forts was regarded as harmless. There was no need to ask the way up to the palace. An unusual feature near the waterside was a huge and ancient yew-tree standing isolated. O'Rourke said that this tree was famous, planted four centuries ago by St Patrick himself, a symbol of immortality. Indeed the name of the town derived from this yew, not from the river, which was called the Clanrye.

With Conall and only two or three others, Kenneth made his way up through the narrow streets. When they reached the monastery, also founded by St Patrick apparently, it proved to be all within the same stockade as the hallhouse-palace, an unusual arrangement, indicating presumably that it had been there first. At a defensive gatehouse they were halted by armed guards, not monks. When Kenneth announced his identity and asked for King Godfrey, it was to be told curtly that the monarch was not present at this time.

Declaring that they had come a long way to see him, and had much of importance to say to him, Kenneth asked was he gone far, and was he expected back soon?

The guards were singularly unhelpful, offering no useful information.

Annoyed, he demanded, at his haughtiest, to be taken forthwith to someone in authority. He was not used, he announced, to chaffering with underlings at a gatehouse, he whose father was King of Galloway, his grandfather King of Dalriada, and coming of the same line as King Godfrey.

This information seemed to make less impression here than it had done at the river-mouth. There was no move to let them past, and Kenneth was wondering what they could do to untie this stupid knot when there was an unexpected development. Instead of the rough, uncompromising voices of the guards, a light and musical feminine voice sounded from above.

"Did I hear you to say Dalriata, friend?"

Surprised, they all glanced up. A youngish woman was looking down on them from the gatehouse parapet. Kenneth raised a hand.

"Dalria*d*a, lady," he called, emphasising the d. "Across

the sea."

"Ah. But Scots then, also. *I* am from Dalriata. Am I sufficient authority for you? I am Cathira."

Kenneth cleared his throat, somewhat embarrassed that his pronouncements about his lofty background should have been overheard by a lady. "I am sorry. I did not know that you were there. I but sought entry, past these. To speak with someone . . . closer to King Godfrey."

"I understand. But we have to be careful. We are wary of strangers, since the Danes have come to harass us."

"They will do that the less now, I think, lady."

"Indeed? Would that I could believe it. We suffer much from them. Come, tell me . . . "

That invitation appeared to be enough for the guards, for they stood aside promptly to allow the visitors to pass in through the gateway.

The lady met them beyond. She was a darkly attractive woman, handsome rather than beautiful, a little older than himself probably, tall, prominent of bosom and of an assured carriage. She eyed Kenneth up and down in frank appraisal.

"I saw you coming up from the ship," she told him. "We get few visitors by water now. You seemingly won past the Danes?"

Conall hooted.

"Say that we caused them to . . . to change direction," Kenneth said.

"You mean that you eluded them?"

"Scarcely that. They eluded *us*. Or some few of them did."

She eyed him searchingly. "You speak somewhat vauntingly, I think, sir prince!"

"I am sorry if you so judge. I would not wish to do so. Especially to a lady. We did exchange blows with the Norsemen. And now they are gone."

She shrugged fine shoulders as though reserving decision. "And now you seek my husband, Godfrey?"

"Husband . . . ? Then – you are the Queen?"

"I told you, sir – I am Cathira."

"I did not know your name, Highness. Yes, I seek King Godfrey. And he is from home?"

"He is gone to Dundrum and Downpatrick. But he should return tomorrow, I think. It is not so very far. He went to encourage them there. Against these Danes."

"Then perhaps he will be back the sooner, Highness. For the folk there may be able to forget the Danes, for a little time at least."

"They will never forget – not after what they have suffered. But . . . do you still speak vauntingly, sir? If you have had some success over the devils, in Carlingford Lough, there are thousands of others, in Dundrum and Strangford and elsewhere."

"I think not, Highness. Not now. You see, we have cleared all these, and more."

"Not with two ships, I swear!"

"No. But with one hundred times that."

The Queen stared. "Tell me," she commanded, with royal enough authority now. Then, "But come – tell me as we go." And she led the way up to the hallhouse.

It took some time to recount even a very abbreviated version of their project and doings – and before it was finished Kenneth was being entertained with food and wine in one of the royal apartments, while his companions fed in the common hall below. Queen Cathira was impressed, and did not seek to hide it. Indeed she became quite frankly appreciative of Kenneth's company, as well as of his story, feeding him titbits the while and filling up his wine-beaker.

It made a pleasant change from seeking to control a fleet of ships.

Kenneth gained some information, too, about this realm of Oriel, its neighbouring kingdoms, the problems facing them, not only from the Norsemen, the weakness of the ageing High King Conchobar, and the difficulty of getting any united action. He learned that Queen Cathira was in fact closer to the ancient royal house of Dalriata than was her husband, and proud of the fact. Also that Godfrey mac Fergus, by implication, was perhaps not the most satisfying of husbands for a spirited woman, a man over-preoccupied with affairs of state.

The said Godfrey did not put in an appearance that evening, and Kenneth's entertainment changed to music on the harp, singing and recitation, with even some dancing. Not that he was clad for dancing, and was well content just to sit and watch – even though he found it difficult to stay awake at times, for he had not done a lot of sleeping recently.

Later still, with the Queen sitting beside him on the snowy-white sheepskin settle, listening to a young woman harpist singing a love-song, he found Cathira's hand coming to rest lightly upon his own, and to remain there. He did not make any response, even though he by no means shook it off. He was far from proof against feminine allure; but the wife of a monarch with whom he had come to negotiate was scarcely an advisable partner. He feigned even more weariness than he felt.

Presently, with the singing over, the Queen seemed to accept the situation. "You are tired, and like to fall asleep on me!" she announced. "You are a personable man, Kenneth mac Alpin, and I could think of worse to happen to a woman than that! Especially if you were less . . . fatigued! But I must ever be the good wife to Godfrey, must I not?"

He inclined his head, touched her shoulder where it swelled to her bosom, and made his escape to his allotted bedchamber.

But it was Eithne of Moray he dreamed of that night, not Cathira.

In the morning, the Queen was her authoritative self again, and took her visitor hawking for wildfowl up the Clanrye River, excellent sport, ahorse, with dogs to retrieve the birds. And when they got back, the King had returned.

Godfrey mac Fergus was a man in his early forties, open-featured and friendly enough, stocky and inclining to stoutness. He had already seen Conall and the others, and so was to some extent prepared for Kenneth's news and announcement. Nevertheless he was scarcely able to credit it all, the scale of the Celtic alliance, the size of the fleet, the numbers of Norsemen disposed of, and the probability that the others would have forsaken the area, at least meantime. When Kenneth told him that he could have two of the captured dragon-ships and as many of the wounded prisoners as he might want, he was much elated, and had to believe it all.

When it came to the suggestion of joining the Celtic alliance, however, he was not so sure, and found various excuses, mainly concerned with how the other Irish kings would react, inter-kingdom rivalry and the like. It was his wife who, rallying him almost scornfully for weakness and indecision, eventually persuaded him to provisional agreement. He would consider what he could do in the matter, would help if and where he could, and would commend the idea to other rulers if opportunity offered.

With that Kenneth had to be content.

His hosts would have had him remain for longer, but he had his waiting host to think of, and many wounded men who should be got home promptly. So Kenneth did not delay thereafter. King Godfrey would accompany him down to the mouth of Carlingford Lough, to collect his dragonships and the prisoners – who could be useful for ransom, barter or revenge. Queen Cathira accompanied them down to the riverside, and gave their guest quite a flattering send-off and warm invitation to return. She would do what she could to further his ambitious project, she assured, but he would be wise to come back, to ensure success.

There were more sorts of success than one, it seemed.

11

Kenneth's eventual return to Galloway was much delayed,
for he felt constrained to pay sundry personal visits on his
way home, to inform the rulers who had responded to his
appeal for ships and men as to the outcome of the expedition. So, leaving the fleet, which was now in process of
breaking up anyway, in the Irish Sea, he headed his own ship
for the Isle of Man, to call on King Howell. That man
expressed himself as well pleased with the report he was
given, and promised further co-operation. Kenneth had difficulty in getting away, with Howell seeking to show his
approval by the way of hospitality.

Thereafter he sailed due southwards for Gwynedd or
North Wales – from whence Howell himself had come, and
where one of his kinsmen ruled. Caernarfon was his capital,
at the head of the great bay behind Mona Isle. Kenneth had
heard of this Mona, but had no idea that it would be so
large, almost thirty miles long, he reckoned, and almost as
wide, but, unlike the Hebridean islands, flat and featureless.
At Caernarfon, sited at the mouth of the narrow Strait of
Menai which separated this Mona from the mainland, he
found that King Mervyn Brych of Gwynedd, and his only
son, Rotri, were gone to a meeting of Welsh monarchs in
Dyfed, one of the southernmost of the kingdoms, this to try
to work out some joint policy regarding the constant inroads
of the Saxons of Wessex, and to a lesser extent the Angles of
Mercia. It was not the Scandinavians who presently preoccupied the Welsh princes, Kenneth was told. He stressed
that his vision of a Celtic alliance would apply against the
Angles and Saxons as well as the Norsemen. This was however received with some scepticism, the point being that the
seaborne forces of the northern nations would not be of
major help in the landward battles amongst the Welsh
mountains. Anyhow, he had no time to go the many miles to

Dyfed. His mission to Gwynedd must wait meantime.

The next visit was to Dunbarton, even though this entailed passing his own Galloway shores on the way. But Roderick of Strathclyde had contributed the largest numbers of men and ships, after Dalriada, and was vital, centrally placed, in any move towards a united Celtic polity, even though he was no enthusiast. His ships would have returned before this, of course, and he would know of the success of the enterprise, but he probably would be pleased to have Kenneth's own account.

And thus it turned out.

So it was with the beginning of wintery weather before Kenneth reached Garlies and his father's house. And there it was his turn to be the recipient of dramatic news. Alpin was not there. He had gone to Dunadd, with Donald. Eochaidh the Poisonous had suddenly died. Kenneth was to come on as soon as possible.

It was back to sea again, therefore. Kenneth did not greatly grieve for his grandfather, never a man to inspire affection, although he had his virtues, and his erudition was notable. But there would be big changes now, that was certain.

Arrival at Dalriada found Port an Deora thronged with shipping, not just the returned squadrons but the personal craft of lords, chiefs and nobles. A great council had been called, it appeared, to appoint Alpin the new King of Dalriada. It would be held in two days' time. Eochaidh had meantime been buried on Iona, amongst his predecessors.

Alpin, a peaceable and unambitious character, was far from elated by this development and his greatly increased responsibilities. But he was glad to see his eldest son, on whom he placed much reliance. He was going to need Kenneth's help, advice and support – even though Kenneth himself would now become sub-King of Galloway, in his place.

That prospect did not alarm his son, who indeed saw all this as strengthening his own hand in working for his cherished project. As a monarch, even a minor one, his voice would carry more weight amongst the other Celtic rulers.

Meantime there was much to be done in preparation for the council and enthronement. It was not thought that there would be any opposition amongst the chiefs to Alpin's elevation. There was really no alternative contender, although some undoubtedly would have preferred a more assertive ruler. But in this respect Kenneth's mounting fame as a leader told, as heir to the throne; there was likely to be almost over-much initiative there.

There was feasting in the palace of Dunadd that night, mourning for Eochaidh only nominal.

Next day, however, there was no feasting. In an afternoon of blustery rain, a large cavalcade arrived, not from ships but on horseback, from the north-east, led by none other than Aed mac Boanta, Mormaor of Moray, Eithne's husband. Only, he was not calling himself mormaor but King of Dalriada, appointed as such by Angus his father-in-law, High King of Alba.

To say that there was consternation at Dunadd would be a major understatement. Utterly unexpected, scarcely believable, this development left the Dalriadan Scots bewildered, angry. How could Angus mac Fergus do this? Why? And on what authority? High King he might be, but of Alba not of Dalriada, an independent realm. He had no right. And who was this Aed, anyway?

Prince Ewan mac Angus had been sent with his brother-in-law, and although Aed himself appeared to consider that no explanations were necessary, Ewan, distinctly apologetically and in private, informed Kenneth of his father's decision. Angus was not actually claiming Alban overlordship of Dalriada, he assured. But *he* had been King of Dalriada before becoming High King of Alba, as had his brother Constantine before him. He said that it was essential that the two realms should remain in close relationship – Kenneth, a believer in unity, would support that? – and considered it best to have one of his own family on the lesser throne. He would have appointed himself, Ewan, but felt that he was too young, with Dalriada requiring a strong king; and frankly, his father did not esteem Alpin sufficiently so. Kenneth would have been different, but he could not appoint him above his father. Aed was strong, his son-in-law, so . . .

And why did Angus mac Fergus think that it was his duty and privilege to appoint anyone to Dalriada? Kenneth demanded. The other could only shrug and repeat what he had said about Angus and Constantine both having themselves been kings of Dalriada.

Discussion, argument, raged fiercely all over Dunadd that night, few indeed prepared to accept the situation. But what could they do? Aed mac Boanta, a forceful man, had not come to discuss, plead or parley. He had come to be enthroned and installed on Dunadd Hill, and that was that. If the chiefs refused, then undoubtedly there would be a violent clash between the two kingdoms, possibly war – and that was unthinkable to most. What, then? Angus was too far committed to change his mind, Ewan said; and Aed certainly would not back down now. Alpin himself appeared to be the least concerned, almost relieved.

Kenneth found all turning to him for leadership. He was the man of decision and drive, was he not? He had influence with Angus mac Fergus also. Could he not resolve this wretched situation somehow? Either go and change the High King's mind, or head up revolt here – since it seemed that his father would not?

Kenneth was in a quandary indeed. Grievously disappointed in King Angus as he was, after all that he had done to help him over St Andrew, he did not see that anything would be served by going to argue the matter with him. A High King, having made such a decision, could by no means climb down over it – all pride would forbid. And if Angus was not going to change his mind, was there any point in contesting the issue with Aed mac Boanta here? An uprising of the Dalriadan chiefs could make it almost impossible for him to rule effectively, yes – but what would be achieved by that? A weakened and strife-torn Dalriada was the last thing wanted, at this or any other stage. Kenneth did not like the man – but that was immaterial. Although he could hardly admit it, Aed might just possibly make a better king than would Alpin. *He* would not have the same influence with him, of course, if any. But if he, Kenneth, was slain in battle, as could so easily happen, then Aed would probably serve the nation as well if not better, than Alpin. And, if he was to be king, Kenneth did not wish to be at odds with him sufficiently to prevent co-operation in the Celtic alliance. The same applied to King Angus. His own great project must not be wrecked by this unfortunate development. And, to be sure, Aed was Eithne's husband. Kenneth again would scarcely admit it even to himself, but away at the back of his mind was the thought that, with Aed here at Dunadd, Eithne would presumably be here also, and he would be able to see her not infrequently.

Kenneth, then, scarcely seemed to live up to his reputation at a hurried conference of the chiefs next day, when he failed to lead the dissentients, and instead advised restraint at present. Let them send a deputation to King Angus, asserting their independence and their right to appoint their own king. But meantime accept this Aed, as it were on trial. If he proved to be unsatisfactory, then it might be necessary to unseat him, as had been done with others before this. But that was for the future. What was the alternative? War? He, Kenneth, was working for Celtic unity, not internal warfare.

Other views were expressed, but no proposals of a practical nature put forward. Alpin and Donald backed up Kenneth's attitude. In the end it was agreed, with marked lack of enthusiasm, to do as suggested, even the most belligerent unable to contest it when the only alternative king and his family accepted. But Kenneth himself recognised that he was sacrificing personal standing on behalf of the greater, wider good, in his opinion.

So two days later the age-old ceremony took place up on the top of Dunadd Hill, before one of the least approving ever of assemblies surely, the installation of King Aed. There, beside the carven wild boar symbol of kingship on the living rock, that man swore the oath to maintain and, with his life itself, protect the kingdom of the Scots of Dalriada, to rule it justly and honourably and to be guided by its chiefs and lords, also to support the Columban Church. Thereafter he placed his bare foot in the incised footprint on a nearby outcrop, into which hollow the said chiefs and lords sprinkled grains of earth brought from their several lands – albeit, brought for a different monarch – so that the King could take and accept their oaths of allegiance for the said lands standing on their soil, to save him having to travel the length and breadth of the entire kingdom and all its isles to do so. Aed performed all this in suitable and quite dignified fashion, well aware that his elevation was less than popular and that hostility had to be overcome. It was traditional, since Columba's first institution, that the newly installed monarch should thereafter go to Iona for the actual coronation ceremony by Columba's successor, the Abbot of Iona, on that sacred isle; but since the present abbot was in fact at Derry in Ireland, and the island's buildings and shrines desecrated by the Norsemen, it was accepted that on this occasion something more modest would have to serve. So the senior cleric available, the prior of the nearby monastery of Ballymeanach, officiated, in the name of the Columban Church of Christ, anointing Aed's head with consecrated oil and then placing the slim golden circlet of kingship over his brows. Normally there were cheers at this stage, but today there were none.

Frequently throughout, Kenneth's gaze had strayed to that magnificent panorama of sea and islands, mountains and headlands, stretching seemingly to all infinity, which all his life had been his favourite and cherished prospect. One day, he had always assumed, this would all be his to care for, himself to be crowned here. And now – what? The man who had taken his woman had now taken his crown also. And he had raised no hand nor voice to deny him either. Whither then, Kenneth mac Alpin?

It was Aed who gave the feast that night, seeking to be as amiable as his nature allowed; but it was a subdued affair, the entertainment confined to the entertainers. Only after the new king retired, Alpin also, did things liven up. Kenneth found himself nominated by the chiefly ones present to lead a delegation to Fortrenn and the High King, and promptly, to acquaint him with their views on it all. Kenneth could hardly object, since it was his own suggestion in the first place. Donald said that he would come with him, and sundry others were appointed.

It transpired that Ewan was going to return to Forteviot without delay, to inform his father as to the situation. Since he and Kenneth had always got on well, they could go together. No leave was sought of King Aed for departure from his royal court.

The weather inclement, they made no very enjoyable

journey of it to Fortrenn, snow already mantling the inland mountains of Drumalban. At Forteviot, four days later, they found Angus absent. He had gone to Kilrymond, in Fife, to superintend the work on the splendid shrine he was erecting to St Andrew, something that he was increasingly apt to do, it seemed, the project there become almost an obsession with him. Nobody knew just when he would return.

If this proved an annoyance for the Dalriadan party, it had its compensations for Kenneth at least. For he learned that Eithne was with her father. When her husband had left Inverness for Dunadd, she had taken the opportunity to come back to Forteviot for a visit, for she worried about her father, whose health was not of the best, their mother having died suddenly a year ago. The news helped considerably to qualify Kenneth's annoyance at having to continue journeying in this weather. His companions were less content.

So it was on eastwards, by the south shores of Tay and across the Rigging of Fife to the Norse Sea.

They saw the fine building towering up on the clifftop even before they crossed the mouth of the Eden River, the shrine of St Andrew, uncompleted as yet but already imposing and a landmark, near but not at the Kilrymond monastery. With the grey seas veined white, and flying spray, it seemed, that day, an odd place to commemorate the patron saint of a great nation.

At the monastery they discovered that King Angus was, as usual, at the building site; but that the energetic Queen Eithne had gone riding along the cliffs. Kenneth would have done the same forthwith, tired as his horse might be, but recognised that this might be injudicious, that he should properly announce his presence to Angus first anyway. However, when they reached the monarch he was fully occupied berating an unfortunate stone-carver who had misinterpreted one of the High King's own decorative designs for a pillar-finial; and Angus paid only scant attention to his visitors, even Ewan, meantime. Kenneth in consequence offered no more than formal courtesies at this stage, and took his leave barely noticed. What *he* noticed was the deterioration in Angus's physical condition and carriage since he had last seen him.

Leaving the others, Kenneth rode the clifftop path

southwards, the way he and Eithne had gone looking for the lost finger-bone of St Andrew those years ago, a somewhat bitter-sweet memory. The conditions were scarcely inviting for such exposed riding, with gusts of wind sending up occasional veils of spume from the breaking seas below; but it might be termed exhilarating, depending on the mood.

He had to go some miles, and he was beginning to wonder whether he had missed her, for although he could see recent hoof-marks on the mud of the path, only going thus southwards, Eithne might have decided to return inland. And then he perceived a single rider approaching from out of a hollow of the cliffs, long hair streaming in the wind. He reined up, to wait.

She came on without slackening pace – and it occurred to the man that she took risks, a woman riding thus alone in such wild places, even the High King's daughter. Watching her, he knew both a great satisfaction and a great sense of loss.

She was almost upon him before abruptly she pulled up her spume-flecked mount, eyes widening in recognition. Shouting something incoherent she came, reining close, to gaze and gaze.

"Highness!" he got out, thickly.

"Oh, Kenneth! Kenneth!" she exclaimed. "Yourself! *You!*" And she kneed her beast alongside his, so that they touched, and her arms reached out to him.

With difficulty he restrained himself from leaning over to embrace her. "Highness!" he said again. That was almost a plea.

She drew back a little, to eye him searchingly, her lip trembling. "Oh, Kenneth – is it . . . ? Is it . . . ? You blame me? My dear – do not blame me, I beseech you. Not that!"

"Blame? How could I blame you, Eithne?"

"You name me Highness. Because . . . because . . . "

"Because, Highness, you are a queen now."

"To my sorrow, yes. And of *your* kingdom. The shame of it, the pain! Kenneth, understand – it is against my every wish. You must believe me . . . "

"Eithne, do not distress yourself." Now he did reach out to hold her. "I come in love and affection, not blame – never that. To call on your father, but hoping, hoping to see you . . . "

They clung to each other, from their two saddles, wordless, and better so.

At length Eithne found her voice again. "Kenneth, how good, how good to see you. Now that I know that I am not blamed. It has been so long . . . "

"Long, yes. And never a day that I have not thought of you. Or a night."

"You, also! My dear." She turned in her saddle, pointing back towards the hollow from which she had appeared. "See – it was more sheltered there. Come."

They reined round and rode back and down into a dip wherein grew a few wind-blown hawthorns; and there, in comparative shelter, by mutual consent, they dismounted. As Kenneth aided her down, they came into each other's arms – but only for a moment or two. Reluctantly he held her away, for she was another man's wife. Eithne, looking at him, first shook her head and then nodded in understanding, a strangely contradictory gesture.

"We are . . . constrained," she said, sadly.

"Yes. But we have this, at least."

Hitching their mounts to a tree, they went to sit in a hollow. Constraint did not prevent them sitting close.

"This of the kingship, Kenneth – of Dalriada," she began, at once. "It is shameful. But I could do nothing to stop it. They would not heed me. My father – I sometimes think that he is not in his right mind, these days. This of St Andrew – it has become a sort of madness. He was wholly set on having a different king for Dalriada, different from Alpin, *your* father. He esteems him weak. You, I think, he might have accepted, but not your father. He believes that Alba and Dalriada should be one. As do you, yes? And sees this as a first step . . . "

"Not how it should be done."

"No, I see that. But he is a sick man, Kenneth, in mind I fear, as well as in body. And Aed was eager, urging him on. I could do nothing to sway them."

"To be sure. Do not trouble yourself, Eithne."

"But I must. I cannot help myself. For me, Eithne nic Angus, to be named Queen of Dalriada, *your* land . . . !"

"Dalriada could scarce have a better queen, at least! But –

enough of this. How goes it with you? Your marriage?"

She looked away. "What can I say to that? I, who never wanted this marriage. I have to bear it, as best I can."

"Is it so grievous, Eithne?"

"How think you? To be wed to a man I do not love, a man who does not think as I think, feel as I feel. Oh, many women have to bear the like, I know. And I could have a worse husband than Aed mac Boanta, no doubt. But . . ."

"He is a forceful man. He treats you . . . well?"

"Since I do not give him all that a wife should, he treats me none so ill. He does not *mistreat* me – for I am the High King's daughter! And . . . he has other women aplenty."

"I see. I am sorry." Inadequate to reply to that, he squeezed her arm.

Almost defiantly, she added, "I have given him no child!"

He shook his head, wordless.

"So, now – let us talk of ourselves . . ."

Strangely, now they had in fact little to say, well enough content meantime just to sit beside each other, listening to the crash of the waves below, and the screaming of the seabirds. By fits and starts they spoke of various happenings and experiences which had affected them since last they had seen each other, but no coherent account. Indeed, more often they referred to their last excursion together along these cliffs, searching the caves. Somehow that seemed more important than what had transpired in the interim.

At length, with the light fading and the cold beginning to get to them, they rose, to hold each other again, briefly, before remounting.

"One more memory to take away, to console me," Eithne said. "Kenneth, what is to become of us? Or, of *me*. You will go on, fighting, winning battles, the hero-prince, seeking to unite the Celts. But me? Tied, held in a marriage I do not want. How to face the years . . . ?"

"My dear. What can I say? Only that, within us we have each other. Not in body – but the body, is it the truest part of us? Is not the heart and mind much the greater? And these we hold secure. None can take that from us. We must hold fast to that. If we can!"

"Brave words!" she said, as she heeled her mount on. "I shall remember them, yes. But whether I can comfort myself with them . . . ?"

"At least, if you come to dwell at Dunadd, we can see each other at times . . . "

Back at the monastery they found King Angus returned, and actually busy drawing more designs for his shrine's decoration, albeit with a shaky hand. Clearly this was his principal interest in life now. He listened to Kenneth and his daughter with only half his attention.

Later, after a meal provided by the prior, the High King did give a sort of audience to the deputation from Dunadd, Eithne listening in. It was scarcely a satisfactory interview, but Kenneth did manage to emphasise that Dalriada was still an entirely independent realm, and gained a testy admission of the fact. He further pointed out, as tactfully as he could, that therefore the High King of Alba had no authority to appoint a king for Dalriada; and that, while on this occasion they had accepted Aed mac Boanta, it was with grave reservations, and if he proved to be an unsatisfactory monarch they would remove him and appoint another in his place. To which Angus announced that he had appointed Aed not in his own capacity as High King but as himself former King of Dalriada, in the cause of unity. Had he not nominated the late Eochaidh as his own successor? Just as Constantine his brother had nominated him? It was all for the good of the two realms. Aed would make a strong and worthy king.

Further discussion seeming profitless, and having made their point, the deputation left it at that.

They departed from Kilrymond next morning, Ewan returning with them to Forteviot. Eithne escorted the party as far as the Eden-mouth. Her parting from Kenneth had to be formal, undemonstrative – but their eyes, locking, said all that their tongues and bodies could not.

12

After a winter spent in Galloway awaiting the weather for wider-spread activities, the spring, when it came, proved to be less than encouraging for Kenneth mac Alpin. He had gone on his first sally of the season, to Cumbria, to try to stir up the dejected and disunited chiefs there towards some sort of concerted action against the Anglian invaders, with the promise of help from the north – this partly in the hope of bringing their Welsh neighbours nearer to a Celtic alliance – when he returned to learn of the death of King Howell of Man, slain in an affray with Norsemen. Kenneth was seeking to discover whether these were some of the Scandinavians left stranded on Man when their ships were sunk, or new raiders, when further tidings reached Garlies, to the effect that there had been another major Norse raid on Iona, with heavy casualties. Other places on the Hebridean seaboard had also been attacked, some alarmingly close to Dunadd itself, even on Jura, and in large force. So it looked as though the Norsemen were back, after the defeats of the year before, and determined on vengeance.

This was serious and challenging news for Kenneth; Howell's death a major blow to his project. He had no knowledge as to who was likely to succeed him, Howell being unmarried and leaving no close heir. Kenneth was concerned, too, that if the Norsemen were thus making a determined come-back in the Celtic area, they might well have returned to Ulster and Oriel also, and King Godfrey mac Fergus be in trouble and so of little use to him.

Kenneth recognised that all this could not but prejudice his cause, seeming to undo much that he had achieved. But he could by no means attempt to assemble another great fleet so soon after the last; that had been a gesture which he could not hope to repeat with any frequency. His own Galloway squadron was not sufficiently large to tackle any major Norse force, well enough for hunting small groups of raiders only. So what was to be done to try to maintain the momentum of his unity campaign?

He decided to try to use Aed mac Boanta, since these latest Norse attacks had come so close to Dunadd. Aed must be worried. He might already have done something about it, of course, but even so would presumably be glad of assistance; and if he had not, might well be prepared to co-operate and contribute a force of Dalriadan ships. Kenneth saw this as his best hope of action meantime.

So, with a flotilla of eight Galloway longships, he sailed north, in fair May weather. And he would see Eithne, he hoped.

Arrival at Dunadd, however, brought further headaches. Eithne was there, and greeted him warmly but less than joyfully; her father had died suddenly, and there was the inevitable resultant upheaval in Alba, as to who was to succeed him. Aed had gone to Fortrenn to take part in the necessary great council meeting on this, just as he had been organising an expedition against the Danes.

Kenneth was concerned for Eithne, but also, to be sure, for his own unity project. Angus had hardly been an enthusiastic supporter, but he had not been hostile. Who was likely to follow him? Ewan?

Eithne thought not, probably. Not yet. The high kingship was a very special and responsible position, scarcely suitable for a young man like Ewan. The *Ard Righ* had to be appointed by the choice of the seven lesser *ri*, sub-kings or mormaors of Alba – of whom of course Aed was one, for he was still Mormaor of Moray even though his brother was deputising for him at Inverness. Aed, ambitious always, undoubtedly would have liked the supreme position for himself, but realised that this would be scarcely likely as a choice. He thought that the probable outcome would be a temporary arrangement, the appointment of an interim ruler, a more experienced man, who would step down in due course, for Ewan to succeed him when he was older. Aed did not see his own chances of such appointment as hopeful, for he was only a son-in-law and distant kinsman of the late monarch, and traditionally the selection was confined to close kin, sons, brothers, uncles, of the royal house.

Kenneth accepted all this, and hoped that whoever succeeded would be favourable towards his own policy. But meantime he saw present opportunity. If Aed had been intending to lead a Dalriadan force against the Norsemen, he might be glad enough for himself, Kenneth, to do it for him. That was why he was here, indeed. Whatever transpired at Fortrenn, these raiders had to be dealt with.

Eithne agreed. As Queen, she gave him full authority to take such ships and men as were assembled. Indeed, she would do better than that; she would come with them.

The man, of course, protested at that. This would be no excursion for women. It was warfare, and the Norse were savage fighters – and fiends if women fell into their hands.

But Eithne was determined. She had always been a forthright and active character, leading her brothers in their adventures; and now she was a queen, and not to be gainsaid. She would lead the Dalriadan ships, under his overall command. Then Aed could not make any objection later.

Distinctly bemused, Kenneth bowed to her decision.

They both went down to Port an Deora to organise the joint venture. Some of the local ships which had been assembled there had gone off whence they had come when Aed departed for Fortrenn; and now Kenneth's friend Conall was sent off in his own vessel to round up such of these as were reasonably near at hand, in the various sealochs and havens. Chiefs and lords were apprised of the situation, and readied, nearly all such welcoming Kenneth's coming. What they thought of Eithne's involvement they did not state.

They would wait three days for late arrivals.

Kenneth was very much aware of the dangers of wagging tongues and assumptions regarding himself and Eithne. Their friendship could hardly be hidden, but it was important that there should be no grounds given for unsuitable talk to be relayed to Aed in due course. So although he and the Queen were much in each other's company those days, it was openly so, and he insisted on spending his nights on his ship, although the young woman declared that to be unnecessary, with the palace large and servants all able to keep an eye on them.

Such precautions, however, did not prevent them much

enjoying the daily proximity.

When eventually they set off, twenty-two ships in all, much as she would have liked to have gone in Kenneth's vessel, Eithne recognised that she ought not to do so. But there was nothing to prevent the two leading craft proceeding more or less side by side, at the head of the fleet. Thus they sailed out into the Sound of Jura, and southwards.

The Norsemen, in their recent raiding, had ravaged places on the two great islands of Jura and Islay, as well as Iona and Mull and further north. So the fleet started its reconnaissance there, calling in at havens and townships at the southern end of Jura, then turning up the narrow Sound of Islay and visiting the harbours of that less mountainous island. Some of their vessels had come from these parts, so they had some idea as to the localities attacked and the damage done. Not that they could do much to help the victims now, save show commiseration and demonstrate avenging strength, with promises of aid in rebuilding and support thereafter – seldom received with any great appreciation by the survivors. Everywhere the reports were the same: brief but savage attacks all along the coasts by small groups of dragon-ships, slayings, burnings, ritual killing of prisoners and decapitating of corpses, raping of women before murder, children not spared, sinking of vessels – then almost hurried departure. From the accounts of those who had escaped, the raiding ships, when last seen, all were heading northwards.

The fleet split up to visit these unhappy communities, as it were spreading the sympathy, for what it was worth; but reassembled for the first night in the sheltered long Jura sealoch of Tarbert. It is to be doubted whether the population there, which escaped the raiders' attentions because of the risk of the dragon-ships getting trapped therein, were especially grateful for this show of strength by their alleged protectors, and the descent of hundreds of warriors and seamen upon their homesteads, eating up their provisions and admiring their womenfolk – even though Kenneth and Eithne insisted on reputable behaviour and payment for all victuals taken.

This pattern was repeated all along the exposed long west coast of Jura, where there were fewer townships, and on to

215

the isles of the quite populous but smaller Colonsay and Oronsay, the Norsemen's conduct fairly consistent, their hate emphatic. Here too the word was that attacks had been of comparably short duration, with no lingering thereafter, and when last seen their ships were heading northwards. That second night, on Colonsay, Kenneth and Eithne were able to spend in a degree of comfort, in the lord of the island's house, set some way inland at Kiloran and thus escaping the raiders' attentions, the son of which house in fact commanded one of the longships of their fleet.

On to Mull and Iona the next day, where the same story was recounted, devastation and the usual array of severed heads greeted them. By now, Kenneth thought that he had discerned the Norse policy. This was no indiscriminate hosting, but a deliberate retaliatory expedition in answer to their own great sweep of the year before, and the various defeats, aimed at covering as wide an area as possible but lingering in none. It was a gesture. The enemy, at this stage, were not seeking battle but vengeance, and the promise of more to come.

They had seen no single dragon-ship throughout.

Iona hit Kenneth hardest, the loveliest isle of all the Hebrides and the most shamefully despoiled. Eithne, strangely, had never been there, and he took her round with mixed feelings, hating for her to see it thus, somehow almost ashamed that he and his like had not been able to save even this jewel of the Celtic Church's crown, whatever his victories. Indeed, possibly his very victories were in some measure responsible for this latest spoliation. He showed her the graves of the kings, where her ancestors and his own were buried, these at least having escaped the general havoc, even though stones and crosses were cast down and defaced. She remained fairly silent throughout.

The Ross of Mull had suffered badly also, but the rest of that great island, the second-largest of all the Hebrides, had escaped fairly lightly, thanks no doubt to the mountainous barrier between north and south. The fleet's last call thereon, at Mishnish, produced the usual report: the last seen of the dragon-ships was half a dozen of them heading north-westwards.

North-westwards of Mull lay Tiree and Coll, Muck and

Eigg and Rhum, and then Skye, with all the lesser isles between. Most of these were not in Dalriada at all, but in Alba. The leaders of this fleet, however, were not going to discriminate. They sailed on.

But after Coll, they found no traces of recent raiding. They went on northwards, right to Skye, but there received similar accounts, no attacks this season, but fishermen having seen dragon-ships heading south-westwards now. There was nothing south-westwards but Ireland.

Kenneth was in two minds as to what he should do. So far they had not seen a Norseman, and after days of sailing the lovely and colourful Hebridean Sea, in the almost consistently fine weather so typical of May and June on that seaboard, much of the urgency and fervour of spirit had gone out of the force, especially once they no longer were seeing the results of Scandinavian savagery. An almost holiday atmosphere indeed was tending to replace it, however unsuitable, even Kenneth himself not being unaffected, with Eithne there to, as it were, seduce him – not that she deliberately did any such thing; but her presence voyaging with him day after day had its effect. So, what? Should he esteem his duty done, and turn back for home? Some would say that this was the obvious course. But in that case, what had they achieved? Nothing of any real value. And raising a fleet, even such a modest one as this, was not easy and could not be repeated very frequently. But, just to sail on, enjoying themselves . . . ?

Ireland again, then? Had that been where the Norsemen had been heading? Probably. Perhaps they might catch up with them there. And if not, at least they could reassure the Irish rulers as to the value of a Celtic alliance.

Of course, nearer than Ireland, and due westwards from Skye, were the far-out islands of the Outer Hebrides, the large isles of Lewis, Harris, Barra and the rest. These represented a major question-mark for Alba. In theory they were part of that realm, but in practice they were Norse territory these days and had been for almost two centuries. For that long they had been more or less occupied by the Scandinavians. But here they had behaved differently from elsewhere. Just why was hard to say. Here they had settled down, after initial conquest, on the land, intermarried with

217

the islanders and become, in the main, farmers and fishermen themselves, giving up hosting and raiding. The High Kings of Alba had been content to leave it so, recognising that, remote as they were from the rest of the country, these isles would be almost impossible to protect effectively. So it was live and let live. No doubt their compatriots, the other raiding Norse, from Orkney, Zetland, Iceland and Scandinavia itself, would avail themselves of facilities here in their hostings, but it was known that they were not welcome to base themselves in the Outer Isles.

Was it worth taking the fleet there, as it were to show the flag? Probably not.

Ireland, then? A brief visit, two days' sail southwards. Eithne had never been to Ireland, and was in favour of prolonging this so pleasant excursion, enjoying her first experience of warfaring. She found shipboard life, in these conditions, not disagreeable in the least, often exhilarating, indeed. She did not suffer from seasickness, had her own privacy under the stern-platform of her longship, and quickly and necessarily had got used to the frankness of men's natural functions.

So they turned southwards, none making objection. The good weather held.

On the second morning they saw their first Norsemen, two dragon-ships well to the west. Not unnaturally these saw them first, a fleet of twenty-two, and sheered off fast. Having greater oar-power than any of Kenneth's craft, he gave no orders to chase.

Approaching thus they came to the north Irish coast not far from the mouth of Lough Foyle. So Kenneth proposed a visit to Derry and Columba's first abbey, Eithne approving.

Up the long lough they saw no raiders; but calling in at Killyleagh, Killinchy and Carrowkeel, they learned that enemy ships had recently appeared again in the lough, made a few attacks on small fishing-villages and then departed – unusual tactics for them. It all went to support Kenneth's theory.

As before, leaving most of their ships at Carrowkeel, Kenneth took Eithne up to Derry. There the reception was considerably more warm than previously, and not wholly because he brought the Queen of Dalriada with him, and even though Abbot Diarmaid had departed again for Kells. It seemed that word of Kenneth's victories on Strangford and Carlingford Loughs, and his reception by King Godfrey, had reached Derry, and his name and fame now meant something here. Eithne was interested in all that they saw, and glad that they had come, the more so when Kenneth told her that this had been the home of Columba's mother, her namesake, the Princess Eithne of Leinster.

Kenneth himself had reason for some satisfaction also, or hoped that he had. For, by chance, he learned that King Feradach of Donegal was at this present nearby, a mere sixteen miles away. Derry was at the extreme western edge of the kingdom of Aileach, with Lough Foyle the border; Carrowkeel, where they had left the fleet, was in fact in Donegal. King Feradach's capital was at the city of Donegal itself, on the western coast, sixty miles away; but Letterkenny, at the head of Lough Swilly, was one of the major towns, and he was there at present, for some reason — or had been two days before. This information much interested Kenneth, for Donegal was one of the largest and most influential of the northern Irish kingdoms, much more so than Oriel, and its monarch's support could be important in any Celtic alliance, especially as he, Feradach, was allegedly hoping to succeed the ageing and feeble High King Conchobar. To reach Letterkenny by sea, back down Lough Foyle, round the great Malin Head and up long Lough Swilly, would be a journey of well over one hundred miles; but across the neck of land between the two lough-heads by land, less than three hours' riding.

With Eithne happy to accompany him, glad of the exercise and change from the cramping conditions of shipboard, Kenneth hired horses, and with a small escort set out south-westwards.

It was good to be riding untrammelled. They had scarcely realised the constrictions of voyaging; but now they appreciated the feeling of release and freedom; also, on the man's part, temporary release from the responsibility for all those ships. The land they traversed was fair, with the oak-woods for which the area was famous, the fresh green of the young leaves burgeoning. They were soon threading hills, and from the high ground could see the blue waters of Lough Swilly ahead, and those of Lough Foyle behind. There was no difficulty in finding their way, at least.

Letterkenny, where the River Swilly joined its lough, proved to be a fair-sized market-town, not walled like Derry but almost as large. There was no palace here, but its O'Neill lord had a commodious hallhouse above the streets. It was evening now, and by the numbers of armed men parading aimlessly about and filling the ale-houses, it looked as though King Feradach was still there. Eithne drew some rude but undoubtedly complimentary attention as they rode by.

Presenting themselves at the hallhouse, the Prince of Galloway and the Queen of Dalriada were received with some astonishment, not to say disbelief. Indeed they were kept waiting on the doorstep while Dungall O'Neill himself was fetched. He, it transpired, had heard of Kenneth's doings in Irish waters, and was prepared to accept his identity. He looked at Eithne admiringly but strangely.

They were led into the crowded hall, where a repast was in progress, no women other than serving-wenches in evidence however. At the head table, none close to him, lounged a hatchet-faced, dark man, in his thirties probably, with strangely ravaged features for that age, and glittering eyes. He stared, and then, grinning, slowly rose to his feet. Tall, he had a distinctly wolfish smile. He barely glanced at Kenneth. When he rose, all others rose likewise. So this was Feradach of Donegal.

Eithne inclined her head only very slightly, and moved forward unhurriedly, Kenneth behind now.

O'Neill announced them.

Feradach flourished a bow of sorts. "Can it be true?" he demanded, glancing about him. "Did we hear aright? Dalriada, not Dalriata? I know Duncan's queen. And she looks . . . otherwise! To his sorrow, no doubt!" That sally raised some laughter.

Since Eithne did not speak, Kenneth did. "The Lady Eithne is Queen of Dalriada across the sea, yes. Also she is the High King of Alba's only daughter." He did not say *was*, in the circumstances, since it was improbable that news of Angus mac Fergus's death would have reached Ireland yet. "I am Kenneth mac Alpin, son to King Alpin of Galloway.

220

You, I judge, must be King Feradach of Donegal? If so, Highness, we greet you with all due regard and respect."

The other spared Kenneth a brief inspection. "Galloway?" he said, almost questioned. "That is somewhere in Strathclyde, is it not? I seem to have heard of it. Or is it in Cumbria?" Having put Kenneth in his place, he turned back to Eithne. "The High King of Alba is to be congratulated on his daughter," he declared, but still with that grin, almost a leer. "Come, lady – sit here at my side, and tell me what I have done to deserve the honour of your presence!"

Eithne turned to O'Neill. "With your permission, sir – since this is *your* house."

That drew breaths, so evident a reproof for the monarch.

O'Neill, an elderly man, looked uncomfortable. But Feradach hooted laughter. "Come!" he repeated.

Eithne awaited O'Neill's gesture, and then smiling to him, moved forward to the table, a hand reaching a little behind her for Kenneth.

The King made a show of pushing back for her the padded bench on which he had been sitting, to stoop to remove the riding-cloak she still wore, with some touching and stroking evidently necessary to undo the catch at her throat. Her companion he continued to ignore.

O'Neill indicated that Kenneth should sit at the other side of Feradach.

Servitors brought food and drink for the new guests.

His shoulder turned ostentatiously on Kenneth, the King addressed himself to Eithne, but in a fashion that was both familiar and less than courteously respectful. For her part, she maintained a cool aloofness, and every now and again leaned forward to seek to bring Kenneth into the conversation. That man's pride did not permit him to seem to push himself forward, in the circumstances, yet he did not forget that he had come here to try to enlist this Feradach in his great cause, and prideful distance-keeping was not going to help in that.

Eithne, recognising this, came to his aid effectively, presently, cutting short Feradach's remarks and raising her voice with sufficiently queenly authority, addressing O'Neill, two places along the table.

"Sir, we come wondering whether you have been suffering the attacks of the Norsemen, in Lough Swilly. It may be that they do not come this far west. Last year, Prince Kenneth came to drive them out of Lough Foyle and other loughs. But he did not get the length of Swilly. Do they trouble you? Or has King Feradach here so assailed them, driven them off, that they do not concern you at Letterkenny?"

Something of a hush greeted that clear and significant enquiry, all but an accusation. For the moment, Donegal's monarch sat silent – as indeed did O'Neill. There had been no word, at Derry or elsewhere, of any particularly vigorous behaviour on Feradach's part against the raiders.

Kenneth, in the pause, took the opportunity thus provided. "After Lough Foyle, we went eastward, to those coasts, to Strangford and Carlingford Loughs, in Oriel. Drove the Norsemen out of these," he said factually. "Perhaps we should have turned westwards first, for Lough Swilly, to aid you here, also? We hold that the Celtic peoples must fight this Norse menace together. No?"

Feradach found his voice. "We do not require assistance," he said curtly.

"That is good, Highness. But others do. And no doubt would be glad of *your* help."

Another pause.

Eithne broke it, speaking again to O'Neill. "No Norsemen come to Lough Swilly, sir?"

That man coughed. "They do, yes. At times."

"But you can deal with them? Send them off?"

There were murmurs, now, in that hall. Undoubtedly there were men there who were not prepared to agree with that.

Kenneth pressed their advantage. "So you need no aid against these killers? As King Feradach says. We are seeking to build an alliance against the Norsemen. Donegal does not require its help?"

Silence.

"It is good that you are so strong. Will you not aid others, Highness?"

The King was in a cleft stick, and knew it. That hall was full of local men, chieftains and leaders of communities, who knew their facts, had suffered raiding, and presumably had

222

not received any major support, seen any large-scale attacks by their ruler's forces. Perhaps the far western seaboard was less troubled by the Vikings, facing the great ocean; but this Lough Swilly could hardly have escaped. So there could well be some resentment.

"What help is called for? And for whom?" Feradach asked, flat-voiced.

"A united stand, opposition against the invaders. When one is attacked, all to rally. Send ships and men, to aid. Not only the Irish kingdoms but those across the narrow seas – Dalriada, Alba, Strathclyde, Galloway, Man, Wales. Last year the fleet I brought was from these, and we cleared the raiders from much of this land. Will Donegal not help? After all, it was of this royal house that Columba came, to bring Christ to Alba. *He* united the Celtic peoples to fight the pagans, then. Should we not seek to do the like?"

Strangely, that reference to Columba seemed to have some effect on Feradach. He rubbed his chin, and looked around him. Perhaps he saw a favourable impression registering on faces in that hall. Columba had been a collateral ancestral kinsman of his own.

"What do you mean by aid?" he asked. "Unity? These are large words. They can mean much, or little. What unity can there be between Donegal and Oriel? Aileach and Dalriata? Connaught and Leinster? These are separate kingdoms, with their own interests and attitudes, ages old. Sometimes at war. Often at odds.

"They at least could unite against the common threat, if in naught else. For the benefits of all. King Godfrey mac Fergus of Oriel has agreed. If you aid also, then Aileach, between the two, would probably join in. And therefore Dalriata would not stand out."

Eithne played her part. She actually laid a hand on Feradach's arm. "*You*, Highness, could lead them. Your name means much. Donegal is important. And Tara, the High Kingship of All Ireland, is to be filled before long, is it not? A leader required . . . ?"

The other looked at her, and caressed the hand on his wrist. "We shall see," he said.

They left it at that, meantime.

In the talk which followed, Eithne and Kenneth were at

some pains to explain their association and why they were here together, emphasising the command of joint fleets and King Aed's absence at a great council of the Albannach. What Feradach made of it was unclear, but he became the more amorously inclined as the evening progressed and the wine flowed, and Eithne was having to fend him off ever more frequently, particularly after an incident when one of the serving wenches, waved forward to fill up his wine-beaker, not for the first time, as she stooped had the royal hand reach up to her bosom and roughly wrench open the bodice she wore, tearing the fabric, to allow her breasts to hang free – this with a grin at Eithne. That young woman wasted no sympathy on the other, who skirled hilariously at the situation and made no effort to cover up, obviously not unused to the like; but Eithne did move further along the bench from the monarch, and caught Kenneth's eye. That man, nodding, broke with custom by rising to his feet before the King, and told O'Neill that the Queen was weary with a long day and much riding, and would now retire. Feradach roared out something incoherent, and sought to get to his own feet. But he collapsed back on the bench, very clearly more under the influence of liquor than had been evident when sitting – possibly some explanation for those ravaged features in a man of his age. At any rate, Eithne was able to bow herself out, and Kenneth after her, with O'Neill playing the good host and offering them accommodation for the night, apologising that it would be unworthy of such illustrious guests, but pointing out that his house was already over-full with the King's people. So Eithne was handed over to a motherly woman whose identity was not explained, and Kenneth allotted a small bare room over stables – which was still more comfortable than his shipboard quarters.

In the morning, Feradach appeared to be quite himself again, with no reference made to the night-time parting. Kenneth said that they had to get back to their ships, already away overlong; but he did not fail to raise the matter of the unity pact against the Norsemen, and found the other not unhelpful in that respect now. He presumably had thought it over in the meantime and found the idea acceptable. He even asserted – admittedly to Eithne, not to Kenneth – that he would seek to bring in the Kings of Aileach and Dalriata in support. Whether this was a genuine commitment they could not tell. But at least it was encouraging and would enable Kenneth to declare that the King of Donegal was in favour. That monarch's farewell to Eithne was physically appreciative to a degree, and she had to cut it short with some firmness. To Kenneth he merely nodded.

"I feared that I would have to fight for my honour before I got away from that man!" she confided, as they rode off eastwards. "If we had stayed longer, there would have been no holding him."

"I think that you would have succeeded in holding him off," Kenneth judged. "You seem to me very able to keep such in their places!"

"Yes? Although I might not be so effective with *you*!"

He considered that, and refrained from comment. Presently he thanked her for the great help she had been to him in bringing Feradach to a state of acceptance of his views on unity. It had been skilfully done.

Back at their ships that night, at Carrowkeel, although Kenneth had contemplated paying a visit to King Godfrey at Newry, they came to the conclusion that they had better not do so. Eithne, much as she had enjoyed the expedition, was just a little concerned that Aed might question over-lengthy an absence, both of his ships and of his wife. Probably they had been away for long enough, much as she would like to prolong it all. Kenneth accepted that. They would sail for home in the morning – but he would meantime hire a messenger, here at Carrowkeel, to go to Newry with his salutations to King Godfrey and Queen Cathira, explaining his presence in these parts and saying that he would have wished to visit them, with Queen Eithne, but had run out of time. Also that King Feradach of Donegal was now in agreement with the idea of mutual support against the invaders.

So they set sail down Lough Foyle next day, feeling that it had been a successful venture as well as a pleasant one – even though they had not slain a single Norseman. They had established that this season's raiding by the Scandinavians had been little more than a gesture, a token, to assert that they were still to be reckoned with and not to be put off by their last year's defeats. But this also implied that they were considerably affected, chastened, and might well restrict their activities in future to larger-scale assaults. Also they, the combined force, had demonstrated to the Irish that they continued to be concerned for their welfare, and a force to be reckoned with. Donegal's adherence to the unity theme, however tentative, was an added advantage gained.

Three days later they moored at Port an Deora. Their approach would have been visible from Dunadd Hill for some time, and Aed mac Boanta had come down to meet them. Kenneth had been, perhaps slightly guiltily, prepared for trouble, but nothing of the sort eventuated. Admittedly Aed was cool towards him, but that was normal. The man seemed pleased, possibly relieved, to see the Dalriadan fleet back intact, and told his wife that she had done well in taking it to sea, to retaliate against the Danes who had assailed his territories, wishing that he had been able to do it himself, and agreeing that Dalriada must lead the way against these wretched Scandinavians. Even though the impression given was that all the initiative had been his queen's, and therefore by implication his own, Kenneth made no complaint. Aed did not seem to suffer the pangs of jealousy, at least.

Later, he told them about the proceedings at the Albannach high council. As anticipated, the *ri* had felt that Ewan mac Angus was too young and inexperienced to be High King, although his time would come, no doubt. So Drust mac Constantine his cousin, Mormaor of Ross, had been appointed meantime, and Talorcan of Angus to be his deputy. There had been great concern over the Norse threat, and Drust urgently required to meet it with all his powers. The Angles also, who had been renewing their raids on Lothian and Fife.

Nothing seemed to have changed after the departure of Angus mac Fergus – save perhaps a lessening preoccupation with St Andrew.

Kenneth did not linger at Dunadd, Eithne acting wife to Aed giving him no pleasure. Besides, his ships and men had to be got back to Galloway.

Their parting was, inevitably, difficult, unsatisfactory, with Aed looking on. But they had had an interlude of some duration which neither would ever forget; nothing could take that from them.

13

Kenneth's concern over Celtic unity had become something of an obsession, persistently occupying his thoughts to the exclusion of much else of some moment – which was, to be sure, all but deliberate; for in the matter of Eithne, he just could not allow his mind to dwell on her and her association with Aed mac Boanta. But this militated against other concerns also, for instance his duties as a prince of Galloway. As his father's eldest son, he had his responsibilities there. Alpin sometimes chided him on the subject, saying that he ought to be of more use to him at home instead of always being off ranging far and wide on great schemes to aid other folk, neglecting Galloway's rule. If he, Alpin, had succeeded his father in Dalriada, as expected, then Kenneth would have been King of Galloway now, and would have *had* to devote his energies to his own realm, and cut down on these expeditions and flourishes – which, in fact, was one reason why Kenneth had not been too much concerned at Aed's appointment. Alpin also accused his son of encouraging his brother Donald to go the same way, to Galloway's detriment.

So, for the rest of that year, Kenneth did seek to carry out his duties in Galloway more effectively, however much his thoughts were apt to stray to wider issues. But even on his perambulations and visitations around Galloway itself, he managed to insert some activity of value to his greater aspirations. On all his voyaging abroad, he had not failed to recognise that Galloway could contribute a much larger force, in ships and seamen, to any combined fleet. Its coastline of enormous bays, huge peninsulas and wide estuaries, extended to hundreds of miles, few parts indeed being more than twenty miles from salt water, its fishing villages and havens unnumbered, its preoccupation with the sea general. It had extensive woodlands and timber, and men who could build fishing-cobles could build longships. Wherever he went, therefore, he sought to encourage the local lords and chief men, not only to build vessels and train crews, but to rival their neighbours in the matter. Fortunately, his reputation as a successful commander had gone before him, and he was greeted fairly consistently as a hero – which helped. He also gave the chiefs some instruction on tactics and ship-handling in a fleet – guidance which was not always gratefully received by his elders, tactful as he tried to be about it. When next a Celtic fleet assembled, then, for a combined venture, the Galloway contingent he hoped would be more impressive. At Garlies itself shipbuilding went on apace.

No word or news came from Dunadd; nor, indeed, from Alba.

By the following spring Kenneth's restlessness was not to be further restrained. Time was passing, and his great unity project not only failing to advance but possibly actually flagging through lack of action. Momentum had to be maintained, he felt, if the idea was ever to come to anything. And nobody else appeared to be prepared to take the initiative. Not that major concerted expeditions could be mounted with any frequency, he recognised. But something should be attempted, surely, to keep the vision alive, something which would be noted, if not to resound, amongst the nations. What?

Cumbria was, he decided, the weakest link in the chain he so ambitiously sought to forge. Although in theory still part of the kingdom of Strathclyde, it was in fact no longer under any Celtic rule or influence, but wholly dominated by the invading Angles. So there was a great gap in the north-south Celtic hegemony, between Galloway and Strathclyde on the north and Wales on the south. If that gap could be filled, the Angles driven out of Cumbria, then the entire alliance theme could be greatly forwarded.

Such endeavour, however, would not be a task for naval forces, for the Angles were not great seamen like the Norse, but land-based warriors, armies not fleets required. Kenneth was less sure of his course here. He was no commander of armies, a captain of horse at best. Occupied Cumbria would demand a different approach.

At least he could go there, as he had done when he went

to Hexham on St Andrew's trail. He was in some doubts as to whether to go, as it were, secretly, as before, to seek out chiefs and lords and try to convince them to rise against the invaders; or to lead a squadron of longships to call in at various Cumbrian ports and harbours, to demonstrate interest and power in the cause of encouragement. He came to the conclusion that the latter would probably be more effective, secret visits thereafter to further inland, perhaps, to individuals, to emphasise and co-ordinate.

So in mid-May he set off due eastwards, with six longships. He could have taken twice as many, and more; but that might be counter-productive. A large fleet cruising off the coast might well alarm the occupying Angles too much, leading them to expect invasion and to send back to Northumbria for additional fighting men and reinforcements generally. Half a dozen ships should be enough to ensure their own effectiveness and safety and to encourage the Cumbrians without too greatly seeming to menace their oppressors at this stage.

Those forty miles to Moricambe Bay again, with a following wind, took them till only mid-afternoon. Openly now they sailed into the wide shallow estuary, between the marshes and the sand-dunes, where Kenneth had gone hidden previously. As its head was Whitrigg hamlet. When there before, he remembered that he had been told that the chief man of this district lived at another and larger village only a mile or two away called Kirkbride. This was not on the waterfront, so its people would not be apt to see the ships. No Angles were billeted there, he was told, so near to their principal base of Carlisle. So Kenneth, with a small escort, borrowed shaggy horses to ride thither.

They found the local chief, one Tormaid, no lord this but a rather dejected youngish man, who showed no elation over the identity of his visitors. It appeared that he had heard of Kenneth of Galloway, and something of his activities, but the main impact this made on him was agitation lest word that he had entertained such a dangerous character might reach Carlisle, with subsequent Anglian wrath descending upon him and his people. When Kenneth explained his squadron's presence in the nearby bay, and the purpose of it, the other was still less delighted, asserting that this could be as good as a death-warrant for himself and family. He refused to go to see the ships, and besought his visitors to depart forthwith. On the subject of a general uprising against the Angles, he was all but appalled. Clearly no warrior, it was apparent that the invaders would have to be in full flight before Tormaid of Kirkbride drew his sword.

It was a disappointing start, especially linked with the name of Kirkbride. For of course St Bride, or Bridget, of Kildare, had been a notable fighter for Christ's cause, and one of Columba's heroines.

They spent the night at Whitrigg, aboard their ships.

Sailing down the coast next morning, they called in at Silloth, Mawbray and Allonby, and in none of these received any encouraging welcome, whatever impression they may have made on the inhabitants. Always, the name of Carlisle was, as it were, raised against them, Anglian vengeance therefrom greatly feared. It came to Kenneth that he was not likely to make any real impact in the area near that great fortress-city, which had once been the famous King Arthur's capital. That hero must be turning in his grave. They would have to go further south.

The Cumbrian coastline was long, almost two hundred miles of it to the Welsh border, and very different in character from that of Galloway or of Strathclyde further north, almost consistently flat and lacking in strong features despite the fine mountains which rose inland further south. After Moricambe Bay there were no great inlets for seventy-odd miles, the river-mouths shallow, fairly level-banked. It tended to be at these that the villages and havens were situated.

Slowly the longships skirted that seaboard, lingering off communities and harbours but not actually landing, their Galloway emblem on sails and banners sufficient to identify them. They met with neither greetings nor signs of opposition. There was nothing like a vessel-of-war in evidence anywhere, and fishing-boats gave them a wide berth. It was not until they reached Parton, within sight of St Bees Head, the greatest landmark on all that undramatic coast, which Kenneth reckoned to be at least fifty miles from Carlisle, that they made a landing.

Here, at a fair-sized village, with a hallhouse and a ruined fort, the first such they had seen, they found an elderly chieftain, obviously of some standing, who was prepared to give them welcome, even though that was all he was prepared to do. But then, he had a son taken hostage by the Angles, for this Lord of Parton's good behaviour apparently, a quite common device, and he would undoubtedly die if his father made any hostile moves – something the Norsemen did not trouble to do. But Cormac mac Cailean at least gave them information and advice. The Angles were, as Kenneth had guessed, less strongly placed as one went southwards towards the Welsh border, the Welsh being vigorous enough to keep them at a distance. Indeed, the entire large area south of the great Morecambe Bay – not to be confused with the lesser Moricambe Bay to the north – where the River Ribble came down to join salt water, was now something of a no-man's-land, with no real rule prevailing. This, although originally of Cumbrian Strathclyde, had early fallen, to become part of the Anglian kingdom of Mercia but now had been largely taken over by the still more aggressive Saxons of Wessex, so that Saxon, Anglian, Welsh and Cumbrian influence here clashed, with predictable results. It was, probably, there that Prince Kenneth should look for support for any rising against the Angles. The men there were wild and unruly, warring amongst themselves but courageous and hating all oppressors. If they would act with some unity, even for a single campaign, they might achieve much and arouse the rest of occupied Cumbria to action.

This made good sense. Kenneth asked if there was no point in seeking to kindle revolt nearer at hand. The old man shrugged, indicating that he was not hopeful. The Angles had a savage way with any who contested their sway – and they had garrisons at a number of points, almost all inland, such as Penrith, Cockermouth, Egremont and Kendal. There were few large communities on the coast between here and Morecambe Bay, save for St Bees and Ravenglass.

They spent the night at Parton, Kenneth in Cormac's house, and in the morning sailed on. Soon they were passing the greatest feature of all that seaboard, St Bees Head, with its three-hundred-foot cliffs. A few miles beyond this they came to the township of St Bees itself, clustered round its quite famous nunnery. Kenneth had heard of this place, founded by St Begha, an Irish princess missionary with a background similar to Columba's, a masterful lady who had made a major impact on these parts a few years after Columba's time, as well as bequeathing a corruption of her name to the place. They put in here, where there was a fair harbour and many fishing-boats.

There appeared to be no hallhouse at St Bees, all being dominated by the nunnery. The shore-going visitors did not have to go seeking admission there, for a group of nuns came down towards the harbour to meet them, led by a woman short of stature but of commanding presence, darkly good-looking and with fine eyes. She halted her group, to size Kenneth up and down.

"I would wish to say God be with you!" she announced firmly. "But first I had better learn who you are and why you come to St Begha's with your ships-of-war. You do not look like Angles nor the Welsh. I am abbess here."

Kenneth bowed. "Permit me to wish *you* God's blessing, Reverend Mother, then," he said – although it seemed absurd to name her that, she so small and seeming little older than himself. "I am Kenneth mac Alpin of Galloway."

"Ah – the Norse-Slayer? We have heard of the bold Prince Kenneth. No Norsemen here for you, Prince. Not yet! I feared at first that you might be such. Although you do not look the part."

"No. No Norse yet, as you say, lady. Although they might well come. But . . . " He took a chance. "There might be Angles!"

"Ha! So you do not confine yourself to hunting Scandinavians, my friend?"

"My aim is not hunting, slaying, but seeking to aid the Celtic peoples to save themselves and their lands from the domination of others."

She looked at him searchingly. "So-o-o! A champion for less spirited folk! And we need such, I do admit. Cumbria has produced few of the like in recent times, I fear."

Encouraged, he nodded. "An occupied land makes difficult soil for challenge and defiance."

"So my father and brother discovered. They were Lords of Greystoke. They both died . . . unpleasantly."

"I am sorry, lady. But I think that their spirit lives on, in you!"

"A woman can only do so much. In especial a religious. But – I try." She turned. "But, come, Prince Kenneth. We can talk in better place than this. My women will entertain your men."

They moved over to St Begha's nunnery, quite an imposing establishment, as large as many an abbey. Here the abbess took Kenneth to her private quarters, whilst her nuns looked after his escort. In the Romish Church this would not have been acceptable, but in the Columban Celtic Church relations between the sexes were much less constrained, the nuns not confined, often actual missionaries, the priests not vowed to celibacy.

Over a meal, plain but substantial, Kenneth told his hostess of his objectives in this venture, his hopes of arousing an uprising amongst the Cumbrians, to be assisted from the north and possibly from Wales and even Man, and his lack of success so far hereabouts. He spoke of Cormac of Parton's advice to go south to the unsettled lands between the Lune and the Ribble, where he would be more likely to find men prepared to fight. The Abbess Bethoc agreed with that, saying that there were many chiefs and small lords down there who, she thought, would not be averse from lending a sword-hand against the Angles, in a major way, given leadership – if they could be diverted from fighting each other. But not to dismiss all nearer at hand as useless. A kinsman of her own was Lord of Ravenglass, some fifteen miles to the south, a young man of some ardour, who might well heed the call. And she herself, when the time came, could probably raise some two score armed men from this vicinity.

Much approving of this female verve and alacrity, from such a small creature, Kenneth was in no hurry to move on; and when she told him that if he cared to spend the night in the nunnery guesthouse she would make arrangements to accompany him on the morrow down to Ravenglass to help him convince her cousin there, this was an offer too good to refuse. His ships would do well enough with the township folks, she assured.

So they spent a pleasant evening together, he attending the vespers service gladly enough. Kenneth told her something of his adventures in Ireland and Man and elsewhere, and of his quest at Hexham and Kirkandrews, in which she was particularly interested, for she knew and liked the deposed bishop there, and St Andrew's name meant a lot in this area. And she told him of conditions in Anglian-held Cumbria, how the invaders fortunately did not greatly trouble the churchmen so long as they paid their dues. She did dwell somewhat on the frustrations of her life, in the circumstances; and Kenneth got the impression that if she had the choice to make again, she would not elect to be a nun. Indeed, when she later conducted him to his room in the guesthouse, and entered it to assure herself that all was in order for his comfort, she seemed to linger a little and then, as she said goodnight, touched his arm and said that sometimes she wondered whether God had really intended her to be a religious, before turning and hurrying off.

In the morning, however, she was all the efficient abbess, organising the establishment as though for an absence longer than seemed required for any mere fifteen-mile journey. When Kenneth asked if she was going to be staying on with her kinsman at Ravenglass, she informed him – no, she had decided to go on, with the Galloway squadron, further south to Morecambe Bay, where she might well be of some help. Just like that. Kenneth by no means questioned this decision, surprised as he was. He was beginning to favour lady voyaging companions. An elderly, motherly prioress was to be left in charge of the nunnery. He gathered that the abbess's departures were not unusual.

What Kenneth's crewmen thought of having a nun for passenger they kept to themselves.

Ravenglass lay at the mouth of a River Esk, one of the many of that name all over the Celtic lands, the word coming merely from *uisge* meaning water. Here, with the hills coming closer to the sea, they found quite a small town, a church and a sizeable hallhouse, to which Kenneth was led by Abbess Bethoc. The lord thereof was named Riagan, it appeared, and they discovered him superintending at his brewhouse, a cheerful young man in his twenties, freckled, red-headed, boyish. He hailed the lady joyfully as Cousin Beth, and seemed quite overawed when she introduced the famous Prince Kenneth of Galloway, Norse-Slayer. He

234

quickly recovered, however, and on being told of Kenneth's mission, became enthusiastic, asserting that this was just what was needed, long overdue indeed, and *he* was to be counted upon for aid. That this was no mere polite gesture was proved, for when he heard that the abbess was going to accompany Kenneth down to the Morecambe Bay and Lancaster area he promptly offered to go too. He knew many of the chief men thereabouts and perhaps could help. He had a ship . . .

When Riagan mac Ewan came in sight of the six longships in the river-mouth, however, he was considerably abashed. He had nothing like these, no longships, only a kind of galley with a dozen oars, not to be compared. Kenneth assured him that he had not come looking for warships but for land forces, since the Angles did not do their fighting by sea. He would be glad of all the armed footmen that could be raised – or the promise of them.

They had to spend the night at Ravenglass while Riagan made his arrangements. When they moved off next day, Kenneth was interested, and more than that, that Abbess Bethoc elected to continue to sail with him rather than to transfer to her kinsman's vessel.

They went in leisurely fashion, necessarily, for Riagan's rather clumsy, and fairly flat-bottomed galley, needed for these waters apparently, was much slower than the lean longships with their great oar-power. They had some twenty miles to go to pass the Furness peninsula and reach the great Morecambe Bay, the largest bight of all this seaboard down to the Welsh border. Bethoc warned Kenneth of its problems as to navigation. It was as shallow as it was wide, worse than the Solway estuary by far, in that the tide went out for miles, shipping having to be very careful not to become stranded, while in wild weather the short seas could be very steep and dangerous. However, a number of large rivers drained into it off the Cumbrian mountains, and these made channels through the sand-flats, which could be used by careful navigators at low water. There were few ports therefore, and the fishing done mainly by stake-nets – indeed, one of the principal sports of the landed men was hunting salmon on horseback with spears, in the shallows, an extraordinary pastime.

Kenneth gained his first experience of this strange coastline when, towards midday, they had to swing out very considerably seawards, at half-tide, to avoid the Duddon Sands at the mouth of the wide estuary of that river. And when, about ten miles further, they passed well clear of the extraordinary sickle-like low Isle of Walney, really only a six-mile-long raised sandbank at the tip of the Furness peninsula, and passed into Morecambe Bay itself, some fifteen miles across, there appeared to be a wide plain of sand between them and the land. They had to heave to for quite some time until the tide changed. Bethoc pointed out a fairly wide channel through it which she said was the outlet of two rivers, the Winster and the Gilpin. If they lined this up with mountain landmarks to the east, in especial one which she called the Old Man of Coniston, it would lead them into the Levens estuary, at higher water. He was thankful now that he had a knowledgeable guide aboard, and understood why the Norsemen had so far avoided this coast, although operating against the Isle of Man not so far to the west.

The longships were fairly shallow of draught, and with that river channel and landmarks to guide them, they did not wait for high water before moving inland. But they went very carefully.

They were making for Arnside, on the Levens estuary, Bethoc informed, who had more or less taken charge. The lord there was another distant relative, although no favourite of hers; whether he would adhere to their cause she could not tell, but at least he would have to give them hospitality and some guidance.

With the making tide they effected their strange landfall, seven ships in line astern all but feeling their way. And at the shallow haven of this Arnside, on the south shore of the estuary, they met with a very different reception than hitherto. Armed men stood at the boatstrand to greet them, swords and spears in hand, and not a smile amongst them. Their approach would have been obvious for long.

It was as well that they had a woman to lead the way ashore from the first vessel, Bethoc, abbess or none, kilting up her skirts and jumping into the shallows without fuss, to wade, waving reassuringly. A heavy-built man of middle years stepped forward, staring from her to the ships, at a loss. Kenneth leapt overside to join the woman, and behind, Riagan followed on.

The abbess introduced Kenneth to Duncan of Arnside, who eyed him suspiciously. He admitted, in surly fashion, to having heard of him, but did not display enthusiasm. When Bethoc explained that Prince Kenneth had come to fight the Angles, he seemed little more impressed, and when Riagan came to add his encomiums, the older man all but mocked him. However, looking at those longships less than favourably and announcing that he wanted no trouble with their crews, he turned to lead the way to his house above the shore, built within the rampart of a former fort.

Despite this unpromising start, over a repast, with a more kindly wife improving the atmosphere, this Duncan of Arnside, questioning Kenneth, became more interested, raising points of practicality and procedure. And clearly he knew what he was talking about, a fighting man. That he hated the Angles and Saxons both was evident. Kenneth began to have hopes of him.

When it was his turn to question, Kenneth established that there were indeed plenty of men in these parts, especially in the Bowland Forest area, who might be prevailed upon to make a nuisance of themselves towards the invaders. They were apt to do that anyway, but not in any concerted way. Whether this would rouse the rest of occupied Cumbria to any sort of large-scale action was doubtful.

When Kenneth declared that he was thinking of making a tour round to meet various chiefs and landholders, and asked the names of those who might prove sympathetic and active, the other shook his head, discouragingly. Going round visiting them was not likely to effect much, mere talk. These were hard men, more concerned with fighting each other, stealing each other's cattle and women, than provoking large-scale retribution from the Angles. They would take a deal of convincing. Some *action*, of course, might have some effect.

What did he mean by action? Kenneth wondered.

Duncan shrugged. A demonstration of strength and purpose. Some assault on the common enemy, as token of intention, he indicated.

"Where?" That was the abbess demandingly. "The Angles are not numerous here, are they? How shall Prince Kenneth find them to assail?"

"They have a garrison at Kendal, on the pass through the mountains. And a small base at Carnforth. And, of course, at Lancaster."

"Carnforth? Would that be possible? Kendal would require many men, almost an army. And Lancaster would be too much also, I fear." She looked at Kenneth. "How many men do you have?"

"Some eighty in each ship. But – these are seamen. Not accustomed to marching and land-fighting. Kendal would never serve. This Carnforth? Where is it?"

"Some ten miles to the south. Inland. On the road to Lancaster."

"Inland. Then I cannot get my ships near to it?"

"No."

"Lancaster you could reach," Bethoc said. "On the Lune estuary. A wide and deep river. But it is a strong place. It was a Roman fortress once. How many Angles will be there, Duncan?"

"It is their main base for South Cumbria. Many hundreds."

"I could put four hundred against it if I could get my ships close. Surprise it. By night."

"You would risk that?" Duncan of Arnside asked.

"To be sure. If it would help to arouse others. But – these shallows and tides? Surprise would only be possible in darkness. And the tide might well not be right for that . . . "

"The tide matters little there. That is why Lancaster is important, and always was on this coast. The River Lune is sufficiently deep. It can be sailed up at all tides. Getting your ships through the sands outside requires guidance, although the channel is fairly wide. Better than any other in the bay. The Romans marked it with posts, they say. But these are gone. But I could guide you. It is not very dark in May . . . "

"You would do that?"

"I will do better than that. I will give one hundred swordsmen to add to your seamen."

The abbess actually clapped her hands. "When, Duncan?" she demanded.

"Give me a day. If this prince will do it."

Riagan said that he could add his two score.

"Then I must come to see it all!" Bethoc asserted.

All the men protested, but that lady jutted out her small chin, and they desisted.

It was half-dark and half-tide both, as the flotilla turned into the Lune channel, from some three miles out, having rowed round from the Levens estuary. The ships might possibly be seen from the shore, near to midnight as it was, but that would be only from the tip of the Lancaster peninsula. The town and fort itself was fully six miles upriver, and the probability of anyone hurrying off all that way at this hour to warn the Anglian garrison was remote indeed.

Duncan stood with Kenneth, Bethoc and Riagan at the prow of the leading longship, to shout directions to the helmsman at the steering-oar. For a mile or so there was little to show that they were in fact in any channel, the waters of the shallows in that faint light seeming all of a sameness to the uninitiated. But evidently the chieftain knew the secret of their approach, for presently they began to see sandbanks appearing on either side and yet deep enough water on their flanks also, and ahead. Soon they were in a recognisable channel, a river almost one hundred yards wide through the sands, winding occasionally but mainly fairly straight.

As the loom of the land neared, it looked as though they were faced with a solid blank barrier. Duncan explained briefly – for he was a man of few words – that the river-mouth proper was narrow, and bent between two small headlands. There would be a strong current here for the oarsmen to contend with, but beyond it opened out considerably.

This proved to be an accurate forecast, and in single file the ships entered the narrows. It was strange how much darker it suddenly seemed, as the rowers strained against the river's rush. Then quite quickly they were out into what they would have called a sea-loch at home, perhaps half a mile wide, and the mirk lightened again somewhat, although not sufficiently to make visible the details of the shores. Lancaster town lay five miles ahead.

Bethoc was most unsuitably excited for any abbess. Always she had wanted to do something like this, she said. She was eager to know Kenneth's plans, but he shook his head. He had to wait until he saw the terrain and problems.

They reckoned that it would be only three hours or so to dawn, and they had still to reach the town. It was impossible to see features once they got that far, even when close to what Duncan called the harbour, although it was scarcely that. But this Lancaster was evidently not a very large place despite its fame, clustering round no very impressive eminence on which would be the fort, the Lune Castra of the Romans.

Silence enforced on all, they made their landing at a riverside wharf, the longships mooring broadside-on to each other so that men could clamber over from one to another and ashore. There appeared to be no stirring in the lanes and alleys of the town, no lights showing.

Kenneth marshalled his force of over five hundred, with whispered commands, Duncan adding his terse warnings. They would move forward and upward in one long file at this stage, but to be ready to divide into two or more groupings for the assault, depending on what they found.

Apart from a barking dog or two they encountered no obvious viewers or attention in the streets. If any were awake to observe them, their numbers would no doubt inhibit any challenge here – although it might well be assumed in the town that they were some new Anglian arrivals. It was when they got up to the fortress ramparts and gates that Kenneth perceived that, as a base, it was much smaller than he had anticipated. He said as much to Duncan, as they halted, peering, in the shadow of the last of the houses.

"You said many hundreds here," he reminded. "There is not room in this fort for such numbers."

"No. Many of the men will be quartered in the town."

That set Kenneth thinking anew. This could both aid and complicate their attempt. The actual fort might be taken the more readily; but with the inevitable noise and strife, garrison-members billeted in the town could be roused and come up to the aid of their fellows, attacking the attackers in the rear. He ordered two groups of about seventy each to detach themselves, therefore, and to act as rearguards to bar any reinforcements from reaching the fort area.

As to the assault itself, he and Duncan made a quiet circuit of the walling. Presumably there were guards, sentries, on duty; but no alarm had been raised. They could be in a guardroom, and making only periodic rounds. Or they could be asleep. After all, presumably Lancaster had never before been attacked, and there would be no reason to fear anything of the sort.

Back at his people, Kenneth, using his skippers as leaders, along with Duncan's men, held a brief council. They had brought grapnels and ropes from the ships. Small groups would go round the perimeter and, as nearly as possible all at the same time, hurl the roped grapnels up and over the ramparts, to fasten within, and use the knotted ropes to haul their members up and over. There were two gates, one north, one south. Grapnel teams to concentrate in the vicinity of these, and if possible, once inside, seek to unbar those massive wooden doors. If that was not feasible, then the rest of the attackers would have to go and follow them up the various ropes. So quiet was the watchword at this stage – and prayers that the Angles slept deeply. The main residue would wait meantime – and the Abbess Bethoc to keep well back and out of harm's way.

It was a strange sensation to stand there in the half-dark of that pre-dawn hour, straining ears for tell-tale sounds, doing nothing, but ready for immediate if unspecified action, expecting any moment to hear shouts, cries, hubbub, before or behind them – but in fact hearing only the swish of the wind and the calls of night-birds. Men fidgeted and shuffled, but very quietly.

In fact, the first sound Kenneth heard was a heavy creaking – and it took him some moments to realise that this was the great gate, some hundred yards in front of him, being opened. Almost immediately afterwards there was a thin scream, which lifted hairs on the backs of men's necks, followed by a shout, then more shouting. But by that time Kenneth was on the move, leading his men in a race for that half-opened gate. In they poured, swords, spears and dirks in hand.

It was chaos thereafter, no coherent leadership or

command possible, as men overran the fortress's hutments and barracks, to kill, kill. It is said that men sleep soundest just before dawn, and certainly those Angles were no exception, most only wakening in time to die. There was noise now aplenty, most of it horrible.

Kenneth did not join in the slaughter, concerned with the overall situation. He stationed himself on the highest point that he could find, where he could, as far as possible, see and be seen by his own people here, and at the same time watch for any approaches from the town, any sound of conflict from there – although it would be hard to identify such, from any distance, from the clamour near at hand. Of the latter, in fact, he got no impression of any unified stand, any real battling, the shrieks and yells and clashes coming from scattered points, mostly muffled by walls, indoors. Nobody came to report to him, any more than the town appeared to erupt defenders.

Presently he heard Duncan's unmistakably gruff voice shouting commands not far away, and he went down to find him. That man was clearly in his element, sword dripping blood, ordering his men, unnecessarily, to spare none. He actually shouted laughter to Kenneth, the first such they had had from him, that it was all over, these Anglian dogs at least now asleep for good.

It seemed to Kenneth all too easy to be true. But everywhere men were shouting the same news. The fort was theirs, no real resistance save by individuals, surprise complete.

Now Kenneth transferred his attentions to the town. Admittedly there was still less probability of any united counter-attack from there, if men were scattered amongst many houses; nevertheless it could be that most of the garrison was in fact there rather than in the fort. But there was still no sign or sound of fighting, above the noise here, and no courier come from the groups sent to deal with the possibility.

He hurried down and out of the gate, to find Bethoc alone – or not quite alone, for she was kneeling beside a fallen man clearly in the last throes, seeking to comfort him, an Angle who must have rushed out through the open gateway, to collapse here. Her voice was trembling and when she recognised Kenneth she rose and flung herself into his arms, sobbing. Undoubtedly she had had enough of warfare, even at long range.

He patted her head, murmured a few words meant to be soothing, and put her away gently, to head off for those town streets. The screams, mainly of women, were beginning to sound from there.

He found no groupings of his men now, only individuals and pairs running around with drawn dirks. He feared that there would have been a certain amount of indiscriminate slaughter in the dark houses, sleeping Angles and Cumbrians not being readily distinguishable in beds and blankets, especially with women alongside. Recognising that this was not his task as commander, he returned to the fort.

It took some time, and dawn had broken, before the jubilant and blood-crazed attackers could be rounded up into some sort of order. By that time the leaders of the town groups had reported that they had faced no organised resistance in the streets. Many Angles had escaped undoubtedly, fled into the night, but no massing to counter-attack, the leaders being probably up at the fort. Full daylight would reveal whether there was any significant assembling of them outside the town.

So, difficult as it was to realise, Kenneth found himself master of Lancaster meantime. He had to adjust his mind to the problems this brought with it.

The first and most pressing, of course, was to prevent his victorious force from indulging in an orgy of sack, loot and rape, in the town. There were few casualties to attend to, on their own side – and the enemy ones were beyond attention. Booty from the fort and the slain was of course allowable, but squabbling over it deplorable. Kenneth was anxious to get his men back to their ships as quickly as possible. Liquor had been discovered in the fort and was having its effect. Duncan's men were a problem, and went their own way.

It was well into the forenoon before he got a somewhat subdued Bethoc down to the harbour, leaving the town in a turmoil, the complaining citizenry scarcely realising how fortunate they were to survive the night. No opposition had developed from the Angles who had escaped, indeed there was no sign of any amongst the surrounding slopes and woodland. Presumably they would be back later; or they might make for Carnforth or Kendal or some other base.

A conference was held at the wharfside. There would be eventual Anglian reaction, most certainly – but how quickly? Carnforth was barely a day's march away, Kendal two. There was no point in seeking to hold Lancaster. Kenneth wondered about making his tour of the chief ones with this news; but both Duncan and Bethoc advised against this meantime. The entire area would be swarming with Angles hereafter, urgent to avenge, and to contain any further threat to their power, out of this their first defeat in years hereabouts. Not only would Kenneth himself be endangered, but his presence would be a danger to the said chiefs and landed men – not the best time to approach them. Much better to leave it, let the tidings of what they had done penetrate to all parts of Cumbria, and rouse the spirits of the folk. Duncan and Bethoc, and Riagan too, would presently make sundry visits; and later, when the hue and cry had died down, Kenneth could come back and try to organise his projected rising, his fame and prowess assured.

On reflection, this seemed sound advice. The Angles everywhere would be on their guard now, and further surprise attacks unlikely to succeed. Sufficient then for the moment.

So it was all aboard, and back down the Lune estuary and into Morecambe Bay, the tidal conditions almost exactly the same as when they had come up, all achieved in twelve hours. They put Duncan and his people ashore at Arnside, hoping that they would not suffer for this adventure, and sailed on to Ravenglass, to spend the night there.

Bethoc had recovered her spirits but clearly had had her eyes opened as to the realities of warfare, and preferred not to talk of them. But she was no less enthusiastic about throwing off the Anglian yoke, and the notion of a Celtic alliance. Even the dream of uniting the Celtic peoples she found acceptable, by the time they said goodnight, and Kenneth decided that he had made a useful partisan as well as a friend.

Next morning, it appeared that she was not yet quite in the mood to resume her duties at the nunnery, and would remain there at Ravenglass for a little longer. So, although

Riagan offered to introduce Kenneth to the sport of spearing salmon in the shallows of Duddon Sands, he declined. His men would be glad to get back to their hay-harvest sooner than anticipated, for they nearly all combined farming with fishing for their livings. And he had his own duties to return to. But he would be back.

The parting with Bethoc was frankly warm, she only remembering to give him an abbatial blessing as something of an afterthought.

14

Kenneth's return to Galloway was to dire news. There had
been a great Norse attack on eastern Alba, in the Moray
area, scarcely just a raid but more of an invasion, allegedly
from Iceland; and in seeking to repel it, the High King Drust
mac Constantine and his deputy, Talorcan of Angus had
both fallen. The Scandinavians were still in possession of
large tracts of the Moray coastline – and the Albannach high
throne was vacant once more, after so brief an interval. The
ri had hastily decided not to appoint another interim, but to
elevate Ewan mac Angus right away. That young man was
now leading forces to repel the invaders, and calling for help
from his brother-in-law, Aed mac Boanta of Dalriada, and
from Alpin of Galloway also. This situation put Kenneth's
Cumbrian venture very much to the back of his mind meantime. Almost certainly this heavy Norse assault on the
Albannach east coast, where there had been only small
sporadic raids previously, would again be a kind of retaliation for Kenneth's own campaigns in the Hebrides, Man
and Ireland; and therefore he felt some responsibility. Also,
his Celtic alliance policy advocated help in such circumstances. And he liked Ewan, Eithne's brother. So he agreed
that Galloway must respond to the appeal. But the Moray
coast of Alba was a long way off, many hundreds of miles.
To lead a marching army thither would take weeks; and to
sail his ships there would mean going right up through the
Hebrides and round the very topmost tip of the land, along
between Orkney and Caithness, and then down the east
coast, not far off eight hundred miles, he reckoned.

In a quandary, Kenneth decided that, despite its length
and difficulties, the sea passage was preferable to the overland marching. It would take no longer, possibly less time,
the latter with endless hills and mountain passes to be
covered and great firths and estuaries to round; moreover, a

fleet would be of more use against the Norsemen, once there, than weary marchers. His father concurred, critical somewhat of Kenneth having been away on this unnecessary Cumbrian affair when he had been needed for a more important service.

So it was a matter of assembling more ships and mustering more men, to make a sizeable force, three times as large as he had taken to Cumbria. It came to him that he might call on Roderick of Strathclyde, to honour his admittedly vague commitment to aid in a common endeavour; but that would take some considerable time, to convince the less-than-war-like monarch, and then to put together a fleet. And Ewan would be needing prompt help, sufficiently delayed as his own must be. Lesser numbers sooner would be of more use than greater later. However, Dalriada might be different. He would have to pass close to Dunadd, on his way, and probably could raise more ships speedily there – that is, if Aed mac Boanta had elected to go overland to Moray rather than by sea, as seemed likely. Eithne would help, for her brother's sake, assuredly.

Only six days after his return therefore, Kenneth and Donald set sail for the north, with a score of longships, the hay-harvest having to be left to the women and oldsters, his crews making only conventional complaint. He assessed that it would take at least twelve days to reach Moray, even at their fastest, and with reasonably favourable winds, this allowing for two days at Dunadd.

All this, however, was made invalid three days later when they arrived in Dalriada, to discover that the situation was entirely changed. Only the day previously a messenger had come from King Aed, now it seemed at Inverness, to an-nounce that the Norsemen had suddenly returned to their ships and sailed off, apparently back to Iceland. This with-out any new major battle, although in the face of Ewan's forces. Why was unclear – but of course these Scandinavians were preferably raiders, pirates, swift slayers rather than campaigners and occupiers of lands. Possibly they had achieved what they had set out to do, to kill, terrorise and punish.

Queen Eithne, greeting Kenneth most warmly, imparted this news. So there was no need to muster Dalriadan ships, no reason for Kenneth to go on northwards. In fact, reason that he should remain there at Dunadd meantime, for Aed's messenger had said that, to celebrate this Norse withdrawal – which could, for purposes of morale, be claimed a victory – and to both emphasise Ewan's leadership and better establish his new kingship, he and Aed had decided to make a sort of pilgrimage of thanksgiving to St Columba's shrine at Iona, there to have the traditional ordination and anointing ceremony. Undoubtedly Kenneth and his father would be invited to attend this – so he might as well just wait for it, for the message was that it was to take place forthwith. No point in going away back to Galloway and then returning almost straight away.

Kenneth was somewhat doubtful – not about the pleasure of remaining in Eithne's company in the interim, but in the propriety of Ewan being anointed at Iona, as High King. Columba had instituted this anointing for the Kings of Dalriada, not Alba. Admittedly Ewan's father and his uncle had both been anointed at Iona, but that was as Kings of Dalriada, before they gained the high kingship. Ewan had never been King here. Might not this seem to establish some sort of overlordship of Dalriada? Especially with Aed mac Boanta, an Albannach, appointed by the late High King Angus as monarch here? Was this a bid for paramountcy – possibly inspired by Aed?

Eithne did not think so, asserting that her brother would never think that way, whatever Aed might do. If Kenneth felt perturbed, then the best thing that he could do was to wait at Dunadd for Ewan's arrival, and then put the matter to him personally. It could be made clear at Iona that the anointing was for the Albannach throne, certainly not for the Dalriadan.

That appeared to be the sensible course, as well as the pleasurable one. But there was no point in keeping all the Galloway men there, idle and probably getting into mischief, when they should be harvesting their hay at home. So, after only a couple of days, Donald was sent back to Garlies with the fleet, Kenneth retaining only a couple of ships at Port an Deora.

Thus commenced a totally unexpected but joyful interlude – although sometimes taxing for them both – all in the cause

248

of good relations between Dalriada and Alba. Eithne, who had very feminine and practical ideas about worship, declared confidently that it was all a direct answer to prayer.

It was on Kenneth's fourth day at Dunadd, with both of them being very discreet and careful in Aed's palace and amongst his councillors – although they did manage to have an unaccompanied ride together on occasion into the hills surrounding on the east – that another courier arrived from Inverness. This was from Aed, announcing that he and Ewan expected to reach Dunadd, with the Dalriadan force, in some ten days' time; and instructing his wife and chief men to have all ready for the High King's reception there, and also to go to Iona and prepare matters there for the ceremonial, making all necessary arrangements with the clerics. Despite this somewhat peremptory demand, neither of them found fault. A visit to Iona together would be no hardship, indeed Kenneth could think of few things more enjoyable. There was much that he wanted to show that young woman on the island.

Next day, then, they set off northwards, in one of Kenneth's ships, taking Conall with them, glad to be able to sail off together without the danger of critical comments, in fact on Aed's orders. They took along with them Prior Phadraig of Ballymeanach, who had performed the ceremony on Dunadd Hill for Aed, since there were now no clerics on Iona itself. They followed the usual route up the Sound of Jura, passing heedfully the Strait of Corryvreckan, and out into the wide ocean just beyond Scarba and Luing, to avoid the Garvellach Isles and proceed due westwards now, parallel with the long Ross of Mull. Rounding the tip of this, with nearly sundown, they came to Iona in the evening light – and Eithne declared that she had never seen anything so lovely in her life, even though she had been here before. They were all a little prejudiced in favour of Iona, of course, that storied isle, Columba's own, the cradle of the faith, burial-place of kings from time immemorial and long before the advent of Christianity, the jewel of the Hebrides. But assuredly, apart from its fame and sacred connections, it was of scenic beauty extraordinary even for that most colourful of seaboards, with its pure white sands shining through translucent water, its marble-green rocks and multi-hued seaweeds, its small bays and scattered skerries, modest green hills rising above the grassy machairs to the heather-clad Dun I. Admittedly closer inspection revealed spoliation, the ravages of the Norsemen, whitewashed cot-houses smoke-stained, barns and byres burned down, walls cast over. But overall the impression was fair beyond words, and Kenneth did not have to extol again his favourite spot on earth. Prior Phadraig, however, who had to visit here on occasion as deputy for the abbot in far-away Ireland, observed that in a winter's gale or under grey storm-clouds, even Iona could look less enchanting.

Columba's abbey being in ruins, the manses destroyed, and no accommodation available for visitors other than in the humble cot-houses, Eithne, queen or none, made no objection to such quarters for the night. Nor did the prior; but Kenneth, ever aware of the dangers of gossip, elected to sleep aboard ship.

The following day sufficed to make the arrangements for the ordination ceremony, orders given for tidying up and clearing wreckage, and ensuring that Tor Abb, where the anointing would take place, was cleared of sheep and cattle droppings, the Reelig Oran swept out, and the tombs of the kings made suitable for inspection. All this completed, they decided that the opportunity to spend another day in simple exploration of the island was too good to miss, with Kenneth eager to show Eithne all that so appealed to him here, she far from objecting. On her previous visit, they had been able to view only a little of it all. They did not think that the elderly Prior Phadraig would mind, nor wish to accompany them.

So, in the morning, the July weather remaining kind, they set off, alone at last, with a satchel of hard-boiled eggs, oatcakes and a comb of honey. Kenneth planned a circular tour of all the bays, headlands, valleys, machairs and so on. Iona was only three miles long and not much more than a mile wide, so that the project was not so daunting as it might sound; and they had all day.

He started by taking her to climb Dun I itself, the highest point of the island, although even so it was no mountain but a quite shapely hill rising some three hundred-odd feet above the sea, no very tiring ascent for an active young woman who had always enjoyed the outdoors – although even so she was panting a little before they reached the summit, at the pace Kenneth led, which however had the effect of giving that man enhanced pleasure in frank appreciation of her heaving bosom.

The views from the top were glorious, with all the Inner Hebrides spread before them and around them, backed by the mighty mainland mountains, with every colour of the spectrum adding to their delight. They sat for a little, companionably, soaking it all in, he pointing out isles, peaks, features, all the way to the Outer Isles. But they did not linger long, for there was so much to do, to see. They went downhill, northwards, hand-in-hand. Nobody would see them up here.

Kenneth particularly wanted to show her features connected with Columba, where he had contrived to make Iona all but self-supporting for his monks and trainee-missionaries. They saw where he had set up mills for grain, dug millponds, instituted a fish-hatchery, smoke-houses and fireplaces for preserving salmon, herring and mackerel, crab and lobster farms, a net manufactory, spinning and weaving sheds, a boat-building yard, even at the extreme northern tip of the island a walled-in enclosure in the waters of a bay, using skerries as breakwater linked by walling, as a haven for breeding seals, useful for their skins and their fat for making candles.

"He was a very practical man was your saint," Eithne commented. "He is your hero, Kenneth, is he not? The priest, not some great warrior, despite all your battlings and leading of men?"

"Columcille was a warrior too, and leader of men. But in a greater cause than any I can aim at. Yes, he was a practical man, although a prince of the Hy-Neill. One of the greatest men who ever lived, I believe. What better hero could a man have?"

After that furthest little peninsula, the scene changed and their mood with it, as they turned to proceed down the west coast. For this was very different from the east, where were the houses, the fields and cultivation rigs, the boatstrands and level ground. Here the shores were steep, rocky, with little cliffs, and hidden coves and tiny bays innumerable, no havens, where the great seas came surging in and broke on the myriad of skerries. They were not likely to see a soul on this side, as they clambered up and down rocky banks, along sea-pink ledges, and descended on to small, brilliant white cockle-shell beaches – all this demanding much masculine assistance and hand-holding. But they did see birds unnumbered, eiders crooning offshore, redshanks and oyster-catchers in the shallows, terns squabbling over tiny fish instead of doing their own fishing, guillemots swimming and diving, gulls of every description, and from behind, the haunting calling of cuckoos still in voice. Eithne, reared inland, was fascinated and delighted. There were many birds to be seen at Dunadd, of course, but not in this variety and in these numbers.

At one of the many sandy coves, where they could watch seals sunning themselves on the weed-hung rocks, they sat on the warm sand to eat their provender. But soon Eithne was up, had her shoes off and her skirts kilted up and was paddling in the clear waters, laughing as she splashed.

"Do you swim, Kenneth?" she called to him. "I like to swim. We had a pool in the Earn, at Forteviot. I swam with my brothers."

"I used to swim much, as a boy. At Port an Deora, and at Garlies too. I have not done if for long," he said, watching her.

She looked back to him. "I – I would swim now. But – I think not. Better not."

"No?"

"No. Not here – a joy as it would be. Crowning all this day's joy. But no. Not here. Not anywhere. With you." She turned away, so that he could only just hear her voice. "I fear, you see – fear that if I took off my clothing, I, we . . . we might well . . . go too far!" She paused. "I think that I know myself, you see. And you?"

He swallowed, but said nothing.

She looked back. "Do I speak foolishly, Kenneth? Unwisely? Immodestly?"

He rose, and went down to the water, and in, boots on, wading to her, to take her hand. "My dear," was all he said, then.

"Am I too frank?"

"Never that. You are brave, honest, truthful – as well as very lovely. And I, I am at once the most blessed and most cursed of men! Blessed in that you can say that to me, accursed in that I cannot have you – another man's wife. Do you think that every moment that I am with you, this is not in my mind, Eithne?"

She gripped that hand tightly. "Why, oh why should this have to be? Because my father thought otherwise, judged differently. It was so . . . wrong!"

"Yes. So wrong. Perhaps if I had spoken earlier? Sought your hand of him. But – who was I, heir only to small Galloway, to ask for the High King of Alba's daughter? I dared not . . . "

"You who have dared so much, my love!" She gulped something less than a laugh. "You see, I name you my love. I have never said that before, have I? Not to you. Only to myself. But – you knew it, I think? Very well?"

He nodded. "I hoped, believed it, yes." He drew her round to gaze into her eyes, gripping her with both hands now, there in the shallows. "But hearing it, I do not know whether my heart sings, or breaks!"

She held up her lips to him.

They clung together for a while, urgent. Then she drew back.

"You see? How it is? We have to be strong. Stronger. Or, or . . . "

"Yes. God help us, yes!" He turned, and led her back out of the water.

They sat again, silent for a little, until Eithne spoke. "Am I a sinful woman? A poor and faithless wife for Aed? I do not give him all that a wife should. He knows that I do not love him. I try to be a fair queen to him, if not a wife. He gets what a man needs from women, elsewhere. Always has done. But – for me to *love* another! Is that a sin?"

"How can love be sin? Real love? Some sorts of what men can call love, yes. But not true affection, the heart's adoring, surely? Not that. Aed married you because you were the High King's daughter. He has got what he wanted . . . "

"But not a child, not an heir! I fail him there."

"For which I thank heaven!"

253

"That could be a sin also, could it not? *Yours*. So many sins. Because we love. But mine the worst. I deprive Aed, in some measure, of what should be his. Even you I may deprive, Kenneth."

"Me? How could that be?"

"You must have a man's needs also. And because of me, fail to receive them. At least, you have not married . . . "

"Nor intend to."

"But you will desire an heir also, one day, will you not? When you are King of Galloway. And meantime? You have a man's body, with its . . . requirements. You can take other women, of course. As Aed does. But . . . that will not fully satisfy, I think?"

He shook his head.

"You must meet many women who could attract you. For you are an attractive man to women, my dear. You must know that. Some must offer themselves? You must often feel the need. That Queen Cathira you told me of, in Oriel? Was I wrong in thinking that she sought to show you . . . special kindness? Even this strange abbess in Cumbria? Do some tempt you? Oh, I should not ask . . . !"

"Thus far, I have not fallen, lass!"

"I am not saying that you should resist, Kenneth. How could I urge that? So long as you always *love* me! And I you. In our strange compact. Other women could not harm that."

"Other women will not have opportunity, I say!"

They thought it safer to leave it at that, and to concentrate, if they could, on the darting swallows and sand-martins and the bobbing eiders. Presently, going to wash their honey-sticky fingers in the ripples, Eithne put on her shoes, and they moved on.

Round a little headland, they came to the largest bay of the island, over half a mile across, called for some reason the Bay of the Twins' Neuk, or Corner. On the heights above this, Kenneth led the way to a great circle of standing-stones, with a central altar-block, and told her that there were others like this on Iona, relics of the days when the island was famed for a different sort of worship, sun-worship and human sacrifice; indeed the seat of a druidical college, where the Reelig Oran was now. Columba's colleagues had wanted to cast them all down, as monuments of evil, sins in

254

stone; but the saint had forbidden it. They represented *worship*, he had insisted, mistaken yes, but man's recognition that there were powers and lights greater than their own. Bless these instead, even use them for the true worship of Almighty God, since they were places that the people turned to. Columba later even built churches within stone circles. Some have declared this folly, even sin on his part, failure to overthrow the evil past. So, there were sins and sins . . .

At the very south-western end of the island they came to Kenneth's most favoured spot of all, the Bay of the Currach, where Columba had first set foot on Iona, a shallow lagoon of sheer loveliness, the sand below the water so pure and smooth that the delicate colours, amethyst, azure, emerald, beryl and golden, were as though painted on white canvas, while the bright ruby, magenta, olive and saffron of the enclosing weed-decked rocks were reflected as a luminous frame. Eithne exclaimed with joy.

"Here is where he arrived, saw, and could not contain himself," Kenneth recounted. "He leapt over the side of the ship which had brought them from Ireland, no coracle but a sea-going vessel, with his twelve companions and the crew, the first to land – or not in fact to land, but to plunge into these shallows and wade ashore, shouting his praise of it all, to kneel and kiss the dry sand, thanking his Creator for bringing him to the fairest place on God's earth. He had seen a heron stalking these shallows, and took it as a sign – for that bird, a crane as he called it, was his symbol. I had hoped that there might be one here today, for I have seen them here . . . "

"Never mind. There are those big birds stretching their wings out there on a skerry. They will do instead . . . "

"Cormorants. They dry their feathers that way. It is said that Columba used tamed cormorants, tied on a line, to dive for fish from a boat. Whether that is true or not, I do not know . . . "

"I think that I will believe anything of your hero, Kenneth! This place is beautiful beyond words. Oh, I could swim here! But, no. *No! Come.*" And taking his arm almost fiercely, she turned inland.

They headed back now for the east-side haven where their

longship lay. On the way, set on the slightly higher ground above the green machair, they passed a small loch, the only one on the island. And there, amongst the reeds, they saw a heron pacing in stately fashion on its long, spindly legs.

"That is all that we needed," Kenneth said simply.

As they came down to the area of the ruined abbey, the Reelig Oran and the royal tombs, Eithne halted. "I want to thank you for this day, Kenneth-of-my-Heart. It has been beyond all in delight. A day to remember all my life. Your care, your sharing all this with me. Aye, and your restraint! Not all men would have behaved so, with a woman. And, I fear, a weak woman. Thank you."

"If you are a weak woman, then I have yet to meet a strong one! But – the thanks are mine. What you have shown me, told me, today, makes me the proudest man in this land – if scarcely the happiest!"

They went to find Prior Phadraig.

On the morrow they sailed back to Port an Deora.

The arrival of the High King and Aed at Dunadd, with the Dalriadan force, created a great flurry and ferment, a major impression, as it was intended to do. For this was to be a victory celebration and demonstration, to help counter the effects of the disasters, defeats and deaths of Drust and Talorcan on the Alba east coast. Morale was to be restored. In fact, there had been no real victory, but the unexpected sailing away of that major Norse invasion fleet was something to celebrate.

Ewan mac Angus was glad to see Kenneth with his sister, whether Aed mac Boanta was or not. He had not changed with his elevation to the high kingship, still the boyish, cheerful enthusiast. Whether he would make the monarch Alba required in present circumstances remained to be seen; but at least he had spirit and energy. He was greatly looking forward to his anointing at Iona. Kenneth told him of his Cumbrian venture, and what success there could mean for the Celtic cause. Aed listened without comment.

There were feasting and parading and sporting contests for the next few days, while notables assembled from near and far, all in the cause of national animation and encouragement, with Aed very much in charge, Eithne acting the

256

gracious queen and Ewan being treated by all as lofty figurehead, despite scarcely looking the part. Donald arrived back from Garlies bringing his father, whose appreciation of it all was only moderate. To Kenneth, although he played his part, the entire performance appeared a little artificial and, worse than that, seemed almost calculated to imply that Dalriada, and therefore Galloway also, was under Albannach overlordship. Not that Ewan personally gave that impression, but Aed did. It occurred to Kenneth that just possibly Aed was looking to the future and, if some disaster was to descend upon Ewan, as clearly could so readily happen, then *he*, married to the High King's sister, might step up to the high throne himself. Perhaps Kenneth was prejudiced.

The day dawned for the great expedition to Iona. Quite a fleet sailed from Port an Deora, with all the notables, Prior Phadraig now distinctly agitated, otherwise a holiday atmosphere prevailing. Passing the Strait of Corryvreckan's entrance, Ewan was eager to see the notorious whirlpool where Kenneth had lured the Norsemen to their doom, and disappointed that they could see nothing very exciting from this distance. None suggested that they should go closer, however.

The weather was less kind than it had been for Eithne's and Kenneth's visit, with grey skies and a strong westerly breeze. But at least it did not rain – which would have made a sorry business out of a wholly out-of-doors programme. The oarsmen were urged to row at their best pace, for even so it would be a six-hour voyage to Iona, and, as there was no suitable accommodation in that ravaged isle for such illustrious company, or indeed for any sizeable company, a return was planned for the same day. The actual ceremony would not take very long; and at least the wind should be in their favour going back.

They reached the island, having started early advisedly, just after midday, and even under these skies the place looked quietly lovely, seeming to glow with its own colours and warmth, those white sands a source of light.

No time was wasted in preliminaries, Aed apparently intent on getting everything over as quickly as possible, not a man for ceremonial. To Kenneth at least it seemed somehow

257

all a waste of Iona's magic, if not a sacrilege.

After paying brief and perfunctory respects at the tombs of the kings, they moved on directly to Tor Abb, the hillock above the abbey ruins where Columba had had his own stark little cell. Here a bench had been brought up, and planks laid on the stones of the cell to form a table of sorts. Prior Phadraig's acolyte brought up a basket, containing a handsome altar-cloth to drape over the planks, bread and wine for the Eucharist, and a flask with the oil. The three kings, Eithne, Kenneth and Donald, climbed up, with the celebrant, and the rest of the company ranged themselves around lower down. The High King sat on the bench.

The prior, whether infected by Aed's attitude, or unsure of himself and anxious to get it all over, certainly did not delay. Ewan was hardly seated, looking self-conscious with everyone else standing, when the cleric plunged straight into a very truncated version of the communion service, many of the onlookers not aware that he was doing so and continuing to chatter and gaze around. Aed barked an order, which although it gave Phadraig a fright, at least stilled the talk. The consecration proceeded expeditiously.

Distribution of the sacred elements thereafter was only for the royal party, and Kenneth, for one, had never experienced less of a feeling of sanctity, despite the spot where it was taking place. Without pause, the prior then picked up the flask of oil, blessed it with a few words and the Sign of the Cross and went with it to Ewan's side. That young man, uncertain whether to stand or remain seated, had the oil promptly poured on his head, above the gold circlet, while still undecided, in the name of Father, Son and Holy Spirit. And that was apparently that. Phadraig stepped back, with evident relief.

It took a few moments for all concerned to realise that this was all, that this was what they had come fifty miles to see. Men eyed each other, wondering.

Aed found his voice first. "Hail, the High King! Hail the High King!" he shouted. "Hail!"

The cry was taken up, almost thankfully, as though this at least was something positive and effective that all could do, and the hailing and cheering went on.

Aed led again. He strode over to Ewan, dropped on one

knee before him, and taking his brother-in-law's hand in his own two, kissed it. Rising, and bowing, he looked over at Alpin, invitingly.

That man hesitated, and glanced at Kenneth, who gave a brief shake of the head. Alpin turned, offered a slight bow to Ewan, and stood still.

There was an uncomfortable pause. Aed stared at Kenneth, who also inclined his head towards Ewan but did not stir from his position. That kneeling and hand-kissing was the sign of fealty, of acceptance of overlordship, paramountcy, of the High King of Alba. The ruler of Dalriada ought not to have done it. Galloway certainly would not.

Eithne it was who brought the situation back to seemly normality. She moved forward to her brother's side, raised him up to his feet and putting her arms round him gave him a sisterly kiss of congratulation. That raised another cheer, and smiling, Ewan waved to all. It is probable that few there recognised the full importance of what had taken place and what had not.

Aed looked grim, and began to stalk downhill, until he recollected and held back for the anointed one to precede him.

The ceremony had had a certain significance after all.

There was a marked coolness between Aed mac Boanta and the Galloway trio, although Ewan and his sister did not show it.

A return was made to the ships forthwith, no further proceedings called for.

The Galloway party did not linger at Dunadd thereafter, despite Ewan's urgings. Next morning they said their goodbyes, and it was noticeable that King Aed did not come down with them to Port an Deora although Ewan and Eithne did. The parting between Kenneth and Eithne, in the circumstances, had to be reserved, formal, however much their eyes spoke. Ewan urged Kenneth to come to visit him at Forteviot before too long.

It was with a very empty feeling that Kenneth sailed southwards down the Sound of Jura.

15

It was the following spring that Kenneth, about to set off on his projected visit to Cumbria again, was constrained to change his mind and plans, and drastically. This was caused by the unlooked for arrival at Garlies of a fleet, a somewhat motley one, not of invaders but of what might almost be called refugees. Not that Godfrey mac Fergus of Oriel would have named them that, allies rather, but in distress. For this was his fighting force, yes – or the survivors thereof, dispossessed, seeking refuge and aid.

It had never occurred to Kenneth that his enrolling of Godfrey in his alliance project would work out thus.

He learned that the dreaded Thorgesr, from Norway itself, had come with an enormous fleet of dragon-ships to Ireland, early in the season for this hosting. Though this in fact had been no hosting but full-scale and determined invasion. The size of the fleet which came to the North might be gauged by the fact that a detachment sent southwards from it to assail the Dublin area itself comprised some sixty-five ships. The main force had remained in the North, sweeping up the loughs, invading one kingdom after another, and before any of them had had time to form any united opposition. All had fallen – Donegal, Connaught, Aileach, Tyrone, Dalriata, then Oriel itself. Complete occupation and control was not won, of course; but the kings were all in hiding if not slain, their capitals taken and forces dispersed. Now Thorgesr was calling himself King of Ulster, or all Northern Ireland, and was seeking to bring Louth, Meath and Dublin under his heathen sway also. He, Godfrey, had only escaped by something of a miracle, with this residue. He had put his wife Cathira on Man, where she had kin, and come on here, seeking the aid of Prince Kenneth, which they had discussed.

That man was, of course, appalled. This was worse than

anything he had visualised, all the Irish North overrun in one swift onslaught, making a mockery of all his own puny and ineffective efforts at a united defence. This great fleet and army, and from Norway itself, under one of their most feared and successful warriors, must represent royal Norse policy, no raiding this but actual invasion and colonisation, to make of Ireland another Iceland, or Zetland, or Orkney. Had that major attack on north-east Alba the previous spring been something of a rehearsal for this?

What to do? To wait, to do nothing meantime, would be fatal for the entire conception of a Celtic alliance, quite apart from failing this Godfrey and the other Irish rulers. Some counter-stroke was necessary, and before long. But it would have to be a strong one, to take on this Thorgesr, no mere demonstration of intent would serve now. Could he persuade the kings on this side of the Irish Sea to join in sending a large enough force to tackle Thorgesr, with any hopes of success? Alba, Dalriada, Strathclyde. It was too soon for Cumbria to be of any use. Howell's successor on Man might join in, for that island must obviously feel greatly threatened. Mervyn of North Wales? All would perceive the Norse menace the more directly now – but would that be sufficient for what was required? And it would take time to organise . . .

Kenneth decided to go forthwith to see Ewan mac Angus at Forteviot. He was the most hopeful. And word of his adherence would help convince others. Almost certainly Aed mac Boanta would join in if Ewan did. With the promise of action from these two, Roderick of Strathclyde could be persuaded perhaps on the way back. He would take Godfrey with him, for added influence. Donald meantime would be assembling the maximum Galloway contingent, with Alpin's authority.

The quickest way to Fortrenn, of course, was up the Clyde estuary to Dunbarton by ship, then north-eastwards on horseback, as done before. So he would have a preliminary word with the always non-enthusiastic Roderick going, then hope to gain the desired adherence on their return. It was already late May. Could all be arranged, and a force assembled, in time to make the attempt in this campaigning season?

The voyage to Dunbarton, new to Godfrey, brought exclamations as to the dramatic isle of Ailsa Craig, the height of the mountains, first of Arran and then of Cowal. Nor had this king ever seen anything like Dunbarton Rock itself, and its extraordinary fortress-palace, which seemed to climb the steep escarpment as though clinging to the rockface. However, King Roderick proved not to be in residence, gone somewhere unspecified up the Clyde valley. So Kenneth hired horses, and leaving the longship to wait for them, set out with a modest escort for Fortrenn. He did not find Godfrey an enlivening companion; and he was not a man to be hurried, it seemed.

The journey through the Kilpatrick and Fintry Hills to the great moss of the infant Forth, therefore, took longer than heretofore. The sight of the mighty barrier of the Highland Line beyond the extensive flats seemed to daunt Godfrey; and Kenneth decided that, in any battle situation, here was not the man to choose to lead, even in a minor skirmish.

It took almost three days to reach Forteviot. Fortunately Ewan was only out hawking, not away in some remote part of his vast kingdom as might well have been, so they had no long wait.

Ewan mac Angus's reaction to their news was as anticipated, astonished, alarmed, but at once eager to try to do something about it all, more than ready to co-operate. He recognised all too clearly that if the Norsemen once became firmly established in Northern Ireland, in major strength, it would not be long before they were crossing those narrow seas to Alba, Dalriada and Strathclyde, in greatly more ambitious fashion than in the raids of the past. He would order immediate and fullest-scale mobilisation of men and ships. It would take time however for all the resources of far-flung Alba to be mustered. Meanwhile he himself would go to Aed mac Boanta at Dunadd, to engage him in the enterprise; he would co-operate to the full, assuredly. This would save Kenneth himself time for his other journeyings, to North Wales and to Man. That man was glad enough to avail himself of this offer, although he would have liked to see Eithne even for a brief meeting. Ewan would send word to Garlies when the Albannach and Dalriadan forces were assembled.

With minimum delay, then, they parted, and Kenneth led Godfrey back whence they had come, reasonably satisfied, assured that Ewan at least would not temporise and tarry.

They found Roderick returned to Dunbarton. Although not eager for involvement, that cautious monarch saw clearly enough the menace of having the Scandinavians actually settled in Ireland a bare score of miles from the entrance to his Firth of Clyde. He reluctantly agreed to contribute his part in the projected expedition, his wealth in shipping, even though not mainly war-vessels, of great value for transporting the armed forces necessary for this attempt, which would demand land warfare as well as sea. Roderick and Godfrey seemed to suit each other. Kenneth was urgent to be off, with so much more to be done. Since the two monarchs seemed to get on well together, he decided to leave Godfrey at Dunbarton meantime, he hoped to spur on Roderick in the assembly of men and vessels, while he himself sailed off southwards at speed. This suggestion was well received.

Back at Garlies, Kenneth found the Galloway mobilis-ation going well, a large contingent already assembled, and proving a nuisance to the Garlies folk, to Alpin's annoyance, the bay there full of ships, Donald coping effectively. Spend-ing only the one night at home, Kenneth set off again, for Cumbria this time.

He had not much hope of any useful Cumbrian assistance, but it was on his way to Wales, and even a token involve-ment in a major venture might help to bring about a greater commitment to the cause. So he called in at St Bees. Abbess Bethoc was delighted to see him, and assured him that she would do all to help that she could. She had no ships, of course, but could raise forty men. Riagan of Ravenglass had two ships, and she could add her people to his – she seemed to have no doubts as to her kinsman's willingness to contrib-ute. So once again she sailed on with Kenneth down the Cumbrian coast to the Esk estuary, and at Ravenglass they did find Riagan mac Ewan entirely ready to play his part. He would personally bring his two vessels to join the Celtic fleet; indeed he thought that he could convince a neighbour to add another ship, which would help to carry the abbess's men.

Encouraged by this reaction, Kenneth was further enheartened to learn that these two had indeed been busy during the past year in seeking to arouse the other Cumbrian chiefs to contemplate armed revolt against the Anglian occupation, they believed with some success. Quite a few, stimulated by the Lancaster affair, had said that they would join in an uprising, if it was adequately organised and led. Not all were too happy with the idea of Duncan of Arnside as leader, for he was scarcely popular; but if Prince Kenneth himself were to come and take part, they thought that there would be a fair response, his fame having spread.

Spending the night at Ravenglass, Kenneth moved on next morning southwards, leaving Riagan to take Bethoc back to her nunnery. He managed to navigate the difficult sands, tides and channels of Morecambe Bay without mishap, and duly reached Arnside in the Levens estuary by midday. As before, he found armed men awaiting him on landing, but these quickly recognised the victor of Lancaster, and escorted him to Duncan's hallhouse in friendly fashion. That man himself was away at one of his other properties a few miles inland; but horses were provided to take Kenneth there.

Duncan was not the sort to express feelings, emotions or positive reactions of any sort, but he did at least exhibit no hostility towards his visitor, and received the news from Northern Ireland with a grim lack of comment. He admitted that he had found satisfaction amongst Cumbrians over the Lancaster victory – although that fortress had been quickly reoccupied and strengthened by the Angles – and some readiness to stage revolt amongst his fellow-landed men. As to joining in the projected attack on the Norsemen in Ulster, he was non-committal; but when Kenneth mentioned that Riagan mac Ewan and the Abbess Bethoc were contributing men, he gained the impression that Duncan would not allow himself to be outdone by such as these. He made no promises, but the impression was that a Cumbrian contingent would not be apt to sail without some element from Arnside and the Levens area.

The Welsh border was no great distance southwards from Morecambe Bay, for originally the two lands had joined. But in the year 613 there had been a grievous Celtic defeat at

264

Chester, and a wedge driven between, this by the Angles of Mercia. The Welsh drew back somewhat thereafter, and the present capital of King Mervyn of Gwynedd, or North Wales, was at Caernarfon beyond the great Isle of Mona. So Kenneth, on Duncan's advice, set sail in a south-by-west direction, well out from the coast, on the seventy-mile voyage to Bangor, at the mouth of the Strait of Menai, which apparently separated this Isle of Mona from the Welsh mainland. This, it seemed, would lead them through to Caernarfon.

It was oar-work all the way, with the wind in their faces. But with darkness very brief at this time of year, they kept going, with relays of rowers, throughout the night, and covered the distance by sun-up next morning.

The scene ahead of them now was not unlike that of their own West Highland coast, with narrow green coastal plains backed by great mountains. No strait, nor indeed any island, was evident as they approached the Welsh seaboard; but they had been warned of this, that Mona was a very flat island, almost featureless from the sea, and the strait-mouth narrow, looking like some modest sea-loch or estuary. The township, port and fort of Bangor were at the mouth of it, and they must call there to gain entrance.

Sure enough, as they neared land, they saw a community at what looked like the entrance to a loch. As they approached this, three galleys came out to meet them, bristling with armed men.

Kenneth's explanation of who he was, and that he had come to visit King Mervyn, was understood and accepted – the language was very similar to their own. Their longship was escorted into the Bangor harbour. There Kenneth had to land, and was taken under guard up to a fort where he was questioned by a suspicious chieftain who appeared to be the guardian of the Strait of Menai. He did not seem to have heard of Kenneth mac Alpin, and was prepared to be difficult. However, when on an inspiration Kenneth mentioned his visit to the late King Howell of Man, this individual's attitude changed. It seemed that Howell had been related to King Mervyn, and had in fact come from these parts. So Kenneth and his ship would be permitted to proceed through the strait, and a pilot provided. It seemed that they would require one.

The need was soon demonstrated. The strait was heavily guarded, by forts and booms, once they entered its narrows their pilot acting more as reassuring envoy than as guide to the waterway, to get them past the defences and defenders. The strait was very irregular in width, varying from over a mile to a mere two hundred yards. Its flanks were frequently quite spectacular, high and rocky and wooded on the mainland side, less so on the Mona banks to the west. Wherever it narrowed there were chains, barrages and fortlets to negotiate. These Welsh certainly did not intend invaders to descend upon them unawares. Another hazard was the tides, which rushed through the narrows at great speed, and with alarming rises and falls, which had to be allowed for in the adjustments of the chain barriers and booms. Their guide told them that there was a normal tidal rise and fall of fifteen feet but on occasion that could be doubled.

Fourteen miles or so of this and they could see ahead the broad waters of Caernarfon Bay, barred by sandspits, and to the mainland side of the strait was the Gwynedd capital of Caernarfon itself, a large town with a great fortress-palace. Once again armed galleys came out to intercept the longship. Kenneth had more explaining to do.

This time, however, he was not taken up to the fortress, for he was informed that King Mervyn was at present at another of his establishments, Harlech, some fifteen miles to the south, when he would return unknown. When Kenneth declared that he would sail thither, he was told that the fifteen miles was by land; by sea it would be nearer fifty, round the long Lleyn peninsula and Ynys Enlli into Tremadoc Bay.

Kenneth debated with himself whether to land and hire a horse to travel thus; but in a strange country, clearly very defence-conscious, he decided that it was better to take the longer sea-journey. Their pilot was quite prepared to accompany them further.

It was out of Caernarfon Bay, therefore, oar-work again into the south-west wind, between Mona and this long Lleyn peninsula. Dusk overtook them before they reached the headland, so not desiring to pass another night at sea, Kenneth put in at a small empty bay of shingle, not far from the point, where they could see a waterfall tumbling from the higher ground, to provide the necessary fresh water. They could all do with a good night's sleep, after stretching their legs.

In the morning, refreshed, they rounded the headland, with its little offshore isle of Ynys Enlli, and sailed down the other side into Tremadoc Bay, at good speed now with the wind behind them. Harlech lay near the head of this bay, its stern fortress rearing high above the town and coastal flats, an impressive place. As usual in this Gwynedd, their vessel was not allowed to approach without challenge. This time however only one craft came out to meet them, from the harbour – and Kenneth was by now sufficiently knowledgeable to recognise a Norse dragon-ship when he saw one, presumably a captured one. Perhaps this had some significance?

When the other craft came close, Kenneth noted that its dragon-prow had been painted bright red, as he had never seen with the Norsemen. A tall and good-looking youngish man stood beside this, gazing over at them.

"Who comes to Harlech in a ship-of-war?" this man demanded, his voice having the pleasant Welsh sibilance.

"If I came on warfare bent, I would come with more ships than this!" Kenneth gave back. "I am Kenneth of Galloway, seeking King Mervyn of Gwynedd."

"Kenneth? Galloway? You are . . . that Kenneth? The Norse-Slayer?"

"Kenneth mac Alpin, yes. And I do not love Norsemen, no! And you are in a Norse dragon-ship?"

"Yes, indeed." The other barked a laugh. "Here is a fair meeting. I am Rotri ap Mervyn. And this ship I was given as a gift by my kinsman, Howell of Man, just before he died. He said that you, Kenneth, had given it to him, after you had captured it!"

It was Kenneth's turn to laugh. "Yes, yes. I left two of these Norse ships with him. Here is a strange chance. I see that you have painted its dragon red."

"To be sure. The Red Dragon is our Welsh symbol. The Scandinavians do not own all the dragons!" He gestured to his steersman to bring his craft's prow round close, so that he could leap nimbly on to the Galloway ship, coming to grasp

Kenneth's hand. "This is a good meeting, friend Kenneth!"

"You are King Mervyn's son?"

"His only son, yes. You have come far to see him? We watched you sail into this bay . . . "

As the two ships were rowed together to the harbour, Kenneth told the Prince Rotri something of his mission and quest. The other heard him with interest, and more than interest, interjecting comments and questions, none in any way hostile. By the time that they landed it was clear that here was a potential ally.

But as they climbed the steep hill to the palace, Rotri warned Kenneth that his father might be less enthusiastic. King Mervyn, as he had grown older, had become less warlike, although he had been quite a fighter in his day. He sought the peaceful life, and was loth to engage in hostilities – too loth, in Rotri's opinion, with the Mercian Angles, and now the Saxons of Wessex, threatening and raiding over their borders, his father too apt to rely on their mountain barriers for protection. He might take some convincing . . .

At the hilltop fortress they found the elderly monarch surrounded by books and scrolls and papers, at work on his chosen task, writing a history of the Welsh people, an unusual occupation for a ruler. He greeted Kenneth kindly enough, however, and learning his identity, after calling for refreshments, plunged almost at once into the subject of the Gododdin, assuming that his visitor would be well versed in this, coming from Galloway. Kenneth, although he had of course heard of the all but legendary Gododdin, knew very little about them, having to explain that although he was Prince of Galloway he was really of the Dalriadan royal house, and had only come to Galloway in his youth, when his father became king there. So Mervyn proceeded to instruct him, while Rotri made faces behind his sire's back.

The Gododdin were, in fact, Southern Picts or Albannach of the Lothian region south of Forth – where the battle with Athelstan had taken place. Kenneth had seen their former capital, Traprain Law or Dunpender, just before that battle. During the Roman occupation, these people were not exactly conquered but did not resort to war against the mighty invaders, as did the Northern Albannach, but chose to co-operate with them in some measure and so live in peace. Mervyn sounded far from apologetic about this, clearly, living in peace being a virtue with him. The Romans trained many of the young men of the Gododdin in their very effective kind of warfare; and at some stage in their relationship, in the early fifth century, persuaded a band of some three hundred of them, under a Prince Cunedda, to move down here to Wales, to help stiffen the resistance of the Welsh to the inroads of raiding bands from Ireland. These young men, warriors all, settled here in Gwynedd and never went back to Lothian, marrying Welsh women and becoming in time a sort of military aristocracy. He himself, Mervyn, was of that line. They had come south on their journey, through Galloway, and he had always understood that they had picked up some more of their band there, for it is said that they were of the same stock, Southern Picts. He was surprised, therefore, that Kenneth did not know more of all this.

Kenneth, recognising that to show interest in the subject was probably as good a way as any to gain the King's sympathy and possible co-operation, asked further questions, and learned how the Gododdin, or Votadini, which seemed to be another form of the word, had given names to a great many places in Gwynedd, indeed Gwynedd itself derived from the name Cunedda.

When, however, Kenneth began tentatively to put forward his proposition about Celtic co-operation, Mervyn accepted that it was a worthy notion but scarcely possible of fulfilment. And when it came to the matter of providing armed forces, the historian monarch was entirely negative. Rotri indicated his support for Kenneth but his father remained intractable. Eventually Mervyn agreed that if his son liked personally to take his dragon-ship to join the allied fleet in a venture against the Norse, he was welcome to do so, but that was all.

It was a very feeble contribution for North Wales, but better than nothing, in that it would imply acceptance in theory of the Celtic alliance. Kenneth had to be content with that.

And that was not all. For Rotri, despite his own support, advised against wasting further time by going south and seeking to enrol the other Welsh kingdoms, Powys, Gwent and Dyfed. He feared that no help would be forthcoming there meantime, for these had weakly entered into some sort of arrangement with their warlike neighbours, the Saxons of Wessex, paying tribute in exchange for non-invasion – although this did not in fact prevent constant localised Saxon raiding. They were not likely to upset this uneasy pact by joining a Celtic alliance. Exasperated, Kenneth pointed out that this was exactly what the projected alliance was for; that if only the Celtic nations would combine to show a united front against the Scandinavians and these Anglo-Saxons, all this raiding and invasion could be halted. Rotri accepted that, but declared that the more southerly Welsh kingdoms would require no little persuasion, and demonstrations of substantial success, before they would be ready to consider joining in. But he did agree that King Guriat of Man, who had succeeded Howell, would almost certainly be more helpful, since he was of all the most endangered by the Norsemen in Ireland. If Kenneth went to Man, now, he himself would accompany him, to add his persuasions.

Glad at least to involve Rotri further, and since time was of the essence, Kenneth said that they would sail next day.

It was only some sixty miles from the Welsh coast, at Llandudno, to the Isle of Man, and there was much coming and going between the two realms, especially with Welsh monarchs on the Manx throne.

With a great Red Dragon banner flying from the mast of Rotri's ship, the two vessels had no difficulty in entering harbour unopposed, and in being conducted up to Rushen's palace two miles inland from St Mary's Bay. King Guriat, a man of middle years, growing portly, was in residence, and welcomed his visitors warmly. There was no question, from the first, of his willingness, indeed almost eagerness, to join in any expedition against the Norsemen in Ireland, for he felt daily endangered by their near presence. It was only a question of time, undoubtedly, before he also was assailed. He would assemble his fullest strength forthwith, and be ready to join the fleet at whatever rendezvous was appointed.

Well satisfied, Kenneth said that probably some weeks would be required for all the various contingents to come together. This would best take place at Dunadd in Dalriada, where a large concentration of shipping could gather behind the lengthy bulk of Jura without becoming evident from seawards; for they did not want the Norse warned, if at all possible. A month hence, therefore, at Port an Deora, Dunadd. They must not delay longer than that.

Now Kenneth was anxious to be off, back to Galloway, for he had been away sufficiently long. But King Guriat was eager to display hospitality, and the civilities demanded that he stay for a day or two, Rotri urging it also. And Kenneth wanted to visit the nuns of St Mary's, who had been so helpful in the very different circumstances of his previous visit.

Two days later, then, they parted company. Rotri would stay a little longer, to help Guriat with his mobilising. They would meet again in one month.

Kenneth and his men, with a westerly wind behind them, covered the fifty-odd miles to Garlies in the one day, to find all going well with the Galloway assembly, Donald competent at the business, indeed all but ready to sail. There was no point, however, in leaving for Dunadd too soon, with the Galloway men at a loose end there, where there would be a sufficient influx of unruly seafarers to disturb the peace, before the expedition finally left Dalriada. He himself would go on to Dunadd, now, with his information, to make plans with Kings Ewan and Aed, and would send for the Galloway contingent, and other forces, when all was more or less ready.

More sailing, then, northwards – but now, whatever problems and decisions had to be made, he would be going to see Eithne again.

He saw Eithne, yes – but with problems and decisions indeed. She came running when she saw him, arms out, to throw herself upon him, all but incoherent, unlike herself. It was some time before she could get it all out. It was disaster. Ewan was dead. Aed also. And so many others. Disaster . . .

16

The grim news had only reached Dunadd the day before, when two of the local ships had limped home. There had been a great battle in one of the Irish loughs, and the Dalriadan and Albannach fleets almost completely destroyed, with appalling loss of life. Aed, always impetuous, had persuaded Ewan and his force not to wait for Kenneth and the others – some sort of jealousy possibly behind that – and they had sailed for Ireland eight days ago. Apparently they had sighted three Norse vessels offshore, and had chased them into one of the loughs, where they had been trapped by a large fleet of dragon-ships, and the battle had gone hopelessly against them. These two Dalriadan vessels had only escaped because they had been sent to the rear to hold the narrow entrance to the lough clear. All the rest had perished.

Horrified, Kenneth heard her out, almost as shaken as she was. It took time for the full impact of it all to dawn on him, but even so he was shocked, all but wordless for a while.

He had to comfort Eithne as best he could – for she had lost not only Ewan but her other two brothers, Nechtan and Bran as well, a shattering loss. Aed's death hit her less direly, to be sure, but the abruptness of it, and her consequent change of circumstances, were also shattering and the terrible personal blow tended to preoccupy her to the exclusion of all else. Bit by bit the less personal repercussions, however, came to Kenneth.

His part in the projected expedition was no longer practical. The Dalriadan and Albannach contingents would have formed the major proportion of the fleet. Lacking them there was no point in leading a minor assault of the Galloway and Manx ships, with token additions from Cumbria and Gwynedd, against such potent forces. One day, yes – but not now. Their assembly would have to be aborted, all his efforts nullified. And by folly – for that was what it had been, sheer folly, to set off lacking full strength and experience of Norse sea-warfare, headstrong folly.

Anyhow, leading expeditions, however important, was not for him at this juncture. For the situation created by this disaster was extraordinary as it was dramatic, and demanding of all his attentions. The thrones of Dalriada and Alba were both suddenly vacant, and would require to be filled swiftly – for nothing was more dangerous than ships-of-state abruptly left without steersmen. Who would be appointed High King of Alba he did not know, with Ewan's two younger brothers dead also, and Finguine not exactly weak in the head but not of kingly material. But as to Dalriada, his father Alpin must surely now succeed, as he should have done when Aed was so unsuitably inserted in his place. Which would leave the throne of Galloway vacant, and *he* was the obvious successor. So now he would become a monarch, even though of but a sub-kingdom of Dalriada. Which would necessarily involve him in duties which would much restrict his preferred activities – although admittedly his elevation might conceivably lend added authority to his quest for Celtic unity. But he recognised, too, that he would almost certainly be called upon to help his father here in Dalriada. Alpin was no strong and vigorous leader and would require support. It all meant major upheaval and change.

And there was Eithne. Almost, Kenneth dared not let his mind dwell on her situation now, and what might become possible.

It was Eithne herself who dared what he did not, presently, when that same evening, having taken herself and her emotions in hand, she suggested that they climbed together to the top of Dunadd Hill to watch the sun at its setting – and to get away from the many chiefs, lords and councillors who felt it their duty to advise, guide and even seek to console their widowed Queen. He acceded gladly; and halfway up the steep incline, she paused for breath.

"Kenneth, am I a heartless, wicked woman?" she demanded, panting a little. "Or, no, not heartless, for it is my heart which is responsible. But seeming uncaring? When, God knows, I care! Yet, grieving for my brothers as I do, I cannot keep my heart from rejoicing. That now, now I can be yours and you mine! At last!"

He gripped her arm, wordless.

"Is that wrong, Kenneth? At such a time."

"No!" he said hoarsely. "No. Surely not. Oh, Eithne, my dear!"

"You want me? Still?"

"*Want* you? I ache for you. Have done all these years. You must know that. I have ached and longed. And now . . . " He drew her to him – and then looking round and down, shook his head. "Not here. Not now. We could be seen . . . " Dunadd Hill's pyramid was not so high that watchers below in palace and township could not observe a couple embracing. "Come!" He did not release her but almost roughly, turning, pulled her up after him. Nor did she hang back.

At the summit, beside those carvings and the footprint in the outcropping rock, they did not linger. They hurried down the other side some way. There, facing the Moss and the Sound of Jura and all the Sea of the Hebrides, beyond the crest, none would see them.

She came into his arms eagerly, all restraint done with, lips upturned to his. Words, coherent words, were neither possible nor necessary. His hand found itself cupping most naturally a warm and rounded breast which heaved rhythmically from climbing and emotion both.

For them, then, the world stood still.

When, at length, in the rosy glow of the sunset, still holding each other, they turned to face all that refulgence, and by unspoken consent sat down on an outcrop of rock.

"Are we selfish, Kenneth?" she asked presently. "Taking to ourselves all this joy. When we, or I, should be mourning. *Am* mourning. Am I failing my brothers?"

"Do not blame yourself, woman," he told her, deep-voiced. "Your brothers have gone to a better place, I think. They will not wish you to be sorry for them. It is *you* who need the comfort, not them. They loved you, therefore they will wish you joy now. Not sorrow and weeping. So if you have joy in – in what I have to give you, they will be happy. As to Aed, I do not know."

"Aed never loved me, only wanted the High King's

daughter. Nor I him, and he knew it well. Whether he knew that I loved you, *I* do not know. If he also is in your better place, he may smile that cold smile of his, at us. But not break his heart, I swear!"

He nodded. "That I accept." He drew a breath. "Eithne, dare I ask that you marry me?"

She raised a hand to turn his face from the sunset to hers. "Dare you refuse to, Kenneth mac Alpin? After all this!"

"My dear! But – consider. We love each other, yes. Beyond telling. Or I do. But – you are a queen. Sister and daughter of High Kings. And very fair. Many greater than me could well seek your hand. Someone will have to be appointed High King of Alba. Not Finguine, I fear. Whoever that is, he could well seek to strengthen his position by wedding you. So you could possibly be High Queen, if that is how you would be called."

"Think you that I care for that? When I could marry Kenneth of Galloway?"

"Galloway is but a small sub-kingdom. A considerable step-down for the Queen of Dalriada. My father will, I think, take over this throne, so I will become a king of sorts myself. And one day I may succeed my father here. So then you would be back as Queen of Dalriada. But that is a far prospect. My father is not an old man . . . "

"Kenneth, do you think that this of being a queen matters so greatly to me? To be your wife, your woman even – that is what matters. Talk no more of this. When we have so much that is good, splendid, to talk of."

"Very well. But I had to put it to you . . . "

Strangely, thereafter, although they left the subject of kings and queens alone, in lieu of better, they did not in fact speak much at all, content to hold each other, and soak in the superlative experience which a Hebridean sunset can provide. They watched and murmured and kissed and watched again, until there was only the afterglow, when, reluctantly, Eithne said that perhaps they ought to be going down, that it would not look well for the widowed Queen and mourning sister to be out alone in the dark with another man, so soon.

Cautiously they descended that steep, rocky hill, in the shadows, hand in hand.

Kenneth, of course, could not linger at Dunadd. All the assemblies of men and ships he had so painstakingly arranged for had now to be disbanded, at least meantime, word be sent to Cumbria, Gwynedd and Man, and his father informed of the dynastic situation. So it was back to Garlies next day. But before he sailed, he spoke with some of the senior Dalriadan nobles, who all agreed that King Alpin was the rightful and obvious occupant for the throne there, and the sooner he ascended it and took up the reins of government, the better.

Kenneth took leave of Eithne at Port an Deora with suitably discreet formality – but both knew that he would soon be back.

A new era was commencing.

PART THREE

17

The enthronement and anointing of Alpin mac Eochaidh as King of Dalriada was very different from that of Aed mac Boanta – Kenneth, for one, saw to that. This was to be seen and accepted by all as the fulfilment of the ages-old tradition, the crowning of the Scots' heritage, in the direct descent from the mac Ercs who had come from Dalriata in Ireland four centuries earlier, no stop-gap or time-server this time. And also emphasising that Dalriada was free and independent of Alba, however friendly the two realms. Anyhow, after the disaster in Ulster, the morale of the Scots required to be raised, and here was opportunity.

So all the notables, not only of Dalriada itself but of most of the Hebridean seaboard area as far north as Mull and Ardnamurchan, Eigg and Rhum and Skye, which, although belonging to Alba, recognised that a strong Dalriada was vital for their own defence against the Norsemen, assembled at Dunadd. Feasting and entertainment were provided at the palace – with, rather strangely, Queen Eithne acting hostess, by Kenneth's persuasion; for he would not hear of her vacating the premises, although they were no longer hers by right. Alpin's wife had been long dead. Prayers were said for good weather for enthronement-day – for the bare summit of Dunadd Hill, in rain and wind, was not a place to linger.

Fortunately it proved to be a hazily golden autumn morning, after a touch of frost, and all was well. The long column of the prominent wound its slow way, to the music of horns and cymbals, up that rocky hill, banners flying. At the top, King Alpin went to stand on the outcropping oatmeal-coloured stone, flanked by Kenneth and Donald, with Eithne behind as indicating both the transference from Aed's regime and friendly Albannach approval. There his descent was read out by the chief sennachie or herald, from Fergus mac Erc himself down all the generations to

Eochaidh the Poisonous, a lengthy recital. Thereafter Alpin took the slender circlet of gold that represented the crown of Galloway, from his own brows, to turn to his eldest son and place it on Kenneth's, to much cheering, a simple but effective gesture. The hereditary crowner or coroner, one Lulach of Craignish, then stepped forward and replaced that circlet with the more ornate Dalriadan one, loudly declaring Alpin undoubted King.

The horns and cymbals sounded, and singers chanted.

Alpin then raised a hand for silence, and pronounced the oath to cherish, maintain and protect the realm of Dalriada to his life's end, to be guided by his chiefs and lords, and to support the Columban Church. That declared, he ceremoniously stooped to take off one of his boots, and to place his bare foot in the hollowed-out footprint in the rock; and the Lord Lulach of Craignish called upon all the chiefs and greater landholders of the kingdom to line up and take the oath of allegiance to their new sovereign-lord, he himself, as crowner, doing so first. Alpin withdrew his foot from the print, and from a little leather bag at his belt, Lulach sprinkled a few grains of earth from Craignish peninsula into the hollow. Then Alpin replaced his foot on this, and the crowner swore his oath of obedience and fealty, with the King standing on his soil, in token that all the land was in theory the monarch's and held of him in trust and submission. Afterwards, one by one, the lords and chief men filed up to do likewise, each taking Alpin's hand between their own, after sprinkling their earth, with the crowner having to stoop and scoop out the accumulated soil from the hollow, time and again. Rhythmic music was rendered throughout, during the lengthy process, punctuated each time the King's foot went down by a single clash of a cymbal.

At last it was over, and the procession reformed to descend the hill, the musicians leading with triumphant flourish. Behind Alpin, Kenneth walked with Eithne, very much aware of that other so private hilltop visit and descent, of a spring sunset. She touched lightly the gold circlet at his brows.

"Do I now walk beside the King of Galloway?" she wondered.

"I suppose it, yes. Although I have to go through some

lesser coronation ceremony at Whithorn in due course."

"Then hail, Highness!" she exclaimed. "May I be the first to name you."

"You shall name me more than that, Eithne nic Angus!" he told her, in suitably regal fashion.

There was more junketing and celebration in the palace thereafter, with outdoor feasting for the common folk round great fires, with oxen and deer roasted whole and ale flowing like water. It was a grim thought, which did not fail to occur to Kenneth more than once, that this was a nation in mourning for a great disaster.

In the morning, early, they would sail for Iona.

In answer to prayer, or otherwise, the good quiet weather held, although the lack of wind did mean oar-work all the way for the many ships. All that colourful seaboard was a delight, in the autumnal scarlets and ochres and purples, the gold and olive and saffron, the sea however retaining its deep blue depths contrasting with the aquamarine of the shallows, Corryvreckan looking as innocent as any babe. Iona itself, when it came in sight, could scarcely have looked more lovely. Surely it was all an excellent augury?

The ceremonial here was again considerably more elaborate than at Aed's anointing, Kenneth having all but bullied Prior Phadraig into devising a stirring and memorable ritual and programme. At the very landing from the ships, the principals stooped low to kiss the sacred soil, as Columba was reputed to have done. From then on it was significance all the way.

They paid calls at the Reelig Oran, the tombs of the kings and the ruins of Columba's abbey, before proceeding up to Tor Abb for the service and anointing. This time the Eucharist was celebrated more fully and with more solemnity than on the last occasion, and the later blessing and application of the oil in suitably impressive fashion. Alpin had an innate dignity which enhanced the proceedings, and the responses of the congregation were less reserved and formal. Kenneth was satisfied.

Not that his attention was as wholly concentrated on this part of the programme as perhaps it should have been. For when the service was over, and Alpin made his brief acknowledgment and assertion of duty and responsibility,

281

after a pause, he had another announcement to make. Hereafter they would all proceed to the remains of the abbey, where his son, Kenneth, King of Galloway, would be married to the Lady Eithne, lately Queen of Dalriada, here on St Columba's blessed isle.

There was a great stir and exclamation at this declaration, totally unexpected, even though not a few present must have known by now of the friendship of these two. Kenneth turned to Eithne, standing behind, and held out his hand in an impulsive gesture more eloquent than any words. Cheers arose from all around Tor Abb.

Singers and instrumentalists leading, the newly anointed monarch was escorted down to the abbey; but it is to be feared that he was no longer the centre of attraction, the prospective bride and bridegroom now sharing that distinction.

In contrast to what had gone before, the wedding ceremony was simplicity itself, at both participants' request, Prior Phadraig well pleased to comply, a man who preferred his pastoral duties, illuminating manuscripts and studying, to great public occasions. This may have been something of a disappointment to some of the onlookers, but most had probably had a sufficiency of ceremonial for these two days.

Eithne looked radiantly happy throughout.

When they rose from their knees after the final blessing, man and woman turned to gaze at each other for long moments, a reaction more revealing and eloquent somehow than any more demonstrative gesture. None watching could doubt that here was a coming together of no ordinary quality.

That royal wedding was unusual in other respects. There could be no feasting thereafter, for Iona in its present state was no place for such, its larger buildings in ruins, its people now few and unable to provide the wherewithal, indeed today much outnumbered by the visitors. Besides, since there was no accommodation available for all these notables, a move away again was indicated, and without overmuch delay. Not that a return to Dunadd that same day was essential, for there were many lords' houses and townships not so far off, on Mull, Luing, Seil and the Lorn mainland, to entertain distinguished travellers. But still more unusual was the announcement made now by the newly-weds. *They* would not be leaving the island with the rest, meantime. They had their own ideas as to wedding-day celebration.

However much eyebrow-raising this decision occasioned, no one was in a position to say them nay. So, while the great company moved off, back to their ships, Kenneth and Eithne walked away alone, in exactly the opposite direction, north-westwards, to climb over the spine of the island, below Dun I.

They were making for that white-sand west-coast bay where, those eighteen months ago, they had, as it were, exchanged their private vows to each other, the marriage of hearts as distinct from bodies – and restrained themselves so vehemently thereafter. Now the time for that restraint was past, and they were going back.

When they came in sight of their destination, the Bay of Calva, they paused to stare. Although it was October, not May, all looked little changed, the water and seaweed and sand colours glowingly the same, even though those of the land held more of gold and scarlet and auburn. No cuckoos called, and the swallows and sand-martins had gone, but the rafts of eiders still floated offshore, cormorants stretched their wings on the skerries and a long, rippling skein of wild geese gabbled their way across the sky, to add a new dimension of delight.

Down on the beach itself, the gleaming sand untrodden save by a roe-deer's dainty tracks, they stood for a little, hand in hand, absorbing all the peace and beauty of it. Then Eithne trilled a laugh.

"The sun shines and the sea will still hold something of its summer warmth," she declared. "Have you ever swum in October, King of Galloway?"

Even as she asked it, she kicked off her shoes and began to undress.

He did not answer, fully occupied in watching her. After all, he could do so now unabashed, for was not this woman his wife?

"Come – do not say that Kenneth Norse-Slayer is fearful!" she rallied him, as he made no move to disrobe. "The sand is warm on my feet, craven one."

"In due course," he got out thickly. "Meantime I use my

time better!"

Laughing again, she threw off the last of her clothing and stood before him as God made her, a most lovely sight indeed, in the fullest bloom of shapely, well-endowed and splendidly proportioned womanhood, graceful of bearing, enticingly breasted, rounded bottomed and long of leg. With no hint of embarrassment she pivoted round for him, held out her arms to him – and then, before he could do anything about it, smiling provokingly, ran off and into the water, splashing, her laughter ringing.

Kenneth probably had never before got rid of his clothing, fine as it was today for the ceremonial, so quickly, leaving it strewn on the warm sand where it fell, to go racing after her, as the nearest eiders squattered away in alarm.

She had begun to swim before he reached her, hair streaming behind, white body reflecting the sunlight and shadows of the white sand below. With a great plunge he grasped her and turned her bodily to him, and there in the water they clung to each other, naked, and entirely themselves, finding that they could just stand tip-toe. If the October water was cold, they did not notice it.

Kissing salt kisses, the man's hands exploring, they bobbed up and down with the tidal surge, unspeaking save with eyes and persons, all joy and appreciation. When she did find words, Eithne panted, "I have wanted . . . to do this . . . for so long!"

He closed her lips with his own.

Presently they went swimming side-by-side further out into the bay. But not far or for long, for Kenneth had an alternative project in mind. They headed for the beach again, and when in the shallows, he grabbed her arm and ran with her, all but dragging, she feigning reluctance, up over the sand to a neuk between lichen-covered rocks, where he pressed her down, gently but very firmly. And whatever the state of his manhood in the chill water, that run up from the tide seemed to have most adequately revived it.

As they sank down, he on top of her, Eithne, hands on his wet back, whispered, "Sand, my dear! Could be . . . intrusive! Uncomfortable."

"Ah!" He jumped up, and ran back to the litter of his clothing, to snatch some of it to bring back and tuck under

284

his woman, she arching herself helpfully, as prelude to fullest co-operation.

Thereafter they followed the course nature laid out for them, in all fulfilment, restraint most evident by its absence.

When, after a satisfactorily delayed interval, words came to be enunciated, it was the man who spoke them, briefly. "I think . . . that cold water . . . may have helped . . . in the end!"

Eyes closed, she nodded.

Thereafter they lay side by side on the sand in the sunshine, Eithne on her back, Kenneth admiring most frankly and occasionally touching, stroking, fondling, both, at least for the moment, at joyful peace with the world.

But an October sun can lose its heat early, and reluctantly they donned their clothing, to leave that little Bay of Calva. As they turned to look back from the higher ground, Eithne sighed, but with content.

"Now I feel truly married," she said. "I have never felt so before. We shall come back here, husband."

Unhurriedly they made their way over to the abbey area and their ship.

18

After the Dalriada initiations and celebrations, the Galloway crowning at Whithorn was very modest and brief, but graced by Eithne's presence and her friendliness towards all, it made a pleasant as well as a significant occasion. Kenneth would have been for getting it over as quickly as was decent, but for her sake made more of it all, and later at Garlies, with feasting and entertainment. He had no wish for his elevation to the kingship to alter his relations and behaviour towards others, but inevitably his subjects did treat him somewhat differently now.

They found that King Godfrey mac Fergus of Oriel had returned from Dunbarton and had then sailed off to Man to rejoin his wife meantime, leaving word that he was ready, with his men and ships, to join in any venture which might lead to the recovery of his kingdom.

Eithne liked Galloway, and wanted to see it all; so, as Kenneth had to show himself to the various areas thereof, as monarch, the couple made a series of progresses, from the long peninsulas of the Rhinns to the inland vales of Nithsdale and Annandale, from the great Bays of Luce, Wigtown and Kirkcudbright, up to the mountains of the Merrick and Kells and Trool, and all along the Solway coast to the verge of Cumbria, even though the winter weather and the short days made travel difficult. To some extent it was exploring for Kenneth also, for he had not been to all the localities of his sub-kingdom in the past, he never having really identified with Galloway fully, Dalriada meaning so much more to him. Now, however, he recognised that he must take his responsibilities and duties here more seriously. And having Eithne to share them with him made it all so much more acceptable, less of a burden. He was much enjoying being a married man.

Nevertheless, at the back of his mind, and not so far back

at that, there were always other preoccupations – Dalriada, Alba, the Norse threat, and the Celtic alliance. Galloway was just not large enough to hold Kenneth mac Alpin.

He knew well that his father would require help in ruling Dalriada, being the man he was. Donald had remained with him at Dunadd meantime, but Donald himself was a better lieutenant than captain. It never occurred to the elder brother that *he* was more captain than lieutenant. Then he had received no word as to what was happening in Alba, and how the high kingship went now. The Norsemen appeared to be leaving this side of the Irish Sea in peace for the time being, no doubt being fully occupied in the new role, for them, of establishing a Northern Ireland kingdom, and seeking to control large areas of occupied territory, a very different task from pirating and sea-raiding. But being the folk they were, it would not be over-long before they reverted to their favourite pastime of hosting – which, since Northern Ireland was no longer apt for their ravaging, would mean assailing Dalriada, Alba, Man and the rest. Celtic unity therefore was as necessary as ever, more so indeed since the Irish kingdoms were crying out to be won back. Also, the Angles and Saxons, by all reports, were less than quiescent.

Ruling Galloway was all very well. But greater calls sounded for that man.

Eithne, although more content with the nearer prospects, and husband-and-wife life, knew her Kenneth sufficiently well not to try to dissuade him from his wider horizons. Without actually encouraging him in his visionary projects, she did listen and discuss them with him – which in fact much aided him in forward planning.

Spring, of course, is the time for stirring the blood in the veins of the active – hence the campaigning season begins, for oppressors as for defenders. Restless, Kenneth decided that it was time for a return to Dunadd.

It was good to be sailing up the Hebridean seaboard again, Eithne enjoying it also, agreeing with her husband that it was the most lovely scenery of the world they knew.

At Dunadd, they found Alpin less than happy, various problems worrying him. A peace-loving man, he was having to consider warlike action – and was therefore thankful for Kenneth's arrival. And the matter concerned Alba, no less.

It seemed that Alba itself was undergoing internal turmoil, after Ewan's death and the Irish disaster, and the turmoil was spilling over into Dalriada.

There had been two contenders amongst the *ri*, the lesser kings, to fill the position of High King, left vacant – Feredith mac Bargoit, Mormaor of Mar, and Brude mac Fochel, who had succeeded Aed mac Boanta as Mormaor of Moray. The seven *ri* had been divided four to three in the vote, and Feredith had won, and been crowned. But Brude had not accepted the decision – and Moray was by far the largest of the mormaordoms. So a state of almost civil war prevailed in Alba, the realm all but cut in two, north and south, Mar dominating the south and east, including Fortrenn; and Moray the north and west, based on the old capital at Inverness. Internal chaos reigned. Unfortunately, the land bordering Dalriada to north and east, with the Hebridean seaboard, paid tribute to Moray, and so was included in the revolt against the new High King. This unrest had produced unruly conditions amongst the local Albannach lords and landed men, some for Brude, some for Feredith; and this disorder had spread over into Dalriadan territory, with raids and pillaging. The last thing that Alpin wanted was to become involved in Alba's internal upheavals; but something would have to be done to aid the molested Dalriadan folk. Donald had taken a small force up to the worst of the trouble spots, but, without actual counter-raids into Alban territory, which was the very way to provoke major trouble, there was not much that he could do. It was all most distressing, and Alpin had been considering sending for Kenneth to see if he could think of something they might do. And to add to it all, there had been another Norse raid on Iona, a minor one, admittedly, and apparently not from Ireland but from Orkney. Donald was to go on there, to seek to console the folk . . .

Kenneth was, of course, much concerned and angry. How in the name of heaven could the Celtic peoples hope to withstand the assaults of their enemies if they fought not only with each other but in internal strife? Was all his work and effort to go for nothing because of dynastic jealousies and insurrection? The Iona raid was bad, but did not represent major threat to his cherished project.

288

He told his father that he would go to see these two Albannach rivals, Feredith and Brude. Eithne, as sister and daughter of high kings, said that she might be helpful, and would go too.

There was some better news, however. Word had come, via Strathclyde, that the Southern Irish kings were fighting back with some success against the Norsemen in Ulster, and had won an important victory over the Scandinavians, in Meath, where twelve hundred of these had fallen, including their leader, the Jarl Hakon. This much interested as well as heartened Kenneth, for two reasons. It meant that the Norse-Irish venture was indeed serious colonisation, for the Jarl Hakon had been no mere piratical leader but one of the greatest men in Norway – therefore this must be royal Norwegian policy. Also, the fact that the Norsemen had been defeated so far south as Meath meant that they were bent on extending their Irish conquests. This could be important, in that it might well indicate a continuing remission of their raids on these coasts, this Iona attack being merely an independent enterprise of some Orkney pirate.

So Kenneth and Eithne, with a modest escort, set off on horseback on the long ride to Fortrenn, across the waist of southern Alba. They halted for the first night at a monkish hospice on an island in the Loch of Monteith in the midst of the Great Moss of Forth.

At Fortrenn they found Feredith mac Bargoit installed in Eithne's old home by the River Earn. He proved to be a somewhat indecisive man of middle years, with a dominant wife, a strange choice for High King, save in that he was kin to the late Drostan. He was quite affable towards his unexpected visitors, indeed seemed glad to see them, especially Eithne, who, with her royal status, might well give further backing to his own position, amongst the uncommitted, his wife making considerable fuss of her. Towards Kenneth they were less forthcoming, anticipating no doubt his likely requests for military involvement against all Gaeldom's enemies.

At this stage, however, Kenneth was concerned with internal unity rather than united armed strength. He commiserated with Feredith over Brude's rebellion, deploring it but urging that every attempt must be made to heal the breach and regularise the position, for the sake of all. To this end, Eithne backing him, he suggested that some gesture and compromise should be made, something to mollify Brude and the two other mormaors, of Ross and Caithness, who supported him. Alba surely could not go on being divided north and south.

This was grudgingly conceded, but no proposals were forthcoming from Feredith.

Kenneth ventured his own. The High King had no son. Brude was a younger man. If Feredith nominated Brude as his eventual successor in the high kingship, might not that smooth out the situation, pacifying Brude and making him hesitant about taking hostile action lest the nomination be revoked?

The new High King tugged at his somewhat slack and protuberant lower lip. Might not Brude then in fact seek to dispose of him, Feredith, in order to succeed to his throne the sooner? Kenneth countered that by pointing out that the High King could be appointed only by the election of the *ri*. Would they install a man who had so behaved?

Only partially reassured, Feredith indicated unenthusiastic acceptance.

It was only after this that Kenneth went on to speak of his Celtic alliance project and the need for it, using Ireland as dire example. He met with very guarded response. Feredith seemed unlikely to prove a very positive ally.

The visitors did not linger long at Fortrenn. Eithne had hoped to see her one remaining brother, Finguine, but learned that he had gone to live with an aunt in Angus. They took the long road to Inverness.

This journey was one which Kenneth had never before taken. But Eithne had, more than once, and she was quite pleased to be able to lead the way for once. It was not new ground for him until they had crossed Tay and passed north of Scone; but thereafter, steadily mounting into the Highland fastnesses, they followed the great river northwards into the wooded valleys and defiles of Birnam and Dunkeld, and on into Strathtay itself. They halted for the first night at Ballinluig in South Atholl, where the River Garry joined Tay, and there was one of the travellers' hospices which were such an excellent service provided by the Columban

Church. Eithne had never stayed at this one before, for, when travelling north with her father they had always lodged for the night at Dunkeld or at the house of the Mormaor of Atholl at Blair, further north. On this occasion, however, they did not want any unavoidable delay, which would follow upon a call on the mormaor. The monks at Ballinluig had never before entertained royalty at their hospice, and sought to amplify their normally plain fare accordingly.

Next day, proceeding up the turbulent, peat-brown Garry, they passed the entrance to the Tilt valley, a little way up which was the mormaor's fortress-hallhouse, and met with no challenge to delay them. Eithne was a practised horsewoman, and quite prepared to ride up to sixty miles in a day. So they pressed on up Garry further, with the mountains ever becoming higher and steeper, right to the bleak and lofty Pass of Drumochter, one of the highest and harshest in all Alba, impassable often in winter snows. Through its grim portals they rode, with the sun already hidden behind the west-side mountains, thankfully to find another hospice at Dalwhinnie, below the northern end of the pass, a stark place this but blessed nevertheless by many a traveller. Kenneth surmised that the monks manning this one must be sent here as a penance.

The following day, however, all was changed, as they rode down into Badenoch, a lovely land of pinewoods and blue lochs and far vistas, ringed with purple mountains, some still snow-capped. Here they were entering the mormaordom of Moray, the most beautiful as well as the largest in Alba. They followed now the River Spey, not yet so noble a stream as it would become, even so much impressing Kenneth. Compared with Northern Atholl, this was a quite populous land, with much farmery, and townships at Glentruim, Ruthven, Kingussie, Kincraig, Alvie and Alviemore. The lords of all this could undoubtedly raise many men. The prospects towards the east, of the Monadh Ruadh, or Red Mountains as Eithne called them, was quite magnificent, the highest Kenneth had ever seen; the Monadh Liath, or Grey Mountains, to the west, being fine but softer, rounder.

They had another of the high passes to thread before they could pass out of this fair basin of Badenoch, not so lofty and bare as Drumochter but narrower and sufficiently steep, known as the Slochd, Eithne said, that is the Wolf's Throat. Beyond it, they reached their third night's hospice, where they crossed the Findhorn River at Tomatin. Kenneth was discovering something of the size of this Alba; they had already come over one hundred and fifty miles from Fortrenn. Inverness, Brude's capital, lay still another forty miles ahead.

However, they did not have to reach Inverness before they met Brude mac Fochel. They had crossed the River Nairn and were on the wastes of Drummossie Muir when a party of horsemen emerged from scrub oak woodland ahead of them, and seeing them, waited. As they neared these, they could see that some of the horses, rough garrons, were laden with the carcasses of deer. So this was a hunting-party.

Riding up, they were challenged by a youngish man, finely mounted and dressed, good-looking save that he had a cast in one eye, and that notably pale blue.

"Who rides through my kingdom with armed men lacking my permission?" this individual demanded.

"We have the permission of the High King of Alba," Kenneth returned, but not aggressively. "Here is the Queen of Galloway, Eithne nic Angus. And I am Kenneth mac Alpin."

That gave the questioner pause. He stared, with those cold blue eyes.

"You speak of *your* kingdom?" Kenneth went on. "Can you then be Brude, Mormaor of Moray?"

The other jerked a nod.

"Then it is well met, friend. For we are on our way to visit you, at Inverness."

"For what purpose, King Kenneth? And lady." That was scarcely welcoming.

"That we can discuss better elsewhere than here," Kenneth gave back. There was reproof in that; but he did not want to get on the wrong side of this man thus early, if at all. "It is sufficiently important," he added.

Brude shrugged. "As you will. I am hunting here . . . "

"We shall go on to Inverness." That was Eithne at her coolest. "Perhaps there we may speak to better purpose."

The mormaor inclined his head, and they parted company.

"I do not like that man," Eithne said, as they rode on. "Nor would I trust him." It was not often that she was thus swift in her criticism.

"No. Yet we have to deal with him."

They approached Inverness down a series of long slopes from Drummossie Muir, seeing ahead a large town lining both banks of a broad tree-lined river, with, on a series of low hills on the far, northern side, what was clearly a large and powerful fortress crowning one of these. In the town, their party was eyed with interest but no animosity. At the river-bank they discovered a wide ford, part artificial causeway, for horses and carts, with a wooden footbridge nearby, or rather two, which used a little island, possibly also artificial, in the mid-shallows as link, for the townsfolk to cross. They splashed over the ford.

The greater part of this community obviously lived on the north side of the river where there was more level ground before the hillocks. They threaded the clustered houses, to climb towards the fortress. This looked very impressive, really three hallhouses grouped within high ramparts with gates, and very considerable outbuildings and domestic extensions. This had been the original palace and seat of the Albannach high kings, Eithne explained, until her uncle, Constantine, had found it convenient and more central to move it to Forteviot in Fortrenn, whereafter it had passed to the Moray mormaors.

They met with some delay at the main gates while guards were sent to gain permission to admit them; but once inside they were treated with respect by a sennachie or chamberlain and his assistants. Brude evidently kept up fairly regal state here. They were installed in a fine guesthouse.

The mormaor returned, in fact, quite soon after their own arrival, possibly having thought better of continuing with his deer-driving in view of the eminence of his visitors. Presently he appeared at the guesthouse, with two of his lords, while the sennachie was serving the visitors with refreshments.

"I hope that your hunting was not unduly disturbed?" Kenneth asked, straight-faced.

The other shrugged. He did this, as before, using only one shoulder, an unusual gesture. "The deer can wait," he said.

"Yes. So we thought," Eithne observed. She was determined, here, to play the high kings' daughter and sister, it seemed. "Have you occupied this palace for long, Brude mac Fochel? I used to come here with my father."

"For three years, lady."

"And before that?" Brude was being put in his place.

"At the Cawdor of Nairn, lady."

"Ah, yes. Cawdor. We never went to Cawdor." Eithne turned to Kenneth, having played her part.

That man thought to sound more friendly now. After all, the Mormaor of Moray almost certainly ranked higher than the King of Galloway. And he had a mission to perform.

"We heard that you lost the high kingship of Alba by one vote, Highness," he said. "Our . . . commiserations!"

Brude nodded curtly.

"My father, Alpin of Dalriada, is much perturbed that there should be disharmony in Alba. Especially when it spills over into his territories, as it has recently done."

"And is that a concern of mine? As you say, I am not the High King."

"But it is from your Moray lands in the west that the troubles come, from which your people raid Dalriada."

"You have not come all the way from Dunadd to tell me that, I think?"

"No. There are greater issues at stake. We, the Celtic nations, must act together, or we may fall. To repel the Norse and Anglian invaders. This we have been learning hardly, the Northern Irish even more hardly. This we cannot do if there is internal conflict within our nations."

"Perhaps. Tell that to Feredith mac Bargoit."

"We have done so. We come here from Forteviot. King Feredith understands the situation, the dangers, and will seek to improve matters."

"Much improvement *that* one will make!"

"More than you may credit him, Highness. And Alba must be made strong again."

"Then Alba should appoint a strong ruler, not a weakling."

"The *ri* have appointed Feredith, by a majority, have they not?"

"More fools they! But *I* do not need someone from

Galloway, or from Dalriada either, to tell me what the *ri* of Alba should do. Or how Alba should be governed."

"That I recognise. Yet Dalriada, yes, and Galloway also, are endangered if Alba is weak and disunited."

Brude looked at his two companions. "This King of Galloway persists," he said.

"The King of Galloway has reason to persist," Eithne put in. "He recognises his responsibilities, if you do not. And it is *your* people who raid into his father's kingdom."

"Not of my will. I will command that it ceases."

"That is good," Kenneth said. "But this of Albannach unity, greatly the more important. So long as there is division in this land, Alba cannot take measures to counter the Norsemen. For one side will not risk to lend its forces while the other might seize the advantage at home." And when Brude made no comment, "And it is in the west, *your* Hebridean coasts, where the Norse danger is apt to be greatest. There was another raid on Iona a month back."

"I will repel any Scandinavian pirates who raid my shores."

"How?" That was almost a bark, unlike Kenneth.

Brude gave his one-sided shrug. "With steel," he gave back.

"None so easy, you will find. They raid and destroy and sail. How will you catch them? They are notable sea-fighters, and the seas are wide. The only way to halt them is to descend upon their bases. I know. I have learned it. And to raid their bases, wherever, you require a large force, many ships, a fleet."

"This is what you came here to tell me?"

"We came because Alba is supremely important in the fight against the Norse. And Alba is divided because *you* refuse to accept Feredith as High King, thereby weakening the entire Celtic cause."

"Go tell that to the other *ri* who voted for Feredith the weakling! *He* will never lead the Albannach power against your Norsemen."

"Not while you oppose him."

"I oppose the wrong choice as High King. And will continue to oppose it."

"Even though you were named heir? To be the next High

King?"

That brought Brude up with a start. "Heir . . . ? What mean you?"

"I mean that Feredith, son-less, could nominate *you* as his successor. There are seven *ri*. Even though the other three who supported him did not want you, Buchan, Angus and Atholl, that would still give you the majority, four votes. And Feredith is not a young man."

"He would do that?"

"We discussed it, yes. And he agreed that we put it to you."

Again Brude looked at the two lords, clearly considering.

"As designated heir, you could take the lead in much," Kenneth went on. "In especial, as commander in warfare, since Feredith appears to be little of a warrior. You could greatly help to lead Alba . . . "

"And by so doing impress the other mormaors to favour your eventual succession to the high throne," Eithne put in. "Since they could unite to deny it to you, otherwise." That was her warning.

"I will think on this," Brude said, and abruptly turned to leave them. "You will find your comfort here meantime, I hope." Obviously he was not considering any invitation to share his table that evening.

Eithne remarked on this when the trio had gone. "I am thankful that we do not have to eat in his hall this night. I mislike him more than any man I have ever met, I think. Those eyes . . . !"

"I do not favour him, either," Kenneth admitted. "A hard and unfriendly man. Yet he might make a notable fighter, where Feredith will not. At this present time, he might be of more aid to Alba than the other. Not a good king, I think, but a strong warrior. He will agree to this of the succession, you think?"

"Oh yes, he will agree. But whether he will serve *your* purposes, my dear, I am less sure. Or keep his word to Feredith, once nominated . . . "

"The other *ri*, I say, will hold him to it . . . "

That was the best that they could do at this time. Perforce they left it at that.

In the morning, Brude came to tell them that he had

decided to accede to their request, as he put it, not elaborating. Kenneth said that they would inform Feredith and hope that hereafter there would be useful co-operation. Further than that they could hardly go.

There was no invitation to stay, indeed Brude seemed glad to see them go. As indeed were they.

Kenneth would have preferred to return to Dalriada by the somewhat more direct and shorter route, down Loch Ness-side, and the other lochs of the Great Glen of Alba, to salt water again at the Firth of Lorn; but Feredith had to be told of the outcome of their mission, and so they had to go back southwards by the way they had come. Not that that was in any way an unpleasant prospect, especially with Eithne as companion.

The vistas of the mighty Monadh Ruadh range, slashed by the spectacular chasm of the Lairig Ghru, viewed from the north were even more impressive than before, with the boiling clouds of an isolated rainstorm churning up the gut thereof.

When they reached him, Feredith mac Bargoit was only moderately elated by their news. He would wait to see how Brude actually behaved before any rejoicing. But if all went well he would be grateful and would co-operate against the Norsemen.

His visitors departed for Dalriada.

Donald was back at Dunadd when they got there, having taken some punitive action against the Albannach despoilers of his father's northern border areas, and thereafter visiting Iona. He reported that the latest Norse raid there had been less harmful than some, more of a token it seemed. Why the Scandinavians sought out this small island for their especial hate was something of a mystery, for there were far richer pickings, in cattle, grain, goods and women elsewhere. Possibly it was because they knew it to be so important a Christian shrine, and so to be the chosen object of their pagan spleen.

Before returning to Galloway, Kenneth decided to conduct a small personal investigation, Eithne eager to co-operate. So he sought out his friend Conall, the shipmaster at Port an Deora, to ask him to take them up to the place at the mouth of Loch Etive where he had hidden the famous

Lia Faill, the Stone of Destiny, which had almost certainly been Columba's portable altar and had been used as the coronation-seat for the Dalriadan kings.

Kenneth desired to see it again and to ensure that it was safe. It might even be safe to bring it back to Dunadd now; but that might just possibly be unwise. If whoever was High King of Alba learned that it was available again, it could still be coveted and demanded. And Kenneth, at the back of his mind, had the secret ambition that, when he eventually succeeded his father as King of Dalriada, he would be crowned on the *Lia Faill*.

Conall was happy to oblige, and they sailed off northwards in his longship, between the islands, for Lorn. They followed the same route as for Iona, save that when they passed the Garvellach Isles where Columba had established his *diseart* or personal retiring-place, with the great Ross of Mull peninsula ahead, they steered to the right, eastwards, instead of left, to enter the mouth of the Firth of Lorn between Mull and the mainland. Up this they proceeded for ten miles or so, until it was narrowed by the Isle of Kerrera before opening out into the wide waters where the firth was joined by the Sound of Mull and Loch Linnhe, a great hub of the island seas. Passing the township of the Oban, they came to the low little green peninsula of Dunstaffnage, beyond which opened the constricted mouth of Loch Etive of the legends, of Deirdre and the sons of Uisneach.

They landed in a shallow bay just round the point and under the frowning but broken-down ramparts of an early fort guarding the loch-mouth. It was evening now, with the light fading, so Conall produced torches of bog-pine. But they did not climb the rocky knoll to the fort itself, for it seemed that the precious stone was not hidden within the ramparts of the fort, since this could well be visited and explored by the curious, but left in a souterrain just below, an underground earth-house once used for storing fish on ice to keep it fresh. This Conall had discovered as a boy; and here the relic would be secure. Certainly, without being shown, no one was likely to discover this secret hiding-place, screened by rock-falls as it was.

Removing a stone slab covering the entrance, Conall stooped, with his torch, to lead the way in. The souterrain was well constructed, carefully stone-lined and stone-floored and ceiled. Whether or not the long-ago builders were small men, the visitors had to bend a little along the entrance-passage. But the earth-house proved to be T-shaped, and once they reached the junction the height increased somewhat and they were able to stand upright, already coughing from the smoke of the pine torches. But they made no complaint as they stood to gaze at the fabled stone, set there in the dark, itself almost black, with its hollows and carvings picked out in the light of the flickering flames.

Eithne was much affected to see it for the first time – as indeed was Kenneth himself, especially thus hidden away in the underground cell of the ancient people.

"It is wonderful to think of all that it has seen, down the ages," she said, leaning over to run her fingers over the upper surfaces. "It is smooth, almost like marble, black marble . . . "

"It is thought to have been made from a meteorite," Kenneth told her. "They are said to be black and to shine as though polished. Since they come down from the sky, from heaven, they are thought to be holy, unearthly, and so suitable for an altar. Why Columba chose it, no doubt – if indeed it was his altar. They say that he had an old white horse to carry it. A strong beast it must have been, for the stone is heavy. I know! We had to move it, secretly, one night. You remember, Conall . . . ?"

"If it is an altar, why does it have this hollow in the top? I have never seen an altar like that. And these curved rolls of stone at the sides?"

"They are for carrying it by, just handles of a sort. They would hoist it on to the horse using slings of rope on these. And the hollow is for holy water. It was used also as a font, for baptism."

"Altars are usually higher. They would have to stoop to use this for celebrations."

"No doubt. But meteorites are not so common that a man can pick and choose the right height and shape. And the fact that this is only seat-height enabled it to be used as a coronation-chair also, on which to sit. Aiden mac Gabhran, the first Dalriadan king Columba anointed, he sat hereon. None could have sat, with any dignity, on the usual altar."

"And you will sit on this, one day!"

"God willing."

"My father did, and my uncle. But Ewan, poor Ewan did not. Nor Aed. Do you think . . . ?"

"You mean that is why they did not live? Died young? Who knows . . . ?"

The fumes from the torches in that enclosed space forced them to cut short their inspection. Backing out, they thankfully filled their lungs with the fresh air of the clear summer evening.

"Listen!" Eithne said. "What is that noise? A sort of quiet rumble, with a hissing. But steady. The sea is not rough tonight . . . "

"That is the Falls of Lora, Highness," Conall explained. "At certain stages of the tide this happens. Loch Etive narrows to its mouth just beyond here. And right in the neck of it, very narrow, there is a great ledge of rock beneath, some reaching the surface at low water. So the outgoing tide pours over that, down like a waterfall, a strange thing. It can drop as much as five feet. I know of no other on all this seaboard like it. Sometimes there is little sound, but tonight it is loud. There are stories about it."

"Ossian wrote of it, in his songs of Deirdre and the Sons of Uisneach," Kenneth added. "They knew of it even in Ireland."

"This is a strange place," Eithne nodded. "Haunted. But not evilly so."

They returned to the bay, to spend the night on the longship. It was like old times, they agreed – save that now husband and wife shared the little cabin under the prow-platform.

19

Back ruling Galloway Kenneth heard nothing of what went on in Alba, until autumn, when a Strathclyde shipmaster told him of a large Norse raid on the eastern coast there, in the Buchan area, which Feredith and the Buchan mormaor had sought to repel, with considerable loss of life apparently, including the mormaor himself. There was no word of Brude mac Fochel having joined in. This was grievous news, especially if Brude was still failing to support Feredith – although renewed Norse raiding there might have the effect of making the Celtic alliance seem more attractive to the Albannach generally.

Then a message came from Godfrey mac Fergus of Oriel, in Man, announcing that the Scandinavian Jarl Thorgesr, now calling himself King of Ulster, was still seeking to extend his domains southward in Ireland, and there had been another major battle in Ossory, with heavy losses on both sides. But Thorgesr had been repulsed. And now Maelsechlaind, High King of All Ireland, in co-operation with the lesser monarchs, was planning to take the war into the enemy's territory, in a drive northwards. This would have to be in the spring, and it was hoped that Kenneth mac Alpin would co-operate to his fullest ability and bring over to Ireland the largest force he could raise from the Celtic lands of the east.

So here were challenge and opportunity both, to demonstrate the advantages of a united front.

That winter, then, Kenneth, while managing the affairs of Galloway to the best of his ability, concerned himself with sending messengers to Dalriada, Alba, Strathclyde, Cumbria and Gwynedd, urging maximum support in men and ships for an expedition in early May.

Eithne, although inevitably apprehensive about the dangers to her husband of his warlike interventions, nevertheless gave him all the aid she could, sending her own messages to the *ri* of Alba, where her name meant much. The ancient matriarchal traditions of that realm still had their influence, and women's roles in the affairs of the state were more important than elsewhere; and as it happened, Eithne was the only female close blood-representative of the high kingship still living.

Despite all this, they held the best Yuletide celebrations, at Garlies that year, that anyone could recollect, Eithne having a great love of Christmas festivities.

The winter weather with its short days and storms over, Kenneth again chose Dunadd, or rather Port an Deora, for the assembly-place for the fleet where, hidden behind its screen of islands, the ships could muster without likely Norse awareness. Eithne would accompany him at least that far. The Cumbrian and Gwynedd contingents would, however, sail to the Isle of Man, to join Kings Guriat and Godfrey there.

In the event, the turn-out at Port an Deora was disappointing, at least to Kenneth, although a sizeable fleet built up. Donald had done well with his father's resources of Dalriada, but Strathclyde and Alba sent only token forces, Brude doing rather better than Feredith. However, it all represented an allied expedition, which was the vital point.

Kenneth bade farewell to Eithne, and some sixty ships set sail southwards for Man, hugging the coasts meantime to avoid, if possible, being spotted by Norse ships.

So far as they were aware the fleet reached St Mary's Bay, at the south tip of Man, without being observed, at least without themselves seeing any dragon-ships. There they found a heartening assembly of vessels, mainly from Gwynedd under Rotri ap Mervyn himself – who, it transpired, was now King of Gwynedd, his father having died. The Cumbrian contribution was inevitably much more modest, but both Duncan of Arnside and Riagan of Ravenglass were present in person.

Southern Man reeled under the impact of all this invasion of all-too-friendly fighting men.

So, when three days later the combined force sailed westwards, it represented the most significant demonstration of Celtic unity yet seen, although not the largest, with no fewer than four kings aboard – of Man, Oriel, Gwynedd and Galloway. Kenneth knew considerable satisfaction.

Godfrey had managed to keep in touch, by means of fishermen from Man, with his people in Oriel, and was reasonably well informed as to the situation prevailing across the Irish Sea. It seemed that the ineffective Conchobar's successor as High King of All Ireland, Maelsechlaind mac Ronald, was a much more energetic character, and he was managing to get the lesser kings south of Ulster to unite against the invaders. One Cerball, King of Ossory, had already won a quite important battle, although himself something of a rebel; and now Maelsechlaind was seeking to organise this present major thrust northwards into Ulster against the so-called Norse King Thorgesr. His forces were to assemble at Drogheda, near the mouth of the River Boyne – and thither they were bound.

It was no lengthy sail from Man, and the motley, straggling fleet made it in a day, on the watch for enemy shipping. Drogheda was not so far south of Godfrey's own Carlingford Lough. And it was suitably near enough to the High King's seat of Tara, in Meath.

But on their evening arrival at the wide mouth of the Boyne river, although they had expected to find a large concentration of shipping already there, only a few vessels were present and no large camp of fighting men encamped ashore. Mooring their fleet in the bay, the four kings' ships moved on up to Drogheda town. And here again there was no sign of an army.

They learned, in answer to their questioning that, in revenge for Cerball of Ossory's victory, Thorgesr had marched south in great strength, not sailed – for Ossory was well inland – and this time the Norsemen had won the day. Cerball had lost most of his men, and had come hastening to the High King for succour and aid, leaving the Norsemen plundering his kingdom. So Maelsechlaind had not waited for the projected full assembly of the Celtic army but had marched off inland right away, for Ossory, intending to catch the Scandinavians while they were dispersed in their orgy of sacking and looting. He had left word for all reinforcements to follow on after him.

Kenneth and his fellow-monarchs, therefore, were faced

303

with a new situation. He and the Dalriadans and the Manx were accustomed to doing their fighting in ships, or at least from ships, although the Welsh and Cumbrians were less so. But it seemed now that they were to be involved in wholly land warfare. Kenneth, for one, was less than happy about this. His shipmen and rowers were not great marchers.

However, needs must, and sailing back to their fleet, they all disembarked and got ready for an early start; Godfrey mac Fergus himself, who knew all this area well, would act guide. All in all, leaving a few to guard the ships, they totalled some four thousand men.

Their march, despite the grumbling of the men, was at least simple, at this stage; they had to follow up the River Boyne for some thirty miles, to Trim, by Slane and Navan, not difficult going in summer weather although liable to be flooded in parts in winter. This part of Meath had not been ravaged by the Norsemen, and it was quite a task to keep it from being so now by the long, straggling host of allies. Discipline was hard to maintain along the winding valley roads in such a composite body. The kings insisted that all food and drink taken from the local population must be paid for; but ensuring that was less easy.

They got only as far as the small town of Slane that first night, a mere dozen miles. There they were met with complaints that the High King's army, passing through six days before, had pillaged and stolen and raped, and the townsfolk wanted no more of that. The kings, hopefully, promised good behaviour, and payment.

Kenneth on this march found Rotri of Gwynedd particularly good company, a man after his own heart. Godfrey and Guriat rode borrowed horses but Kenneth, Rotri and Donald marched together on foot, as encouragement to the men.

The second day they did rather better, passing Navan, where the Boyne swung southwards and was joined by the Blackwater, getting as far as Bective, near to Tara itself, some fifteen miles, still in fairly level country with grassy slopes, cattle-dotted; so there was no lack of beef for hungry marchers that night.

They were not far from the borders of Ossory now, Godfrey said. At Trim they passed the venerable abbey founded by St Patrick himself. And now they began to see signs of devastation, territory over which the Norsemen had swept. Frightened local folk told of atrocities. Also they said that the High King's army had come this way only two days previously, and there were rumours of a battle being fought none so far off to the south-west, near Mullingar, between Loughs Ennells and Owel.

At Raharney that night, still on the Boyne, the leaders held a conference. If a battle was in progress, the sooner reinforcements arrived the better. On the other hand, this Mullingar appeared to be still some eight or nine miles ahead, which would take most of another day to reach, and their men tired after a long march. It was decided that they would march at dawn, but meanwhile Kenneth, Donald, Rotri and a few others would get horses and ride on, to discover the situation.

Through the evening, then, they rode on westwards. After the days of slow walking at the pace of the least active, it was good to be able to canter fast and free to cover ground, to get away from grumbling men, even through territory showing ever increasing signs of war and destruction.

Water was becoming ever more evident, in sluggish streams and pools and marshland. Quite soon, with dusk settling, they saw the glow of fires ahead. Going warily now, they recognised that this was not the conflagration of burning homesteads but small cooking-fires of an encampment. Presently, on slightly higher ground amongst scrub-woodland, they dismounted to creep forward cautiously on foot to investigate. They heard Irish voices, and, reassured, revealed themselves to patrolling sentries. It proved to be a camp mainly of wounded, under an elderly chieftain. He told them that there had been a great battle fought not far off, in the swampy ground between the loughs of Ennells and Owel. It had been indecisive, however bloody, and both sides had meantime withdrawn to regroup. Numbers had appeared to be roughly evenly matched, but those Norse were hard fighters.

When the chieftain heard that there were four thousand more men coming to help, he was much encouraged. He said that Cerball mac Dungall, who evidently was his own leader, and the High King were encamped about two miles ahead, with the army, and would be glad to hear of this timely support, wherever from.

Kenneth decided that they must ride on this short distance and report to Maelsechlaind.

They saw more fires ahead, many more, and came to the outskirts of a great camp, being challenged by guards as they approached. But, a small band on horseback, they were quickly accepted – for the Norsemen seldom used horses – and conducted through the lines of sleeping men to the group round the fire of the High King.

Maelsechlaind proved to be a man of early middle age, stocky, thick-set, with extraordinarily long arms. Although at first unresponsive, almost forbidding, when he learned the identity of his visitors, especially that of Kenneth Norse-Slayer, he thawed and became almost affable. He introduced Cerball of Ossory, a voluble, urgent young man, and the kings of Meath, Munster and Offaly. The reaction to the news that there were four thousand more fighting men nearby was, needless to say, favourable, although there were regrets that they were still almost ten miles away.

A discussion as to tactics had been in progress when they arrived, and there were differing views on this, Cerball being strongly for one course, others opposing, the High King seeking to weigh up the pros and cons. The newcomers listened as the discussion resumed.

As was to be expected, the keynote of both plans was surprise, or the need for it. It appeared that the Norse host was in fact somewhat larger than their own, and Thorgesr was an able commander, his fighters tough, and bold. The battle, which had gone on from first light, when Maelsechlaind had attacked, until midday, had been hard and costly, with eventually both sides withdrawing out of sheer weariness and losses. But the Scandinavians were still there, camped on somewhat higher ground than they were, just east of Lough Owel, about three miles away, and able to overlook this Irish position. Surprise was going to be difficult.

Cerball's proposal was that they should seem to retire southwards, down to the shores of Lough Ennells, the two loughs being about five miles apart, thus coaxing the enemy to leave their higher ground and follow them. And at the lough-side, turn and face them, where at least one flank would be safe. Those against this strategy held that they could still be all too easily surrounded there, their backs to the water, with no escape in the event of failure but to be driven into the lough. Cerball scorned this as defeatist talk. The alternative proposal was to wait where they were, dig ditches and banks, ramparts, and let the Norse expend their strength against these manned defences, making a kind of fort of the position. Especially now that reinforcements were coming, who could assail the foe from flank and rear.

Kenneth heeded it all intently. He, a stranger, was reluctant to intervene – but he did have a suggestion to make. He caught the High King's eye, and that stern man nodded.

"Highness, I agree with King Cerball that a seeming retiral would probably serve best to deceive and surprise the Norsemen. I do not know this Lough Ennells and its shores. But coming here, I saw a place which I noted as a good site for an ambush. I was thinking of our own march – that, if the Norse knew of it, they could trap and destroy our four thousand all too readily. But – it could serve the other way. If the Norse could be led thither, the trapping could be on *our* side."

"Where is this?"

"It was about two miles east of where we came to your camp for the wounded, yonder. Where the Boyne flows sluggishly through a long, narrow valley of marshland and pools, low hills to the north, the river on the south of the road. Any force threading that valley would have to string out at great length, difficult to command and control. That is what struck me – the danger to our long marching column. If you could coax Thorgesr to follow you there . . . "

"That is the valley of Killucan," Cerball interrupted. "I know it well. But Thorgesr is no fool. He would see the danger. That we could seem to flee down it but turn at the far end and come back against him, over the high ground."

"Yes. He would have to be assured that you did not do that. He would assuredly send scouts ahead, after you, to inform him. No commander could fail to do so. Your army, therefore, must be seen to go on beyond, not to be waiting or turning back. So Thorgesr will believe the valley clear. And there is well over a mile of it, I reckon . . . "

"So . . . ?"

"*Our* force could come forward. Early. Get behind those small hills. Thorgesr will not know of it, of us – since you did not. Then, in position above, when the Norse are strung out along the valley's narrows, with the hillside on their left and the Boyne on their right, we would descend upon them. And you then turn and come back on them."

For a little there was silence as men considered this proposal, visualising the territory and the conditions.

Maelsechlaind beat a fist on his knee. "I like that!" he exclaimed. "But – could you get your people there in time? They are near ten miles away, are they not?"

"If we went straight back now. Fast. Roused our camp at Raharney. Marched through the night. From there it is only five or six miles. We could, God willing, be in position by sun-up, I think. When would *you* move?"

"We could not delay overlong. Or Thorgesr will be here to seek to trap us. If we are going to move, we need to do so fairly soon after daylight."

The others made agreeing noises.

"You will have about four miles to march before you reach this valley. You say that you will be in view of the Norsemen. It will take us all our time, but it ought to be possible. If Thorgesr does *not* follow you, no harm is done. We can join up at the east end of the valley. And make a different plan."

"Yes. That is good. I say King Kenneth's advice is best. Is it agreed?"

There were nods of acceptance, Cerball's grudging.

The visitors rose. The sooner they were back to their own camp at Raharney, the better.

If the march hitherto had been productive of much grumbling from men who were seafarers rather than land-fighters, the arousing of the sleeping camp and the forced night-march thereafter brought complaints to a crescendo, even Godfrey and Guriat protesting. But there was no actual refusal, Kenneth's reputation sufficient to carry the necessary persuasion. The actual march in the semi-dark of a summer night was no orderly progress, to be sure, but with royal encouragement the ground was covered. Fortunately, having ridden over it, twice, at least as far as the road was concerned, the leaders knew what was ahead.

Dawn was beginning to lighten the sky behind them when they reached the beginnings of the low hills and the entrance to the Killucan valley. Now it became more difficult, new ground for Kenneth amongst the shadowy trackless slopes, where mists lingered. Keeping thousands of men approximately together in these circumstances was not easy.

As the light strengthened and they could see further, it was to reveal that the little hills levelled off northwards quite quickly to more waterlogged moorland, almost impossible country for any army to traverse. Which at least meant that they were unlikely to see or be seen by any Norsemen on that side. And, thankfully, the hill formation to the south, although forming no continuous ridge or escarpment, was sufficiently solid to create a recognisable barrier between them and the Boyne valley.

A mile of this upland, stumbling and plowtering, and Kenneth called the scattered force to a halt, to well-earned rest meantime, while he, with Rotri, Donald and Riagan strode off upwards and southwards for what had to serve as a ridge, or part of it. The sun was beginning to rise now and mists were lifting from the damp hollows.

When they attained the rounded grassy summits above the valley, it was with some misgivings that they discovered that the slopes down to the road were longer, less steep and less continuous than they had thought in the half-dark, averaging perhaps a quarter-mile, with a drop of some two hundred feet. However, charging men could race down that in two or three minutes, which ought to serve for surprise, certainly not giving time for any long, strung-out host to attempt consolidation. Reasonably satisfied, Kenneth was telling Donald and Riagan to return to the men and bring them up in a lengthy line to man these heights, just out of sight from below, when Rotri gripped his arm and pointed. Away to the west, the first ranks of a great array of men were coming into view.

"The High King and our friends," he said. "Or – I hope so!"

"It will not be the Norse. What would bring them here, save to follow the Irish? This is the time that Maelsechlaind said they would move. But – how far behind will be Thorgesr?"

While the other two hurried down to order their waiting people up to their positions, Kenneth and Rotri watched. Soon it was apparent that this was the High King's army, by the number of horsemen at its head.

Kenneth's forecast as to the very narrow and elongated nature of any force coming down this valley was amply fulfilled presently, with the mounted vanguard able to ride only three abreast and the following ranks of marchers four or five. Soon the Irish host became a lengthy, attenuated file winding along between hillsides and river, most obviously vulnerable to attack – although that only from the high ground; any assault from rear or front would be faced by the same constrictions. The High King's army developed into a thin column well over a mile long, its head emerging from the valley-mouth before its tail could enter at the other end.

There were lessons to be learned by the watchers, as to how far to let the enemy leadership pass through – assuming that they attempted to do so – before attacking. Obviously, if the Norse army was larger than the Irish one, all of it would not be in the valley by the time that its leaders were emerging beyond. Kenneth assessed the options.

They had not long to wait before evidence of enemy reaction was forthcoming for, with the inevitable delay at that western end, as the Irish rear waited to gain entrance, Norse forward troops in chase caught up and fighting developed. Kenneth had not visualised this; but although it was unfortunate for those so caught, it nowise prejudiced the outcome; indeed it tended to confirm his strategy.

However, when the battling rearguard of the Irish managed to detach itself from its attackers and to escape into the valley's constrictions, the enemy did not follow, or not immediately, no doubt waiting for their leaders to come up with their main strength. It was difficult, at that range, for Kenneth and Rotri to make out just what went on there, but they could see numbers building up to the west, and could watch the last of the High King's people come hurrying down the valley road below.

Further development was not long delayed. After an interval, a party of about twenty of the enemy came warily on the trail of the Irish, most evidently prepared for trouble, cautiously prospecting every bend and corner, very ambush-minded. These necessarily took a considerable time to cover the length of the valley. Kenneth hoped that no over-enthusiastic warriors of his own force would be tempted to descend on these scouts. Meanwhile, the last of the Irish rearguard had emerged from the narrows and pressed on after their fellows.

At length the Norse scouting party reached the eastern mouth, and there would be able to see that the Irish army was still moving away, with no aspect of halting or turning back. Leaving half of their number there, to keep watch, the others came hurrying back westwards at the run. If any of them glanced upwards to the hilltops, they would not see the ranks of men hiding there just behind the crests.

Now, for the test of Kenneth's planning.

The main Norse army began to enter that valley. The watchers peered, to try to identify the leadership grouping, no flags or banners showing. But since the way forward had been prospected, and there were scouts still ahead who would return to inform of any danger, there seemed no reason why Thorgesr and his chiefs should not be at the front, in order to make decisions promptly.

This presently proved to be the case – at least, after an initial group of about forty, a sort of vanguard, came a party whose great winged helmets identified them as Viking leaders, stalking three by three. Behind came the long, coiling column of troop upon troop of fighting men.

Kenneth and Rotri moved at last, backing belly-down over the skyline, where the long ranks of their men waited. A final word to each other and they separated, Kenneth to run eastwards, Rotri the other way, shouting to their people, as they ran, to await the signals to move.

A little way from the far eastern end where the hills dwindled and drew back, Kenneth, choosing a summit, pantingly crept up to it, to peer over. It was insufficiently steep a drop to see over and down into the valley. Cursing, he ran forward until he had a view, then dropping flat. The advance party of the enemy was directly below now, and the leaders not far behind. Give them another hundred yards . . .

He was about to creep back when he found Cerball of Ossory lying at his side.

"We have them," that young man jerked. "Where is Thorgesr?"

Kenneth pointed. "The winged helmets are there, coming beneath us now. We must not let them get too near the mouth of the valley, or they might escape, fight their way out."

"I will see that they do not, by God!" the other said grimly. "I have scores to settle!"

"Come, then . . . "

They worked their way back until a curve of the hill hid them from below, and then they rose to run. On the summit they halted, to raise arms and wave, and went on waving, pointing forwards, southwards. And, all along those rolling hilltops, the four thousand rose, swords and stabbing-spears in hand, and surged upwards and over. Far to the west, on a similar summit, Kenneth could just see Rotri at his own signalling.

That charge down the hillsides could not be described as disciplined or orderly – but then few charges are, especially if involving thousands of men over rough, broken ground and extending for a mile's length. Some men ran faster than others, some sections reached the road before others. There were gaps and bunchings. But on the whole it was successful, and certainly it was highly impressive as threat and assault on the surprised marchers below.

The Norsemen had some little warning, of course, with their attackers having to cover four hundred downhill yards to reach them. But that did not do them much good, strung out as they were and their column only four or five men deep. They had nowhere to go to escape the impact, left and right their fellows to collide with, behind them the wide, deep river. And no one close enough to take charge, to command. It was every man for himself. And they had to be more or less stationary, whilst the assault came down on them with yelling impetus. They were fighters and fought bravely enough, but few had any chance to survive. Some preferred to drown.

Cerball led his own men down, aiming specifically at the Norse leadership grouping. They made a greater, denser

mass of attackers than elsewhere, some hundreds strong. And however fierce and puissant the Viking chiefs, they could no more withstand the headlong onslaught than could lesser men. They were overwhelmed in one furious rush, by sheer weight of numbers and impetus and trampled down with little opportunity to defend themselves, those winged helmets flying.

Knots of Scandinavians here and there lasted longer than others. Some at the extreme west end escaped. But at the east valley-mouth none did, for now, almost too late to be involved, the High King's people came running back, their mounted leaders well in front, swords slashing. In only a matter of minutes it was total victory, thousands dying, many driven inexorably into the river to drown, the wounded underfoot, only a few actually throwing down their arms and yielding.

Kenneth himself had no opportunity to strike a blow, since he had waited behind somewhat to survey overall in case leadership or aid was required anywhere. None appeared to be, so far as he could see. By the time that he reached the blood-streaming roadway, all was practically over, although stabbing and stamping and finishing off were still in progress.

It took some time for the victorious leaders to restore order amongst blood-crazed men. They had suffered some casualties, of course, few dead but quite a number wounded. There was more confusion with the fighting over than in the actual assault itself. Most of the Irish army had not been engaged at all; and these coming up only added to the chaos.

There were not a few captives, to be sure, despite the prevalent finishing off, few unwounded. Amongst these were a number of the Norse leaders, including Thorgesr himself, a huge, hairy, bull-necked man with a gashed forehead and a broken arm. Cerball of Ossory had to be restrained from personally running his sword through him there and then, in revenge for his having raped his sister. Maelsechlaind said no, he had other plans for him.

When eventually some order was established along that narrow valley, with the dead enemy unceremoniously thrown into the Boyne, a move was made by the combined forces, with prisoners, back westwards, to head for the

various camps left there, the High King now having eight other monarchs in his company, apart from the self-appointed 'King' Thorgesr, who was strapped on a horse's back since he could not walk.

Kenneth was made much of.

At Maelsechlaind's camp an impromptu feast of newly slain cattle, scores of them, was conjured up for the victorious warriors – to the distress of the local population. Then the High King announced that the day would be completed by an especial ceremony. The kings and chiefs and a few of the men's leaders would march north with him some three miles to Lough Owel, to where the Norse camp had been, and where, if he knew the Scandinavians, a number of captive women might be found, Cerball's people. They would take the captives with them.

So, leaving the riotously celebrating armies, the leaders moved off.

Sure enough, they found women, some hundreds of them at or near the former camp, although many had apparently already disappeared into the safety of the surrounding countryside when their captors, left to guard them, had fled northwards when informed by fugitives of the defeat. Most of the women were too distressed to demonstrate relief and gratitude to their rescuers, but some were sufficiently active to rail at, claw and spit upon the captives, their late rapers and ravagers. They were allowed a free hand.

But the High King had further ideas as to justice. He ordered a move down to the lough-shore for all.

There he had men collect two or three small boats, used for the fishing, and having these manned by rowers then had the Norse prisoners tied together with lengths of rope, in lines, Thorgesr foremost. The rope-ends were attached to the boats, and the oarsmen commanded to pull.

To mingled cheers, hoots, skirls and vituperation the boats drew out into the loch, dragging the stumbling prisoners after them, and went on and on until the last splashing, gasping Viking disappeared beneath the surface, to prolonged acclaim from the shore.

Kenneth mac Alpin, for one, watched this scene with distaste, although he recognised that these Norsemen had done far worse to innocent men, women and children times

without number. It was as kind a justice, perhaps, as would have been hanging.

A return was made to their own camp.

Two days with the High King's company and the Irish army began to break up. The hay-harvest was now ready and men anxious to get home and get it in, for the winter-feed for their cattle. Kenneth and his fellow-monarchs were invited back to Maelsechlaind's capital at Tara; but they decided that a return promptly to their own various realms was called for, hay being important there also, and their men having been away from home for long enough. So leave was taken of a grateful High King, who was loud in his praises for a Celtic alliance. He assured that he would not cease to punish further the Norsemen in the north.

Kenneth led his people back eastwards down Boyne to their ships at Drogheda, his name and fame undoubtedly further enhanced – and, he hoped, his unity project also.

20

All the drama and excitement of that summer had not taken place in Ireland. Kenneth returned to Garlies to rousing news, good and bad. The good was that Eithne was pregnant – a joy to them both. The bad was that Feredith mac Bargoit had been slain, assassinated, in mysterious circumstances, and Brude mac Fochel was now High King of Alba.

This last, of course, disturbed Kenneth greatly. It seemed likely that Brude was behind the death of his rival, and this was a sure recipe for internal strife in Alba and consequent weakening of that realm. Brude was a fighter, but an unruly man, and unlikely therefore to prove a good ruler, or a good neighbour for Dalriada. And there had been a further Norse raid on Alba's Buchan coast, apparently again from Orkney.

There was little that Kenneth could do about this situation but hope for the best, concerned and frustrated though he was.

Eithne was much concerned also about the state of Alba, her homeland. Since her father died, there had been an extraordinary succession of high kings, none reigning more than a year or two, to the detriment of the realm. Desperately the nation required a strong monarch with an extended reign, to give stability, continuity and, it was to be hoped, peace internally and externally. Brude was unlikely to provide these, she felt. She almost wished that Kenneth, so successful in his ventures in other lands, would, or could, take a hand in Alba.

Their fears of trouble were not long in being substantiated, trouble in Alba itself but also spilling over into Dalriada again, general lawlessness rife. Another mormaor, Drostan of Angus, had some of his lands overrun by the Moray men, and when he complained to Brude, was insulted before a large company. Angry, he was now in a state of revolt, and urging the other *ri* to join him in it, and dethrone

Brude.

Of more personal concern to Kenneth were the now frequent and quite widespread incursions into Dalriadan territory by Albannach bands, clearly unchecked by Brude, these now beginning to rival the Norse raids. Donald was kept busy repulsing and chasing them. Some of the island chieftains were now joining in these assaults, as a sort of sport, and Alpin called upon Kenneth to come and teach such folk a lesson.

His father's plea posed a problem indeed. Kenneth's concern was with the *uniting* of the Celtic peoples, not with punitive expeditions against them. Yet he could not ignore Alpin's call altogether, and he did recognise that these raids had to be halted. What to do? He had no illusions that any visit to Brude would be productive.

It was Eithne's suggestion that a *show* of strength round the islands, without actual hostilities, might be effective and serve as warning and persuasion, visiting the troublemakers and others who might be tempted to join in. She would come with him, in support; her name might help. Kenneth's fears about possible ill effects on her pregnancy she dismissed with amusement. An excuse to sail the Hebridean seaboard in late summer was welcome, admittedly.

Towards the end of August, then, they set out in a longship, to call at Dunadd and pick up Conall and another three ships, which they felt would be about the right number to show strength without aggression. Alpin was thankful to see them, with Donald away on the tracks of raiders from the Morvern area on their northern border.

This northern border situation of Dalriada was itself something of a problem and source of trouble, and always had been, for the dividing line was not clear-cut, amongst all the plethora of peninsulas, islands and sea-lochs, neither realm prepared to yield debatable land. Dalriada, being by comparison small, was the more reluctant. The Ardnamurchan peninsula, the longest of all, stretching furthest out into the Western Sea just north of Loch Sunart, was generally accepted as Dalriada's ultimate limit; yet much of the great island of Mull, to the south of this, off which lay Iona, was claimed by Alba. And some of the lesser isles were of doubtful allegiance. But because Dalriada

317

always maintained a large and comparatively powerful fleet, indeed was apt to do its fighting by sea, while Alba did not, at least on this seaboard, the islesmen tended to defer to Dunadd. Now, it seemed that Brude was encouraging a different alignment.

It was a little difficult, therefore, for Kenneth to know where to start: whether to support Donald operating by land, in Ardnamurchan, or to proceed further north and west, towards Skye. However, according to reports, the worst of the spasmodic and localised raiding had emanated from the islands of Eigg and Rhum, north of Ardnamurchan but south of Skye. So it was decided to visit these first.

In fact, sailing up that colourful and beautiful Sea of the Hebrides in August sunshine, amongst the jewelled islands set in painted waters, it was difficult likewise to feel any sense of conflict or danger. Especially when they passed Iona and went close enough inshore, on the west side, for Kenneth and Eithne to view the white sands of Calva's Bay, where, for them, peace and joy seemed always enshrined.

It was evening of that first day before, passing seawards of the astonishing columnar island of Staffa and the picturesque cluster of the Treshnish Isles, they came to sizeable Coll, where, those years ago, Kenneth had obtained his first victory over the Norsemen. It seemed a long time ago as they approached Arinagour, the chief haven.

That approach apparently alarmed the islanders, for nobody was to be seen when the four vessels entered the bay. However, when only a token few of the visitors landed, with a woman, people began to appear; and presently Kenneth's identity was recognised and a welcome of sorts was forthcoming.

Coll, they discovered, had been one of the sufferers in the latest lawlessness, the raiders being their own neighbours to the north, from the Albannach isles of Muck, Eigg and Rhum. It had been nothing like the Norse attacks, admittedly, mainly cattle and sheep stealing and some molesting of women, but grievous for the victims nevertheless. These hoped that King Kenneth was going to go and teach the wretches a lesson. They themselves had been thinking of combining with the men of Colonsay, Oronsay and Tiree, also assailed, to mount a retaliatory attack on the offenders to the north.

Kenneth urged them not to attempt this meantime; mutual warfare amongst the islanders would be a sorry outcome. Leave it to him, at this stage.

They sailed on the score or so of miles. The vistas ahead were becoming ever more dramatic, with the shapes of the islands changing notably, mountains rising to more than rival in height and outline those of the mainland. Far north soared the jagged Cuillins of Skye, a fiercely lovely blue barrier. Somewhat nearer, further to the west, the lofty, shapely peaks of Rhum challenged them. And nearer still, Eigg's thrusting prow-like tor, abruptly steep and proud, at one end, dominated the closer scene.

Passing the smaller island of Muck, the Swine's Isle, of this group, which did not support sufficient folk to seem worth any demonstration, they sailed under the towering isolated pinnacle of the Sgurr of Eigg, to the central bay and haven of Kildonnan, on the sheltered east side of the larger isle. Here the martyred St Donnan, one of Columba's more headstrong disciples, had rebelliously established his own church almost three centuries before, and where there was now quite a large township. The four longships coming into the bay, and flying the banners of Dalriada and Galloway, created something of a stir ashore, if not a panic.

This time Kenneth and Eithne landed most of their crews, all armed, so that there would be no doubt about their ability to take strong measures if necessary. The chieftain's hallhouse was very obvious, set on a mound near the church and a great cairn of stones which was St Donnan's grave. From here the visitors were watched warily by a small group. Having a woman with them must have mystified the waiting party.

As they came up, Kenneth raised an arm in greeting – but with a clenched fist at the end of it and no smile on his face. "I seek Findon mac Derile, lord of this Eigg," he announced. "Is he here? I am Kenneth mac Alpin of Galloway. And this is Eithne, my queen, daughter and sister of high kings of Alba."

"I am Findon," a burly giant of a man answered, without any assurance for one so large. "I – I greet you, Highnesses."

"Reserve your welcome," Kenneth told him flatly. "We come on no kindly visit. That is – if you were one of those who raided the Isle of Coll, in my father's realm, as we have been told. Were you, Findon mac Derile?"

The other coughed. "I . . . we went with Cormac of Rhum. It – it was scarcely a raid, Highness. The Coll folk have been a trouble to us, on occasion. We went to warn them, that is all . . . "

"Your warning included burning houses and barns, stealing cattle and sheep, raping women and taking goods and gear. If that is warning, what is it warning of?"

There was no answer.

"*I* could warn you here, on Eigg, similarly!" And Kenneth gestured towards his hundreds of armed men. "Coll is Dalriadan territory. Warfare against my father's realm."

"It was not like that, Highness – not warfare," Findon assured earnestly. "We, Cormac and myself, meant no great ill. Just warning, as I said. Some of our men may have been – been over-eager. The drink, you know. No great hurt was intended . . . "

"Yet great hurt was done." That was Eithne. "Not only to the Coll folk but more seriously, to friendly relations between Alba and Dalriada. Such raiding *is* warfare. And not to be tolerated by the princes of nations."

Silence.

"Other Dalriadan islands have been raided. Tiree and Colonsay," Kenneth went on. "And on the mainland, in Morvern and Ardnamurchan . . . "

"Not by me, Highness – not by me."

"Who, then?"

"What Cormac of Rhum may do, or Brendan of Skye, is not my responsibility, Highnesses."

"I think that you hide behind others? Scarcely praiseworthy, Findon mac Derile!" Eithne put in.

"Your responsibility as to Coll will serve us, meantime!" Kenneth said. "For that, I am here to see that you pay. For all cattle and sheep that you stole you will return two of each. You will make restitution for goods taken. You will give assurance that you will raid no more Dalriadan territory. And you will feed us and our men this night. Is it understood?"

The other nodded.

"So be it. Tomorrow we will see Cormac of Rhum."

Presumably relieved that he had got off thus lightly, Findon thereafter sought to make himself affable. It turned out that he had a pleasant, motherly wife, who entertained her uninvited guests well in the hallhouse. Their crews fared adequately down at the shore and in some of the houses.

In the morning, they sailed on the ten miles to Rhum, a still larger and very mountainous island, its fine peaks renowned for possessing their own small white captive clouds, which either sat on the summit tips or hovered like haloes just above, source of many a story. Kenneth was aware that Rhum had only the one really sheltered anchorage on its cliff-girt, rock-bound perimeter, the east-facing Loch Scresort, its main community at the head of this.

They were still a couple of miles from the island when they saw two galleys leaving the mouth of this Loch Scresort and immediately turning off northwards, to depart at speed.

Eying these, Kenneth scratched his chin. "These appear to have seen us. And do not want to meet us!"

"Perhaps they think that we are Norsemen?" Eithne suggested.

"It is possible. But if so, would they not be more likely to retire into their own mountains and valleys? It is a large island. Driving their cattle with them. And there should be sufficient men on Rhum to defend it from four dragonships."

"These could be not Rhum men. Possibly Skye ships. They seem to be heading for Skye."

When they entered Loch Scresort, over a mile long, they found the shores of it dotted with cot-houses all the way up to the sizeable haven and township at the head. Quite a number of fishing-boats were in evidence, and a single larger vessel. No crowd awaited the visitors here.

They landed under the shadow of the high mountains, so close were they, disembarking a fair proportion of their force, very much aware of the lack of visible population. There was a hallhouse behind the township, larger than that at Eigg. Kenneth and Eithne made for this, recognising that they were being watched from doorways and sheds.

At the hallhouse door it was a young woman who opened

to them, seeming nervous. She did not speak.

"This is the house of Cormac of Rhum, lady?" Kenneth asked.

"Yes."

"Is he here? At home?"

"No, Highness."

Eithne touched his arm. "So you know who we are!" she said. "How that, I wonder?"

The other woman looked confused. "I – I spoke without thought. I am sorry. I . . . " She spread her hands.

"We are the King and Queen of Galloway. So your unthinking served you well!" Kenneth smiled. "Are you kin to Cormac?"

"His wife, Highness. Moninne."

"Then you will know where he is. We have come to see him." And when she did not meet his eye, "We saw two galleys leaving here, to sail north. They must have seen us. Would Cormac be in one of those, I wonder?"

"He had to go to Skye. To speak with King Brendan."

"In haste, it appears! And you knew that I was on my way here. He did not wait to see me. So he feared meeting us. I think that you must have been warned, from Eigg. A boat must have come, early. Before us?"

She did not answer.

"So, Lady Moninne, your husband has a guilty conscience! As well he might. For he has been raiding Coll, with Findon of Eigg, and did much hurt there, in Dalriada, my father's kingdom. You will know of that? He must pay for it. Has he left any man here in charge?"

She shook her head.

"Then you will have to tell him what he must pay. Now, how will we ensure that you do so, and that he pays? This elusive Cormac! Some hostage, perhaps?"

"The Lady Moninne herself perhaps should come with us, I think. To Skye – to see her husband," Eithne proposed. "Would not that be best?"

This time it was Kenneth who hesitated, concerned as to two aspects of this suggestion. One, that he should seem to be using a woman to bring pressure to bear. And also Skye was scarcely a place to seem to challenge with four longships. The largest of all the Hebridean islands and the

322

most populous, it called itself a kingdom although part of Alba and its rulers not of the seven *ri*. King Brendan was said to be a fierce character.

He could hardly voice his doubts there and then. "We shall see," he said.

In the end, he decided that, since nothing was to be gained there on Rhum, in the circumstances, lacking Cormac's presence, he would indeed proceed to Skye, but in as non-aggressive fashion as possible, to seek to involve King Brendan in his alliance project, and hope to make his point with Cormac of Rhum while he was there. In this last, Eithne reasserted that having the wife with them would be of help, even though they did not call her hostage.

That young woman was clearly very reluctant to accompany them, but was not in a position to resist. No doubt Eithne's presence was of some comfort for her.

They sailed out of Loch Scresort and turned northwards.

It was a further ten miles to the nearest point on Skye, the Sleat peninsula. So large was this island that it seemed to block all ahead of them, a mighty barrier of harsh-seeming mountains. But Conall had been here before, and knew the way into and up the narrow Sound of Sleat, which the uninformed would have found it difficult to locate. He pointed out that, as on all the Hebridean islands, the havens and larger townships were situated on the sheltered eastern side, facing the mainland and not the wide ocean. Skye's *Port-an-ri*, or Portree, the Haven of the King, was no exception.

The ships had to face strong tide-races in the narrows of that sound, and distances were longer than they had calculated, so that it was late evening before they emerged into the almost inland sea to the east of Skye, with a brilliant crimson and gold sunset blazing behind the black fangs of the Cuillins. Conall said that it could still be a score of miles to Portree – and anyway, night was no time to approach, on their present project. So they anchored at a fishing-community, not on Skye itself but on the mainland shore opposite, where they sought to allay the alarm of the folk, and where Eithne took Moninne to sleep in one of the cot-houses.

They awoke to mist and rain, with the mountains

shrouded and the sea a leaden level grey, and made a dreary voyage of it north-westwards, to get behind the long, narrow isle of Raasay which lay between Skye and the mainland here. Some way up this lesser arm of the sea, the bay of Portree opened.

Kenneth was somewhat surprised to have got thus far without challenge, possibly their night-time arrival and the day's poor visibility responsible. But entering the mouth of the bay they were met by two longships and four galleys, a sufficient force to bar their way if nothing more. Kenneth had his rowers raise their oars high, while they waited for this squadron to come up.

A young man hailed them from the leading longship. "I am Colum mac Brendan. Who are you who enters my father's waters lacking invitation?"

"If the banners of Dalriada and Galloway mean nothing to you, you lack knowledge, Colum mac Brendan," Kenneth called back. "Which is a pity, for you have a good name."

"What do you mean by that, stranger?"

"I mean that Colum, Columcille, St Columba, names the greatest man who ever came to this land, friend. If you are called after him, you are to be congratulated. Even though you do not know the devices we show on our banners."

"I *am* named for Columcille. He came here and saved Skye from the evil. Delivered us from the Fell Hound." The young man gestured towards where the Cuillin Mountains were hidden in cloud, and spoke almost as though Columba had visited his island the day before. "Who then are you, who speaks so bold?"

"I am Kenneth mac Alpin of Galloway. And this is Eithne of Alba, my queen. Come to visit King Brendan."

"Not . . . not . . . the Norse-Slayer?"

"I have been called that."

They could see great commotion aboard the other vessel.

"We have nothing to fear here, I think," Eithne said.

"We are come to escort you in," the young prince shouted, belatedly. "Follow us, Highnesses."

So they entered the hammer-head-shaped bay of Portree in style, ten ships now. At the head, the community round the double harbour was large enough to be called a town, mist-shrouded hilly ground behind, and nearby, to the north, a fort crowned an isolated summit overlooking all. On a clear day the views would be stupendous.

The intention had been to keep the young Moninne aboard, in their charge, as a bargaining-counter; but it looked as though this would not be necessary. So Kenneth decided, as they disembarked, that she should come with them – to her evident relief.

Colum mac Brendan, a fresh-faced, eager character in his early twenties, was flatteringly impressed by his visitors' identity, bowing low to Eithne and looking questioningly at Moninne, whom he obviously knew. He pointed to the fort-crowned hill.

"Dun Torvaig," he said. "My father's house. He sent me . . ."

"This lady's husband, Cormac of Rhum – is he here?"

"Yes. He is up at the palace, Highness."

Actually, that was not quite accurate, for, as they set off to walk to the hill-foot, a party could be seen coming down the spiralling road from the fort.

As the two groups drew close, Colum called out, "Here is King Kenneth mac Alpin, Norse-Slayer. And the Queen of Galloway. Come visiting." And to Kenneth, "My father, King Brendan."

At first they took the swarthy, black-browed individual, good-looking in a harsh way, to be the allegedly fierce King of Skye; but when this character seemed to have no eyes for any but their hostage, they assumed that he must be Cormac, and therefore Brendan was the shrivelled-looking limping, smaller man at his side. He it was who spoke.

"The Norse-Slayer? Himself?"

"And his lady! The Queen Eithne nic Angus of Alba," Kenneth emphasised.

"Ah, yes – yes, to be sure, Highness. Here is a surprise. What brings you to Skye?"

Kenneth had to choose. He could say that Cormac of Rhum brought him to Skye, and why. Or he could take the longer view. He chose the latter.

"We are sailing the Hebridean Sea, Highness, in the cause of defence against raiders, all raiders," he answered carefully. "I seek, as you may have heard, to unite all the Celtic peoples against those who oppress and harass us. The Norse and the Angles in especial, but also other and lesser evildoers." And he looked directly at Cormac, the swarthy one presumably. "I think that so potent a monarch as Brendan of Skye, with many fighting men, should be glad to join the forces of Dalriada, Alba, Galloway, Strathclyde, Cumbria, Gwynedd, Man and the Irish kingdoms, in our alliance. Is it not so?" That, putting this Brendan on a par with all the greater rulers, might have its effect.

The small, twisted man inclined his head. "I have heard of this. And much of yourself, Kenneth mac Alpin. And of Queen Eithne also, to be sure." That was a little hurried. "We will discuss it, your alliance – but not here. I see that you have the Lady Moninne with you?"

"Yes. We had reason to call at Rhum. And found her husband gone. She, I think, has matters to put to him."

"M'mm." Brendan looked from wife to husband. "Then let us go to my house, yonder."

In their progress through the town and climb up to the fort-palace, Kenneth ignored Cormac and walked beside Brendan. Colum escorted Eithne, and the pair from Rhum followed on, whispering to each other.

Kenneth decided that he could like Brendan, who appeared undeserving of his hard reputation; perhaps, as a younger man, he had gone in for piracy and aggression, but now he gave a different impression. Or it may have been merely that he approved of what he had heard of Kenneth himself. And when pointing out where Columcille the saint had delivered the Skye of his day from the dreaded Fell Hound, he learned that Columba was Kenneth's hero also, Brendan recognised fellowship in this. He promised to show his guest a notable relic, up at the palace. In return, Kenneth informed him that he had the famous *Lia Faill*, the coronation stone, hidden away in a secret place, for safety from the Norsemen, as he put it, rather than the Albannach, in these circumstances.

By the time they reached Dun Torvaig they were on excellent terms, so much so that Kenneth was disinclined to spoil things by crossing swords with Cormac meantime. Rather feebly, as he felt himself, he asked Eithne to deputise for him and have a quiet word with that man, to the effect that compensation must be made to the Coll folk, and promptly, and no further raiding into Dalriadan territory, or Rhum would suffer.

At the palace, then, they were made very welcome, and Brendan proudly produced an enormous wild-boar's tusk, which he claimed had come from an animal slain by Columba himself, in the Cuillin Mountains. Somehow this creature had come to be associated with the aforementioned and dire Fell Hound of those mountains, the fear of which had apparently held the islanders in thrall, a fear nourished by the pagan druids for their own ends. The saint, in allegedly slaying this boar miraculously, armed only with a little woman's knife presented to him by the then Queen of Skye, had rid the island of its bugbear, to the dismay of the druid priests and the advance of Christianity. On how much of all this was truth and how much legend, Kenneth reserved judgment; but the tusk was real enough, and impressive.

They stayed three enjoyable days with Brendan and his large and laughter-loving wife, and were shown something of the great island, which, with the weather fortunately improving, they discovered to be highly dramatic as to scenery, not only the mighty mountains but the coastline of cliffs and towering stacks, fine bays and sea-lochs.

Cormac and his wife quietly took themselves off on the second day. King Brendan made no reference to what Kenneth's business with Rhum had been, although quite possibly he had a fair idea. But he did agree to contribute to any allied force against the Norsemen – who could on occasion be a menace to outlying parts of Skye also, although they apparently never attacked Portree itself.

Well satisfied, Kenneth and Eithne took their leave, and sailed on.

They still headed northwards, for although the Albannach chieftains and islanders up here were too far off to be of much trouble to Dalriada, Eithne was eager to see something of this remote Wester Ross seaboard, and Kenneth himself far from averse. Anyway, their purpose was to demonstrate a Dalriadan presence, in strength, in these waters. The mormaors of Ross had their capital on the east side of this great province, in the Cromarty area, so there was little chance of seeing the present incumbent, a supporter of Brude.

In leisurely fashion, then, the four longships cruised up the scenic coast for another hundred miles or so, past localities which Conall could name for them, some quite famous, some unknown to them: Torridon, Loch Ewe, Gruinard, Coigach, Edrachillis, Handa. They called in at communities here and there, careful to show friendship and to pay for such food and drink as needed and obtained, and met with no hostility although a certain amount of local concern until their identity was established. They kept a sharp look-out for Norse dragon-ships, for they were getting none so far from the Orkney Isles now, but saw only fishing-boats.

When they reached the topmost western tip of Alba, at the thrusting headland of An Garbh, so called because of its great thrusting promontory like the prow of a ship, Kenneth was tempted to sail on and make a demonstration round the Orkney Isles themselves, now to be seen hull-down to the north. But Eithne, and caution, prevailed. They would be better with a deal more than four ships to venture thither. One day . . .

So they turned westwards now, to visit the Outer Hebrides instead – Lewis, Harris, Benbecula, Barra and the rest. These remote isles constituted a strange territory, in theory still part of Alba but in fact all but independent – more, part Norse now, for numbers of the raiders from Orkney in the past had stayed on, settled down and inter-married with the local population, in a taming process. Tamed or not, however, Kenneth decided that they would be none the worse for a sight of Dalriadan ships-of-war making their presence felt in these waters.

It was about fifty miles out from the mainland to Lewis, the most northerly and largest of the Outer Isles, the chain of which, with no large gaps between, unlike their Inner counterparts, extended southwards for over one hundred and fifty miles. Down and amongst these the squadron sailed for a full week thereafter, meeting with no opposition and themselves making no real challenge. They called in at various havens and townships, Eithne's presence a great help in reassuring folk on first arrival, at Stornoway and Ranish on Lewis, Tarbert and Luskentyre and Rodel on mountainous Harris, Lochmaddy, Locheport and Lochboisdale on the loch-strewn Uists, Eoligarry and Kisimul on Barra, and finally at the little Mingulay and Berneray, the southernmost outposts. For the visitors it was all but sheer vacation, the weather in the main good, the people not unfriendly, the scenery remarkably varied for islands, but trees notably lacking, except for small patches here and there in very sheltered corners. In that lengthy chain of isles, they were more than usually aware of the vast empty ocean to the west, and although they encountered no storms, the swell was enormous even on almost windless days.

Well aware that they had been away from their duties in Galloway and elsewhere for overlong already, Kenneth ordered a return now to Dalriada, almost reluctantly.

At Dunadd the holiday atmosphere terminated abruptly. They had barely landed at Port an Deora when the dire news was broken to them. King Alpin was dead, ambushed and slain. Troubled by further raiding from Alba in the east, and with Donald still away in Morvern and Ardnamurchan, Alpin had himself led a punitive force inland, and had been trapped in a pass called Brander, between Lochs Etive and Awe, beneath the mighty Ben Cruachan. Who was responsible was not clear, but since the raiders were in large numbers and almost certainly Moraymen, Brude himself was being blamed.

Kenneth was appalled. Although he did not always see eye to eye, and he had little respect for his father's warlike abilities, he was fond of him and recognised his many virtues and good-natured tolerance. Kenneth now blamed himself. He had been away cruising unconcernedly in the Hebridean Sea, enjoying himself, when he had been needed here. Eithne, while sympathising, declared that attitude to be nonsense. If they had not gone off round the islands they would have gone back to Galloway, would they not? So they would not have been at Dunadd when the call came, anyway. His father's death was tragic, but no fault of his. He must now do what was required, what was best – but not to blame himself.

And there was much to do, in the circumstances, there at Dunadd left suddenly rulerless. It was a little while before it really dawned on Kenneth mac Alpin that *he* was now that ruler, King of Dalriada, not of Galloway.

21

Coronation and enthronement could wait. More pressing was not the revenge which so many Dalriadans demanded, but to settle the situation with Alba. It was maddening, after all Kenneth's efforts, that there should now be almost warfare between the two neighbouring realms, and chaos within Alba itself. This Brude was a disaster as High King. Whether or not he was personally responsible for Alpin's death, he was responsible for the unruly conditions prevailing in his kingdom, amounting to civil war. Something had to be done.

Kenneth was loth to invade Alba with an army, as the Dalriadan lords were clamouring for him to do. That could destroy all that he had worked for in Celtic unity. Yet, what else would be effective? No personal mission by himself or by an envoy was likely to have any effect on Brude, even his safety problematical. More mere chasing and chastising of raiding parties would be quite insufficient and would not affect the High King. But he could not just accept the situation, or send protests. And there was Galloway, the sub-kingdom, to think of.

He sent for Donald to return from the north. He would appoint him King of Galloway now, and despatch him back to Garlies. Meanwhile, on second thoughts, he would go ahead with the arrangements for his own coronation. He would have the greater authority over Dalriada when that was done, undoubtedly. As a first step towards this he sent Conall to Dunstaffnage to unearth and bring back the hidden *Lia Faill*.

Eithne was a great help and comfort to him in all this; but she could not guide him as to what to do about Brude mac Fochel.

When Donald arrived back at Dunadd he was as outraged and incensed as was his brother, and all for an immediate expedition in fullest strength into Alba, as far as Inverness itself, if need be. Kenneth said to wait. It was autumn now, and soon the inland mountain passes would be snow-bound, no time to start any major campaign on land. Nor was it the time to sail a great fleet all the way up and round, through the stormy Pentland Firth between Alba and Orkney and down the east coast, to attack Inverness from the sea. Better to hold back until the spring, and decide on action then, meantime sending a courier to Brude registering anger, demanding satisfaction and conveying warning. For the present, they would hold a joint coronation ceremony at Iona, to better establish their two regnal positions.

So one more pilgrimage to Iona was embarked on, for all the notables of Dalriada. Kenneth decided that it was more appropriate to hold the coronation and anointing service *before* the actual enthroning and fealty-swearing up on the top of Dunadd Hill, when he would be the more undoubtedly monarch and fealty fully due. Eithne, although now heavy with child, insisted on coming along too, asserting that if the voyage in choppy autumnal seas brought on a somewhat premature birth, what better than for their son to be born on Iona? She was confident that it *was* to be a son.

No such circumstances arose, however, and they all reached the sacred isle safely, in quietly grey weather, solidly overcast but not wet, Prior Phadraig now, with practice, attaining a mastery of the proceedings. It gave Kenneth great satisfaction to have the *Lia Faill* placed back on the summit of Tor Abb for the occasion, where it must frequently have rested in Columba's time, as well as at earlier coronations.

After the Eucharist and the anointing, with the former abbot's chair now used as seat for Eithne just behind the coronation stone, Kenneth himself performed a little enthroning of his father's devising, appointing his brother as King of Galloway and placing his own former golden circlet around Donald's brows, an innovation here.

There was no time, nor was this a suitable occasion, for Kenneth and Eithne to make their own private pilgrimage to Calva's Bay; but that could wait.

The feasting this time was provided by the lord of Bunessan, on Mull nearby, where there was a sheltered haven for the shipping.

When all got back to Dunadd for the fealty-giving and enthronement up at the Boar-stone, it was to learn news which changed the entire situation with regard to Alba. Brude was no longer a problem. He was dead, slain in battle with Drostan, Mormaor of Angus; and the latter had now assumed the high kingship – although apparently not with unanimous support.

Brude's reign, if it could be called that, had been mercifully short. Would this Drostan's be longer, better? Poor disunited Alba.

So there was no need meantime to prepare any avenging invasion from Dalriada for the spring, unless Drostan proved as awkward as his predecessor, or was unseated by another of the *ri* who might in turn be inimical.

Donald sailed off for Galloway.

Kenneth's taking over of the throne at Dunadd, after Alpin, was less difficult, despite their very different characters and ideas as to rule, than might have been, for of course he had been leading Dalriadan forces in warfare for long, and knew and was known to most of the chiefs and lords. Also his reputation was such that his authority was respected. So the change-over presented few problems, although some of the more independent characters recognised that there would probably be stricter control over their activities than in the previous two reigns. There was fairly general disappointment that the puissant Kenneth had not led a suitably spectacular attack into Alba – that was all.

He held a great conference of his chief men and landholders before all returned to their glens, peninsulas and islands, wanting to hear their views on the governance of the nation as well as projecting his own. His visits to all the other Celtic states had given him an especial insight into the customs and usages, good and less good, prevailing elsewhere, some of which he was eager to introduce in Dalriada. He emphasised, of course, his vision of Celtic unity, and the onus this laid upon them to try to restrain their reactions to Albannach raiding, difficult as this might be. It was to be hoped that, under the new regime of Drostan, this would diminish, if not cease altogether.

On the whole he achieved fairly general agreement and

backing.

He did not retain the *Lia Faill* at Iona, or even at Dunadd, in case of disaster to himself or the nation, from whatever cause, but sent Conall back with it to its former hiding-place at Dunstaffnage.

Just before the start of the Yuletide festivities, Eithne was at last brought to bed. Births are seldom as easy as men can assume, for women concerned, however natural the process may be esteemed, and Kenneth was more anxious than over campaigns and battles where the life or death of hundreds could be at stake. But there were no complications, and after a fairly lengthy labour the promised son was delivered, in good shape and sound condition. Eithne, handing him over to his proud father, urged that he should be called Conn, or Constantine, after the uncle of whom she had been fond and who had made a good king for Dalriada and then for Alba also. Kenneth was well enough content with that, although he would have granted her anything, there and then.

So they made a happy Christmastide at Dunadd; and the Yule celebrations thereafter, which dated from pre-Christian days, had their own fulfilment. Kenneth mac Alpin could rejoice and make merry as well as plan, persuade and fight.

He was in fact already planning how he would and could best use his new authority and status in the cause he had at heart. He was part encouraged, part troubled, by a message from Drostan, seeking his help against rebellious Moraymen. Brude, it seemed, had been succeeded as Mormaor of Moray by a brother, Tadg mac Fochel, who was made in something of the same mould, and, with Fergus, Mormaor of Ross, had opposed Drostan's elevation to the high kingship. He might prove awkward hereafter, and again no good neighbour to Dalriada.

At least Drostan seemed to want to be friends, and appeared to have the support of the remaining *ri*, which was hopeful.

22

In the spring, there were tidings of renewed Norse activity, and on two fronts. In Ireland, Thorgesr's successor was on the rampage, but Maelsechlaind was proving a strong High King and was again personally leading the defending forces. There had also been another assault on the east coast of Alba, thought to be from Orkney, this on the Easter Ross and Moray seaboards – which Drostan appeared almost to welcome, as it would serve to keep those two mormaors preoccupied with their own problems and less likely to trouble *him*. The which Kenneth considered to be a mistaken and dangerous attitude, knowing Norsemen.

He decided that a visit to Drostan, at Forteviot, was called for.

In May he set out, with a small party only strong enough to protect him if attacked while passing through the border-line country with Moray, in the Drumalban area – where indeed his father had met his end. Eithne would have liked to have come with him, needless to say, but now she had a six-month-old warrior to deal with who seemed to demand prior attention. So Kenneth proceeded to her homeland without her, up Loch Awe-side to the Glens Orchy and Lochy and over the watershed to Strathfillan, down to Glens Dochart and Ogle and so into Strathearn, to follow the Earn down almost to salt water at the Tay estuary.

At Forteviot, he found Drostan to be a solemn, unsmiling man of middle years, with a slight impediment in his speech. But however uneloquent, he was clearly glad to see his visitor and anxious to have his help and guidance. His problems were many, having taken over the rule with Alba in a divided and unsettled state and central authority lacking. But his main fears were connected with the hostility of the mormaors of Moray and Ross – which, because of the geographical position, meant that Caithness also was apt to be of no support to him, which left only the four southern mormaordoms of Buchan, Mar, Atholl and Angus, with the lesser provinces of Fife, Strathearn and the Lennox, to be relied upon. The Norse threat seemed to worry Drostan less, a sad commentary on the state of Alba.

Kenneth was sympathetic but suggested that the Scandinavians were really the major menace, and that leaving Moray and Ross to deal with their own Norse raiding was a mistaken policy. If there were further attacks there, would it not be wiser to go to these mormaors' aid and so commend his rule to them, and at the same time warn off the real enemy?

It was strange to be at Forteviot and Eithne not there. Oddly, Drostan, like Angus mac Fergus, took his guest eastwards, after a day or two, to the Fife Ness neighbourhood, not to Kilrymond and St Andrew's shrine but to the marshy expanses of the Tents Muir area to the north of it, where they hawked for wildfowl, this High King's favourite pastime it seemed.

They had been at this sport for a couple of days when a messenger arrived hot-foot from Forteviot. He announced that a call for help had come, not from Moray or Ross but from Gartnait, Mormaor of Mar, much nearer at hand. A major invasion of Norsemen was in progress in the area south of Aberdeen, hundreds of dragon-ships involved and great devastation being committed. The Mar forces desperately needed aid.

Drostan was much concerned, and they hastened back to Forteviot. The Scandinavians had never before come so far south as this – and the territory concerned was neighbouring on his own former mormaordom of Angus. He would have to go there and mobilise its fighting men – for the high kings as such did not have at their disposal large numbers of troops, being dependent on those of the other *ri*. Would Kenneth mac Alpin help them, in this crisis, with his advice?

That was not to be refused, of course. But Kenneth suggested that it might be best if he went directly to Mar, to discover the tactical situation there, rather than delaying by going to Angus, with Drostan, to raise forces. This was accepted.

So, from Forteviot, with only about three hundred men,

all horsed, they headed north-eastwards two days later. Kenneth would accompany the High King as far as Forfar, the Angus capital, where Drostan's young son Nechtan was now acting mormaor, more or less on his way to the Dee valley and Kildrummy where Gartnait of Mar had his main seat.

It was no great distance to Forfar, less than fifty miles, and they made it in a day, crossing Tay near Scone and passing Dunsinane and Coupar to enter the great valley of Strathmore, halfway down which lay Forfar on its loch. There they found that Nechtan, a vigorous young man, already knew of the Norse attack to the north and was assembling his manpower, not so much to go to Mar's aid as to protect his own territories should the Scandinavians move southwards. His father convinced him to use only half his force, when fully mustered, for defending Angus, and to send the rest north to Gartnait's assistance, to think of Alba not just Angus. Leaving them to it, Kenneth and his party, with a guide, rode on.

This was all new country for him, often heard of but never visited. Strathmore was fair, settled and populous, with much tillable land and wide pastures, hemmed in on the west by tall mountains and on the east by low green hills between it and the sea. It was, oddly enough, not the channel for any major river, but instead was crossed diagonally by many, Isla, the Esks, Lunan, Bervie. The strath narrowed and petered out as at length it neared the sea close to Dunnottar, an impressive rock-top fortress. Here the travellers could at least have open vistas northwards over comparatively low-lying coastal country – and what they saw witnessed that they were nearing their destination, for ahead, a dozen miles and more, a great black-brown smoke-cloud covered the landscape and drifted far out to sea. The Norsemen were busy, as ever.

Their guide, at the haven below Fetteresso, advised that they should here swing off, west by north, to take a pass called the Slug or Slochd, through the foothills of the high mountains. To continue on as they were doing would bring them into the lower Dee valley, which was obviously alight and being ravaged. Kildrummy, their ultimate destination, was well up the Don, the Dee's neighbouring vale to the north, and they could best approach it by seeking to cross Dee higher, hoping that the Norse would not have penetrated that far from their ships.

Thereafter they traversed wild upland country, untouched by invasion, although the pall ahead was ever present and the reek of burning tainting the air. When, after a dozen miles, the long pass began to drop to lower ground, the smoke made it all too clear that the Norsemen had got as far up Dee as this Banchory ahead. They decided to turn away due westwards, keeping still to the higher ground, until the long, wide valley below might be clear enough to cross. This meant going, as it were, against the grain of the land, and slowed their progress. They were, of course, limited by the need for fords over Dee; but fortunately these were apparently fairly frequent.

It was not until early evening and they had got as far as opposite Dinnet, between Aboyne and Ballater, that they decided that they might risk going down to the levels and crossing the ford there. In the dusk it was easy to see where the red glow of fire ended, and that presumably the invaders were still two or three miles to the east. They loosened their swords, however, prepared for trouble.

In fact, they saw no Norsemen – nor anybody else, although there were many villages and houses in the rich valley. Wood and peat smoke still rose from many a chimney, but the householders were gone, no doubt fled for safety into the hills, taking their beasts and poultry with them. The travellers did not linger, either.

Leaving Dee, they hurried northwards into the shadowy low hills between it and Don, and after a mile or two found a deserted hamlet at the side of Loch Kinord, which they took over for the night. The houses had been left in haste obviously, with even food on tables and fires smouldering on hearths. The owners would have been surprised at the identity of the present occupiers.

At first light they were off again, climbing by Logie and Migvie to the dip to the parallel Don valley, more winding and with a less settled aspect to it, but beautiful. Here the houses and farmsteads had not as yet been abandoned, and the travellers were eyed with some alarm.

Kildrummy, set amongst fair-sized hills, proved to be a

strongly placed palace-fortress surrounded by quite a large township, at present overflowing with armed men. The visitors were challenged well before they reached it, but had little difficulty in gaining passage since they certainly did not look like Norsemen, horsed and dressed as they were. Gartnait of Mar Kenneth found to be a red-headed, fiery-faced youngish man with, however, a disarming and unlikely friendliness of manner, although clearly a very worried individual at present. Kenneth's name and fame were known to him, and he was much encouraged by such unexpected adherence – although he was disappointed that Drostan and a reinforcing army had not yet appeared. He was urgently calling up all his manpower from his far-flung domains, but much of his territory was mountainous and assembling his support from the remote glens a slow process.

He was well informed as to the enemy's activities and progress. He reckoned that there were at least two thousand Norsemen involved. They had made their landings, not at the mouth of the Dee itself but just to the south, at Nigg Bay, this no doubt because Aberdeen was protected by walls and ramparts, a major town at the river-mouth, which would demand a deal of taking – and the Scandinavians were not apt to go in for siegery. But on the other hand it was a commercial centre of merchants and traders, not fighting men, and the surrounded Aberdeen was not of any great help to its overrun hinterland. The invaders had thus far not moved up the Don valley, concentrating on the easier pickings of the Dee. But it was only a matter of time – and time might not work in Gartnait's favour, with his very scattered support to be assembled, for his best fighters were the mountain men. Meanwhile, the more settled folk suffered.

Kenneth, of course, after telling that the Angus force would be coming to help, under the High King, asked what Gartnait's plans were to counter the enemy. He gathered that in fact the mormaor had no strategy mapped out other than to amass an army large enough to attack and beat back the invaders in simple confrontation. Had the King of Dalriada any suggestions?

That man had not failed to consider the tactical situation as he rode north, and had indeed ideas beyond mere straightforward clash of strength, out of his experiences of

338

dealing with the Scandinavians. He pointed out that the enemy, despite their fighting abilities, had certain weaknesses. One was their dependence on their ships. Another that, intent on ravishment and plunder as they always were, they tended to separate into groups rather than remain together as a unified force. And they were apt to become very drunken of a night. In present circumstances, he saw distinct possibilities. That long and populous Dee strath which they were presently harrying – that could present opportunities for the defenders. As he had ridden along its southern flanks, his guide had pointed out various valleys and glens entering from the north. Since, by the nature of it all, the Norsemen would be strung out along it for some time yet, if Gartnait's forces, instead of making one head-on assault, split into sections and attacked down these valleys, they could effectively carve up the enemy into small parties and prevent them from massing. Especially if this could be done while the Scandinavians were preoccupied by the oncoming Angus force threatening on the *south* side of the river. These would require to use the fords, to cross, and the Norsemen would almost certainly man all such to prevent any traverse. Gartnait's men could then be attacking, as it were, from behind, out of the different glens all along the strath, and so be greatly advantaged.

The mormaor was much impressed by this conception. He would send messengers, then, to inform Drostan and Nechtan of the strategy, and seek their co-operation.

His visitor had a further suggestion. Their ships were both the Norsemen's strength and weakness. If these had been left at Nigg Bay, south of the Dee-mouth, they could be vulnerable. They would be guarded, of course, but probably by only small numbers of men. If they could be assailed and captured, or even just dispersed, the effect on the enemy's morale would be great.

Gartnait pointed out that there were reputedly one hundred and more of the dragon-ships involved. He had no fleet to challenge these.

Kenneth answered that he had heard that Aberdeen was the greatest trading town on all the east coast of Alba. There must be many merchanters and trading-ships in its harbours, deep-sea fishing craft also. And at least one or two galleys.

Enough to form some sort of naval force which could make a surprise descent on the crowded, moored dragon-ships and cause chaos amongst them.

Gartnait was doubtful still. But when Kenneth said that since *he* was used to fighting from ships, and had no real armed force to lead here, he was prepared to go and attempt a sea sally from Aberdeen, whilst Gartnait and Drostan dealt with the land situation, the other acceded. He could go to Aberdeen and do what he could. He could take Aidan, his uncle, with him, as guide and to commend him to the townsfolk. When would he go?

The sooner the better, Kenneth said. If the Norsemen in the Dee valley and elsewhere heard that their shipping was endangered, they would be worried and might well send back part of their force to deal with the situation, thus weakening them against the land assault. How long it would be before Drostan's army reached Dee they did not know, although it was to be hoped, very soon. So time should not be lost.

Next morning, then, the visitors rode off again, with Aidan mac Aidan, a genial, plump, elderly man who seemed quite content with the role allotted to him. They went east by south now, down Don, through, Kenneth noted, very defensible country, the river running through a number of pass-like defiles and narrows, apt for ambushes – no doubt why the invaders had chosen to advance up the easier Dee. Past the Corbouies and Brux they went, and through the fertile Howe of Alford, to more passes at Forbes, and Tilliefoure and Pitfichie, to emerge from the larger hills on to the wider rolling plain at Monymusk, still a score of miles from the sea.

Now they could see the smoke-cloud again, various thicknesses and shades of it, from old burnings and new, covering much of the land to the south. How much anguish and sorrow that smoke represented, and how much fear for those as yet unassailed.

By Inverurie, where another large river joined Don, and Kintore and Dyce they rode, and now the sea was not far off. At Balgownie where the Don began to widen to its mouth, they could see the large town of Aberdeen ahead. It could equally well have been called Aberdon, for it lay midway between the two river-mouths, these less than two miles apart.

A system of walls, ramparts and gates guarded the town, these presently being patrolled by citizen-bands. The travellers were challenged, but the banner of Mar and the presence of Aidan gained them entry, and they rode through the lanes and alleys for the harbour area, which lay southwards of the main town.

They came to the largest port that Kenneth had ever seen, where the Dee opened into a sort of double bay before it was narrowed again at its actual mouth by a curving, horn-like headland, to form a spacious expanse of sheltered water, into which projected many quays and piers, these all served by warehouses and stores and fish-curing sheds, these jetties themselves lined with shipping of various kinds.

Aidan knew his way around here, and leaving the horses at an open market-place, he took Kenneth to a row of stone and timber buildings, which all appeared to be ale-houses and eating-places. These, entered, proved to be full of men drinking and talking, the noise considerable.

The newcomers' arrival went largely unnoticed at first until, weaving through the crowd, Aidan brough Kenneth to a table at the back whereat a group of men sat a little apart. At sight of the mormaor's uncle, these set down their mugs of ale and rose to their feet. Their respectful greetings changed to a staring silence when Aidan introduced them to the King of Dalriada, Kenneth Norse-Slayer.

That man sought to put them at ease by picking up one of the jugs of ale, gesturing to them all with it, and quaffing a mouthful. Hastily more drink was poured for the newcomers, and they all sat down.

It appeared that these were the harbour-master and his deputies, with some of the more senior shipmasters. They had been discussing how best to defend the harbour and shipping should the Norse decide to attack it. They were clearly relieved at the appearance of the distinguished visitors, which they took to mean help from the mormaor.

That relief changed to doubt and something like alarm when Kenneth explained what he had come for, and there were assertions if not protests that they were traders and peaceful seafarers not fighting men, to assault Norse dragon-ships. To which Kenneth countered that they had been planning to defend the harbour and ships anyway; why not do so by destroying the enemy vessels moored in Nigg Bay? The guards of these would probably be all, or mainly, ashore, and the task would probably not be too difficult. And, he added, there might well be considerable booty to be gained in the process.

They listened to him, at least.

His plan was this. The Norsemen might well sleep on their ships, but surely would not spend the days cooped up on board. So an early evening attack, when they would be apt to be eating the last meal of the day and probably not a few drunken. Any look-outs would by then tend to be less alert. A descent on Nigg Bay, round the headland from Dee-mouth, by as many assorted craft as they could muster, laden with tinder, pitch and torches to burn the dragon-ships. They would send up a new smoke-cloud to rival all the burning homesteads, and put doubts and anxiety into the black hearts of the Norse invaders up the Dee valley. He made it all sound fairly simple.

His hearers were soon intrigued and began debating amongst themselves, some growing enthusiastic now, some still doubtful, but none actually rejecting. Kenneth encouraged by saying that Norsemen without their ships had their menace halved, and with the Mormaor Gartnait and the High King, and Angus forces attacking inland, their guards would be preoccupied with the situation westwards, not seawards.

Asked when this would take place, Kenneth said that they must wait for word from Kildrummy that action there was imminent. That would probably not be for a couple of days yet, time for support to muster and the Angus force to reach Dee. So, three evenings after this one? That should allow them to arrange all.

It was agreed. How all the shipmen of Aberdeen would react was another matter, of course.

Quarters were found for the distinguished visitors and provender provided.

Next day Kenneth, with Aidan and the harbour-master, moved amongst the skippers, crews and fishermen, explaining, persuading, daring them. His status and renown greatly helped, of course, and they met with a fair amount of acceptance, all recognising that Aberdeen itself could be a target for the invaders soon if they were not dealt with. It was a new role for Kenneth, persuading and convincing ordinary folk, not commanding. All was not enthusiasm, but agreement grew as the day went on, and by nightfall they knew that there was sufficient support for the attempt to go ahead.

The following day it was a matter of organisation, planning and assembling the necessary materials for combustion, pitch, tar, torches, flints and steel. Also weaponry of whatever sort could be found.

It was well that they had not delayed over all this, for that afternoon messengers arrived from Kildrummy to announce that the High King's force was on the south bank of Dee and that Gartnait therefore had no option but to move into action at once without waiting longer for reinforcements. The couriers said that battle by this time might well be in progress.

So the shipping venture had to go ahead at once, a day earlier than planned, if it was to have its fullest effect. All was haste and bustle now. Kenneth held a hurried meeting with the many skippers, taking them over his plans and telling them approximately what was required of them and their crews, and explaining the signals he would give from the leading ship, an old galley of two dozen oars. No elaborate tactics were possible in the circumstances.

As the sun began to sink behind the great hills to the west, its colours in competition with the red glow of fires, the very odd expedition set sail for the harbour-mouth, a strangely assorted, straggling fleet of some forty vessels of every type and size, from large traders to ferry barges and fishing-boats. A less warlike assembly would have been hard to imagine, and a small squadron of dragon-ships could have demolished it with laughable ease – but it was to be hoped that the moored Norse fleet would make it all a very different proposition.

Through the channel between the enclosing headlands, Kenneth led this motley flotilla, to swing round southwards in a curve, close inshore, to use the land as screen for as long as possible. Girdle Point projected almost a mile beyond

Dee-mouth, with Nigg Bay on its southern flank, so no distances were involved. Kenneth kept his galley oarsmen at their slowest, or he would have rounded the point before the last of his tail had left the harbour.

The prospect, when they did turn the headland, was extraordinary, and even Kenneth had not visualised it quite like this. Nigg Bay was a comparatively shallow crescent, half a mile across and less than that in depth, with a sandy shore. Now, however, it was more like a winter's forest than a bay, so full of ships and their rearing masts and dragon-prows. Row upon row they were packed, hulls so close-seeming as to touch each other.

Kenneth bit his lip. Because of that screen of masts and shrouds he was prevented from seeing the beach. Were most of the guards ashore? That could be so important.

Then he noticed, in the evening light, a thin haze of blue smoke rising behind the masts, not the black-brown of burning thatches. That could be the cooking-fires of the guards, he decided thankfully. Also he now became thankful for that mast-screen itself, for that could serve to hide the Aberdeen flotilla from the men on shore. The guards would soon perceive what was going on, to be sure, but any time given the attackers before the alarm sounded was precious.

Kenneth let his nearest supporting craft line up on either side of his galley so that they could descend on the moored vessels in line, these only a couple of hundred yards ahead now.

There appeared to be no men watching them from those first dragon-ships, no sign of movement other than the sway of the tide. So Kenneth ran his galley alongside one in the centre of the line, and was the first to leap over, the other craft moving in left and right to do the same, men, with torches already lighted, clambering on to the enemy ships.

As Kenneth knew from experience, vessels, whether dragon-ships or lesser craft, were not difficult to set alight, fire indeed a constant hazard, being built of wood, their timbers sealed with pitch, the shrouds and rigging tarred for protection against the salt weather. So the fire-raisers in those first vessels had no great problems. The problems were otherwise, those of further access and of crowding, as was quickly apparent. The Norse ships admittedly were

344

ranked across the bay, but inevitably most were behind the first row. Now all the Aberdeen craft, as it were, piled up against this frontal barrier and could get no further, all the men having to come pouring out and over first their own ships and then the enemy ones, to get at the next ranks. So there was fairly general chaos of crowding men with lighted torches scrambling over the sides and getting in each other's way, tripping over ropes, rowing-benches and sail-cloth and the like, the confusion added to by the smoke of the pitch-pine torches and, soon thereafter, by the fires started on the first vessels.

Kenneth himself, although aware of something of it all, behind him, was not greatly impeded, for he led onwards, ahead. His trouble was otherwise, the getting from one dragon-ship to the next. Although they had looked tightly packed from a distance, in fact there were often fair-sized gaps between the rows, too wide to leap. All had gangplanks aboard, of course, some already lashed in position, for the Norse crews themselves to use to reach land, but getting all these into effective use was a delaying factor. Also there were gaps, much too wide to be bridged, and this involved detours, as it were, or actually getting out the enemy's oars and rowing the vessels closer. So the process was far from speedy. In none of the dragon-ships, however, did they find any men to oppose them.

Kenneth was not forgetting the opposition. However unprepared as the men ashore must have been for this attack, the smoke of their burning ships would have alerted them almost at once and they would not be backward in seeking to take counter-action. But, of course, the same difficulties of access and transference from ship to ship would face them as their adversaries, so no concentrated confrontation was possible.

Kenneth perceived the first of them when about halfway to the shore, five or six men clambering on to a ship in front of him, swords and axes in hand. Fortunately for the attackers, the wind was south-westerly, so the smoke was not obscuring their view, being blown seawards; but it would confuse the Norsemen, prevent them from seeing just what went on and the scale of the assault.

Not all the Aberdonians were concerned with the fire

raising, and Kenneth now paused to gather some of them, more than enough to challenge the half-dozen in front. He saw more of the enemy appearing on other ships, and recognised that from now on they would have to fight their way, difficult as this would be – although the defence would be equally hampered.

So an extraordinary struggle developed, with much more shouting, gesticulating and threatening than actual fighting, the contestants often only a few yards apart but unable to get at each other. Throwing-spears would have been the most effective weapons, but not many of these were available – oddly enough, more on the attacking than defending side, for they found not a few stored on the dragon-ships. And all the time, as the daylight faded, the red blaze and black smoke of the burning ships behind contributed its own grim impact.

Kenneth, seeking to command effectively, did not let himself become involved in any hand-to-hand fighting that eventuated, trying to ensure that his fire-raisers were able to keep on advancing. But in the utter confusion of it all, leadership was all but impossible, and no recognisable line could be maintained. Some incendiaries got well forward of others, some fell before much more effective Norse warriors, some no doubt held back prudently. Nevertheless, presently, it was apparent that the majority of the enemy ships were on fire, a dire sight.

No doubt this recognition came also to whoever was in command of the Norsemen, in due course. Whether some sort of recall was sounded or not, or whether it was more or less by mutual consent, the Scandinavians became less evident and some could even be seen heading shorewards from ship to ship. They would, of course, be quite ignorant of the numbers and composition of the attacking force and might well assume that it was a major fleet and army. And probably there was no great force of guards left there in the first place. So it dawned on Kenneth, eventually, that he had won the day, strange victory as it might be. When he stood at the side of a dragon-ship and saw only the fire-reflecting shallows between him and the beach, he recognised the fact. With others, he leapt over the side into the water to wade ashore, sword at the ready.

But there was no opposition awaiting them up on the grassy shelf above the beach. Cooking-fires still glowed, feeble in contrast to the huge conflagration seawards – that was all. The surviving Norsemen had fled the scene.

When sufficient men had gathered around him to form a tight group, they moved up to the camp, based on two or three fishermen's cot-houses. Here they found only a few bodies lying, which they assumed at first to be wounded or corpses but which on inspection proved to be merely drunken.

Kenneth, although well pleased with the evening's work, realised that there were still dangers. The Aberdeen men, elated by their achievements, could lose all sense of caution and in their search for booty be an easy prey to any counter-attack, if the Norsemen had not gone far, and perceived their opportunity. So, unpopular as his commands were now, he insisted on some sort of discipline and order, difficult as this was. All those blazing ships in the bay created an atmosphere of savagery and licence, somehow, hard to counter. Also liquor was found in the encampment and not left unsampled. Moreover, women presently began to creep out of corners where they had been hiding, again normal where the Scandinavians were concerned, and although these were their own countrywomen, the fact that they had been Norse playthings seemed to constitute them equally suitable for some of the victors, and fighting developed over them. Kenneth had to use his own escort in an attempt to enforce his will.

At the same time, he sought to plan ahead, to attempt to visualise probable developments now. Those fleeing Norsemen, if they did not come back and attempt a counter-attack, what would they do? Presumably go on up Dee, to rejoin their fellows. And if these latter were engaged in battle? How were Drostan's and Gartnait's forces faring? Had battle in fact joined yet? Or might it be all over? Victory, or no clear decision? It was all so uncertain and his own duty now equally so, in consequence. If the Albannach forces had fought and won the day, then presumably the defeated enemy would be retiring down Dee, to gain their ships here. If, on the contrary, *they* had triumphed, they would probably press on westwards. If they were returning, and these fleeing guards joined them, how soon would that come about? The Dee valley was long, and any joining up might be many miles inland. So much would depend on when battle, if any, had taken place, and where. If it had been fairly early in the day, and the Albannach winning, then the beaten Norse host's survivors could be no great distance off. Or quite otherwise. It all presented a most difficult problem for Kenneth.

Also, of course, he had to consider these Aberdeen ship-men who had served his purpose so well and who were now so vulnerable. In their present state they could be over-whelmed and cut down by even a small band of disciplined fighters. Almost certainly his own prime duty now was to try to get them safely back to Aberdeen harbour as speedily as possible. After all, they had achieved their objective. If he had had any, even a modest, force of trained fighting men with him now, he would have headed on up Dee through the night, to seek to aid in the greater struggle. But . . .

There was another question to concern him. What would the returning Norse, defeated or victorious, do when they reached Nigg Bay and found their fleet destroyed? Presum-ably, out of all those scores of ships there would be some not so seriously damaged as to be unsailable? But enough to transport the surviving Vikings back to Orkney or Iceland or wherever they came from? If not, what? Presumably they would range up and down this seaboard seeking to find craft of some sort, mainly just fishing-boats probably, to get them home. But they might attempt an attack on Aberdeen har-bour itself, to win larger ships there, defended walled town as it served.

Out of all this debate with himself, Kenneth came to the conclusion that he should try to get his motley and excited company back where they came from forthwith, and then seek to organise them and their fellow-citizens to guard and watch, and to improvise some sort of boom across the Dee-mouth to prevent any usable dragon-ships from getting in. In fact, he could have some of the burned hulks towed, and either sunken or tied across the harbour entrance, as barrier. Then merely wait.

This, then, he endeavoured to organise, no easy task in the circumstances. Some of the Aberdonians wanted to go back and board such of the ships as were not too badly ablaze, to search for booty, in especial the gold ornaments, necklets, arm-bands and bracelets of which the Norsemen were so fond. But this would cause great delay and danger, and Kenneth had to forbid it. Back to their own vessels, he ordered, with only such loot as they had managed to garner so far; the Norsemen might descend upon them at any time. That warning had some effect.

Now there was, of course, a new problem. How to return to their own vessels over all the burning dragon-ships? This difficulty was resolved by heading round the horns of the bay, on foot, and there, beyond the conflagration, shout and signal for their shallow-bottomed fishing-boats to come and ferry them out to their larger ships. With a few wounded, and more drunken, speed was no more in evidence than order.

Needless to say, Kenneth fretted throughout. He was thankful when, at length, he had most of his people aboard their vessels, and was able to lead the way back round Girdle Point to the harbour. Even so, they left some behind, determined looters and, he was told, others ambitious to find unburned enemy ships to tow in as trophies and prizes.

It was not far off dawn before Kenneth, posting himself at Dee-mouth, saw what he hoped was the last of the stragglers come in, and gave orders for four smouldering hulks to be chained together across the entrance. What went on at Nigg Bay now, or up Dee-side, he did not know, and could only hope for the best. He must snatch an hour or two's sleep, if he could.

In the event he slept longer than intended, and was wakened to be presented with a message from Gartnait of Mar. It was victory. The strategy in the Dee valley had worked well, the enemy preoccupied with the presence of the High King's force across the river, and not knowing which fords and crossings they might use, had been cut up all along their extended length, as it were from behind, by Gartnait's groups descending on them down the re-entrant glens and passes. But it had been a bloody business, in especial for Drostan's people, who had had to cross the fords in the end, and these the Norsemen had defended effectively. There were heavy casualties, and amongst the many,

Drostan's son Nechtan was seriously wounded. But the day was theirs, the enemy fleeing eventually, leaving large numbers slain.

Heartened by the news, Kenneth now wondered what the Norse survivors would do about shipping. He sent the messenger back to Gartnait congratulating him and urging him to despatch parties to all coastal areas, especially Nigg Bay, of course, to try to protect the fisher-folk, who were almost certain to have their boats taken, the larger ones. He also suggested that the Aberdonians send out bands south and north, to help their coastal neighbours.

There was little more that he could do here, he decided. He collected his escort and took his leave of the harbour folk, to ride back to Kildrummy first, and then south-westwards. Aims achieved, after a fashion, the sooner he returned to Dunadd, and Eithne, the better he would be pleased.

23

Dalriada took much more ruling than had Galloway, not only in that it was much larger but because of the terrain: mountains, sea-lochs, peninsulas and islands, which made for very remote communities – and the lords of these all too apt to go their own ways and ignore central authority. Kenneth therefore was kept much more busy and tied down than heretofore, and in consequence was unable to embark on many of the united Celtic ventures which had made his name famous, although he did try to maintain that policy by keeping in fairly constant touch with his fellow-monarchs in Strathclyde, Man, Gwynedd and Ireland, as well as Alba, and when these were assailed by Norsemen or Anglo-Saxons, sending fleets to aid them, although he did not go himself. He was discovering the trammels and responsibilities of being the king of a major nation. Eithne at least was the happier for it. Not that, in the months that followed, he was not personally engaged in armed sallies, for on three occasions, twice into the Hebridean Sea and once inland, he led attacks on the Scandinavians who were assailing the Albannach.

The pattern of the Norse raiding was interesting in its alteration from formerly. Dalriada itself was left comparatively untouched, presumably on account of Kenneth's reputation and the recognition that it was liable to be dangerous; and because of the fact that Ulster and the north of Ireland were now dominated by their more settled compatriots, and so no longer apt for hosting, and the south had the effective High King Maelsechlaind operating against them, the raiders were more and more turning their attentions to Alba, where civil strife and disunity gave them ample opportunity. It was worse on the east than on the west coasts, and Drostan was greatly concerned, and disappointed that the Deeside victory had not discouraged the wretched Vikings.

The trouble was that they came from so many different lands – Orkney, Zetland, Iceland, the Faroes, Norway itself, Denmark and Sweden; and lessons taught to one did not necessarily apply to others. The fact that it was the rebellious mortuaths of Moray, Ross and Caithness which suffered most was only some small consolation for the High King.

Man was suffering also, these days, but from bands raiding out of Ulster apparently. Gwynedd was enjoying a respite, it seemed, although the Welsh kingdoms to the south were under constant assault from the Saxons. The embattled Celtic nations therefore required unity as much as ever, as Kenneth lost no opportunity of declaring. And he made a point of sailing the Sea of the Hebrides very frequently, with a sizeable flotilla, as warning to all that Dalriada at least was alert and prepared – jaunts on which Eithne was very ready to accompany him, even though she was again pregnant.

It was some eighteen months after the Deeside battle that the direst news reached Dunadd. Drostan had been assassinated at Forteviot, and Alba was in complete turmoil and confusion.

Details of it all took some time to assemble. The High King had been attacked and slain while hawking and separated from the rest of his party. Who was responsible was not known, although most assumed that Tadg mac Fochel, Mormaor of Moray, brother of the late Brude, was behind it. Now Alba was again without a supreme ruler and chaos prevailed, the *ri* more divided than ever. Tadg, to be sure, was claiming the high throne, but even Ross was not supporting him, asserting that *he* was senior and had the better right. The other mormaors would not have him either, naming him traitor. Yet none of them wanted the so dangerous position and responsibility themselves, especially Nechtan, Drostan's son, who had never fully recovered from the wounds sustained on Deeside. And who would blame any of them? It was an utterly appalling situation, seemingly defying solution; and once the Norsemen heard of it, they would descend on Alba like any flock of carrion crows.

Kenneth was much exercised and concerned.

It was Eithne, however, who put forward the drastic, the

extraordinary, the eye-widening suggestion. "Why do not *you* make yourself High King of Alba, Kenneth?" she asked.

He stared at her.

"Would that not be the answer? Solve so many problems?"

"But . . . *me*? What are you saying, lass? Myself, the High King!"

"Yes, Kenneth Norse-Slayer. High King of Alba. Why not? Alba needs you. Nothing surer than that, my dear."

"I have no right . . . "

"You *have* a right. More than one. You are wed to a High King's daughter. And sister. And by our Albannach traditions, our son Conn could one day claim the high kingship as of right. Why not his father, now, who could save Alba for him? Alba which needs saving! And other kings of Dalriada have gone on to become high kings. My father himself. And my uncle, Constantine."

"They were themselves Albannach. Acting kings of Dalriada while they awaited the greater call."

"You have some Albannach blood. But, much more important, Alba *needs* you. Has done for long. A strong hand. I have thought on this, often, although I have not spoken of it."

He shook his head.

"Give me one good reason why not, Kenneth."

"I would be . . . usurper."

"Not if the majority of the *ri* voted you in."

"Are they likely to do that? An incomer?"

"I say that they well might. I think that none, other than Tadg of Moray and Fergus of Ross desire the position. I think that they dread it, indeed. But want neither of these two. Too many high kings have fallen, of these last years. But *you* would not fall, I swear! Tadg and Fergus are not suitable, all know. And the other mormaors would not have them, without war. Who, then? Who has the stature, the ability, the experience? Kenneth mac Alpin has all that, and more. You cannot deny it."

"But . . . I have no desire to be High King."

"You desire Alba's unity, do you not? Her preservation from the Norsemen, her very survival? You do not want to see Alba become another Ulster? Nor ever racked by civil strife. You could save her. And, I think, only you. And I speak as an Albannach princess."

"I am a Dalriadan. *This* is my nation, not Alba. My father, grandsire, all my forebears, were kings of the Scots of Dalriada. Think you that I could give that up, for the troubles and uncertainties of being High King of strife-torn Alba? Would wish to?"

"You could be both, could you not? King of both realms."

"Dalriada would never agree to become part of Alba. Never! We have always prided ourselves on our independence, the Scots, as you know well."

"Not part, then. Remaining independent. But sharing the same monarch."

Kenneth rubbed his chin, gnawing his lip.

"If you do not, what is to become of Alba? And you have worked and fought and pleaded, for long, for Celtic unity. Here is opportunity to take that unity a step forward, a great step. You must see that? If Alba and Dalriada were as one, under your rule, how great an example to show to the other kings. Then you could speak with the greater authority. Lead in more than battles. Is it not true?"

He could not deny that. "I shall think on it," he told her, head ashake.

"Do that. You are not usually so slow of wits!" And she left him to it.

It made sense, of course, he could not contest that. In fact, the more he considered it, the more sense it did make. Yet his reluctance did not abate.

And it might all be impossible, anyway. The *ri* might well be outraged at the idea. And he was not going to try to convince them, that was sure. Yet . . . what was the alternative, for Alba?

He did not decide yea or nay, there and then. What he did decide was to pay a visit to Alba. He would probably have done that anyway, to discover the true position and to see what help he might offer, if any. And while there, he might learn the answer to Eithne's suggestion.

That young woman, four months pregnant as she was, insisted that she would come with him. Had she not the right? Alba was *her* country.

So, in mid-June they set out, spurred on by word of another raid by Scandinavians on Easter Ross, the start of the new hosting season.

They made a rather slower journey of it, to Forteviot, than usual, for whatever Eithne might say, Kenneth was determined that there should be no avoidable danger to his pregnant wife in the long horseback travel. But that was no hardship in the lovely early summer weather, with the countryside looking fair indeed, Loch Awe-side, Drumalban, Strathfillan and the rest, demanding not to be hurried through.

At Forteviot they found no one there but the great palace's chamberlain and caretaker. Nechtan, it seemed, remained in his own mortuath of Angus, and no one else had, as yet, any right to occupy the High King's seat, however ambitious.

They decided to proceed to Angus. It was the nearest of the mortuaths, anyway. Forfar, its capital, was only some forty-five miles away north-eastwards, once Tay was crossed, up the great Strathmore. Eithne would have liked to have lingered awhile at her old home, but recognised that this was not the time for that.

When they reached Forfar, with its loch-protected fortress, it was to learn that the Mormaor Nechtan now spent most of his time at the hunting-seat of Kincardine, up in the Mearns, to the north – not for the hunting they gathered, for it seemed that he was all but housebound, crippled, the wounds he had received at Deeside leaving him that way. But he loved the peace and quiet of Kincardine, and left most of the day-to-day running of his mortuath to his illegitimate half-brother Donnan, who, it seemed, was very able.

It was on, therefore, the further twenty-five miles into the foothill country of the great mountains, forested valleys, heather moors and deer-haunted slopes, to a sequestered large hallhouse, not particularly strongly placed, since major defence was not its function.

Kenneth was shocked at the appearance of Nechtan mac Drostan, so changed was he from the cheerful, impulsive young man of heretofore, thin, twisted, bent, old before his time, thanks to Norsemen's throwing-spears and axes, a man now finding his satisfactions in working with his hands, drawing, painting, carving in wood and stone and horn, discovering talents, especially in the delineation of birds and animals and Celtic designs incorporating these. But he welcomed his visitors warmly, and introduced them to Donnan, a stolid, stocky individual, but shrewd-eyed, who appeared to take after his miller's-daughter mother rather than his royal father.

It was not long before the all-important matter of the rule, governance and state of Alba came up, and Nechtan was not so distanced from national affairs that he was not greatly distressed and concerned, not only over his father's death but over the prevailing anarchy and danger for the realm. From the first, he took it for granted that Kenneth had come to aid in the relief and saving of Alba, his faith in the other's prowess and abilities all but childlike. All would be well now, was his attitude. His half-brother was less confident.

Kenneth, of course, raised the question of the other *ri* and the high kingship. Nechtan spread his hands helplessly. None desired the responsibility, he declared – except of course Tadg of Moray and Fergus of Ross, rogues both and now opposing each other, God be praised! Gartnait of Mar would be the best choice, probably, but he was set against it. He said that he was not eager to be the next to be assassinated! Dungall of Atholl was too old, and no warrior anyway. Malcolm of Buchan suffered from gloomy fits, when he was impossible to deal with; he would never do as High King. And Fillan of Caithness was the most junior of all the *ri*, all but unknown to the rest in his remote northern mortuath, youthful and not to be considered. The lords of Fife, Strathearn and Lennox were not mormaors and therefore not of the required status. It was a dire situation. He himself, Nechtan, to be sure could not possibly seek or hold the position; and he had no hopes of Gartnait being persuaded to stand. Anyway, good màn as Gartnait was, could he take on the task of uniting the nation? Had he the ability and strength to withstand the Norsemen, and to quell internal revolt? The only fighting he had ever done was at that Deeside battle.

Into the silence which followed that sorry summary, it was Eithne who spoke. "I, as a princess of Alba, not as Queen of Dalriada, propose another name to consider. Kenneth mac

Alpin, Norse-Slayer."

Two breaths were sharply indrawn at that.

The half-brother, Donnan, looked searchingly at Kenneth, who gazed anywhere but at his host.

It was Donnan who found voice first. "Is that . . . possible?" he asked.

"It is," Eithne asserted. "For the very reasons, friend, that *you* cannot be Mormaor of Angus! Because, in our polity and tradition, the female descent is all-important. Your mother was not of the *ri*. I am daughter, niece and sister of high kings. And Kenneth and I have a son, Constantine, who is in the direct succession. None with more right, when he is of age to be High King, Constantine the Second. Meanwhile, he has a father who could save Alba – and whose grandmother, Fergusiana, King Alpin's mother, was herself an Albannach princess."

Donnan inclined his head, silent.

Not so Nechtan. "You would do this, Highness?" he demanded. "You would take the high kingship?"

Kenneth spoke carefully. "Not take. If offered it, I would . . . consider the matter. But only if it was desired. By sufficient."

"Save us – this would be of all things best! What Alba needs, as never before. A strong, warrior High King. For the saving of the nation!"

Kenneth cleared his throat. "That I could not promise," he declared. "I am no miracle-worker. I would do my best, but . . . "

"If *you* could not do it, none could, I say! Kenneth Norse-Slayer."

"The Norsemen I can try to hold off. But enmity and strife *within* Alba is another matter. Am I the man to heal that sickness? Might not I, an incomer and a Scot, make it worse? Cause only further strife?"

"With whom? With Moray and Ross, yes. But whoever becomes High King will face their enmity. But no others, I swear."

Kenneth was surprised at Nechtan's enthusiasm. But then, of course, he had no ambitions for himself. The reverse indeed. The other *ri* might feel very differently. He looked over at Donnan. That young man was clearly less impressed. But he did not venture a comment.

"I believe it is what should be," Eithne added. "I see no other to meet our needs, Alba's needs. Alba has suffered enough. It was *my* suggestion, not Kenneth's. He is doubtful, but I am not."

"Nor I," Nechtan exclaimed. "It is God-sent, I do believe! Donnan, do you not agree?"

His brother shrugged. "It is not for me to say. I am not . . . concerned. But others are. What the other mormaors say is what signifies."

"I agree," Kenneth said. "I will not seek to impose myself against any of the wishes of these. Except those of Moray and Ross, who would be a disaster for Alba and whom the others would not accept, either. But – how to discover these others' wishes?"

"I, as the last High King's son, can summon a council of the *ri*, here. Tadg and Fergus will not come, I think. But the others will. And I shall be surprised if they do not acclaim Kenneth mac Alpin as High King!"

"It is none so far to Kildrummy from here. I would welcome the advice of Gartnait of Mar. And we might return by Atholl."

"No need to consult at Atholl. All that one seeks is to be left in peace in his mountains . . . "

They left it at that. They would travel north to Donside, another sixty miles or so, to see Gartnait, before returning to Dunadd.

They went up over the Cairn of the Mount pass through the high mountains, then down the Dye Water to the Dee, across it and through lesser hills to the Don valley, new ground for Eithne. At Kildrummy they found Gartnait of Mar delighted to see Kenneth again and impressed by the presence of his queen. From the first mention of the subject of the monarchy, his agitation was evident, and his relief, at Eithne's suggestion, still more so. For King Kenneth to accept the high throne would be the very best solution for Alba, he declared. He would vote for that with great satisfaction, and he was sure that the other mormaors would do likewise, with gratitude. Or sufficient of them to ensure the appointment. When would Kenneth move to Fortrenn?

That was all going too fast for that man. He announced

that he was honoured, but that the matter was still only a possibility, an interesting proposal on Queen Eithne's part, but something which would require a deal of thinking through before decision could be arrived at. Apart from the Albannach acceptance, there was that of Dalriada. It could not just be assumed that his own people would agree to this, fiercely independent as they were. And the welfare of Dalriada must come first in his decision-making. His forebears had been Kings of Scots for four hundred years.

Gartnait was somewhat crestfallen at that.

They did not linger at Kildrummy, despite urgings to stay, and gave up any notion of visiting Atholl on the way home, assured that Dungall thereof would be well content to take the other's advice as to voting. As for Malcolm of Buchan, all agreed that no call there was necessary. So it was back across the mountains of Drumalban, by devious ways, winding glens and passes innumerable, to the sea-lochs and peninsulas of the west.

Eithne was well pleased with what they had learned and established, Kenneth less confident. Now it was not so much the Albannach reaction which was concerning him as the Dalriadan one.

"I cannot see the lords and chiefs rejoicing at this joint kingship," he told her. "Alba is so much the larger, the greater. They are bound to fear being swallowed up. Nor would I blame them. Nor wish to be the one responsible, after all the centuries of fighting to maintain Dalriada as the kingdom of the Scots. To seem to sell it to the Albannach, for the sake of power, or even Celtic unity."

"But the two kingdoms can remain separate, Kenneth."

"Can they? In fact? In name, at first, they might. But in time must not the greater take over the lesser? That is my great fear."

"In name . . . ?" Eithne repeated, thoughtfully. "In name . . . ?"

24

The great council called at Dunadd that October was one of the best attended Dalriada had ever seen, undoubtedly – and that, as well as the urgency of the royal summons, because of rumours and whispers as to the reasons for it. For, despite all the efforts on Kenneth's part to keep the main subject of debate secret at this stage, to avoid prejudging and entrenched attitudes, the matter had somehow leaked out, and inevitably less than accurately, indeed in various forms and misconceptions. Widespread was the anxiety and foreboding.

So there was a large crowd of lords and chiefs and landholders there, too many for the great hall of the palace, so that the meeting had to be held in Prior Phadraig's church. Kenneth came in to sit at a table placed before the altar, with his brother Donald, as King of Galloway, on his right, and Eithne, now in her seventh month, on his left. Normally women did not take part in Dalriadan councils, but this one was special and the matrilinear connection important.

After the prior had opened the proceedings with prayer, and one or two formalities disposed of, Kenneth made no beatings about the bush. He told the gathering that, as all now probably knew well, Alba was in a dire state of anarchy and division, with resultant weakness, and this at a time when the Norse were more and more turning their savage attentions on that realm, in especial on its eastern seaboard. This situation, as well as being grievous for their neighbour and ally, constituted a serious danger for Dalriada also. They had, of late, been suffering less at the Scandinavians' bloodstained hands; but if these won any major foothold in Alba, as they had done in Ulster, and were seeking to do in the Irish south, then Dalriada would most certainly be endangered. All must recognise that.

There was no contesting this summary. None, even from

the most remote of holdings, was wholly ignorant of the gravity of the Albannach position, and unaware of what Norsemen, based in Alba, might do.

The disunity and enmity amongst the present mormaors of Alba, Kenneth went on, and indeed their incompetence as commanders of fighting men, with all their best leaders slain or assassinated, meant that no acceptable High King was forthcoming to succeed Drostan mac Bargoit, his son now a cripple from wounds. None of the other *ri* were prepared to take the high throne, save for Tadg of Moray, who would be a disaster and whom the others would not accept anyway. So the nation's leadership was void, and with no prospect of any satisfactory filling. Violent taking, war, invasion were inevitable – to the Norsemen's evil delight.

Silence.

In the circumstances, he, Kenneth, was being offered the high kingship by some of the mormaors. He . . .

Clamour and exclamation erupted. He let it continue for a little, before banging fist on table for quiet.

"Hear me!" he commanded. "I said offered, not that I would take it. I am no Albannach, nor greatly desire the high throne, with all its promise of trouble and difficulty and danger. But I do desire Celtic unity, as should you all, and this would be a great step in that direction. I could, God willing, perhaps save Alba. To the much advantage of Dalriada also. And I have a certain right to it, through my wife and son, Constantine. Conn, a grandson of the High King Angus mac Fergus, is in the direct line of succession. You all know of the Albannach custom and tradition of succession through the female descent . . . "

The shouting began again. What of Dalriada? He was *their* king. Not Alba's. The Scots were a proud people, not to be swallowed up by the Albannach. Who would rule here, if he went to Fortrenn or Inverness? He had sworn his solemn oath on Columba's stone to cherish and defend, not Alba but Dalriada. Was this how he kept his word? And so on.

Kenneth let them have their say, as patiently as he might, before raising his hand. "I will not desert Dalriada," he declared strongly. "I am a Scot, and will, must, remain one. I would remain King of Dalriada as well as be High King of

Alba. Only as such would I agree to it."

That did not still the outcry. Such a claim would be in name only. The greater would include the lesser, nothing more sure. Once Kenneth sat on Alba's throne, Dalriada would cease to be an independent realm. There were ten and more Albannach to every Scot. Numbers would prevail. Dalriada would become but a small province of Alba. They would all be Albannach, in time, not Scots.

"Not so," Kenneth asserted. "I would never allow that. I am a Scot, I tell you, in direct descent from Fergus mac Erc himself. And a score of kings since. Think you that I would ever forswear my ancestry?"

"Even if you did not, others might," one lord cried. "Your sons and grandsons. In time we would all be known as Albannach."

"If you were slain by the Norse? Or assassinated, like the others? What then?" another demanded. "How would Dalriada fare?"

"My brother Donald, here, King of Galloway, would become King of Dalriada, independent. And in time young Constantine become High King."

"You are set on this, Highness?" he was asked.

"No, I am not. I am in two minds on the matter. And it may all come to naught. I seek guidance, in a great matter . . . "

Eithne touched his arm. "May I speak?" She raised her voice. "My friends, hear me. This was *my* suggestion, in the first place. And the mormaors took it up gladly. I am a princess of Alba, and have responsibility in the matter. The woman's responsibility. How many of you here know that at one time, for many centuries, High Kings of Alba were forbidden to marry? So that the succession must pass through the line of their mothers or sisters or female cousins. There is none so close to the high throne as I am. Therefore my husband should hold that throne for my son. If he will. And if you let him."

There was a general murmur at that last, acknowledgment of their rights and privileges, an olive-branch.

She went on. "You are concerned that Dalriada may be lost within Alba. King Kenneth says that Dalriada and Alba should remain each independent, separate, under his joint rule. This I would agree. You fear that in time the greater must swallow the smaller, and all here become known only as Albannach. In name." She paused. "I have a suggestion as to that. Alba and Dalriada to remain entirely separate kingdoms, yes, for all to recognise. But the new realm ruled over by the High King to have a new name. Just as Wales has the independent kingdoms of Gwynedd, Dyfed, Powis and Morgannwg and Gwent. So Alba and Dalriada would retain their own names and rule, within an overall new style . . ."

"But the Welsh have no High King over all," someone objected. "None is greater than other."

"No. Perhaps better for Wales if they *had* a High King. To unite their resistance to the invading Anglo-Saxons. *We* could show the way, I say. Suppose King Kenneth's new title was not High King of Alba. Nor of Dalriada. But of another joint name?"

"It would become Alba again, in time, Highness. To the Albannach."

"Not, my friend, if he was High King of Scots. The new style, the land of the Scots. Scotland!"

Utter hush descended on all in that church. Men stared at each other, tasting it, considering, savouring the sound of that, wondering – and the significance of it. There was no question as to the impact that Eithne had made.

At the high table, the trio waited, watching, calculating.

Oddly, it was Prior Phadraig who raised voice first. "Highness, the mormaors would never accept that."

There were mutters of agreement.

"They would, I think, if it was made a condition of King Kenneth's taking of the high throne."

The talk and debate became general as the chiefs and lords and clerics discussed and questioned amongst themselves. Kenneth gave them their head now, while shrewdly assessing. At length he stood up – and all others must therefore rise also.

"What then do I tell the mormaors?" he asked, simply. "And what do I tell myself?"

Out of the various shoutings, it was clear that one theme prevailed – High King of Scots they would accept. Not otherwise. If the Albannach would do likewise, they would agree.

Satisfied, Kenneth escorted Eithne from the church.

They did not require to convince Nechtan and the other
mormaors as to the strange terms for Kenneth's acceptance
of the high throne – the Norsemen did that for them. Late in
the season as it was, a series of attacks on the Buchan coast
of Alba had developed, not just piratical raids but large-
scale invasions, penetrating a fair distance inland. In seeking
to repel these, Malcolm, Mormaor of Buchan, had been
killed, leaving only a child heir. The Norsemen were still
there, almost giving the impression that they intended to
settle down in Buchan, at least for the winter. King
Kenneth's aid was therefore direly needed. Would he come,
in force? His leadership was never more necessary. As to the
high kingship, any conditions he put forward would be
acceptable, Nechtan assured.

Kenneth was loth to go, in this late October, and to take
an army with him. It was still golden autumn weather, but
could change at any time. Early winter snows could block
the passes through the mountains, and even without that,
conditions for marching men could become grievous. How
long might any such venture take? It could be mid-winter
before his force could head for home. And Eithne's second
child was due before Yuletide.

The sea? Could he risk the sea-voyaging right round
Alba? With a great fleet, in early winter? Five hundred miles
at least, to Buchan. And get his ships back again, in winter
storms? Would that be folly? How long would it take, those
five hundred miles? So much would depend on the weather,
on the winds in especial. Longships, in favourable conditions, and with relays of oarsmen, could cover if necessary
up to eighty miles in twelve hours, even more. But not day
after day. Could a fleet average, say, fifty miles a day? Ten
days, some days doing less, some more. The Norsemen
themselves ventured on far longer voyages than that – but
seldom in winter. Would it be worth trying? At least no risk
of his being trapped in Alba on account of snow-filled
passes.

Eithne was in favour of the sea venture. After all,
Kenneth's principal victories had all been gained from ships.

Although she was, as ever, concerned for his safety, in these armed sallies, she did not voice this.

So Kenneth assembled a fleet of some forty vessels, carrying around three thousand men, all he had time to collect, and set off northwards, promising to try to be back before Eithne's lying-in. The weather remained reasonably kind, dull, with poor visibility, but fairly calm, with the winds light and south-westerly, in their favour at this north-going stage.

They had to go, as ever, at the speed of the slowest, however galling that could be; but even so they made good time that first day, reaching the shelter of Arisaig Bay, north of the great Ardnamurchan peninsula, for the night. They required a fairly large shelter-area for a fleet of this size. The second day they got as far as Loch Dunvegan, near the north of Skye. Then, with the wind freshening, and this now directly behind them as they headed north-eastwards out of the Minch for the very tip of Alba, An Garbh, the Prow, they could dispense with oars most of the time. Despite rising seas, they made the mouth of Loch Eriboll, actually on the shore of the Pentland Firth between Orkney and Alba, that night, their best day yet, whatever the stormy reputation of these waters. This was much better going than Kenneth had reckoned on. They had seen no sign of Norse ships, only the usual coastal fishing-boats.

It was fifty miles from Eriboll to Duncansby Head, the extreme north-east corner of Alba, which they covered easily, and some way beyond, to Freswick Bay in Caithness, for the fourth night. It was now only some sixty miles due southwards, leaving their coast-hugging, to the Buchan area; but now the wind would not be in their favour, so it was oar-work again, this first day of November. But there were plenty of relays of rowers, men glad enough of the exercise, for it had turned colder.

They saw the smoke-clouds to the south when they were only halfway across the great bight of the Moray Firth, these seeming to rise from fairly far inland. So the Norsemen were still there, and active.

That inland smoke well pleased Kenneth, in some fashion, whatever misery it represented to the unfortunate inhabitants of Buchan. For it seemed to imply that the invaders remained at their usual ravaging, and would not be settled down in any numbers near the coast and their ships. These therefore should again be vulnerable. They would not be anticipating any assault by sea, for the Albannach were not really sea-fighters.

In these circumstances, Kenneth decided that his best course would be to head inshore almost at once, and to lie up overnight in some remote shelter, so as not to give any warning to enemy look-outs. Then, well before daylight next morning, sail out, eastwards now, along the Buchan seaboard, splitting his fleet into four groups each of some ten longships, to search the bays and inlets of that Buchan coast, when day broke, to try to destroy Norse vessels moored therein, proceeding along that seaboard, aiding or by-passing each other. He himself, in his command-ship, would remain well to seaward, to try to direct proceedings, send help where required or, if necessary, summon a reassembly of the fleet. It was unlikely that the Scandinavians would have moored all their ships in one place, but possible. The principal port and harbour of Buchan was at Kinnaird, just beyond where the coast made its mighty bend southwards from the Moray Firth, near to the mormaor's seat of Dundarg. But the smoke-clouds rose from areas consider-ably to the west of that, so it seemed unlikely that the invaders' ships would be concentrated there.

So, well before dawn, the fleet crept out of Garmouth, on the great Spey Bay, and divided into four sections, to scour that coastline's havens, while Kenneth's own ship headed north-eastwards, alone, to take up a position three or four miles offshore, where he could, as far as possible, oversee all, and be available for guidance and reinforcement. It was not the sort of role which Kenneth found to his taste, pre-ferring to be a deal more active; but it provided overall leadership and control, his part nowadays as a monarch.

That day, in fact, his part proved to be singularly unevent-ful, dull, and in a way frustrating. Nothing at all happened to involve his ship, no calls on his command, no other vessels came out to seek aid or instructions, no signals were sent. They *saw* vessels of their fleet, from time to time, as the day wore on, against the loom of the land, always moving east-wards, as it were leap-frogging other groups' activities; but the only indications of progress and success were the columns of new black smoke which arose from this bay or that and presumably represented burning dragon-ships, these so much nearer and darker than the great brown banks of smoke inland which came from blazing thatches and roof-timbers. It was galling indeed for the inactive watchers to have to gaze and assess and wait, the price of leadership.

The fact that those black smokes kept rising, ever eastwards, was of course an excellent sign; and every hour or so Kenneth moved his own ship in that direction also, to keep abreast of operations. In the late afternoon he was nearing Kinnaird Head, at that mighty turning-point of the entire seaboard where Alba thrust its fist furthest out into the Norse Sea. The main Buchan port was just round the corner from there, and Kenneth decided that he had waited long enough. He ordered Conall to sail in towards the headland. If there was any Norse fleet moored in Kinnaird's haven, and with enough men to man the ships, these must be aware by now of what was going on along the coast, and might put out to counter it. He had ordered that none of his own vessels should proceed as far as Kinnaird.

When, with the short day's light already fading, he reached the bay of Phingask, between Troup Head and Kinnaird, it was to find one of his groups already waiting there, its people in high spirits. They had found, surprised and burned eight dragon-ships altogether, five and three, in Portsoy and Pennan inlets, the few Norse guards either fleeing or putting up inadequate resistance against overwhelming odds. Considerable booty had fallen to them and no casualties worth mentioning. They had seen other smokes, so presumably their colleagues were being successful also.

Two other sections of ten came in together soon afterwards, with the same sort of tale, claiming six and four dragon-ships respectively, in Cullen and Banff and lesser havens. The last flotilla to arrive came in comparative disgruntlement – they had found only two Norse vessels, at Aberdour, which had managed to get away before they reached them, and they had had to chase after them. They had caught up eventually, the enemy craft being, of course, under-manned, and had duly boarded and then sunk them. But all that had taken time, and meanwhile the other groups had been clearing the coast, so that there were no pickings left for them, a sad tale productive of much mirth amongst the others.

Kenneth, bemused by how easy it all sounded, was nevertheless well pleased. They had disposed of no less than a score of dragon-ships all told, at little cost and apparently with almost laughable ease. What proportion of the total Norse strength that represented he could not tell, but these vessels, being half as large again as his longships, should have made up a substantial part of the whole. Those ravaging Scandinavians inland were now without most of their means of transport.

What next, then? There had been no Norse sallies out of Kinnaird, that they had seen – which could mean much or little. There might be none there, or so few as not to risk any confrontation. Folk there could hardly have failed to see the new smoke-clouds along the coast westwards – although they *could* assume that these represented merely more Norse burnings of townships.

He was in two minds as to whether to move on in force now, to Kinnaird, with darkness falling, or to wait until morning and attack at dawn. Probably the latter, to give his men a rest.

Careful watch kept, they spent an undisturbed night.

Well before sun-up the fleet, in tight formation now, rounded Kinnaird Head and turned into the half-mile-wide inlet, hardly a bay, which formed the large haven. There were fishing-boats and two larger craft to be seen – but no dragon-ships.

Kenneth, well escorted, went ashore. The township was half-burned and obviously had been savaged; but, although at first all seemed to be deserted, they soon discovered surviving residents hiding in fear. These, reassured and questioned, declared that there had been four Norse ships with their devilish crews in their town and harbour until last night, when they had slipped out to sea in the darkness, taking a number of women with them, God's curse on them. Where they had gone was not known.

Kenneth cursed also. He had made a mistake in waiting, then. He could have trapped those ruffians, who had clearly been warned by the coastal burnings, and could have saved those unhappy women.

He questioned the locals further. Did they know the situation as regards the main Norse force? They had accounted for two dozen dragon-ships now. There could not have been many more than that, surely? Were the enemy all now engaged in looting and rapine inland? Had they a guarded base somewhere?

The townsfolk did not know. They assumed, by all the smoke, that all Buchan was being harried. A great battle had been fought at Boyndlie, not far from the Mormaor Malcolm's palace of Dundarg, where he had been slain and his force defeated. But after that, they knew naught, save that the burnings went on.

Kenneth faced a considerable problem. Word would not be long in getting to the ravaging Scandinavians that their ships had been destroyed, and that there was a large fleet operating against them. They might well guess that it was the Norse-Slayer himself. What would they do? Come together again to form a united force, or stream off in groups down to where they had left their ships? This might well depend on how scattered they were now, and how much in command was their leadership. He, Kenneth, had come here not only to destroy dragon-ships but to slay Norsemen and to free Buchan from the scourge. How best could this be achieved?

He decided that he must again divide his force. The long-ships, with their normal crews, would patrol the coastline, to seek out returning raiders and deal with them if possible. He himself would disembark the large numbers of extra fighting men he had brought, more than half of the total, and march with them inland, to try to find the Norse nucleus – and hope that many of the defeated and dispersed Buchan fighters would join him in the process.

The Dalriadan troops, cooped up for too long aboard, were only too glad to get ashore – and the shipmen to be rid of them. Kenneth ordered the fleet to return here to Kinnaird when they had finished their sweep of the coastline, to wait for him.

Then, at the head of nearly two thousand men, he marched, west by south, since that was the direction towards the great smoke-clouds. They took a couple of local men with them as guides.

Over undulating countryside they went, by Cardno and Ardler, making first, advisedly, for Boyndlie and the Water of Tyrie, where the battle had been fought – this so that they might follow up the tracks of the Norse victors, Kenneth hoped.

They progressed on into hilly terrain now, the Aberdour area, with everywhere signs of destruction and ruin, burned farmeries, mills, barns and unburied corpses, many of these beheaded and nailed up against walls. It was widespread devastation. What made men wish to behave thus to those who had done them no harm?

They saw no raiders. Nor indeed did any local volunteers come to join their force. And the survivors of the terror remained discreetly in hiding.

Presently the hills dwindled to an extraordinarily deep, branching valley which the guides called the Tore of Troup; and here they obtained their first word of the Norsemen, at a still-smouldering group of cot-houses in the gut of the glen, whose owners had apparently crept back to see what could be salvaged and who, because of the constrictions of the valley, did not see the newcomers before they rounded a bend. Reassured by the guides, they informed that the raiders had been there only the day previously, but had left hurriedly, in the direction of the coast, in the late afternoon. And yes, they themselves had seen black smoke-columns rising seawards.

Pressing on, into more level and populous country now, called apparently Cushnie and Gamrie, they came across still more recently ravaged communities and farmeries. Here too the word was that the devilish invaders had departed coastwards late the previous day, evidently in groups and small numbers and not in any organised fashion. It looked as though the Vikings' weakness, their concern for and reliance on their ships, had taken over and caused a piecemeal and hasty retreat to where they had left their vessels, rather than any mustering to form a unified force again.

Kenneth assessed that his shipmen, therefore, would be the ones who played the useful part in this operation, and his larger force here was being unprofitably employed. So he divided his people into four parties of approximately five hundred each, and sent them off coastwards, for different destinations, to make for those various havens and inlets where they had destroyed the dragon-ships. He himself went with a central party, aiming to try to co-ordinate efforts.

In fact, there was little that he could do in that respect, the coastline being so cut up by cliffs, headlands and deep ravines, so that there could be little or no communication and co-operation between groups. But this, of course, applied equally to the enemy, and each unit had to operate on its own.

Kenneth's party arrived down at the fishing-village of Pennan, to find a small battle already in progress, five of his longships moored in the shallows and their crews engaging Norsemen in hand-to-hand fighting, on the beach, amongst the houses and even in the water itself. The arrival of nearly five hundred Scots, of course, altered the picture entirely and promptly, and soon there were no raiders left alive.

The light was beginning to fade by this time, but Kenneth permitted no congratulatory delay over this modest victory. He sent half of his people eastwards and half westwards, to assist at neighbouring encounters, whilst he himself embarked on one of the longships, and with the other four vessels put out to see what could be done seawards.

In the event, not a great deal was possible, or necessary. In the separate havens, the dispersed and outnumbered Vikings were being effectively mauled, attacked from front and rear, and unable to join forces with their compatriots elsewhere. Few fled. These devils were good at dying bravely, whatever else.

With darkness descending, Kenneth came to the conclusion that it was total, if scattered, victory. He sent orders for all his ships to pick up the land-based men and then return to Kinnaird harbour.

That night they celebrated.

Kenneth would have wished to visit Dundarg, to commiserate with the Mormaor Malcolm's family and inform them that Buchan should now be free of any but odd Norse stragglers. But he was concerned to get his fleet back to Dalriada as soon as possible. And he had another visit to pay, first.

Next day, then, he sailed his ships down the Buchan coast southwards the forty miles to Aberdeen, in Mar. There his men would be well entertained by grateful citizens, while he hired horses to ride up Don to see Gartnait of Mar.

At Kildrummy, with his news, he was hailed as conquering deliverer, saviour, Alba's protector. Nothing was too good for Kenneth mac Alpin, no reward too great. His assumption of the high kingship was now taken for granted, and the overall name of Scotland accepted, if that was his wish. Kenneth gathered that so long as Mar and the other mormaordoms retained their distinctive identities, the other name did not greatly signify. And there would be no question of any adverse vote amongst the *ri*, with Mar, Angus and Atholl assured, Buchan's appointed representative now bound to support him, and Ross and Caithness only concerned to keep Tadg of Moray out. The sooner Kenneth moved to Fortrenn the better.

Satisfied, as far as it was possible for him to be, Kenneth returned to Aberdeen. Now, to get his ships back to Dalriada before the winter's storms really set in.

25

Eithne produced a daughter as Yuletide gift, and the delighted parents named her Deirdre. Young Conn was jealous at first but soon became fond of his little sister. They made a happy family.

It was March before a courier arrived from Alba. A meeting of the *ri*, at Forteviot, also attended by the lords of Fife, Strathearn and the Lennox, but shunned by Tadg of Moray, had unanimously elected Kenneth mac Alpin to be High King, with fullest powers and all promises of support. The name of the united kingdom, with each component retaining its own identity, to be whatever he chose. He was urged to come to take over his throne as soon as possible, in case Tadg made himself awkward in the interim. The inauguration ceremonies would be held at Scone, if he was agreeable.

Kenneth sent back word that he would come to Forteviot and Scone in April, before the Norse hosting season began, in case they still had not learned their lesson. It would be a pity if this so significant occasion was to be spoiled by having to go and repel raiders.

So all was planning and bustle at Dunadd. Not that the royal family were going to desert the palace there for good; it would remain their favoured home. But much of their time hereafter inevitably would have to be spent at Forteviot; and Eithne's childhood quarters would become their second home. So there was much of domestic nature to be seen to. Also dynastic, for a standing council of chiefs had to be established, to see to the day-to-day running of Dalriada while Kenneth was elsewhere. Donald, underemployed in Galloway, would spend more of his time at Dunadd. Also, the *Lia Faill*, the Stone of Destiny, had to be retrieved from Dunstaffnage and taken with them, for Kenneth to be crowned on, a second time. He had a feeling, rather than a theory, that this had been intended for him, all along, that

373

his destiny was linked with it, and the uniting of the kingdoms part of its mystical influence, destined indeed. There was no need to hide it now, from Albannach or Norsemen. It would be safe at Scone.

So in mid-April a great company set out on the long journey to Forteviot, a slow, deliberate progress on this occasion, with women, children and many pack-horses laden with gear and goods, not to mention the Stone of Destiny itself, a cavalcade stretching for almost a mile along the narrow and winding roads through mountains, glens and passes. None of their route, by Loch Awe-side, Glenorchy and Drumalban to Strathfillan and Strathearn passed through Moray territory; nevertheless Kenneth had strong armed escorting files out before and behind, just in case ill-wishers thought to interfere.

In fact it took longer for that entourage to reach Fortrenn than it had done for the Dalriadan fleet to sail right round Alba the previous autumn, nine days, with some of their overnight stops primitive to say the least. But there were no complaints, none at least made to Kenneth or Eithne; and young Conn found it all a great adventure.

Well warned in advance, a large gathering of Albannach notables had assembled at Forteviot to greet them, all the mormaors save those of Moray and Caithness, including the child Aidan of Buchan with his guardian and mother, even Fergus of Ross, a gross hulk of a man whom Kenneth decided that he would not trust one yard. Crippled Nechtan of Angus acted as host meantime, although Eithne required no introduction to her old home.

There was much feasting and celebration for a day or two, as preparations were made for the all-important ceremonial at Scone, and late-comers arrived. The fabled Stone was on exhibition, and attracted much attention and examination.

The great day dawned and, dressed in their best, all set out on the twelve-mile ride to Scone, crossing Tay at the Derder's ford, a huge company, probably the largest, save for actual armies, ever seen in Alba. Bands of musicians and singers accompanied the cavalcade at intervals.

At Scone, where Eithne's uncle, Constantine, had established a sanctuary and abbey, all was ready. Kenneth himself had planned most of the ceremony, based on both the traditional Albannach and Dalriadan coronation rituals, with one or two of his own and Eithne's ideas added. The abbey-church was much too small to accommodate all concerned, so the proceedings were held outside. Fortunately the weather, although dull, remained dry.

When all were assembled, the Abbot of Scone, assisted by Prior Phadraig from Dunadd, opened with prayer and psalm-singing from a small mound near the church. Then the mormaors, led by the limping Nechtan, came forward to take up their positions, the young Aidan being led by the hand by his tutor or guardian, this to the rhythmic clash of cymbals.

When silence descended, Nechtan, on behalf of his fellow *ri*, made a prepared and quite lengthy statement, not particularly impressively announced but of the most vital significance. This to the effect that Alba desperately needed a strong hand at its helm at this dire stage of its long story, with unending Norse assault, internal unrest and the un-timely deaths of so many of its natural leaders. A great warrior and able governor was required, one who could unite all factions as well as defeat the raiders and invaders – and who better to do that than Kenneth mac Alpin, King of Dalriada and famed Norse-Slayer? King Kenneth was wed to the daughter of the renowned and well-loved High King Angus mac Fergus, and he had a son by her, another Constantine, here present, who was therefore in direct line of succession to the high throne. Queen Eithne, whose authority none could question, had urged King Kenneth to accept this position, duty and responsibility. After pressure, he had agreed. On condition that he remained King of Dalriada as well as High King of Alba, a joint kingship. It was with pride and satisfaction, therefore, in the name of the *ri*, the lesser kings of Alba, that he requested Kenneth mac Alpin to come forward and occupy the high throne.

Nechtan sighed with relief to have got that over.

Kenneth paced out, features set almost sternly, to climb the mound, amidst cheering, Eithne a few paces behind, with Conn by the hand and baby Deirdre in her arm, the line of succession and authority to be thus apparent to all. Bow-ing to the mormaors, Kenneth went to stand beside, but not to sit on, the massive throne-like chair placed there, between it and the Stone of Destiny, which was now covered with the great black and white wild boar banner of Alba. When he gestured for Eithne to sit on the throne, with the children, a murmur of surprise ran through the assembly. It had clearly been expected that he himself would sit.

He raised his hand for silence. "I, Kenneth, call upon the High Sennachie of Alba, Murdoch mac Congall, to pronounce before you all my identity and descent, that there be no mistake. Hear you him."

An old stooping man wearing a splendid robe embroidered with the black boar, supported by elaborate mystical animals representing the mormaordoms, and all enhanced by colourful and elaborate Celtic tracery, shuffled out from the side, carrying a long parchment roll. Making obeisance to Eithne first, then to the mormaors and finally to Kenneth, he began to read, in a remarkably resonant voice for one who seemed so aged and feeble.

"I, Murdoch, name you this man, Kenneth," he intoned. "Kenneth son of Alpin, son of Eochaidh, son of Aed Find, son of Eochaidh, son of Domangart, son of Donald Breac, son of Eochaidh Buide, son of Aidan, son of Gabhran, son of Domangart, son of Fergus Mor, son of Erc – all these kings of Dalriada. The said Erc came from Dalriata in Ireland, and was son of Eochaidh Muin-remor, of the line of the mighty Niall of the Nine Hostages, High King of All Ireland. Of such is this Kenneth!"

The High Sennachie stood back.

"You have heard," Kenneth said then. "Now, hear this. Today a great deed is to be done, and you all are witnesses to it. Under God, a new realm is to be created. Alba will remain, as will Dalriada, two separate and distinct kingdoms. But together they will have a unity under one monarch. And that united realm will require a name. It is part of my acceptance of this high throne that I give this realm a name. I name it Scotia, the land of the Scots. Scotland, I say. Hear you – Scotland!"

He gazed around him, almost challengingly.

There was staring, stirring, exclamation from the crowd, but no actual voiced protest.

He went on. "The Scots, you may say, came from Ireland. Fergus mac Erc, my forebear from Dalriata, led them, as you have heard. But so, my friends, did come the Albannach long before, whom the Romans called the Picts, because they spelled their language in pictures, as still you do. But the Albannach, the Picts, also came here from Ireland, the ancients tell us. They too were Scotti. So we are all Scots, now in a unity."

He paused, as though prepared for counter-challenge. None was forthcoming.

"Heed that word, unity. This is what is important, whatever the name. The unity of our Celtic peoples. Long I have fought for this. Only in a unity will we preserve our freedom and our lands from the invaders. From the Scandinavians, the Angles and the Saxons, who seek to dominate and destroy us. The Celtic nations *must* act together, work together, fight together. Unite in some form. Today, a great step is being taken in that good cause. Two of the nations coming together in a unity. I rejoice. So should you. But the Norsemen will not – that I swear!"

This time he gained acclaim.

"As sign of this uniting, this marriage of two realms, I give you two tokens." He half-turned, and stooped to draw the boar banner from off the stone. "Here is the Stone of Destiny itself. It has been the Dalriadan coronation-seat since Columba's time, our most precious relic. Now it is Alba's also, the Stone of the Scots, enduring mystic symbol of kingship. Dalriada brings it to Alba, to Scotland . . . "

Clamour drowned his voice as all stared, pointed and cried out. That renowned stone had hitherto been only a name, a legend, to the vast majority there. Now they saw it, and gazed in a kind of awe.

When he could be heard, Kenneth resumed. He handed the boar standard to Eithne and from her received in exchange another folded banner. This he shook out, to display the white St Andrew's Cross on the blue background, Angus mac Fergus's flag, representing that celebrated victory over Athelstan, when Andrew had come to the rescue, and thereafter had been named patron saint of Alba.

"This is Alba's token, given by the daughter of Angus mac Fergus, to match and add to Dalriada's Stone," he declared, in ringing tones, now. "This shall be Scotland's standard from now on, a fair exchange!" And he draped that blue and white saltire flag over the gleaming black stone.

To cheers upon cheers he bowed to the company, and then, turning, gestured towards the Abbot of Scone and Prior Phadraig. Then to a third man, standing a little way back, Duffus, Lord of Fife, the senior of the Albannach nobles after the mormaors. He carried a cushion on which gleamed the golden circlet of a royal crown.

The abbot raised voice, to pray eloquently that Almighty God would bless and prosper what they were about to do this day. Then he came to take Kenneth's hand and lead him to sit on the stone. There, he laid hand on Kenneth's head and blessed him. Then Phadraig came forward to do the same, his hand on top of the abbot's, in symbolical union. Standing thus together they waited, while cymbals clashed and singers chanted a verse of Columba's psalmody.

The clerics stood back and Duffus of Fife took their place. He bowed to Eithne, then to the mormaors, and handing his cushion to the abbot, took the golden circlet and carefully placed it about Kenneth's brows.

"Hail, Kenneth, High King of All Scots!" he cried, and sinking on one knee, took Kenneth's hand between both his own, in gesture of allegiance.

The mormaors took up the cry. "Hail, High King, Hail, High King!" And the entire company raised voice to repeat and repeat it, on and on, with the clashing of cymbals joining in, as Kenneth sat, set-faced, crowned head high, tense. Then he turned, to smile to Eithne.

That had been a difficult ceremony to devise and arrange. After all, Kenneth had already been crowned and anointed as a monarch, and this could not be repeated; anything such would have offended the Dalriadans, implying that *their* coronation at Iona and Dunadd was somehow less than adequate. The unity theme had to be stressed, and the stone's and the flag's significance emphasised, the Columban Church's essential role brought out, for it had been Columba himself who instituted the anointing of the Dalriadan monarchs, a feature of major importance.

They were not quite finished yet. When the cheering and shouting at length died away, Eithne rose and came, baby crooked in one arm, Conn by the hand. Relinquishing her son, she took Kenneth's hand instead, to raise him up and lead him over to the throne she had been occupying. Conn, intrigued, got rather in the way here.

Then Nechtan led the mormaors forward to kneel before the enthroned High King and take their oaths of allegiance, as Duffus had done, Eithne standing behind, seeking to restrain the now excited Conn. The long file of the nobles, chiefs and lords of Alba lined up to offer their fealty, while the musicians played and the choristers sang.

At length it was over, and the principals repaired, in procession, to the abbot's house, for refreshment, while open-air feasting was provided for the large assembly.

When they could be alone for a little while, Eithne held out her arms to her husband.

"My dear, my dear," she exclaimed. "At last, you are where I have longed to see you. Kenneth of my heart, are you as happy as I am? At this great outcome?"

He looked at her, brows puckered. "That I do not know, lass. For you mistake in that, I fear. This is not an outcome, only a start, a beginning. My road has today crossed a ford that is all. A great ford, but only that. The road goes on, and I with it. So much to be done still . . . "

"Oh, you will do it, Kenneth, *Ard Righ*, founder of a new nation. Few men achieve that. Does it not feel good to you?"

"Ask me that ten years hence! Or twenty, God willing! But, meanwhile, so long as I have you at my side, in my arms, I can face my fate."

And he took her and held her to him.

HISTORICAL NOTE

Kenneth's recognition and concern with the tasks ahead of him were fully justified. He reigned for sixteen years as High King of the new Scotland, and they were action-filled years indeed. He had to defeat Norse assaults a number of times thereafter before those determined invaders came to perceive that Alba was not for them. Dalriada was not immune either, especially the Hebridean islands so easily reached from Ulster. Indeed Iona was raided again and again, so that Kenneth in the end transferred all the remaining Columban relics to Scone, for safety.

Once he had discouraged the Scandinavians he still had the Angles to deal with, these growing increasingly aggressive. He never actually incorporated Lothian and what is now the Scottish Borderland into his kingdom but sought to keep it under his control as a sort of occupied territory, a buffer zone. Six times he invaded Northumbria and Cumbria, in retaliation.

As well as all this, it was four years before he finally subdued the last Albannach opposition to his rule, although this was on a comparatively minor scale and apt to surface only when he was away battling elsewhere, never really endangering his occupancy of the throne.

It was not all warfare, of course. Kenneth drew up and imposed the first Code of Laws for Scotland, which indeed remained more or less unaltered until, two centuries later, his descendant, MacBeth, devised an amended version. His rule thereafter was much more complete, the nation more unified, than ever before, the mormaors content to play a more subsidiary and supportive role.

Abroad, in Ireland, Maelsechlaind proved to be a successful High King also, and preserved the land south of Ulster from Norse domination, although later the invaders achieved control of the Tara and Dublin areas. The Celtic unity vision never developed to full fruition, but the alliance did help to restrict the invasions and attempts at Anglo-Saxon colonisation.

Kenneth and his wife had more children, just how many is not recorded. But one daughter married the King of Strathclyde, Run by name, a grandson of Roderick, it seems; and another wed Aed Find-liath, King of Ireland, a successor of Maelsechlaind, linking the two realms more closely. Kenneth may have had a son called Gregor, from whom the Clan MacGregor, or Clan Alpine, claim descent; but there seems to be doubt about this, some historians suggesting that this Gregor was a younger *brother* of Kenneth. Strathclyde in due course became part of Scotland.

Kenneth died, of a tumour we are told, at Forteviot in 858, so he would be just under sixty years. Conn would then be about nineteen years, and presumably considered too young to take over as High King, for Kenneth's brother Donald mac Alpin succeeded in the interim, ruling for four years; and then *his* nephew took the throne as Constantine the Second, reigning for twenty years. So the line became well established.

Kenneth was buried, beside his forefathers, on Iona – as indeed were his successors.

A verse has come down to us from the ancient chroniclers:

> That Kenneth, of many stables, is dead
>   Causes weeping in every house.
> There is not under Heaven one king so good,
>   As far as the borders of Rome.

Leave it at that.